CRITICAL RAVES FOR THE *NEW YORK TIMES* BESTSELLER

RUN FOR YOUR LIFE

"Sexual tension sizzles as the danger heats up."
—*Cosmopolitan*

"An impressive foray into modern romantic suspense... fast-paced...dynamic... sensuous."
—*Booklist*

Extraordinary Praise for Andrea Kane's Blockbuster Works of Romance and Suspence

RUN FOR YOUR LIFE

"A knockout! Andrea Kane expertly juggles suspense and romance in this fast-paced story of good vs. evil."

—Iris Johansen

"Kane's strong suit is her ability to create memorable characters. . . . What sets this book apart from other romantic thrillers is Kane's deft skill in defining the actions of her lead characters: her love scenes, for example, are exceptional."

—*Publishers Weekly*

"This is a suspense thriller that will keep you guessing right up to the explosive ending."

—*Rendezvous*

"A thriller of intrigue and romance. . . . A keeper for certain, and I believe it to be a 'Perfect Ten.' Needless to say, it's one you will not want to put down, and one I very highly recommend."

—*Romance Reviews Today*

"A real page-turner! *Run for Your Life* is a keep-you-up-all-night romantic suspense."

—Karen Robards

"Historical favorite Andrea Kane chooses to explore a whole new genre as she deftly tackles the world of romantic suspense. *Run for Your Life* packs action, drama, romance, and suspense into a rousing read."

—*Romantic Times*

"A very, very gifted writer. . . . *Run for Your Life* is a top-notch suspense story that keeps your fingers busy turning the pages. The premise of the story is intriguing. Mrs. Kane has developed fleshed-out characters that are as real as your next-door neighbors. The love story of Victoria and Zach is woven throughout this exciting tale. This is one book that you should run to your favorite bookstore and get as soon as you can."

—New and Previously Owned Books

"A thrilling ride, and the author is adept at weaving in layers of suspense without sacrificing other elements of the story."

—CompuServe Romance Reviews

"Andrea Kane has written a great, action-packed story with plenty of suspense, mystery, and love. I enjoyed her first contemporary immensely and had difficulty putting it down."

—Old Book Barn Gazette

THE SILVER COIN

"*The Silver Coin* leaves readers wondering what Andrea Kane can do next. . . . The action-packed story line never eases up."

—*Affaire de Coeur*

"The tension and suspense remain at a high level throughout the book, punctuated by the escalating romance and passionate love scenes."

—Bookbug on the Web

THE GOLD COIN

"Kane's engrossing plot and her quick-witted, passionate characters should make readers eagerly await this novel's companion. . . ."

—*Publishers Weekly*

"A superb novel. . . . The story line is nonstop and loaded with romantic tension and intrigue."

—*Affaire de Coeur*

Also by Andrea Kane

My Heart's Desire
Dream Castle
Masque of Betrayal
Echoes in the Mist
Samantha
The Last Duke
Emerald Garden
Wishes in the Wind
Legacy of the Diamond
The Black Diamond
The Music Box
Gift of Love (anthology)
The Theft
The Gold Coin
The Silver Coin
Run for Your Life
Wait until Dark (anthology)

Published by POCKET BOOKS

ANDREA KANE

NO WAY OUT

POCKET **STAR** BOOKS
New York London Toronto Sydney Singapore

For information regarding special discounts for bulk purchases, please contact Simon & Schuster Special Sales at 1-800-456-6798 or business@simonandschuster.com

An *Original* Publication of POCKET BOOKS

A Pocket Star Book published by
POCKET BOOKS, a division of Simon & Schuster, Inc.
1230 Avenue of the Americas, New York, NY 10020

ISBN: 0-7434-1275-3

First Pocket Books printing November 2001

10 9 8 7 6 5 4 3 2 1

POCKET STAR BOOKS and colophon are registered trademarks of Simon & Schuster, Inc.

Cover art by Brian Bailey

Printed in the U.S.A.

To new beginnings—at any age, at any stage—
and all the hope and promise they represent.

Acknowledgments

With thanks to the following:

The American Professional Society on the Abuse of Children (APSAC) for their dedication in researching and responding to all facets of child maltreatment: prevention, assessment, intervention, and treatment. Through their network of medical, legal, law enforcement, social service, and research professionals, they ensure that those affected by child mistreatment receive the help they need. Their publications, legal research, and educational training provide an invaluable medium promoting public awareness of the complexities of child maltreatment.

Teachers everywhere, both those I interviewed and the thousands I couldn't, for nurturing, educating, and protecting our greatest gifts—our children.

Dr. Hillel Ben-Asher, for medical consultation given with unfailing patience and incomparable wisdom.

And the greatest brainstorming partners anywhere—my family. You define teamwork, and I love you.

NO WAY OUT

1

April 14
Leaf Brook Mall
Westchester County, New York

Wrong place. Wrong time.

She had to get out of here.

Julia gritted her teeth as she fought the crowd surging back and forth through the mall. She shoved her way to the door leading to the twelve-story parking garage. Wall-to-wall people. Everything was called a grand opening. This felt more like Mardi Gras in New Orleans.

Coming here today had been stupid. The Stratfords were enveloped by spectators, surrounded by members of the press. And the mayor was flanked by his father and brother—a clear message that the Stratfords represented a unified front. Even Julia's desperation hadn't been enough to get her through. She'd have to find another way.

Taking an elevator wasn't an option. There was already a huge line waiting, and as each car opened, Julia could see they were all filled to capacity. The stairwell wasn't much better, but it was her only choice. She scaled each level as quickly as she could, wincing as the deejay's music rocked the concrete walls and vibrated through her head.

Eventually, the throngs of people began to thin out and the music started to fade as she put more distance between herself and the celebration. She was worried sick and frustrated as hell. If what she suspected was true, then an hourglass was running out. It was up to her to stop the flow of the sand.

She exited the stairwell on the eleventh floor, where she'd wedged her car into the only available parking space—a space that was far away from the opening-day pandemonium. Reflexively, she groped for her keys as she walked.

The screech of tires was what alerted her.

Her chin came up just as the silver Mercedes blasted around the corner, bearing down on her with lightning speed.

She knew she was its target. She also knew why.

Her hunch had been right. And she was about to be silenced.

A frozen moment of fear paralyzed her. Abruptly, it shattered. A surge of adrenaline jolted through her, and she tried to jump out of the way.

She couldn't make it.

She felt the stunning impact and then a dazed awareness as she was hurled through the air. The concrete floor came rushing up to meet her.

Brian, she thought, shards of pain piercing her skull. *Who's going to save Brian?*

2

March 30
Poughkeepsie, New York

"Honey, are you sure you don't want to stay over?" Meredith Talbot asked her daughter as they finished their late-evening cup of coffee at the town's cozy, home-style diner. "You have over an hour's drive back to your apartment. Tomorrow's Saturday. That means your father isn't scheduled to teach any classes at Vassar, and your elementary school is closed. You can spend the weekend with us."

"Thanks, Mom, but I have to get back." Julia Talbot shot her mother a grateful look, well aware that this invitation was prompted by more than the hope of a quiet family weekend. Julia would need no prompting for that. She enjoyed going home, spending long evenings swapping classroom anecdotes with her father, and debating everything from books to politics to the pitfalls of modern society with her parents. But tonight, her mother's invitation wasn't about conversation. It was about lifting Julia's spirits.

Unfortunately, her efforts weren't going to work.

"That workshop was more draining than most," Meredith said gently.

"That's an understatement." Julia's breath expelled on a sigh. "Each week when I walk into that hospital and stand next to you, I tell myself that our workshops are making a difference. Then I hear reports like Dr. Garber's, and I wonder if it's all a pipe dream, if what we're trying to do is like trying to boil the ocean."

"You don't believe that. Besides, with enough pilot lights turned up, even the ocean will eventually start to boil. We're gaining awareness. It's a beginning."

"You're a lot more patient than I am. And listening to those statistics—it hurts so much."

Julia pushed aside her empty coffee cup, remembering the frustration in Dr. Garber's voice as he'd issued his findings to the handful of workshop attendees. An on-staff psychologist, he'd just conducted a study on emotional child abuse and neglect. The results were chilling, and they weren't restricted to any one cultural, demographic, or socioeconomic group. Just as there were all forms of abuse, there were all types of people who resorted to it. Two educators had spoken up in support of his case studies, one a preschool teacher and the other a middle-school guidance counselor. Their stories of the impaired personality traits of psychologically abused kids had twisted Julia's insides into knots.

The fact that some parents physically violated their children was unthinkable. Almost as unthinkable was the fact that large numbers of them battered their kids emotionally and got away with it, since there were no tangible scars to submit as evidence. Not to mention that many of them didn't even consider their behavior to be abusive.

How could someone fail to realize that neglect and psychological battering were as destructive as physical aggression? Especially when it came to young children, who were impressionable and who wanted nothing more than to please their parents?

The very concept tore at Julia's heart. Sometimes so much so that she wondered if she was strong enough to continue giving these workshops with her mother. Her mother handled the emotional fallout better—maybe because she was a nurse, and maybe because she was older and more seasoned. Not that Julia had been sheltered. She'd seen the effects of abuse firsthand, and at a very young age. The impact had left an indelible imprint on her mind and heart and helped shape the direction of her life. But that didn't mean she'd ever be immune to the horror stories.

Regardless, the workshops were necessary. Someone had to heighten the awareness of educators and healthcare providers, especially to the more subtle—and easily missed—forms of emotional child abuse. Meredith Talbot had embraced the task for the past five years, offering these weekly meetings on a pro bono basis in conjunction with the American Professional Society on the Abuse of Children. Julia had joined her right after finishing graduate school. With a double major in child psychology and early childhood education, it was the perfect way to augment her teaching career and make a difference in an area so close to her heart.

But the path seemed endless . . .

"I'm not patient. I'm practical," Meredith was saying. "And, in your own way, so are you. You're just more emotional than I am—at least on the outside." She squeezed her daughter's hand. "Why not come back to the house? Just for the night, if not the whole weekend."

"I really can't, Mom." Julia rushed on to dissuade her mother's fears. "I'm not being a martyr—honest. It's just that I'm expecting a call from Greg tonight. Something about theater tickets. And I've got Brian's Little League game first thing in the morning. It's the season opener. He's pitching. I can't miss it."

"No, of course not." Her mother's smile was filled with fondness. "I hate to think what will happen when Brian Stratford moves up to middle school. On second thought, I know what will happen. He'll be dropping by your classroom once a week to introduce you to his friends, and you'll be driving to the middle school every Saturday of the spring sports season to cheer him on to a no-hitter."

For the first time that night, Julia grinned. "Probably. There's part of me that hates the thought of Brian's father running for the state senate. Especially since I'm sure he'll win. He's a great mayor, and he'll make an equally fine senator. I just hope he has no plans to move closer to Albany. I'd miss Brian terribly—even though he won't be in my class anymore by then. He'll have moved up to third grade."

"Since when has not being in your class stopped him?" Meredith questioned with another smile. "He's been a fixture in your classroom since he was in kindergarten, starting from that week in September when you taught him how to throw a curve ball during recess. He's been a true-blue friend ever since."

"Brian is a very special kid. He's warm, open, and sensitive, not to mention intelligent and mature. One day, he's going to make a difference in this world. Heaven knows, we need more people like that." Julia strove for a lighter tone. "As for true blue, that's more than I can say for most men. Other than Dad, of course."

"What about Greg?" Meredith inquired carefully. Although she and Julia were close, she tried to respect her twenty-seven-year-old daughter's privacy. Still, this particular aspect of Julia's life, well founded or not, troubled her. "Does Greg fall into that category, or have you even given him a chance?"

A quick shrug sent masses of Julia's silky, mahogany-brown hair tumbling onto her shoulders. "It's not a question of giving him a chance," she hedged. "The truth is, I really don't know Greg that well yet. We've only been seeing each other about a month. Which, in our case, means six dates. He's even busier than I am. I manage a classroom. He manages a city—not politically but organizationally and financially. He's swamped."

"In that case, there's no chemistry between you."

Julia looked startled. "I didn't say that."

"You didn't have to." Meredith inclined her head, the shiny dark hair much the same color and texture as her daughter's, only cut short in a sleek, tapered style. "I'm not ancient. I remember attraction. It happens in a lot less than a month, and it doesn't wait for your input or your approval. It just happens, sometimes in ways that seem to make no sense at all. Then again, I think you know that already, don't you?"

An uncomfortable pause.

"Julia, life's filled with surprises. Sometimes they pull you off track. That can mean taking risks. Risks aren't always bad, they're just unsettling—especially when taking them conflicts with a plan you're sure is right. Go with your instincts. Don't let fear get in the way."

An uncomfortable pause. "There's nothing getting in the way, Mom. Nothing but work."

"If you say so."

Another pause. "I have to get going." Julia rose hastily, avoiding her mother's astute gaze. The last thing she wanted was to have this particular discussion. It hit too close to home. These days, she wasn't sure where ideology ended and unsettling awareness began. And she wasn't about to find out.

She gathered up her purse and notes. "Thanks for the coffee. And for cheering me up by talking about Brian. Your maternal medicine worked. I feel much better." She stood, leaning over to kiss her mother's cheek. "Give Dad a hug. I'll call you during the week."

"See that you do." Meredith's tone was playful, although she continued scrutinizing her daughter's expression, as if she had a lot more to say but was wisely refraining from doing so. "I want to know who wins that season opener."

"You will."

Julia left the diner, crossing over to where her Volkswagen Beetle was parked. For a moment, she paused, glancing around at the familiar streets where she'd grown up. She felt a sudden pang of loss as she recalled the absolute faith she'd known here as a child—a faith that not every child was lucky enough to know. She was determined to change that, to ensure that more and more kids were given the secure foundation they deserved. Maybe that goal was idealistic, but it was what drove her.

Still, she mused, thinking about the results of tonight's workshop. Sometimes idealism got harder and harder to cling to.

But cling she would.

"Really. You're sure the shots are clear?" Greg Matthews stretched his long legs out in front of him. Leaning back in his living room's leather recliner, he gripped the telephone, listening intently to the information coming to him from the other end. "That's just what I was hoping to hear. Messenger them over here now. Yes—tonight. I'll need the leverage for tomorrow's meeting."

He hung up, mulling over the best strategy for his upcoming breakfast meeting. Normally, he didn't schedule Saturday business appointments. But in this case, he had no choice. And if things went as planned, it would definitely be worth it. He would set the wheels in motion Monday. An insurance policy—one that would result in a solid investment for the city and a solid investment for himself.

All in all, he was satisfied. His professional life was finally coming together. Time for his personal life to follow suit.

Pensive, he stood, turning to glance at the clock. Nine-thirty. And Julia still wasn't home. He'd left two messages on her machine since dinner. No reply. That meant she hadn't gotten home from Poughkeepsie yet. He hoped she hadn't decided to stay over at her parents' house. He had Broadway theater tickets for tomorrow night, given to him at the last minute by a local businessman. He'd mentioned that to Julia when he spoke to her earlier in the day. She'd promised to save Saturday night for him. The problem was, she'd sounded rushed and preoccupied when she said it. Her mind was already on the workshop she was giving later that evening. So he didn't have much faith in her remembering their date.

He'd wait until ten. Then he'd call her again. Julia Talbot was a gorgeous breath of fresh air. He had no intentions of letting her get away.

Especially not now.

3

March 31
Leaf Brook, New York

Stephen Stratford glanced at his car phone, half tempted to make the call he was itching to make while driving the last few blocks to the baseball field. Neither his wife nor his son would notice. They were both in the backseat of the family's Ford Explorer, sidetracked by the pregame crisis that had just occurred.

A button had popped off Brian's uniform.

Unfortunately, this particular button had popped off the dead center of the shirt, rather than off a less conspicuous spot where its absence might have gone unnoticed for this one game. On the plus side, Nancy never traveled anywhere without a first aid kit and a sewing kit—not since Brian's toddler days, when he first became the whirlwind of activity he was now.

Having already helped her son squirm out of his shirt and into his warm-up jacket, Nancy was bent over her task, fighting the clock to get the job done in time. And Brian was making her job harder by bouncing around on the backseat like a jumping bean, his open jacket flapping against his bare chest with fast, impatient thwacks.

"Mom, we're almost there," he protested, staring out the car window. "The game's starting in a few minutes. I gotta have my shirt."

"Here it is." Nancy flourished the good-as-new top, tossing it playfully at her son. "Now, quick, take off your jacket, and we'll get you back into full uniform. By the time Dad parks, you'll look like the pro-ball pitcher you are. The Yanks will have nothing on you. Except that they've stopped growing, so their uniforms fit. If you'd tell your muscles to slow down, maybe this sort of thing wouldn't happen so often."

"Thanks, Mom." Brian tore off his jacket, gazing at Nancy with the utter relief of a seven-year-old who's been saved from public humiliation.

Nancy tousled his hair as he squirmed into the shirt. "Let's get you buttoned up so you can make a dash for the pitcher's mound."

No time for phone calls now, Stephen noted, popping the cell phone out of its cradle and into his shirt pocket. The Little League field was in sight. His promising investment would have to wait.

Frustrated, he steered the car into the parking lot, where it bounced over gravel as he headed for the shaded area near the bleachers.

Brian's nose was pressed to the car window. "Is Miss Talbot here?"

"I don't know, sweetheart." Nancy followed his gaze, trying to pick out Brian's teacher from the dozens of people milling toward their seats. The stands were always packed on opening day. The parents of Leaf Brook's elementary-school students were very involved in their kids' lives. Baseball season was a big deal here. Which meant everyone came out for opening day, parents and grandparents alike.

"I don't see Miss Talbot," Nancy continued, unfastening her seat belt as the car came to a stop. "But that doesn't mean anything. There are too many people on their way to the bleachers to tell one person from another."

"If I know Miss Talbot, she'll be here," Stephen assured his son, turning off the motor and mentally shoving aside his problems. There would be time during the game to make his call. When Brian's team—but not Brian—was at bat, that's when he'd excuse himself and slip away for a minute or two. "Especially if she promised, like you said. She's never broken a promise to you yet."

"I know." Brian still looked worried. "But it's the first game of the season. What if she forgot to come? Winter's long. There haven't been any games for her to come to since September. She's out of practice."

Stephen's lips twitched as he climbed out of the car, opening the back door for Nancy and grabbing the bottle of water his son inevitably forgot. Only Brian would think in terms of a spectator being out of practice.

His wife slid out of the backseat, searching her husband's face briefly before helping Brian gather up his gear. "It's Little League opening day," she reminded Stephen. "And it's no secret who's pitching. With the senatorial campaign under way, I'm assuming the press will be looking for you."

"Probably." Stephen shrugged. "I'll talk to them—*after* the game. Right now, I'm Brian's father. Not the mayor. And not a candidate for the state senate."

Nancy flashed him a quick smile that brought back memories of the happy young woman he'd married ten years ago. He found himself wishing he could make her smile like that more often. These days, she usually looked tired and drawn.

He hated being the cause of that.

But dammit, he was drowning.

They were heading for the field when a silver Mercedes SL500 pulled into the lot, top down. Its driver honked, then stuck his arm in the air to wave.

"Uncle Connor!" Brian's entire face lit up, and he waved back wildly. He jumped from one foot to the other, watching his uncle park the car and trying to have enough patience to wait. Ultimately, he lost the battle and rushed forward to meet the tall, dark-haired man who'd unfolded himself from behind the wheel and was now heading toward them.

"I didn't know you were coming," Brian exclaimed, slapping him five and grinning ear to ear as the two of them rejoined Stephen and Nancy.

"Fat chance I'd miss your opening day." Connor Stratford smiled one of his rare smiles, something he reserved for his nephew. "Cool glove," he added, inspecting the mitt Brian had gotten for Christmas. "But your uniform's looking a little snug. I think you've grown since last month."

"I did. Especially my muscles. I popped a button off my uniform. Mom had to sew it on in the car."

"That must have been fun." Connor leaned over to kiss his sister-in-law's cheek. "Lucky woman. Manipulating a sharp object with this dynamo in tow and my brother doing fifty to get here on time. I don't envy you."

"Forty," Stephen corrected, grasping Connor's hand. "And look who's talking. How many lights did you run between Manhattan and here? And how many cars did you leave behind in the dust?"

"Not too many." Connor draped an arm around Brian's shoulders and headed toward the field. "Saturday mornings, the West Side Highway's fairly quiet. I don't think I did too much damage."

Stephen linked his fingers with Nancy's and followed suit, automatically scanning the area for reporters. They were there, all right, camera equipment and all. The good news was, they hadn't seen him yet. Maybe he could actually enjoy a few innings before he was accosted. Better yet, maybe Connor could run interference for him. No one was better at thinking up creative strategies than his younger brother. It was in his blood, just as it was in their father's. It had made Harrison Stratford a multimillionaire and the business mogul he was today. And it made Connor the extraordinarily successful venture capitalist he was.

A venture capitalist who was busy as hell. Much too busy to take off a good portion of Saturday to be with his family.

Normally, that realization would raise a red flag in Stephen's mind. If Connor showed up in Leaf Brook for an unexpected visit, it was usually to check up on him. But not today. Today was about Brian. And when it came to Brian, Connor's feelings were real and intense. The two of them were nuts about each other.

So the red flag remained down. And the tensions between the brothers were held at bay.

"I'm glad you're here," Stephen murmured to Connor. "I thought work might keep you."

"Work can wait. My ace pitcher can't." Connor tugged at the rim of Brian's baseball cap, which had been hastily yanked on by the ace pitcher in question.

"My arm's in great form," Brian announced. "The coach said so. So did Miss Talbot. Did you know she had the fastest curve ball in her whole neighborhood when she was a kid? Her dad taught her. He was a Little

League pitcher, too, about a zillion years ago. Did you know that?"

"I think you might have mentioned it thirty or forty times," Connor assured him.

"Anyway, Miss Talbot knows all about curve balls. And she said mine is even better this year than last."

"I don't doubt it." Connor shaded his eyes, reflexively peering around as they reached the stands, assessing the way the members of the press had positioned themselves.

Abruptly, Brian pointed, excitement rippling through him once again. "There's Miss Talbot! She's up front. In the first row. Let's go say hi."

Unfortunately, Miss Talbot wasn't the only one in the front row, Connor noted. Three reporters and two photographers were right next to her—pretty heavy media attendance for a Little League game. Obviously, they were there to speak with the mayor, or, rather, the senatorial candidate. They had yet to catch sight of the Stratfords, but that would change the minute they walked over there. Normally, that would be fine. Stephen was in his glory when he was in front of the cameras. His natural charisma captured the public like a magnet. Effortlessly, he charmed reporters, photographers, and the voting public alike, making their dreams his, their hopes his intended reality. Without trying, Stephen always became the center of attention.

Today that wouldn't fly. It was Brian's day, Brian's moment in the sun. His father would want it no other way.

As if to verify that fact, Stephen tensed up, his gaze fixed on the waiting reporters, his body language confirming Connor's assessment: he wanted to keep a low profile until after the game. Then he'd talk to the press.

"Brian, your coach is signaling you," Connor announced, inserting himself and heading off the problem. "The team's waiting. Wave at Miss Talbot as you take the field. She'll understand. We can say hi afterward. Right now, you'd better warm up, and we'd better grab some seats or we'll miss your opening pitch. We'll sit over there." He pointed to a section of bleachers just behind home plate. "That way, we'll have the best view of the pitcher's mound."

"Okay . . . I guess." Brian looked reluctant, torn between his urge to see Miss Talbot and his unwillingness to disappoint the uncle who was his hero.

The scales tipped in Connor's favor when Brian saw his teammates motioning him on.

"Yeah, okay," he agreed, this time with conviction. Flashing his family a thumbs-up, he took off. He stopped halfway to the dugout area, turned, and gave Miss Talbot a huge wave. She sat up straighter, a bright smile lighting her face, and waved back.

"Thanks," Stephen muttered to Connor as they all settled themselves at the end of the second row of the bleachers he'd selected—which happened to be two sets of bleachers away from the press. "If that had come from Nancy or me, it never would have flown."

"You're his parents. I'm his uncle. I've got the easy job. You do the work. I win the popularity contests." Connor watched the exchange between Brian and his teacher. "Speaking of popularity contests, I see our guy's still crazy about Miss Talbot."

"Yup," Stephen concurred. "The sun rises and sets on her. Rightfully so. She's an amazing teacher, motivates the kids like I've never seen."

"Ah, so it is more than her curve ball," Connor returned dryly.

"No question," Nancy chimed in, her admiration for Brian's teacher clear and unmistakable. "Although her skill with the curve ball doesn't hurt. Neither does all the time she spends unofficially coaching the kids at practice. But Stephen's right. She's quite an educator. She's smart and enthusiastic. She's also able to see the world through the eyes of a child. I'm sure you can't relate to that, given the world you work in, but believe me, it's a remarkable trait, one that takes insight and sensitivity. Put all those qualities together, and you've got a rare combination."

"Rare? I'd sooner say extinct." Connor slanted a baffled look in Julia's direction. It was far from the first look he'd given her. Julia Talbot might be an anomaly, but she was hard not to notice, even from a distance. And from up close, she was a knockout. He knew that firsthand, having met her five or six times, thanks to Brian's zealous introductions.

They'd never exchanged more than a few words. That wasn't a surprise. As Nancy's description attested, his world and hers were polar opposites. She lived in an idealistic, sheltered environment dictated by children's laughter. He lived in a cold reality where money was king and power was god, a world that, long ago, would have stripped away his rose-colored glasses—if he'd had any to begin with. But being a Stratford, he'd learned from the start that life was one increasingly formidable challenge, one you either beat or were beaten by.

Opposites was putting it mildly. He couldn't fathom that someone as naive as Julia Talbot existed. And, judging from the wall she put up whenever they spoke, she was as stumped by him as he was by her, and whatever small aspect of him she did understand, she didn't like.

That didn't stop him from looking.

She was beautiful, all right, in a real and natural way that differed sharply from the women who traveled in his circles. Her features were delicate and almost makeup-free, enhanced by a pair of sunglasses perched on the bridge of her slightly upturned nose. Her silky dark hair with its deep red highlights was pulled back in a French braid, although a few wisps had escaped and were clinging to her cheeks. She wore a tan spring jacket and a pair of jeans that did a pretty good job of concealing her slender curves. But Connor had seen her at Brian's summer games, during the hotter months of July and August, when she'd worn only a T-shirt and shorts. Her body was the kind men fantasized about.

Right now, her back was to them, her concentration entirely fixed on Brian. She whooped and cheered as he and his team took the field.

"She's seeing Greg Matthews."

"Hmm?" Connor slanted his brother a puzzled look. "Who is?"

"Julia Talbot. Greg mentioned it to me at the city council meeting this week. He sounded pretty intense about the whole thing."

"You're kidding. That's an unlikely pair. He's a smooth businessman with enough political savvy to run for office himself. And she's . . ." Connor shook his head. "Talk about a lamb in a lion's den."

"Yeah, I thought so, too."

"How long have they been seeing each other?"

"About a month. They met at a reception for the principal of her school."

Connor's shoulders lifted in a shrug. "There's no figuring out what attracts one person to another. Then again,

I'm hardly an expert. My track record with women stinks."

"That's because you're married to your work, and so are the women you've been involved with. Not a formula for happily-ever-after, if there is such a thing."

There was a definite trace of bitterness in Stephen's tone, one Connor picked up on loud and clear. He would have called his brother on it, point blank, if Brian hadn't been warming up to make his first pitch.

Questions would have to wait.

But the uneasiness that had begun gnawing at Connor's gut during his last visit to Leaf Brook intensified.

It was the bottom of the fifth inning, and Brian's team was winning, 3–1, when Stephen began fidgeting. Connor frowned, recognizing the signs, and hoping he was misreading them.

What Stephen did next told him he wasn't.

Half rising, Stephen climbed past Nancy, who was seated on the aisle. Simultaneously, he reached into his pocket and pulled out his cell phone. "I have a quick call to make," he said tersely. "I'll be back in a minute."

"Now?" Connor demanded. "Brian's team is up."

Stephen's cold stare told Connor to mind his own business. "There are five batters ahead of Brian and two more outs before he's back on the mound. I won't miss a thing."

He swung down and headed away from the crowd.

Connor saw Nancy's lips tighten, and she swallowed hard, as if to fight back tears. But her gaze never shifted from the ball field.

Another warning sign.

"Nance?" Connor kept his voice low. "What's going on?"

He knew she heard him. But she didn't answer.

"Nancy." Connor wasn't letting this go. "Is my brother in trouble?"

She turned her head slightly, enough so he could see the pain on her face. "Leave it alone, Connor. It's just the pressure of the election. It's getting to him. He'll be fine."

How many times had Connor heard those words in the past? "Dammit," he hissed.

"It's okay," Nancy reassured him quickly. "Really. It's nothing I can't handle. And politically, Cliff has things under control. He's laying out most of the campaign, making things run smoothly. That way, Stephen has less on his plate. Once the preliminary polls show the numbers we're hoping for, everything will settle down."

Everything. What she really meant was Stephen.

Connor cast a quick look around, seeing no eavesdroppers, only cheering parents and absorbed spectators. Even so, he forced himself not to push the matter. He was a Stratford, conditioned from birth to protect the family at all costs. Part of that meant not airing their dirty laundry in public. Any specifics would have to wait until later—assuming he could get them at all. Neither his brother nor his sister-in-law was inclined to open up. Nancy was busy protecting Stephen, and Stephen was busy protecting himself. Both of them were in denial.

The only good news was that Cliff Henderson was on top of the campaign. That would minimize Stephen's pressures, which, in turn, would curb the downward spiral of his behavior.

That prospect eased Connor's mind a little. Cliff was Stephen's oldest and closest friend. He was also his attorney, and now his campaign manager. Their friendship dated back to college, when they'd attended Yale together. They'd both continued on to Yale Law, during which time they met Nancy, who'd been a junior undergrad when the two men were in their second year of law school. Actually, she'd met Cliff first, even dated him a few times, but the relationship hadn't taken off, and when she and Stephen met, it was love at first sight. They'd gotten married after she graduated and after Stephen was admitted to both the Connecticut and the New York Bar. First, they'd settled in Connecticut, using Harrison Stratford's connections to get Stephen's career off the ground. Then, when Harrison deemed it time to launch his son's political career, they'd moved to Leaf Brook, the up-and-coming city Harrison chose as a prime location for Stephen's political roots to take hold.

Throughout these changes—and the establishment of his own private practice—Cliff had remained a loyal friend to Stephen, eventually moving to upper Westchester, where he could live at a commutable distance to his office and a mere half hour's drive to Stephen and his family.

Connor liked the man. He was a sharp, honorable guy with a quick mind and the ability to see the big picture. He believed in Stephen and his future, and when the time had come for Stephen to fulfill his father's directive to run for office, Cliff had been right there, supporting him and helping get his campaign off the ground.

Cliff was smart. Too smart, given that he and Stephen went back twenty years together, not to know about Stephen's compulsion—or at least to suspect. But whatever he knew, or thought he knew, about the skeleton in Stephen's closet, he kept that knowledge to himself. Instead, he quietly applied himself, showing up where he was needed, doing what had to be done.

Doing what had to be done. Now, *that* was the catch.

Connor pressed his palms together, feeling an overwhelming sense of frustration. The bottom line was, Stephen's compulsion wasn't going away. It peaked and ebbed, depending on the pressures in his life. And the people closest to him had to peak and ebb with it, acting as his crutch, helping him survive while hiding the ugliness from the public eye—*and* from Harrison Stratford.

That was becoming harder and harder to do.

"All taken care of," Stephen announced, scooting back into his seat. "I didn't miss anything, did I?"

"Apparently not," Connor muttered.

Stephen shot his brother a sideways look. "It was a business call."

"Really." Skepticism laced Connor's tone.

"Yes. Really." Stephen turned his full attention to the game. "So chill out."

Again, Connor bit back his concerns—for now. But this subject was far from closed. He'd originally intended to head back to the city after Brian's game was over and a victory celebration had been shared. But the behavior he'd just witnessed had changed all that. Now, his plan was to stay through the afternoon, go back to Stephen's house, and find a few minutes to talk to his brother alone—whether or not Stephen was in the mood for a heart-to-heart.

The final score was 7–2, with Brian's team—and his curve ball—emerging the victors.

Julia cheered and whistled as Brian accepted his teammates' back-slapping and high fives. He deserved the praise. He'd pitched an amazing game, even driving in two of the seven runs. She felt a tug of pride as he broke up his group of celebrating teammates, leading them over to slap hands with their opponents in a customary display of sportsmanship. Even at his tender age, Brian never forgot to consider other people's feelings. That was a trait that would carry him long after his enviable pitching arm had faded into a fond memory.

She watched his team disperse, her heart warming as he darted over to his family, who'd climbed down from the bleachers to wait for him. His mom, a graceful, slender woman with sleek blond hair and a radiant smile, hugged him tightly, squatting down to say something that made him beam. And his dad, Mayor Stratford, was right behind her, tugging at Brian's baseball cap and smiling a proud, paternal smile.

He'd barely said three words to Brian before the press descended.

"Mr. Mayor, how does it feel to have a champion pitcher in the family?" Julia heard one pushy reporter ask, bearing down on the mayor in a way that clearly indicated this was just her lead-in question, to be closely followed by the questions she *really* wanted to ask.

Stephen Stratford smiled that charming smile that could melt an iceberg. He was an astonishingly handsome man—tall, broad-shouldered, with jet-black hair and sapphire-blue eyes that altered from warm and welcoming to shrewd and insightful. With those incredible looks, natural charisma, and impressive family connections, he'd probably manage to get elected to the state senate without anything more. But he did have more: an impeccable five-year record as mayor. After a full term and then some, he'd proven himself to be an outstanding leader, one who'd significantly improved Leaf Brook's economy, its schools, its parks, and its environment. In Julia's mind, he was a shoo-in for the senate. And he wouldn't stop there. Julia had a strong feeling that the next decade would see Stephen Stratford advance from Albany to the U.S. Senate in Washington, D.C.

"Hello, Cheryl." He was greeting the overbearing reporter, retaining his good humor despite the intrusion on his family time. "If you'll give me a minute to congratulate my son, I think you'll see how I feel." Without waiting for an answer, he turned and gave Brian a huge bear hug. "Great game, ace," Julia heard him say. "And great curve ball."

"Thanks." Brian was grinning from ear to ear. Interesting how he scarcely seemed to notice the press. Julia supposed he was just used to having them around. With a bigger-than-life grandfather and father and an entire family who was constantly in the news and the public eye, being hounded by reporters was probably par for the course, even for a seven-year-old. Still, Julia herself couldn't imagine living in the spotlight that way.

On a different note, though, she could completely identify with his current frame of mind. He was flying on his win. She chuckled inwardly as he jumped around, incapable of standing still, too filled with energy and excitement. He zipped away from his parents, rushing over to give a rousing high five to the other tall man who was with them.

Connor Stratford.

Julia's smile faded a bit as that unnerving awareness set in, along with the resulting confusion, neither of which she could shake, both of which plagued her only around Brian's uncle.

This was what her mother had picked up on the other night, the "something" she'd perceived as an obstacle to whatever might or might not develop with Greg. Chemistry, she'd said. Well, maybe. More like unwelcome fascination, in Julia's opinion. Unwelcome fascination without any basis whatsoever, other than physical attraction.

Yes, Connor Stratford was good-looking—*very* good-looking—in a hard, arrogant sort of way. And he had a personality to match. Well, she hated arrogance. It was enough to turn her off to any man, handsome or otherwise. At least, it always had been. It didn't seem to be working that way in this case. Why not, she hadn't a clue. All she knew was that she'd met Connor Stratford just a handful of times, yet each and every time, he'd managed to throw her off balance.

She lowered her gaze, trying to understand her unprecedented response to a man who, on the whole, she didn't even like.

It was hard to believe he and Stephen Stratford were brothers. Oh, physically it was obvious. They looked a lot alike, feature for feature. Same dark hair, same height and build, same blue eyes. No, actually, different blue eyes. The mayor's were a vivid, brilliant blue, warm and open. His brother's eyes were lighter, more of a blue-gray, veiled and unreadable. They matched his personality—aloof and guarded, coolly enigmatic, with a brooding sort of intensity Julia couldn't begin to relate to, which seemed to hold all human contact at bay.

As if that wasn't enough, he was a venture capitalist—a fancy name for someone who invested money to make more money. Like his father's, his name appeared regularly in the financial columns, articles that recounted windfalls he'd made, the details of which Julia couldn't begin to decipher, much less understand. All she knew was that at age thirty-five, he'd already made millions, which he chose to reinvest in bigger and more lucrative ventures.

What a waste. At least Mayor Stratford had opted to use the advantages life afforded him to make a difference, to give back and make the world a better place. He dealt with people. His brother dealt with cash. That notion left Julia cold. Connor Stratford left her cold.

Most of the time.

Then she'd watch him with Brian, and she'd see an entirely different man, one who fed into her irrational fascination. His wall of reserve would lift, his arrogance would vanish, and he'd light up like a Christmas tree, all warm and vital. Clearly, he was crazy about his nephew, and Brian's love for his uncle was nothing short of hero worship.

Now was a perfect example of that.

"Wasn't it an awesome game, Uncle Connor?" Brian was demanding.

"Beyond awesome," his uncle assured him, returning his high five and grinning that rare grin that transformed his entire face from chiseled to magnificent. "You're one step from the pros. Give it another year. Two, tops." He winked. "On the other hand, maybe you better stay in school. That way, your mind will be as sharp as your arm."

The reference to school seemed to remind Brian of something. And Julia had a sinking feeling she knew what—or *who*—that something was.

Sure enough, Brian spun around, his gaze darting

toward the set of bleachers where she still stood. He found her, and his eyes gleamed. "Miss Talbot!" he bellowed, waving. "Miss Talbot! I'm over here!"

Julia felt Connor's stare shift until it fixed on her. She swallowed, wishing she could disappear. Automatically, she waved back at Brian, racking her brain for a way to slip off without joining them. There was none.

Yes, there was. The press. They were converged around the mayor like a swarm of bees. And she didn't want to intrude.

Nancy Stratford closed off that avenue of escape.

"By all means, join us, Miss Talbot," she called out, gesturing her over. "There's no victory celebration without you."

On wooden legs, Julia complied.

"Mr. Mayor." One determined reporter was addressing him. "I know you support the funding of after-school programs for kids. Would you advocate those programs on a state level?"

"Definitely," Stephen replied in that smooth, confident voice that said he knew exactly what he was talking about. "Not every family has the financial means to send their children to private after-school programs, whether those programs are sports, arts, academic, community service, or social in nature. It's up to the state to make those programs available to all families." He shot a quick smile in Julia's direction. "Thanks for the curve-ball lessons. They really paid off."

"Any time." She smiled back, squatting down to give Brian a warm hug. "You were sensational."

"Thanks. Say hi to Uncle Connor."

Why did kids always manage to zero in on exactly what you wish they wouldn't?

Resigned, Julia stood, raising her chin to meet Connor's coolly assessing stare. "Nice to see you."

"You, too." He gave a tight nod. "I hear you did some great last-minute coaching."

"It wasn't necessary. All Brian needed was another loud set of lungs to cheer him on. I provided that."

There were the same clipped sentences and strained discomfort that underscored all of their exchanges.

Julia was dying to get out of there.

Brian had other ideas. "Once Dad's finished talking, we're going out for ice cream," he announced. "Oh, and lunch, too. Can you come?"

Julia gave a rueful shake of her head. "I'm sorry, but I can't. I've got lots of spelling tests to grade, and I'm meeting a friend after that."

The last part was a mistake. Julia knew it the minute she saw Brian's eyes light up with interest.

"What friend?" he demanded. "Miss Haley?"

"No, sweetie, not Miss Haley," Julia replied, torn between amusement and a desperate urge to extricate herself. She should have anticipated this. Robin Haley was the computer teacher at their elementary school, and, yes, she and Julia were friends. It followed suit, then, in the eyes of a second grader who couldn't visualize his teacher having a life outside school, that *all* her friends would have to be found there. So Robin was the logical choice as the friend she must be meeting.

It was also the wrong choice. And Julia had no intention of setting Brian straight by telling him she had a date—and certainly not with whom. Greg worked with the mayor. She taught the mayor's son. It was an awkward coincidence, one she'd prefer didn't become the topic around the water cooler.

"Not Miss Haley?" Brian pressed, on cue. "Then who?"

"Brian, I think you've asked Miss Talbot enough questions for one morning." It was Connor who saved her, although his tone was more amused than censuring, and Julia got the distinct impression that he enjoyed watching her squirm. He leaned over, hissing in his nephew's ear. "You're starting to sound like one of them." He jerked his head ever so slightly in the direction of the reporters.

Brian rolled his eyes and shared a grin with his uncle. "Yeah, I guess you're right. Sorry, Miss Talbot."

Julia had just opened her mouth to reply, when the reporter named Cheryl turned in their direction. "Mr. Stratford," she said, addressing Connor. "My name is Cheryl Lager, and I'm with the *Leaf Brook News*. It's no secret that your father and you are the Stratford millionaires. So tell me, will you be contributing heavily to your brother's senatorial campaign? Or will most of the financial backing come from your father?"

There was a heartbeat of silence, during which time Julia could feel a blanket of tension settle over the group. She glanced at the mayor and saw a flicker of surprised annoyance flash in his eyes, then vanish. His wife looked startled, stepping closer to her husband's side in a reflexive show of support. The rest of the reporters leaned in with great interest, glad they hadn't asked the question, equally glad someone else had.

Connor's expression never changed, although Julia was standing close enough to him to see his jaw tighten.

"Ms. Lager, I believe my brother will make an exceptional senator," he replied. "He has my full support in any way I can offer it, including financially, should it be needed. My father shares those sentiments, as I'm sure he'll gladly tell you." One dark brow rose. "Imagine that. A family investment in a candidate's campaign. A refreshing concept, wouldn't you say? Sure beats campaign financing from special-interest groups."

There were a few titters, and for an instant Julia thought the taut moment had ended.

But Cheryl Lager wasn't ready to throw in the towel. "In theory, yes, that sounds commendable. But it occurs to me that, given your numerous business interests, you might have a few ideas of your own on how state finances should be allocated."

This time, she got a reaction. Connor's features went rigid, and the glare he aimed at her was positively lethal. "My ideas—and my ethics—are mine and have no place in this election. Further, they're not up for sale, for discussion, or for compromise. Does that answer your question, Ms. Lager?"

"Apparently, it does." She backed off, sensing she'd overstepped her bounds.

"Uncle Connor." Brian tugged at his arm. "Why do you look mad? I thought we were celebrating."

Something inside Julia snapped. Maybe it was the ugly, unwarranted line of questioning, and maybe it was the fact that Brian's victory was being shoved aside by an insolent reporter going for a few cheap, political shots. "We are," she heard herself say. Placing a hand on Brian's shoulder, she added, "Do you know, now that I think about it, I have enough time for a quick ice cream cone. Besides, I have a favor to ask your dad." She inclined her head quizzically at Mayor Stratford. "I was hoping he'd come in and talk to our class about running for office. Class elections are coming up, and we need lots of help."

"You've got it." The mayor's smile returned, but it seemed forced, and he looked distinctly unnerved. So, for that matter, did his wife. And Connor Stratford was drawn so tight, Julia could almost feel him vibrate.

"Great. Thank you," she replied, addressing the mayor. "Then maybe we can pick a date while Brian picks a flavor."

"Good idea." It was Connor who spoke, breaking in as if he'd had enough. "No more questions this morning, folks," he flatly informed the reporters. "We're on family time. So, if you'll excuse us . . ."

There was no arguing with that tone. The press complied, gathering up their things and disbanding.

"Thanks," Stephen said quietly to his brother. There were dots of perspiration on his brow.

"Yeah." Connor stared after Cheryl Lager, his jaw still working with anger. "She was sickening. But who am I to argue with freedom of the press?" His head swung around, and he shot his brother a quick, hard look. "Then again, we should expect more of that, right?" Without waiting for a reply, he averted his gaze, his demeanor softening as he tugged at the rim of Brian's baseball cap. "Come on, ace. We've got some celebrating to do."

"Miss Talbot, too," Brian reminded him.

Those frosty blue eyes flickered across Julia's face. "Yes, Miss Talbot, too. But only for a quick cone. She's got spelling tests to grade, and you and I have lots of catching up to do."

"Okay," Brian agreed. Clearly, the thought of spending time with his uncle was enough to offset his disappointment over the brevity of Julia's visit. "We're going to the Big Scoop," he informed her. "It's my favorite."

"Mine, too," she agreed.

"I'm starving." Brian gazed expectantly at his parents. "Can we go now?"

Stephen Stratford was staring off into space, his brows knit in concentration.

"Stephen?" His wife squeezed his arm.

He blinked, recovering himself in a heartbeat. "Sure, we can go. Everybody's set? Then we're on our way." Beckoning to the group as a whole, he looped an arm around his wife's shoulders and headed off toward the car.

Connor paused, his lids hooded as he watched them go. "Do you have your car?" he asked brusquely.

Since she was the only other adult standing there, Julia had to assume he was talking to her. "Yes."

"Good. That way, you can get going whenever you need to."

He planted a hand on Brian's shoulder and led him toward the parking lot.

Julia held back a moment, struck by the tension still crackling in the air.

Connor Stratford hadn't even tried to hide the fact that he was eager to get rid of her. But this time, it had nothing to do with the odd vibes that existed between them. This time, it had to do with his family, with his brother.

This time, something was wrong.

4

April 2

Elbows propped on his desk, Stephen massaged his temples, wishing the phone would ring, wishing his gut instinct would pay off. He needed this win. He needed something good after the lousy weekend he'd just been through. First, that pain-in-the-ass reporter on Saturday, followed by an inquisition from Connor. Then, Sunday, finding out his pick had fallen through, big time. All culminating last night in a knock-down, drag-out fight with Nancy.

She was worried about him. Connor was worried about him. The whole damned world was worried about him.

If they'd all just go away and leave him alone, he'd be fine. He knew what he was doing. He was always on top of things. After all, he was a Stratford, right?

Bitterly, he pushed his chair away from the desk, swiveling it around so he could stare out the window. Five stories below, the city of Leaf Brook moved briskly through its morning. The hub that surrounded the City Municipal Building was hopping. Business people zipped off to work, parents drove their kids to school or day care, and shoppers carted their groceries home from supermarkets.

It all looked so simple.

Maybe for some people it was.

His cell phone rang. Stephen snatched it up. "Yes?"

"No good. The team didn't make the trade."

Stephen's fingers tightened on the receiver. "What do you mean, they didn't make the trade? They were about to sign."

"Well, they didn't. He renegotiated his contract. He's staying."

"Shit." Stephen punched END and stuffed the phone in his jacket pocket. There went ten thousand dollars down the toilet. How much worse could it get?

There was a rap on his door.

He swallowed, folded his hands tightly on his desk. Control. He had to get himself under control.

"Mayor Stratford?" Celeste, his secretary, poked her head through the doorway. "I'm sorry to bother you, sir, but your nine-thirty appointment is here. So is Mr. Henderson. Shall I send him in first?"

Automatically, Stephen's gaze darted to his calendar. Nine-thirty. Philip Walker, one of Leaf Brook's wealthiest real estate developers. He'd orchestrated the building of two-thirds of the city's strip malls, several of its office complexes, its main recreational center, and two of its movie theaters. He'd also invested big bucks in the super mall that had just been completed downtown and was scheduled to open in less than two weeks. Greg had mentioned something about Walker wanting to speak with them about a substantial business proposition that would greatly benefit the city.

"Sir?" Celeste prompted.

Stephen raised his head, giving his secretary a genuinely appreciative look. "Yes, send Cliff in first. And buzz Greg. Let him know Mr. Walker's here. He'll want to join us."

"Very good, sir."

"Oh, and Celeste? Tell Mr. Walker I'll be with him in five minutes. In the meantime, see if he wants some coffee."

"Of course."

"Thanks a lot." Stephen warmed her with his smile. "You're indispensable."

She smiled back. "I try."

An instant later, Cliff Henderson strode in, briefcase in hand. He was tall and lean, with sandy hair and affable brown eyes. Cliff's clean-cut appearance and easy manner added up to a boy-next-door charm. He used that all-American appeal to his advantage, lulling his legal adversaries into a false sense of security by fooling them into believing he was just an average legal counsel in a conservative Brooks Brothers suit. The truth was, there was nothing average about him. He was an extraordinary attorney, with exceptional insight, fine-tuned instincts, and a mind like a steel trap.

He set his briefcase on the desk, darting Stephen a quick look as he snapped open the case. "You okay?"

"Yeah, fine. Why?"

"You look a little tired." A corner of Cliff's mouth lifted. "Probably the stress of being the father of a game-winning, superstar pitcher. It was a pretty impressive game, followed by a pretty impressive celebration, from what Nancy said."

Stephen relaxed, his expression softening. "Yeah, the game was great. As for the celebration, that's probably why I look a little off today. I ate an entire three-scoop banana split on my own. My thirty-six-year-old stomach isn't as resilient as it used to be."

"Tell me about it. The days of downing a whole pizza

with everything on it are long over." Cliff pulled out a file, opening it as he sank into one of the cushioned chairs across from Stephen's desk. "I've got some preliminary numbers. They look good, even this early in the campaign. The voters like you. They like what you stand for. Braxton knows it, too. He's been campaigning hard, which is unusual this many months before the election. That means he's worried. He should be. Take a look." He slid a page across the desk.

Stephen scanned the information. "It's not exactly a slam-dunk lead. Yeah, I'm ahead, but only by fifteen points. That's not enough to start planning the victory party. And let's not forget, Braxton's the incumbent. We've got our work cut out for us." *And we need major dollars to back us,* he added silently. *Dollars I don't have because they've been slipping away, along with my luck.*

"I spoke to your father this morning," Cliff continued. "He likes the way things are shaping up. He's optimistic about the outcome."

"Glad to hear it." Stephen had to work to keep the sarcasm out of his voice. Optimistic. That was his father's way of saying, not bad but not quite there. The usual, when it came to his opinion of Stephen. And that would deteriorate into outrage and disgust if the omnipotent Harrison Stratford knew what his son had done with the cash he'd provided to back this campaign.

The thought made Stephen's insides twist.

He had to recoup that money—and fast.

"Do you want to prep for this meeting with Walker?" Cliff was asking.

"Do you know what it's about?"

"Nothing specific. Other than that it concerns a new proposal, something that's not on the table yet."

"Yeah, Greg mentioned that. But that's all he mentioned. So we can't do much prepping." Stephen leaned back in his chair. "I'm not too worried. Every one of Walker's ventures has been good for the city. I'm assuming this one will be, too."

Cliff nodded. "I'm eager to hear what he has to say. And not only because he's been good for the city, but because he's been good for you." He slipped the senatorial campaign file back into his briefcase and took out a pad and pen. "He's a solid ally, Steve—affluent, well connected, a good source of new revenue for Leaf Brook, and an equally good source of potential campaign contributions."

"Understood. Anything else before we get this meeting started?"

Another searching look. "Nope. Except I suggest you go home early and get some sleep. And lay off the banana splits."

"I'll try." Stephen punched the intercom button on his phone. "Celeste, you can show Mr. Walker and Mr. Matthews in now."

"Right away," his secretary replied.

A minute later, she gave the usual perfunctory knock, then opened the door and showed the two men in.

Stephen rose, greeting Philip Walker, meeting the older man's firm handshake with one of his own. "Good to see you, Philip. Greg, thanks for joining us." He shifted his handshake to the city manager, a gesture that was more a matter of protocol than anything else. He and Greg Matthews had long since passed the formality stage. They'd worked together in this municipal building for five years. Besides interacting on the city's budget and policies, they shared an occasional lunch, a friendly rivalry over the Mets and the Yankees, and snatches of personal conversation in the parking lot. Greg was bright and ambitious, and Stephen felt confident knowing Leaf Brook's fiscal well-being was in his hands.

He completed the social amenities with, "You both know Cliff Henderson," motioning toward Cliff.

"Of course." Another round of handshakes.

"Have a seat." Stephen indicated the cluster of chairs across from him. He waited until everyone was settled before opening with a reminder that was sure to set an upbeat tone for the meeting. "The mall's set to open on April 14th. The celebration we're planning should bring out the whole city."

Philip Walker nodded, looking pleased—or at least as pleased as he ever looked. With his deep-set dark eyes and watchful expression, he appeared to be perpetually intense, almost grim, as if he were contemplating what was being discussed and evaluating it for loopholes. "Good," he replied. "That's what we're aiming for." He ran an impatient hand through his thick head of salt-and-pepper hair. "Actually, I'm here about another idea, one I think will be equally profitable. So, if it's okay with you, I'll get right down to business."

No surprise. Walker was known for his shoot-from-the-hip delivery. And in this case, it was more than fine with Stephen. The way his head was throbbing, the last thing he felt like doing was shooting the breeze. What he really needed was some strong coffee and a plan. "Go ahead."

"It occurred to me that Leaf Brook has grown a lot since you took office. It's now got office buildings, shops, and traffic congestion, especially in the heavily populated areas. Municipal lots have sprung up everywhere to accommodate people's parking needs."

"True." Stephen frowned, wondering where this was going.

Philip leaned forward, his forehead creased in concentration. "Walker Development has an affiliated real estate services company. We offer things like landscaping, snow removal, and security services to those who own or lease the facilities we built. We'd like to expand to a more public domain—namely, the city's municipal parking lots. We'd revamp the lots, tearing out the meters and putting up booths with attendants at all exits. We'd reorganize the way the lots are set up, making parking more accessible and expedient. And we'd implement round-the-clock security for safety purposes."

He folded his hands. "Here's how I see it. Based on my estimates, Leaf Brook currently grosses just shy of a million a year off the lots, then pays tens of thousands to maintain them. If, instead, you leased those facilities to my company, we'd pay Leaf Brook the same million, plus five percent of the gross revenue we'd generate on top of that. The city would have safer and better parking facilities, lose the headache of maintaining them, and make a nice profit in the process."

"So would you," Stephen commented, his mind rapidly processing everything Walker had said.

"True." Philip's gaze remained steady. "Then again, that's what I'm in business for."

Stephen picked up his pen, rolled it thoughtfully between his fingers. "It's an interesting idea. Certainly worth considering."

"Considering. Does that mean you support it?"

"Unofficially, my initial reaction would be to say yes. Of course, I'd have to run through the numbers with

Greg, and then pass the proposal on to the city council. As you know, their authorization is necessary."

"And I'm sure, as presiding officer, you'll get that authorization without a problem. After all, what I've suggested is a win-win situation—as I'm sure Mr. Matthews's numbers will confirm." Philip rose, smoothing the jacket of his expensive suit. "So, the next city council meeting is Thursday. Bring it up then. When you get their feedback, give me a call."

"I will."

"Oh." Philip paused, as if something had just occurred to him. "Speaking of win-win situations, congratulations on your candidacy for state senate. New York will be lucky to get you."

"Thank you." Stephen came to his feet as well, although his instincts told him something more was coming.

His instincts were right.

Philip slipped his hand into his coat pocket, fishing out a checkbook and pen. "If I may, I'd like to make a contribution to your campaign. I'm sure you can put it to good use, even though you're probably swimming in contribution money. But I'd like to be part of your winning campaign." Without waiting for a reply, he wrote out a check, tearing it off and passing it across the desk. "There. With my best wishes."

The number of zeroes struck Stephen squarely between the eyes. Five of them. Philip Walker had just handed him a check for a hundred thousand dollars.

He raised his head, his features carefully schooled as he accepted the check and folded it in half. "That's very generous of you, Philip. I appreciate your support."

"My pleasure." A hint of a smile curved his hard

mouth. "I'll let you get back to your work." He gripped Stephen's hand in another firm handshake. "Thanks for taking the time to see me. Gentlemen," he said, acknowledging Cliff and Greg. "Nice seeing you."

He crossed over and left the office.

Greg unfolded his lanky frame from the chair, rising to stare after him. When the door was firmly shut, he turned and gave Stephen a measured look. "I thought this would be about breaking ground on another office development. I wasn't expecting this. Sorry if it blindsided you."

"No problem." Stephen was fighting to keep his mind on the conversation. It was all he could do not to start jumping up and down. A hundred thousand dollars. It was just the spark he needed. "I wasn't expecting this, either. But the idea does have merit. Our municipal lots are decaying. And maintaining them has become a royal pain for the city. Not to mention the amount of taxpayer dollars we're spending. This could be a good deal for Leaf Brook all the way around."

"I can't argue with that." Greg's sharp gray eyes assessed the mayor's reaction, interpreted it as positive. "I'll run through some numbers. If they come out as I expect, we'll raise the subject with the city council. I can't imagine they'd object."

"I can't, either."

Cliff said nothing, just scribbled some notes before setting down his pad and making a steeple with his fingers, resting his chin atop them.

Greg cleared his throat. "I'll get back to my desk and get started. I'll check your schedule with Celeste and see when you're free to go over the results."

"Sounds good," Stephen agreed. "Let's shoot for late this afternoon."

"Fine."

The room was silent until after Greg had left.

"Interesting timing on Walker's part," Cliff offered when he and Stephen were alone. "How much did he give you?"

Wordlessly, Stephen handed him the check.

Cliff let out a low whistle. "A pretty serious contribution."

"No argument there." Stephen's conscience made him ask the obvious. "So tell me, was I just bribed?"

A corner of Cliff's mouth lifted. "I think Philip Walker would call it an incentive. Whether or not that amounts to the same thing is a matter of interpretation. He didn't threaten to pull the funds if you ultimately refused his business proposal. And since you could technically cash this now, long before the council makes any final decision, I don't think it constitutes a bribe. That doesn't mean he won't like you a whole lot better if you manage to pull this off for him."

That was just the answer Stephen wanted to hear. His conscience was off the hook.

"No question about that," he acknowledged, seeing a ray of hope that had been painfully absent a half hour ago. "But the truth is, his idea's a good one. Good for Walker, yeah, but good for Leaf Brook. Incentive or not."

"Then you have your answer."

"I guess I do. Now all that's left is getting Greg's corroboration and the council's authorization."

"And one other thing. Deciding how to allocate your latest contribution."

Oh, Stephen knew how to allocate it, all right. He'd make a few strategic bets that would increase the contribution and help him recoup his losses.

Correction: his *father's* losses.

He'd be off the hook. Everything would be okay.

"Right," he murmured, his mind racing from one possibility to the next. "I expect Walker's contribution will go a long way."

5

There was something magical about recess. It took problems and inhibitions and made them vanish with that first scoot down the slide or that first scramble up the monkey bars.

Ah, to be seven again.

Julia smiled, watching three of her students negotiating the two empty swings. Krissy, as usual, was bossing the other two girls around. But this time, her tactics were being met with resistance. Jenny, who was normally very shy, wanted the swing enough to stand her ground. And Lori's keen sense of competition was kicking in.

This was going to be a dead heat.

Realizing they'd reached an impasse, the three girls resorted to the only possible solution that wouldn't waste precious recess time arguing: they did "once twice three shoot" to decide who the two lucky takers would be. Nothing more equitable than that.

A minute later, Krissy flounced off to try bossing the boys around.

Julia's gaze shifted, automatically making its rounds to ensure the safety of all her eighteen pupils. All well.

She frowned a little as she spotted Brian, standing off to the side and tossing a baseball in the air, catching it in his glove, then throwing it again. It wasn't like him to hang out alone. Or to be so quiet. Yet he'd done both all day. Even after Saturday's overwhelming victory.

For the dozenth time, she wondered what had happened the rest of the weekend to alter his mood so dramatically. Whatever it was, it had begun with that bitchy reporter and her intrusive questions. Mayor Stratford had been out of sorts from that moment on. The celebration at the Big Scoop, while outwardly jovial, had been underscored with that same tension she'd sensed at the ball field. Both of Brian's parents had done their best to hide it, but Julia could feel their emotional strain. And Connor Stratford had been positively glacial during those infrequent moments when he wasn't interacting with Brian.

She'd gotten out of there as soon as she could. But she'd felt distinctly uneasy all weekend, and she'd worried about Brian. With good cause, it seemed.

"Hi." Robin Haley strolled over to Julia, shading her eyes from the sun. "I had a break. My next class isn't due in the computer lab for twenty minutes. So I thought I'd see how your date went."

For a moment, Julia almost asked what date. Then she realized Robin meant her evening with Greg.

"The show was excellent," she replied. "Afterward, we grabbed a late-night bite in midtown. Considering how exhausted I was, I had a lot of fun."

Robin tucked a strand of honey-blond hair behind her ear. "And?"

"And what?"

Her friend sighed. "Julia, I've met Greg Matthews. He's an incredible-looking guy. He's also pursuing you like crazy. He calls, he sends flowers, he takes you to great places. So what's the problem?"

Julia avoided meeting her friend's gaze by keeping her own watchful stare on her kids. She hated this conversation. Robin was a good friend, but she harped on Julia's social life—or lack thereof—far too much. If Julia didn't know she meant well, she'd tell her to butt out. But she did mean well. And to Robin, who was the proverbial party girl, a healthy social life meant dating lots of men and exploring each relationship to its fullest. Which was fine—for Robin. But it wouldn't work for Julia.

"There is no problem," she stated flatly. "Yes, Greg's a nice guy. And yes, he's been very attentive. I enjoy his company. I don't know what you expect to hear. We've only gone out a handful of times."

"Yeah, I know. And Greg doesn't strike me as the type who's used to waiting."

That part was true. Greg was a man who was used to getting what he wanted. But he was also pretty astute. He'd picked up on the fact that Julia wasn't the type to separate physical and emotional commitment. At the beginning, he'd been very patient, tangibly restraining himself from pushing her. This time had been a little more difficult. When he'd taken her home Saturday night, he'd wanted to come in—and not for coffee. She'd put him off, explaining that she was tired. It was the truth.

Okay, part of the truth.

The rest would have sounded like melodramatic drivel or soapbox spouting to a man as seasoned, as fundamental about "taking the next step," as Greg.

She realized it wasn't fair. But she couldn't help who she was. So she'd suggested to Greg that they see a little less of each other. That hadn't flown. He'd eased up the pressure immediately, apologizing for rushing her and assuring her that he was more than willing to wait, to back off and give her as much time as she needed.

The problem was, she wasn't sure time would change anything. Especially if what her mother had said the other night was true. Whatever spark was supposed to be there between her and Greg—at least from her perspective—still hadn't ignited. Nor had any real feelings started to develop. She liked the man. Period.

"Julia?" Robin prompted.

"There's nothing else to tell, Rob." Julia closed the subject firmly, her troubled gaze drifting back to Brian. "Sorry to disappoint you, but . . ."

"That's not it." Her friend was peering past her, scrutinizing the far section of the playground. "There's a guy watching the kids. Over there by the fence. Behind the trees."

"A guy?" Julia whipped around, angling herself so she could see past the cluster of oaks. She spotted the tall man who was leaning against the fence, arms crossed atop it as he gazed steadily toward where the children were playing.

Recognition was immediate.

"That's Connor Stratford," she murmured. "Brian's uncle." She turned to Robin. "Will you watch the kids for me for a minute?"

"Sure."

"Thanks." Julia headed straight for the fence, rounding the trees that shielded Connor from view. He must have seen her coming, but he gave no sign of that fact.

"Hi," Julia greeted tersely as she came up to him. "Can I help you?"

Those cool blue eyes flickered over her. "I don't remember asking for help."

"True. Does that mean you're here to observe recess? Or are you just waiting for a swing to free up?"

His lips quirked ever so slightly, as if the response was against his will. "The swings were never my thing. I was more of a dodge ball guy myself."

"Dodge ball. Now, why doesn't that surprise me? You could aggressively go after people, then calculate the direction of their return swipes so you could sidestep them and win. Sounds right."

This time, he surprised her by chuckling. "You don't have a very high opinion of me, I gather."

"I don't know you well enough to have *any* opinion of you. Except where it comes to Brian. You obviously adore him." She paused and glanced quickly over her shoulder to see the boy still playing alone. "You're also worried about him," she surmised quietly. "So am I. He's been uncharacteristically withdrawn today. I tried to talk to him but without much luck." She turned back to Connor. "I don't suppose you want to give me some insight into what's bothering him."

She didn't hold out much hope of getting a response.

Sure enough, Brian's uncle met her request with a tight-lipped silence.

"Does it have something to do with his father's campaign?" she pressed, stating the obvious. "Are things becoming tense at home? It certainly seemed that way the other day. And the signs are there."

"Are they?" Connor straightened, his expression closed.

"Yes." Julia gripped the fence, frustrated at the wall that was being erected to shut her out. "Mr. Stratford, I have experience in this field. I know when a child is hurting."

"Really. You're a psychologist? I thought you were a teacher."

"I'm both. I have degrees in child psychology and early childhood education. I also give lectures at hospitals on topics that involve children's emotional well-being. I'm more than qualified. So, believe me, I'm not just blowing smoke."

A hint of interest lit his eyes. "Childhood psych *and* elementary ed. I'm impressed."

"Somehow I doubt it. Neither profession commands the kind of income that would impress you. And the workshops are pro bono."

"You just finished saying you don't know me. How would you know what I'd find impressive?"

"A shrewd guess. Venture capitalists value money and opportunities to make more of it. That's a far cry from what teachers and psychologists value."

Rather than annoyed, he looked intrigued, inclining his head to study her. "I take it you know quite a few venture capitalists?"

She flushed, realizing he had her there and he knew it. She was speaking out of anger and frustration, not fact. What's more, it wasn't like her to be so judgmental.

"Don't look so guilty," he said bluntly, reading her expression. "Your assessment's accurate. I was just wondering if it was based on your observations of anyone other than me. But let me clue you in. There's a big, ugly world out there. It's not only financial types who are driven by greed and power. Most everyone is. Take a peek outside your classroom sometime. You'd be surprised."

With that, he pushed away from the fence. "I'm going to take off before Brian sees me. I'd prefer he didn't know I was here."

Why? she wanted to ask. *Because it would upset him when you had to say good-bye? Or because he'd tell his father about your visit?*

"Mr. Stratford." Without thinking, Julia grabbed his arm, needing to have her say before he left.

He paused, his smoky-blue stare focusing on her fingers, then shifting to her face. "What?"

Hastily, she released him. "I know you dislike me. That's your prerogative. But it has nothing to do with Brian. Your nephew is very special to me. So, if he's in pain, I want to help."

Connor's features hardened. "I realize that. But you can't. So stay out of it." He retreated a few steps, then halted, turning until their eyes met. "For the record, I don't dislike you. And my name is Connor."

6

Connor didn't get back to the city until late Monday afternoon.

He drove around for hours after leaving Brian's school, bothered as hell by the dejected slump of his normally exuberant nephew's shoulders. It killed him to see Brian so low. And it made him want to beat some sense and, more important, some priorities into his brother.

Couldn't Stephen see what he was doing to his son?

Striding into his Upper West Side apartment, Connor shrugged out of his jacket and tossed it onto the couch. He was beat. He'd left the apartment at dawn, been in the office before seven, and taken off at ten to drive back to a suburb he'd roared out of two days ago. And why? Because he'd hoped to find something there that would ease his mind. Instead, he'd found Brian worse than he'd been on Saturday. Obviously, the tension between Stephen and Nancy had blown wide open sometime between Saturday afternoon—after the biting words he and Stephen had exchanged behind closed doors—and Monday morning when Brian left for school. Being as sensitive as he was, Brian would internalize every drop of his parents' stress. Stress that was totally preventable, if Stephen wanted it to be.

Goddammit. The man was gambling again.

With a muttered curse, Connor stalked over to the sideboard to pour himself a drink. He took it with him, going over to stand by the stretch of windows in the living room, gazing across Manhattan's skyline.

Stephen's gambling had started in high school. Even before, if you counted small-time stuff like betting with his buddies on whether or not the school team was going to walk away with the year's trophy. From there, it was on to bigger bets and pro ball clubs—smaller wagers for regular-season games, up to thousands for Super Bowl and World Series wins. The compulsion got worse as time passed. With it, Stephen's personality became more and more erratic, sometimes exuberant, sometimes withdrawn. His dramatic highs and lows spoke volumes.

Connor understood the root of his brother's problem better than anyone. Stephen needed to prove himself, to come out a winner.

To live up to their father's expectations.

Connor harbored no illusions. Harrison Stratford was an overbearing son of a bitch, whose fixation with making money was dwarfed only by his fixation with power. He believed in winning, always and regardless of the odds. He'd accept no less from his sons.

Stephen had the bad luck of being born first. A year older than Connor, he was immediately slated as his father's golden boy. The best schools, the best grades, the captain of the most competitive varsity teams. From there, it was on to Yale and Yale Law. The plan was a series of stepping stones: first, attorney extraordinaire; next, strong local political figure; then a jump to the state senate, then to Congress and—with the right record, image, platforms, and backing—straight to the White House.

What Stephen himself wanted was never discussed, since, in their father's mind, it was of no consequence. Neither were his aptitudes, his areas of interest, or his backbone. Harrison Stratford called the shots. And Stephen fell in line.

Connor's path had been easier. To begin with, he was the second child. The expectations were different. Also, he fit his father's professional mold admirably. He had a natural inclination for making money. In Harrison's mind, that made him a chip off the old block. And with no role to fulfill, no national mark to make, Connor was free to pursue his goal, plowing his way through Harvard and right up through its graduate business school. From the start, it was clear he had a talent for making just the right investments. That earned him high-powered jobs and huge financial returns. By the time he was thirty, he'd formed his own company and was out on his own. By thirty-three, he was a millionaire. As a result, he'd earned his father's respect and fulfilled his expectations.

The expectations for Stephen were much higher and much longer-term. Connor was a fait accompli; Stephen was a work in progress.

Harrison had no idea of his son's gambling problem. Connor made damned sure of that, bailing Stephen out whenever he got in over his head, covering for him as needed. More important, he talked to him, or maybe *lectured* was a better word. Professional help wasn't an option—if the press got wind of the reasons behind the therapy, Stephen would be finished. So it was up to those who cared about Stephen—initially Connor, eventually Nancy—to give him the strength he needed to abstain.

With marriage, fatherhood, a successful mayorship, and Connor's badgering, Stephen finally improved. He managed to take control of his life, locking away his gambling in a dark corner of his past, where it stayed.

Until this damned senatorial race got under way.

Suddenly, the pressure of having to succeed, to be bigger than life, to win, was back in his face, looming over him like some predatory animal.

Connor sensed the transition in his brother's personality around New Year's, when plans for the campaign were launched. He observed Stephen quietly, saying nothing to anyone—even Nancy, whose overly bright eyes and too sunny smile told him she already knew. Connor prayed he was wrong. But his every instinct screamed that Stephen's old ghosts were rearing their heads. Unable to shake his concerns, he began visiting Leaf Brook more frequently, studying Stephen's behavior and, even more crucial, scrutinizing its possible effects on Brian.

Until now, Brian had seemed okay.

But this past Saturday, everything unraveled. Stephen's behavior—the urgent phone call he left the ball game to make, his hypersensitivity over the topic of his financial backing—confirmed the worst of Connor's suspicions. And Brian's adverse reaction confirmed the worst of his fears.

That terrific kid was becoming a casualty of Stephen's war.

Connor's argument with Stephen hadn't been pretty. He hadn't minced words, brutally reminding his brother of past binges that had cost a fortune and put one hell of a strain on Stephen's marriage. He further reminded Stephen that he now had a son who was old enough and insightful enough to sense his father's behavior and, consequently, to bear the subsequent emotional scars.

Stephen had snapped, and the two men had had a knock-down, drag-out shouting match. It had ended with Stephen accusing Connor of being a sanctimonious bastard and, in plain words, telling him to mind his own business, to take his damned money and his patronizing lectures, and to go straight to hell.

Connor was furious. He was sorely tempted to walk away and not look back. And he just might have, if it weren't for Brian.

But he couldn't stand the thought of his nephew suffering as a result of Stephen's weakness and Nancy's refusal to face the truth. Brian needed stability in his life, someone he could count on. And, for now, his Uncle Connor was it.

His Uncle Connor and Julia Talbot.

No doubt, Brian had an ally in Miss Talbot. Her devotion to Brian these past few years spoke for itself. And today—well, she'd certainly made it clear how much she cared about him. Not to mention her protectiveness toward him. It was admirable how deep her commitment ran.

Rolling the tumbler between his palms, Connor contemplated Brian's teacher, reflecting on their brief interaction earlier today.

Julia Talbot wasn't exactly what he'd originally surmised. Oh, some of his observations had been accurate. Her unaffected manner, for one. She viewed the world through eyes that were startlingly unclouded by cynicism or the desire to realize a personal agenda. Her physical attributes were equally natural and equally remarkable—a reality Connor couldn't help but notice even with his mind preoccupied with Brian. And, of course, there were her feelings for Brian, which were genuine to the core.

On the other hand, she was more gutsy than he'd originally thought, with some bite to her humor and an impressive directness to her approach. In his experience, people were glib, sometimes caustic, but rarely direct. And coming from an idealistic elementary-school teacher, it surprised him.

As for her take on Brian, it had been dead-on. In one way, that was good. She'd be keeping an eye on him, watching him like a hawk for signs of stress. On the other hand, if she didn't like what she saw, she might take the matter a step further. She might contact Nancy and Stephen or discuss her concerns with one of her superiors. And that could snowball into trouble.

For Julia Talbot to become any more deeply involved in this problem wasn't an option. She had to stay out of this.

It was up to him to see that she did.

Using whatever means he had to.

7

April 5

Panic was setting in.

Stephen paced around his office, sweat dampening his shirt. He yanked off his sports coat and tie, threw them onto the chair, and rolled up his sleeves.

Think. He had to think.

Everything was going wrong. He was in too damned deep, and he had nowhere to turn. Even turning to Connor was no longer an option. Not after insulting him and throwing him out the other day. And not with this massive debt. It was three times more than he'd ever owed. Connor would have his head.

Half a million dollars. How was it possible for his losses to add up to such a staggering sum? He'd only made a few damned bets. They'd all been sure things, strategically placed, carefully researched. The problem was, he'd bet on hockey games. And he didn't have the natural instinct for hockey that he had for football and baseball. But the timing of things had stunk, and he'd had no choice. With the Stanley Cup drawing close, hockey was the only sport yielding stakes high enough for his purposes. Football season was long over, and baseball's opening day had just taken place this week. As for the preseason games, they didn't yield a damn.

So hockey it had been.

And now he owed five hundred thousand dollars.

He dragged a palm across his forehead. Bad enough that a little more than one hundred fifty thousand of that money had come from his personal accounts. But the rest of it—three hundred forty-seven thousand, six hundred and fifty dollars, to be exact—had come from his campaign funds. And a huge chunk of those funds were his father's investment.

He wasn't sure which would be worse, going to jail or facing his father.

What in the hell was he going to do?

He had to get that money back—and fast. Before Cliff found the discrepancies, before the press dug deep enough to uncover his questionable activities. He didn't have much time, but he did have some—a few days, maybe a week. He *had* to get that cash back where it belonged.

But how? Where could he go for help?

The thought of Connor reasserted itself. Did he have the guts to call his brother?

Did he have the option not to?

He was still deliberating when his private line rang.

Numbly, he stared at the phone, making no move to answer it. The business day was long over, which meant the call was personal. Well, he didn't want to talk to anyone. If he had to bet—not that his picks were worth much these days—he'd bet it was Nancy, wondering where he was and when he was coming home for dinner. He couldn't talk to her. Not now. He certainly couldn't face her. And Brian—how could he meet his son's eyes, knowing what a mess he'd made of their lives?

Brian thought his father was a hero.

Well, he was no hero. He was a crooked, spineless fraud. Brian would find that out eventually.

But did he have to learn the truth before he was eight?

The phone stopped ringing, then started again, this time without letting up.

Fine. He'd get this over with.

Clearing his throat in an attempt to sound normal, he leaned over, plucked the receiver from its cradle. "Nance?"

"No, Mr. Mayor, it's Philip Walker. Sorry to call on your private line, but I just hung up with Greg Matthews. He passed along the results of the city council meeting. I must say, I'm not very pleased."

Great. This was the last thing Stephen had expected. In the frenzy of the past few hours, he'd completely forgotten about the city council meeting that had taken place earlier. He'd asked Greg to call Walker with its outcome. He should have anticipated this return call. Although how Walker had gotten his private number, he hadn't a clue.

What difference did it make? The man was sitting at the other end of the phone waiting for an answer.

And Stephen was in no state to deal with him.

"Hi, Philip," he said, switching to automatic pilot and trying desperately to keep his voice even. "I was just on my way home. I'm glad Greg reached you. Yes, I was surprised, too. I had no idea one of our members was checking into alternatives for the municipal parking lots. Still, what he proposed does have merit. I don't know if Greg went into detail, but the proposal is to get rid of hourly and daily payments altogether. The city would issue long-term parking permits. The fees for those permits would be collected by the city clerk on either an annual or semiannual basis. It's a low-cost, painless alternative to what we have now."

"Perhaps." A thoughtful pause. "On the other hand, that system doesn't provide any security for the cars or the people walking to them."

"I pointed that out at the meeting," Stephen answered, barely able to think over the pounding in his head. "And your proposal is still on the table. But I have to be honest. Most of the council members are leaning toward the permit option. It's cost-effective and less drastic than turning the entire parking system over to a private company."

"I see." A drawn-out silence. "Well, I hope you'll change their minds. In fact, I'm sure you will."

Maybe it was Stephen's state of mind, but the words sounded more like an order than a request.

"Anyway, I won't keep you. Go home to your family." Philip coughed. "But before we hang up, I have another reason for calling. It's a little embarrassing, but I just realized I made a huge error on that campaign contribution check I gave you. I must have been preoccupied when I wrote it. I accidently added an extra zero. I'd appreciate your tearing it up. Of course, I'll write you a new check for the sum I'd intended—ten thousand dollars."

Stephen felt bile rise in his throat. Slowly, he sank into a chair, his whole body trembling. This had to be some kind of cruel joke. Tear up the check? He couldn't. Thirty thousand dollars of it had already been gambled away.

"Mr. Mayor?"

"I'm here," Stephen heard himself say.

"Don't be offended. I wish I could contribute more.

But we don't always get what we wish for. Let's face it, life is a crap shoot. If we're lucky, we come out ahead. If not, we wind up losers. It's usually in the hands of dumb luck—which, as you know from recent personal experience, can mean one long bad streak. Once in a while, we can control the way things turn out. Like, for instance, when one hand washes the other and everybody gets what he wants. Then again, how often does a situation like that present itself?"

This time, there was no missing Walker's message. It came through loud and clear.

All of it.

Icy chills shot up Stephen's spine. "Are you suggesting that the hundred thousand is contingent upon . . ."

"We have a terrible connection," Philip interrupted to announce. "Damn, I hate phones. In any case, you were on your way out. I'll let you get home to your wife and son."

A quiet click, followed by a dial tone.

Stephen sat alone in his dark office, his head buried in his hands, long after Philip Walker had hung up.

He was being blackmailed. That was bad enough. But how much did Walker know? A whole lot, obviously.

For starters, this whole scenario wouldn't make sense otherwise. Based solely on their previous dealings together, Walker's perceptions of Stephen would have to lead him to conclude that the mayor was a squeaky-clean, ethical leader. Therefore, it followed suit that he'd expect Stephen to be outraged by his innuendos. He'd expect him to tear up the check, refuse any further offers, and report Walker's extortion attempts to the police.

That's not the way it had played out.

Which led to the more damning part. That pointed reference to life being a crap shoot and the equally pointed mention of recent personal experience and a long streak of bad luck. The whole gambling analogy was too precise to have been a coincidence.

No, the handwriting was on the wall. Philip Walker knew Stephen was in trouble. But how? More important, how extensive was his information? Did he know Stephen was up to his neck in gambling debts? Did he know those debts had come from campaign funds and had yet to be reimbursed? Worse, did he know that his own contribution was among the losses? Was that why he was so sure that blackmail would work—because Stephen couldn't return money he no longer had?

Stephen's breath was coming so fast he could feel the rise and fall of his chest. He had to find out how much Walker knew. If it was as bad as he feared, he had to convince Walker to be patient and not demand his money back. He'd promise to throw all his weight behind Walker's municipal parking proposal. Hell, it didn't matter to him which motion the city approved. Both had their benefits. So he'd actively endorse Walker's—for security reasons, he'd claim. It was a valid argument. Somehow he'd win over the other council members. He had to.

He picked up his private line and dialed.

"Yes?" Walker answered on the first ring, obviously expecting the call.

"I need to see you," Stephen said without preliminaries. "Tonight."

"Mr. Mayor?" Feigned surprise. "I thought you'd be sitting at your dinner table by now."

"I'm not. Apparently, neither are you. When can we meet?"

A pensive pause. "How's half an hour, at the bar on the corner of North and Third?"

"I'll be there."

Stephen had downed half his gin and tonic by the time Philip strolled in and slid into the dark corner booth. Unbelting his trench coat, he ordered a bourbon, awaited its arrival, then took a healthy swallow before meeting Stephen's gaze.

"You wanted to see me?"

"I'd like an explanation."

"About?"

With trembling fingers, Stephen set down his glass. "I'm not interested in playing games. I want to know what you meant by one hand washing the other."

Philip's brittle stare bored into his. "I think the statement is self-explanatory. You have something I want. I have something you want. We help each other." Another swallow. "Simple."

"What makes you think I'd stoop to dirty dealing just to collect a campaign donation?"

A corner of Philip's hard mouth lifted. "Not just any donation. A one-hundred-thousand-dollar donation. One you can't return because you've already invested it in sports betting."

Stephen's insides wrenched. "You don't know what you're talking about."

"Don't I? Then I tell you what. Call my bluff. Tip the cops off to the fact that you're being blackmailed." He offered Stephen his cell phone. "Go ahead. I'll wait here for them to show up and take me in."

With a heavy sigh, Stephen lowered his gaze, staring

at his drink. "You want the municipal parking contract with Leaf Brook."

"That's the idea."

"I can't force the council to vote my way. But I can make a damned good pitch."

"You do that." Philip polished off his bourbon, shoved aside the glass, and rose. "Call them each individually. It'll be easier that way. After you've won them all over, take a vote. You've got a week to deliver good news."

"Or to give you back your money," Stephen reminded him.

Another grim smile. "We've passed that point, Mr. Mayor. What I have on you would ruin your career and send you to prison, whether or not you managed to scramble together what you owe me. So keep the money. Use it for your campaign or your compulsion—I don't care which. I don't want reimbursement. I want the contract. So find a way to make it happen." He rebelted his trench coat. "I'll expect to hear from you next Thursday. Have a nice evening."

Connor was asleep when the phone rang.

He groped around on his night table until he found the receiver, dragging it to his ear. "Hello?"

"Connor, it's me." Nancy's voice was muffled and choked with tears.

He was instantly awake. "What's wrong?" he demanded, his gaze finding the lighted dial of the clock. It was four-fifteen.

"I'm sorry to wake you. But I didn't know what to do. I couldn't call Cliff, not about this."

"Nancy, calm down." Connor was already throwing

back the covers and climbing out of bed. "Tell me what's going on."

"It's Stephen," she whispered. "He doesn't know I'm calling. But I'm scared to death. He didn't come home until after three. And when he did, he was so drunk he could hardly walk. I tried to talk to him, but he told me to leave him alone. He said some horrible things. Then he passed out on the couch. I don't want Brian to find him like that in the morning, but he's too heavy for me to carry upstairs. And with the state he was in when he passed out, I'm afraid to wake him." A shaky pause. "He's in trouble, Connor. I've never seen him like this. And I don't know what to do."

"Is Brian okay?"

"Yes. He doesn't know about any of this. He went to bed at nine. I told him Stephen had a late meeting. He slept through the rest."

"Good. I'm on my way. I'll be there before Brian wakes up."

After slamming down the phone, Connor flipped on a light and went into the hall to yank down his suitcase from the closet. He flung the case onto his bed and randomly tossed in some clothes, his mind racing a mile a minute as he packed. It was Friday. That bought him the weekend. But the way things sounded, he'd need more than that.

He made a swift decision.

His deals were all running smoothly. Thank God for modern technology. With that new state-of-the-art unified messaging system he'd just gotten, he could go to Europe for a month and no one would miss him. The hi-tech gizmo integrated his voice mail, e-mail, and faxes and displayed them all on his computer screen. He would forward his private line to his cell phone. Then he could work from anywhere.

It was time for an extended stay in Leaf Brook.

Twenty minutes later, Connor tossed his laptop and suitcase into his Mercedes, and, with dawn a mere glint on the horizon, he zoomed up the West Side Highway and toward the crisis that awaited him.

8

Nancy looked close to collapse when Connor walked through the front door forty-five minutes later. He frowned, not used to seeing his always-put-together sister-in-law in an old pair of sweats, her face blotchy and her eyes swollen from crying.

"Hey." He dropped his bag and gripped her shoulders. "Are you okay?"

She nodded, clearly struggling for control. "Thanks for coming. Stephen might kill me for calling you, but I had to do something. I couldn't let Brian see his father like this." With a shaky breath, she glanced down at herself. "Speaking of Brian seeing us like this, I think I'll go up and shower now that you're here. That way, I'll look seminormal when my son comes downstairs." She gestured toward the living room. "Stephen's still on the couch. Also, I made a pot of coffee. You're going to need it."

"I'm sure I will."

"Connor?" Nancy touched his arm as he started to move toward the living room. "I can't tell you how much I appreciate . . ."

"I know." Connor covered her hand in a brief gesture of comfort. "Go on upstairs. I'll handle it from here."

Stephen was still out cold, crumpled over the arm of the sofa. He was fully dressed from his coat to his shoes.

Swearing under his breath, Connor seized his brother's arms and shook him. "Stephen." Another hard shake, followed by a few light but insistent slaps on his face. *"Stephen."*

Stephen's eyes cracked open long enough for him to mutter something unintelligible. Then they slid shut.

"Dammit, Stephen, wake up." Connor ground out the order from between clenched teeth. What he really wanted was to shout the house down. But that would wake Brian.

It took him a full five minutes to get a coherent response out of his brother.

Scowling, Stephen forced open his lids, his bloodshot eyes focusing vaguely. "Connor?"

"Yeah, it's me." He clasped Stephen's chin and gave it a hard shake, then another. "Stay awake," he commanded.

"What're you doing here?" Stephen slurred.

"Saving your ass." Connor dragged his brother to his feet, anchoring him by draping one of Stephen's arms around his own shoulders. "Walk with me."

"What?" Stephen complied unsteadily. "To where?"

"The kitchen. You're going to down about three cups of black coffee. Then I'm throwing you in the shower. You reek of booze."

A flash of irritated resentment crossed Stephen's face.

"Before you start fighting me, think of this," Connor advised in a tight, angry voice. "In about one hour, your son is going to come down here for breakfast. Is this the way you want him to see you?"

The resentment vanished, replaced by a haunted look that made Connor's own anger fade. Whatever the hell was going on, his brother was in torment.

Stephen drank his coffee in silence, shuddering from the bitterness of the taste. Slowly, sobriety returned, and the glazed look disappeared from his eyes.

"What time is it?" he asked at last.

Connor checked his watch. "Almost six."

"Barely dawn." Realization tightened Stephen's mouth into a grim line. "Obviously, Nancy called you."

"Damned right she did. And don't even think of being pissed. Your wife loves you. She was worried sick. She turned to me because I'm the only one who knows the situation. She was protecting you, the same way she always does."

Stephen stared into his coffee mug. "I know," he said in a strangled voice.

It was the perfect opening for Connor to start firing his questions. Unfortunately, the timing stank.

The inquisition would have to wait.

He rose. "Let's get you shaved and showered. We'll all have breakfast together when Brian comes down. After Nancy takes him to school, you and I will talk."

At that moment, Nancy walked in, looking infinitely more put together than she had a half hour ago.

Tension crackled in the air as her wary gaze met Stephen's. Neither of them spoke.

"The shower's free?" Connor's light question sliced the silence.

Nancy nodded. "Ready and waiting."

With a shaky sigh, Stephen came to his feet, more worn out than unsteady. "I don't remember much about what happened when I came in last night, but I doubt it was pleasant," he said quietly to his wife. "I'm sorry. More sorry than you can imagine."

He was talking about much more than coming home drunk, and they all knew it.

Nancy swallowed hard. "I know."

"I'd better get myself together." Stephen walked toward the doorway, regaining his equilibrium as he did. He shot Connor a quick look. "I can manage alone."

Yeah, right, Connor wanted to say. *Maybe with your shower. But not with your life.* "Fine," he said instead. "I'll hang out down here and grab a cup of coffee with Nancy."

Brian slept through his alarm clock that day, a first-time occurrence.

When seven-fifteen came and went with no telltale stomping overhead, Nancy went up to wake him. She came down, her expression bleak. Meeting Stephen's questioning gaze, she reported that their son had been dead asleep, that he looked exhausted, that his covers looked worse—as if they'd survived a war—and that his first question had been whether or not his dad was home. Wincing at the implications, Stephen reacted immediately, going right upstairs to reassure his son. The ensuing sounds of thudding closets and running water told Connor that his brother had taken over Nancy's morning rituals—choosing clothes that matched and overseeing tooth-brushing and shoe tying.

Still, Connor could hear Brian's voice, and it was a poor echo of his normal exuberance. Until he and Stephen were halfway down the stairs and Stephen announced that there was a surprise waiting at the breakfast table.

That got Brian's attention.

"What is it?" he demanded.

"Go down and see for yourself." Stephen sounded relieved.

Brian ran on ahead, scurrying into the kitchen and peering around expectantly.

He wasn't disappointed.

"Uncle Connor!" A huge grin split his face when he saw his uncle hunched over the table, polishing off a slice of toast.

"Hey, ace," Connor greeted him. "You got down here in the nick of time. I was about to gobble down those amazing pancakes your mom just made you."

Brian dropped his bookbag with a plunk. "I didn't know you were coming today."

"That's why they call it a surprise." Connor tousled his nephew's hair, then patted the cushion of the adjacent chair. "Sit down and talk to me while you eat."

"I've only got five minutes. I get marked down if I'm late." Brian's grin vanished. "I wish it wasn't a weekday. Then I wouldn't have to go to school."

"Ah, that's part of the surprise. I'm not just staying for today. I'm here for a nice long visit."

"Really? How long?"

"Long enough so I had to pack a whole bag of clothes *and* my laptop. Take a look in the guest room. You'll see my stuff on the bed."

"All right!" Brian celebrated that news by pouring syrup on his pancakes until they floated. "So you'll be here when I get home?"

"I'll do one better. I'll pick you up at school—that is, if it's okay with your mom." Connor glanced quizzically at Nancy, seeking permission.

"It's fine with me," she assured him, leaning over Brian to cut the pancakes into bite-size chunks. "It'll give me a few extra hours at the shop. I need to finalize expenses for the quarter." Nancy owned and ran a small upscale boutique in one of Leaf Brook's prime shopping districts. "So I'll drop Brian at school this morning, then meet you two guys home around five. How's that?"

"Sounds good." Connor was more than pleased with that scenario. He wanted as much time alone with his nephew as possible, so he could figure out exactly what Brian's state of mind was.

"What about Dad?" Brian piped up. His earlier uneasiness returned, and he shot a quick glance at his father, seeking some measure of reassurance. "Will you be late again tonight? Or can you come home for dinner?"

An anguished look crossed Stephen's face, the look of a father who knew he'd caused his child pain. "I'll be home before seven," he confirmed. "Okay?"

Brian's relief was tangible. "Okay."

"Better than okay," Connor informed his nephew. "It'll give you four hours to work up an appetite. And we won't waste a minute of them. We'll go straight to the park after school and practice that running slide of yours so you can reach base without breaking any bones or swallowing an entire infield of dirt. After that, we'll go home and get going on your homework. Maybe we can even help your mom with dinner. Before you know it, your dad will be here. What do you say?"

"Great!" Brian was shoveling down food, looking like his old self. "I'll meet you at the playground gate," he got out between mouthfuls. "At three."

"It's a date."

* * *

All levity vanished the minute Connor and Stephen were alone, the fading thrum of Nancy's car engine confirming that she and Brian had headed off to school.

"Let's not waste time," Connor said quietly, perching at the edge of his chair. "How bad is it?"

Stephen jammed a hand through his hair, turning away to stare out the kitchen window. "Bad."

"Stephen, talk to me. I'm not going away. Neither is the problem. We'll work something out. Just tell me where things stand."

A humorless laugh. "How magnanimous. And heroic. Here I threw you out on Monday, and Friday you ride back, a twenty-first-century Lancelot galloping to my rescue."

"Cut it out." Connor stalked over to his brother, slapping his palms on the edge of the counter. "Stop feeling so goddamned sorry for yourself. It's Brian you should be worrying about. He's the reason I'm here." A pained pause, after which Connor added, "That and the fact that you're my brother, and you're screwing up your life."

"*Screwed* up my life," Stephen corrected. "Past tense. I've really buried myself this time." He lowered his head, interlacing his fingers behind his neck. "This one's going to be tough to swallow, even for you."

Connor studied the dejected slump of his brother's shoulders. "I'm not judging you. I want to help. For God's sake, let me."

"Sure, why not," Stephen returned, his tone rife with self-derision. "Let's see, do you happen to have a half million dollars lying around? You know, money you can get your hands on that's not tied up in stocks or bonds? If so, it would be damned useful right around now."

Sucking in his breath, Connor tried to keep the shock

from coming through in his tone. "You're in the hole for five hundred thousand dollars?"

"That's about the size of it."

Connor forced out the next question. "That can't all be on sports bets. Are you involved in something else?"

"Like what, drug dealing? No, Connor, I haven't sunk that low. It's just bigger bets, bad choices, bigger losses." A bitter laugh. "I always did suck when it came to hockey."

"Your bookie's waiting for the money?"

"No, he already has it. Unfortunately, I don't. So I need to put it back where I got it from."

A sick knot formed in Connor's gut. "Which is where?"

"Where else? My campaign." Stephen turned to face his brother. "By the way, did I mention that most of that money is Dad's?"

"Shit."

"My sentiments exactly." Stephen turned his palms up. "So, who gets my head first, the authorities or our loving father?"

Connor's mind did a quick scan, first of the overall situation, then of the immediate options. There was nothing to deliberate about. The long term would have to wait. For now, plugging the hole was all that mattered. He'd sell some stocks, drain some money-market accounts. He'd spread it across a couple of different banks and brokerage houses. There'd be no single drastic depletion of funds. No questions from anxious bank officers or stockbrokers. It could be done.

"You'll have the money by the end of the banking day," he informed Stephen.

His brother's jaw dropped. "Just like that?"

"No, not just like that." Shards of ice glittered in Connor's eyes. "Getting you the money is my problem. Holding on to it is yours."

"I realize that." Stephen swallowed, that haunted look back on his face. Clearly, he was at the very edge of his control. He was about to snap. "I'll find a way to pay you back," he said. "It'll take some time, but . . ."

"Pay me back by stopping." Connor had to get through to his brother. He just didn't know how. "Stephen, this isn't just a bad habit. Not anymore. We can't pretend otherwise. This is a compulsion. We've got to get you some help."

That elicited a response—although not the one Connor had hoped for. "Great. A shrink. One who specializes in luckless gamblers. Or, better yet, a bunch of inspirational meetings at Gamblers Anonymous." Stephen walked away, refilled his coffee cup. "How long do you think it'd be before the news leaked out that a Stratford was attending those? Particularly this Stratford. The tabloids would have a field day. So would Braxton. I could kiss the senate seat good-bye."

"Stephen . . ."

"Connor, please." Stephen slammed down the cup, sending coffee sloshing all over the counter. "I'm not up for the healing pep talk. It was hard enough for me to ask you for the money. Don't make it any harder." His hands trembled as they balled into fists. "I need to get past this election. Once I'm in, once I'm not under Braxton's microscope, then we'll talk about long-term solutions. For now, let's compromise. You're lending me a fortune. In return, I'll promise you I won't gamble it away."

"Not good enough. You'll promise me you won't gamble at all." Anticipating the cursory agreement he was about to receive—pure lip service without foundation—Connor added, "Let me warn you that I don't take that promise lightly. Nor should you. Because I intend to stick around here and make sure that you keep it. I know all the signs, big brother. I'll know if you're back in the game. And I'll stop you. You can bet on it, and that's a bet you'd win."

Stephen drew a long, slow breath, then released it in a rush. "I was away from it for a long time, you know."

"Yes, I know. And you will be again. For Nancy's sake, and for Brian's. He knows something's wrong. The last thing we need is for him to start thinking that whatever's going on is his fault."

Another of those pained expressions tightened Stephen's features, as if his worry ran far deeper than the eye could see. "We can't let Brian find out about any of this. We've got to nip it in the bud while we still can."

The words had a ring of desperation to them, a desperation that sent prickles of uneasiness crawling up Connor's spine. Why was Stephen still so agitated when he'd just been thrown the very life preserver he needed?

Something didn't fit.

Connor frowned, trying to zero in on the parameters of Stephen's crisis. "We *are* nipping it in the bud. At least, I think we are. I said you'd have the money today. You'll make sure it stays where it belongs. And that's that—isn't it?"

"Yeah. It has to be." Stephen's jaw set. "I'll fix things. I won't let them impact Brian. I swore I'd never put him in a position where he has to question his self-worth. Not after having lived my whole life that way. I love that kid more than anything. It's up to me to stop things before they get out of hand. I have to, and I will."

9

Julia was on edge.

She massaged her temples, walking the periphery of the computer lab and giving the room a quick once-over to make sure all her students were okay with their assignments. Heads bent, they were punching away on the keyboards, entering their two-paragraph essays on "What I Wish For" into their PCs under Robin's watchful supervision.

Right now, all Julia wished for was a good night's sleep.

She hadn't gotten one last night, or the night before, for that matter.

Maybe it was anticipation over tonight's workshop—a continuation of Dr. Garber's findings on child neglect and emotional abuse. And maybe it was her worry over Brian Stratford.

Either way, her dreams had been flashbacks to the past, filled with broken memories that hadn't resurfaced in years, not in such vivid detail. As a kid, she'd had these dreams a lot. It had been a traumatic time in her life, one that had influenced the entire course of her future.

No surprise that the memories had chosen now to resume.

She and Franny hadn't been in touch for ages. Franny had left home at sixteen—run away was more like it. She'd written to Julia for a while, letters that were postmarked San Francisco, Los Angeles, and finally San Diego—places that were as far from Poughkeepsie as possible. Then the letters had stopped, and somehow Julia knew that, despite how close she and Franny had once been, despite how much Franny cared about their friendship, the ties with the past were too painful to maintain.

Not that Julia could blame her. After all she'd been through, how could she not want to erase her childhood?

It had started when Franny was not much older than Brian. At first, the signs had been subtle, too subtle for her eight-year-old best friend to notice. But Meredith Talbot had noticed. And later, when they'd escalated, she'd acted.

Reality had never been so ugly.

Sighing, Julia cast a glance at the wall clock in the computer lab.

Two-forty. Almost weekend time.

A bunch of the kids were starting to fidget. She didn't blame them. It was a Friday afternoon in spring, the birds were chirping, and the weekend was calling.

"Almost done?" she asked.

Lots of key tapping, a few nods, and one or two hands waving in the air.

"I tell you what. Five more minutes. If Miss Haley can get you all wrapped up by then, we'll go outside and use the playground for fifteen minutes to celebrate the start of the weekend."

A round of whoops greeted her announcement, and Robin shot her a grin. "A well-received option," she observed. "Okay, guys, who needs help?"

Eight minutes later, the class spilled onto the playground, flinging their bookbags against the side of the building and dashing off to play.

"No wonder you're so popular." Robin chuckled, coming to stand beside Julia. "I'd love you, too, if you let me start my weekend early." A rueful sigh. "Although maybe not *this* weekend. I have to work both days. I've got a project to finish up. My Visa bill needs paying."

Julia nodded her understanding. Robin was a computer whiz, not only technically but creatively. She had a degree in electrical engineering, and she'd spent the first few years after college designing circuits and wireless devices for major communications clients. It was lucrative, but it wasn't her. Not the pressure. Not the detached work environment. Not the boring social life of the geeks she worked with. So she'd turned to her other love: children. She'd gone back to school and gotten her teaching certification. Now she was happy, with a job she enjoyed and a thriving social life. The only thing missing was the huge salary she'd collected in industry. She tried to compensate for that by earning extra money writing sophisticated computer programs for small companies, programs that looked like Greek to a non-techno-genius like Julia.

Robin's talents were impressive. More impressive was the fact that she regarded them as secondary to what she could offer the kids she taught. That said a lot about her character, at least from Julia's viewpoint.

"Is this a big project?" Julia asked, intentionally refraining from asking specifics. She was well aware that confidentiality was part of what Robin agreed to in her contracts.

A shrug. "The company I'm working for thinks so. All I know is I'll get three thousand dollars when I'm done. That'll take care of the charges I've racked up during spring sales. Including that ice-blue silk dress I told you about, the one that cost an arm and a leg. I'm wearing it Saturday night, by the way."

Julia smiled. "Ah, so you are taking time out for recreation. Who's the lucky guy?"

"Someone new and very promising. That's all I'm going to say for now. I don't want to jinx it. Anyway, he's taking me to a posh French restaurant in Manhattan."

"Sounds like the silk dress will come in handy."

"Hope so." A questioning look. "What about you—are you seeing Greg?"

"We're having brunch on Sunday." Julia didn't add that she'd purposely made it a morning date, in a restaurant that was centrally located. That way, they could meet at the restaurant, and she wouldn't have to deal with managing Greg's expectations.

"Julia, at some point, you have to sleep with this guy."

So much for avoiding the subject. Good old blunt Robin had just eliminated that possibility by grabbing the bull by the horns.

With a resigned sigh, Julia met bluntness with bluntness. "Why? Because he's male, I'm female, and we've gone out to dinner a few times?"

"No, because he's good-looking, he's successful, and, crazy as he is about you, he's not going to keep up this monk routine forever."

"Then I guess he'll have to take it elsewhere." Julia was surprised to hear herself snap out such a stinging retort. Her surprise was compounded by a twinge of guilt at the startled, slightly put-off look on Robin's face. But only a twinge. The truth was, she was tired of being told she had to sleep with someone just because he was a good catch and they'd spent enough time together for him to expect it. She didn't give a damn what year this was or what other people did. She wasn't hopping into bed with someone unless she was good and ready.

"Wow, that was pretty intense," Robin replied mildly. "Did I hit a raw nerve? Has Greg been pressuring you?"

"No. Nothing like that." Julia ran both hands through her hair. "Rob, I'm sorry. I didn't mean to bite your head off. But this argument is getting old. I know you mean well. But sex is the farthest thing from my mind, at least these days. These days, when I hit the bed, all I want is a good night's sleep. Which I'm not getting. I slept three hours last night. Maybe that explains my bitchy mood."

"Don't worry about it." Robin waved away the apology with her customary live-and-let-live attitude. "And you're right. Whether or not you sleep with Greg isn't any of my business. I just don't want life passing you by while you wait for Mr. Right. But that's your choice, not mine." She glanced thoughtfully at her friend. "But now that you mention it, you do look kind of peaked. Anything in particular bothering you?"

"As a matter of fact, yes." She cocked her head, watching as Brian Stratford raced across the playground and lunged at the monkey bars, climbing them with a vengeance. He seemed himself—for the moment. But there had been times—too many times today—when he seemed troubled and far away. She'd noticed it all week. But it had been more frequent today, and certainly more pronounced. Plus, he looked tired, not just lack-of-sleep tired but drained tired, as if there was something major on his mind, something that was eating at him and keeping him awake. Julia knew in her gut that whatever it was, it bore some connection to his father.

"You're still worried about Brian," Robin deduced, following her friend's gaze.

"Yes, I am. He's not himself. I wish I could find a minute to talk to him alone, although Connor Stratford practically forbid me to interfere."

"Like that would stop you if you thought one of your kids was hurting."

"You're right, it wouldn't. What stopped me was the fact that there hasn't been a single opening today that lent itself to a private talk. I won't risk upsetting Brian. Which means I won't pull him aside or make an issue out of his change in behavior. The timing has to be right. And today it wasn't. There wasn't a quiet moment since the first bell rang."

"What about now?" Robin suggested. "That is, if you can peel him off the monkey bars."

Julia turned to scan the blacktop area, frowning and shaking her head as she saw that the buses were starting to arrive and line up across the way to receive their passengers. Behind them, carpooling parents were driving in slowly, pulling into the designated spots to await their cargo. "Now won't work. There's not enough time, and there's too much going on. Besides, Brian's mom will be here any minute to pick him up. It'll have to wait till Monday."

"Why not speak with Mrs. Stratford? Not in front of Brian, of course, but arrange to give her a call. She's always been receptive."

"In the past, yes." Julia's frown deepened. "But this time's different. Based on everything I've seen—from the mayor's tension to his brother's protectiveness—my guess is this problem's close to home. And if I'm right, then Mrs. Stratford might not be the right person to . . ."

She broke off as a blue coupe drove all the way up to the playground gate. Its driver, an official-looking woman in a gray business suit, got out and headed purposefully toward them. She looked familiar, but Julia couldn't quite place her. She wasn't one of the parents, at least not any Julia had met. Besides, she looked too detached, walking stiffly with her notebook and a small black box that, upon closer scrutiny, Julia realized was a tape recorder.

The tape recorder was what made the woman's identity click into place.

"Ms. Talbot!"

Recognition occurred at the precise second that the woman spotted her and called her name. "Ms. Talbot, may I speak with you?"

It was Cheryl Lager, that slimy reporter with the *Leaf Brook News* who'd descended on Brian's baseball game last Saturday.

What on earth did she want with her?

Julia shot Robin a quick puzzled look. "That's the reporter I told you about," she muttered. Turning, she braced herself for whatever this seedy newswoman had in mind. "What can I do for you?" she asked coolly.

"I'm not sure you remember me," Ms. Lager began. "I'm . . ."

"I remember you, Ms. Lager. I'm just not sure why you're here."

The reporter looked mildly surprised. "That's easily clarified." She scanned the area swiftly, her gaze fixing on the monkey bars, which Brian had scaled for the third time. "Ah, there he is. That's Brian Stratford, isn't it?"

Julia folded her arms across her chest. "I think you know it is."

"I also know he's immensely fond of you. That was clear at the game on Saturday." Cheryl Lager studied her notes, as if contemplating her next question. With one deft motion, she clicked on her tape recorder. "Tell me, Ms. Talbot, have you noticed anything unusual about the boy's behavior lately? Any unusual strain? I have a hunch he confides in you, which wouldn't surprise me. I adored my second-grade teacher. I would have told her anything, especially if there were a problem at home. Like if I sensed any unusual tension that I couldn't understand. Maybe even what I thought was causing that tension."

She rushed on, not even waiting for a reply. "I'm sure you know the mayor and Mrs. Stratford quite well through the school. You certainly felt comfortable enough with Mayor Stratford to invite him to your classroom for a presentation to your students. So, tell me, based on your personal impressions of him, both past and present, did it seem to you he was unusually defensive the other day? Specifically when the subject of campaign financing came up? Is that a particularly sensitive topic to the mayor—in your opinion, of course?"

"I have no idea what you're talking about, Ms. Lager," Julia returned, her voice trembling with outrage. "Nor do I have any idea where you get your nerve. This is a school. I am a teacher. You're invading my work space during teaching hours. Please excuse yourself and leave."

Rather than be put off, Cheryl Lager seemed hopeful. "Does that mean I can call you at home?" she asked. "If so, that's fine with me. We can work out a convenient time, at which point we can . . ."

"Ms. Lager, let *me* ask *you* a question. How would your newspaper feel about a lawsuit? Because you're bordering on one right now."

The voice emerged out of nowhere, but Julia knew without looking who it belonged to.

Connor Stratford.

Based on her white-faced reaction, Cheryl Lager recognized it, too.

"Mr. Stratford," she managed, veering about to face him. "I was just asking Ms. Talbot . . ."

"Interrogating her, you mean." He jerked his head in the direction of her tape recorder. "I suggest you turn that thing off. Now." The instant she complied, he turned his ice-blue gaze on Julia. "You don't have to answer anything. Nor do you have to put up with harassment by overbearing reporters."

"I don't intend to," she assured him. "In fact, I was just telling Ms. Lager to leave. Which she was about to do. Weren't you, Ms. Lager?" Julia's eyes sparked fire.

Reluctantly, the reporter nodded. "All right." She began walking away, pausing to aim a quick, contemplative look in Brian's direction.

"Don't even think about it," Connor warned, obliterating any notion she might have of approaching Brian directly. "Go within ten feet of my nephew, and I'll have you arrested. Think how attractive *that* headline would read."

His threat had the desired effect. Cheryl Lager marched off to her car and drove away.

"What nerve," Julia breathed, still infuriated. "No wonder the media gets a bad name. Bloodsuckers like that see to it."

"She's scum, all right," Connor agreed, glaring after the reporter. "Then again, she's far from unique. And that applies to more than just the press. Most people have an agenda. You'd be shocked at what lengths they'd go to to achieve them."

"That's pretty cynical, wouldn't you say?" Julia inquired.

"Nope." He met her gaze and shrugged. "Pretty realistic—when you're dealing with people over the age of twelve and outside a classroom, that is."

Julia was getting very tired of his condescending attitude. "Then I'm glad I'm *inside* a classroom and dealing with seven- and eight-year-olds. In fact, I think more people should work in elementary schools. It might do them—and their agendas—some good."

"Could be."

There was that charged air again, hovering between them like repelling magnets.

Or was it attracting magnets that were so totally opposite in their charges?

"Yoo-hoo, hello." Robin cut through the thick wall of tension, sticking out her hand and smiling at Connor, her pert, all-American features coming to life at the sight of a good-looking man. "I'm Robin Haley. I work in the computer lab here. And I think your nephew is great."

Connor reacted with a mildly apologetic look and a firm handshake. "Connor Stratford. And forgive my bad manners. I was sidetracked by that reporter and my urge to choke her."

"If you say so." Robin's grin turned impish. "To me, it seemed as if it was Julia you wanted to choke. I guess that was just spill-over from your anger at Ms. Lager. Right?"

Her implication found its mark, and Connor's dark brows shot up. "I think I've just been accused of venting at the wrong person. If I did, I apologize."

"Julia accepts your apology," Robin assured him. "Don't you, Julia?"

Julia was actually wishing the ground would swallow her up. "No apology is necessary. Brian's uncle and I just don't see eye to eye."

"Ah, is that the problem?" Robin's tone said she knew better. "I got a different impression. No matter. As for Ms. Lager," she continued to Connor, "I don't blame you. Her questions bordered on slander."

"And maybe struck too close to home," Julia said under her breath.

She hadn't meant for Connor to overhear her. Unfortunately, he did.

He stiffened, turning to level that piercing stare on her. "Miss Talbot, may I speak with you alone?"

A knot formed in the pit of Julia's stomach. She'd definitely overstepped her bounds. But somehow she didn't care. Maybe because she was worried about Brian. Maybe because she was pissed off at his uncle. Probably both.

"All right." She raised her chin, her gaze sweeping the playground before meeting his. "But only for a minute. I've got to watch the kids. Not to mention that any second now, Brian's going to notice you and come charging over."

"A minute, then." He looked politely at Robin. "Would you excuse us?"

"By all means." Robin looked as if she was biting back laughter. "And I'll watch the kids, too. So you two can take a full minute and concentrate on killing each other. Or whatever."

Julia walked the short distance to the building, pausing in an alcove that was as private as you got on a Friday afternoon at three.

"Let me guess," she began, pivoting around to face Connor. She folded her arms across her breasts, ready and willing to do battle. "You didn't like my comment. Correction, you didn't like the fact that it was true."

His piercing gaze narrowed, and he studied her intently for a moment. "This isn't about me and what I do or don't like. This is about protecting my family."

"Isn't Brian part of that family?"

"You know the answer to that."

"Then he deserves your protection, too."

"He has it."

"Does he?" Julia's chin came up another notch. She wasn't going to back down, not this time. "He's hurting. He's exhausted; he looks as if he didn't shut an eye last night. He's quiet and withdrawn. We both know that's not Brian. Something's wrong. The fact that you're here today is evidence of that. That's twice this week you've left your financial empire to drive up here and see Brian. You're worried about him, too. Only you know what the problem is. I don't."

A muscle worked in Connor's jaw. "You didn't mention any of this to that reporter, did you?"

"Of course not. I didn't tell her anything, except to get lost. But Cheryl Lager's not the problem. She can be kept away, by legal means, if necessary. The problem is Brian, his state of mind. What's going on at home? Is it the campaign? Is it chewing up too much of the mayor's time? Is the emotional pressure too great for his family to take in stride? I can understand that. A tough campaign, long hours. But Brian doesn't fall apart that easily. He's used to his father being in the public eye. So my instincts tell me it's more. Is it?"

"Brian was up late," Connor replied, his expression never changing. "He's tired. He'll be fine after a weekend's rest."

Julia's final vestige of patience snapped. "Stop trying to placate me. This isn't fatigue. It's more. And the fact that you're evading my questions makes me wonder if Cheryl Lager was right about the problem being financial. I saw the mayor's reaction to her questions about monetary backing. He was upset. So were you."

Anger glinted in his eyes. "She questioned my integrity. I shot her down. And I wasn't upset. I was furious. There's a difference."

"You didn't answer my question."

"I don't like its implications."

"There *are* no implications," Julia exclaimed, utterly frustrated. "I like your brother. I voted for him. I'll vote for him again. He's a fine man, and an honest one. He's done great things for Leaf Brook, and I have no doubt he'll do even greater things for New York. I don't care if you and your father bankroll him to Albany. Just tell me why Brian is being impacted by all this, and I'll go away."

"For the last time, Brian is fine. He just needs some sleep. As for Stephen's schedule, yes, he's insanely busy. And yes, Brian misses him. But we've taken steps to fix that. I'll be there to fill in for my brother wherever and whenever Brian needs me."

"How are you going to do that from Manhattan?"

"I won't be in Manhattan. I'm staying at Stephen and Nancy's house."

That brought Julia up short. "You're staying there? For how long?"

"Like I said, for as long as I'm needed."

"What about your company? Your clients?"

A corner of Connor's mouth lifted. "Why? Worried about me losing money? Don't be. Technology is amazing. I can do everything right from my laptop. My unified messaging system integrates my voice mail, e-mail, and faxes, all in one. It can even automatically forward calls to my cell phone. It's one of the perks of being part of the vicious non-elementary-school environment. Impressed?"

"You're goading me."

"Yeah, as a matter of fact, I am."

Julia felt herself smile, despite her best intentions. "That's honest. Okay, then, yes, I am a little impressed."

"By what, my technical sophistication or my frankness?"

"Both. Although the state-of-the-art status I expected. The frankness, that's another story."

A subtle shift of expression, one that had nothing to do with the current topic. "I have many sides," he said, his gaze moving briefly to her mouth before lifting back to meet hers. "As, I'm beginning to suspect, do you."

Julia wished she could deny the pull that existed between them. But there was no point. It was there, with or without basis. She felt it. And so did Connor.

He cleared his throat and groped in his jacket pocket for a pen and paper. "I'm going to ask you a favor."

"All right."

"My brother is committed to his campaign *and* to running the city. He scarcely has time to breathe. Nancy's an amazing wife and mother, but she's dancing as fast as she can." Connor scribbled something down on the paper. "This is my private cell phone number. If you have any concerns about Brian, if you see a recurrence of any of the symptoms you described before, call me. I'll take care of it."

Julia took the slip of paper, glanced down at it. "I wish

I could get over the nagging feeling that there's more to this than . . ."

"Get over it. For Brian's sake and for yours."

Her head snapped up. "Are you *threatening* me?"

"I'm trying to keep you from needlessly screwing up a lot of lives. Including your own. I appreciate your concern for Brian. But I'm on top of this, and I'll continue to be."

It wasn't a request. It was a demand.

Julia folded the paper in two and slid it into her pocket. "I believe your intentions are good, at least when it comes to Brian. So I'll try it your way. But if you and I clash, if I don't agree with the way you're handling things, or if Brian gets worse, I reserve the right to change my mind. Whether it means involving the school or telling Brian's parents, I'll do whatever it takes."

Before Connor could respond, their attention was diverted by a happy shout of "Uncle Connor!"

"It looks as if you've been spotted," Julia observed, spying the blur of color rushing in their direction and recognizing it as Brian. She glanced quickly at her watch, just as the first bell rang. "I've got to go get my kids in line for their buses and carpool groups."

"Are you free later for a drink?"

Now, *that* was the last thing Julia had expected. "What?"

"I asked if you were free for a drink. Unless, of course, you still dislike me more than you like me. Or, more important, unless you and Greg Matthews have an exclusive arrangement of some kind."

A flush stained Julia's cheeks. "How did you know about . . . ?"

"Hi, Uncle Connor." Brian collided with his uncle's

leg. "How come you're waiting here instead of at the playground gate?"

"Because I needed to talk to Miss Talbot." Connor squeezed his nephew's shoulder. "Did you have a good day?"

"Uh-huh."

"Great. Why don't you grab your bookbag and your mitt? I'll finish up with Miss Talbot, and we can go straight to the park."

"Can Miss Talbot come?" Brian demanded. "Maybe her running slide's as good as her curve ball."

Julia drew a slow breath. "No, sweetie, I can't come. I've got to meet my mom for a workshop. I won't be home until very late tonight," she added, talking to Brian but speaking to Connor. "Besides, my slide is awful. The first time I tried it, I broke my big toe."

"Your toe?" Brian looked incredulous.

"I know what you mean." Julia grinned. "It was pretty humiliating. I zoomed in feet first and jammed my foot between the bag and the second baseman's sneaker. All that pain, and I had nothing to show for it but a broken toe. I didn't even get to wear a cast, in which case everyone would have felt sorry for me. I spent two weeks wishing I had broken something major in my leg. At least that would have looked and sounded impressive. But breaking my big toe? All that accomplished was keeping me off the pitcher's mound and making me the object of some pretty cruel jokes."

"Wow." Brian patted her arm as sympathetically as if she'd told him she'd been flattened by an eighteen-wheeler. "Don't feel bad. If it had been your leg, you would have been out for a lot longer than two weeks. And don't worry about the running slide. Uncle Connor can teach me."

"Good idea," Julia acknowledged ruefully.

"I'll be right back." Brian scooted off to collect his things.

"How about Saturday night?" Connor demanded. "Are you free?"

Julia found herself answering before she could weigh her decision—probably because if she weighed it, she might change her mind. "Yes, I'm free."

"Just for drinks, or can I talk you into dinner?"

"You can try."

His eyes glinted as he took on her challenge. "I know a little Italian place about a half hour from here. It's casual. The food is great. And the wine's superb. Oh, and they make a tiramisu that's so good it'll straighten your curve ball."

"That good?" Julia wondered what she was getting herself into.

Probably a whole lot more than she could handle.

"In that case," she heard herself reply, "how can I refuse? Dinner it is."

A flicker of triumph. "Excellent. How's seven o'clock?"

"Perfect."

Connor handed her his pen. "Rip off a piece of that paper I just gave you with my cell number on it, and write down your address. I'll pick you up. Write down your phone number, too, while you're at it."

She'd just scribbled down both when Brian reappeared.

"I'm ready," he announced.

"Great." Connor pocketed the scrap of paper and his pen. "Miss Talbot and I just finished talking. So let's get going." He gave Julia a long, searching look. "See you."

She nodded. "See you. And have a great time at the park, both of you."

They were a few steps away when she remembered something. "Connor?"

"Hmm?" He turned.

Her lips curved slightly as she echoed the words he'd tossed her way at the end of their last meeting. "For the record, I never disliked you. And my name is Julia."

10

~

6:55 P.M.

Greg Matthews was in a foul mood.

He'd planned on leaving the office early, going home, and getting some sleep. Instead, here he was, at seven o'-clock on a Friday night, still sitting at his desk, working on a revised budget for the school district cafeterias. Boy, talk about high-level excitement.

He tossed down his pencil and rolled his head in a slow circle meant to relax the tight muscles at his neck. He was beat. It had been a roller coaster of a week, and tomorrow promised to be just as bad. So much for taking Saturdays off. Last week, it had been that breakfast meeting; tomorrow, it was the hours of schmoozing he had to do—some of it on the golf course, the rest on the phone.

He was in no mood for walking a six-way political tightrope.

But that's what he had to do. There was no other choice. Not if he meant to get what he wanted out of all this.

Pain in the ass or not, it should be interesting to see how this little drama played out.

As if on cue, an office door shut in the distance, and familiar footsteps echoed down the hall, turned in the direction of the elevator.

The mayor was on his way home.

Greg pursed his lips, staring idly at his own closed door as the ding of the elevator indicated it had arrived. Next came the slow, gliding sound of its doors as they opened, a prolonged pause, and a repeat of the gliding sound as they shut. Then silence.

If it had been a rough week for him, it had been hell on wheels for Stephen Stratford.

And the fun was just beginning.

He wouldn't trade places with the mayor for all the seats in the senate combined. Political notoriety was great; he was all for it. And sure, one of the prices you paid was exposing your soft underbelly to the world and leaving yourself wide open for attack. But if those attacks could bare secrets bad enough to land you in real trouble, and if that trouble meant pissing off men like Philip Walker, hell, it just wasn't worth the price.

With a weary sigh, Greg bent back over his work, marking up the last of his preliminary numbers for the budget. That did it. He'd work up a detailed spreadsheet when he got home. He'd shove last night's Chinese food into the microwave and knock off the budget while he ate. That would leave him more than enough time to plan tomorrow's agenda over a cup of decaf and hit the sack early. He had to be alert for a seven A.M. tee-off.

It was going to be a long, productive weekend—in more ways than one.

Tomorrow, he'd make the necessary headway with the city council.

And Sunday, he'd do the same with Julia.

10:15 P.M.

It was drizzling when Julia veered off the Leaf Brook exit on the Taconic Parkway and made a right onto Main Street.

She was glad that home was just a few more driving minutes away, and not only because the rain was picking up. Her mind was on overload. It had started out that way, and tonight's workshop hadn't helped.

Dr. Garber had presented the final details of his research, then opened the floor to questions. As fate would have it, most of those questions had dealt with recognizing the preliminary signs of emotional distress in young children so that the problem—and its cause—could be nipped in the bud. The answers only served to fuel Julia's worry over Brian. Oh, she realized his symptoms lacked the severity and long-term manifestation of Dr. Garber's case studies. Still, the entire workshop might have served as a red flag to Brian's parents, had they been there.

But they weren't. For all Julia knew, they didn't even notice the glaring signs. They were loving parents, but if they were absorbed in their own problems, it was possible Brian's symptoms weren't being recognized, much less contended with. It was all speculation on her part. And if she kept her agreement with Connor, it would continue to be.

Damn, she was so confused.

She knew Connor wasn't giving her all the facts. That didn't bother her nearly as much as the reasons behind his evasiveness. Okay, he was protecting his family. He'd as much as said so.

But from what?

She couldn't force him to confide in her. On the other

hand, he couldn't force her to stop asking. And even though she'd agreed to do things his way—for now—she'd also emphasized that she wasn't making any promises.

He'd never had time to respond to her stipulation before Brian returned, bookbag in hand. Then again, his reaction couldn't have been *too* severe. He'd still asked her out to dinner. But how much of that invitation stemmed from his wanting another chance to drive home his point, and how much from his urge to explore the undercurrents simmering between them?

It would be interesting to find out.

A chain reaction of screeching tires and sudden brake lights ahead of her jerked Julia back to the moment. Reflexively, she slammed her foot down, bringing her Beetle to a halt. What was going on? It was after ten o'clock—why was she sitting in rush-hour traffic?

She rolled down her window and peered out to see if she could make out the problem.

About a quarter-mile ahead, she could make out some flashing red lights. Police cars. God, she hoped that didn't mean there'd been an accident. But it was a possibility. It was raining. The streets were slick. And it was Friday night. While DWI-related crashes weren't common occurrences in Leaf Brook, they did happen.

The section of Main Street she was approaching led to one of the corporate mini-centers. There were two or three popular bars across the way, where the corporate employees went for Friday happy hour. A few stupid ones sometimes drank too much and then got behind the wheels of their cars. Once in a while, someone got hurt.

Julia clutched the wheel tightly, hoping this was just a fender bender and nothing more.

The traffic crawled forward, and Julia went with it.

It took fifteen minutes before she reached the spot where the two cop cars were positioned, just outside the entrance to a municipal lot. One police car was blocking off the lot, the other was parked across the street. There were two officers standing in the road directing traffic. Julia scrutinized the area but didn't see any sign of broken glass, a mangled vehicle, or an ambulance. That suggested that whatever had happened had happened in the lot.

She was half tempted to question the policeman who was briskly gesturing the drivers along, just to reassure herself that there were no fatalities. But he looked tense and preoccupied, and his rain slicker was getting wetter by the minute. Now was definitely not the time. Whatever had happened would no doubt show up in tomorrow's newspaper. In fact, Julia thought with a grim frown, reporters like Cheryl Lager had probably been at the scene and gone, heading back to their offices to get a jump on writing up the story. The messier the better.

Inside the municipal lot, Officer Benjamin Parks followed up with the last potential witness, jotting down a few additional facts. Detective Frank Taylor circled the area, making a final check for any evidence that might have been overlooked.

He doubted he'd find any. Whoever had done this was a pro.

Car thefts in Leaf Brook were rare, although the number had been picking up these past few months. But this one didn't fit the usual pattern. Usually, the cars that were stolen were current, popular models, worth a good price and with parts that were easily fenced. Like the Toyota Camry that was stolen from the lot on Maple Avenue last month, or the Honda Accord that was ripped off from the Water Street shopping center a few months back. Not so this time. According to the police report he'd been handed, this time the car in question had been a classic—a 1955 two-tone pewter and white Chevrolet Bel Air sedan. Its owner—or, rather, its driver, since the car belonged to the man's son—ran a small temp agency in the corporate center. Albert Kirson, his name was. Poor guy—he'd been a real mess when he came into the station to file his report. Seems he'd borrowed the car for work only because his own Ford Taurus was in the shop. And now he felt lousy about facing his twenty-three-year-old son with the news. The kid had saved for six years to earn enough for a down payment on that car. Sure, his father made a decent living, but that classic cost fifty grand. Not the kind of cash a small-business owner with two kids in college and one in grad school had lying around.

Detective Taylor shook his head ruefully. It always happened to the decent guys. Albert Kirson was a perfect example of that. Even the timing hadn't played in his favor. If it had been an election year, he might have gotten the kind of press that would have drummed up a big sympathy vote. As it was, he'd get nothing but an insurance check and a lot of grief from his son.

Well, for his part, he was glad he'd voted for Kirson in the last election. The man made a damned fine city council member. Taylor hoped he'd stay on even after the mayor moved up to the state senate.

11:00 P.M.

Stephen was sitting at the edge of his bed, getting ready to catch the late-night news, when the phone rang.

Automatically, his head jerked around, his gaze focusing on the bathroom door. Still shut. And the sound of running water meant Nancy hadn't finished her shower.

He groped for the phone, feeling an immediate constriction in his chest. These days, phone calls at odd hours could mean nothing but trouble.

He lifted the receiver. "Hello?"

"Ah, good. I can hear the local news playing in the background," Philip Walker said in a conversational tone. "Check out the *very* local late-breaking incident they'll be reporting before the weather. You'll find it fascinating."

Click.

Sweat beaded on Stephen's brow. What the hell had Walker done now?

He sat through the international and national highlights, his fists clenched in his lap. When he saw the words *late-breaking,* followed by a shot of Albert Kirson's face, he turned up the volume, listening intently as the chiseled, unemotional anchorwoman gave the details of the city council member's stolen vehicle.

Stolen from one of Leaf Brook's municipal lots.

Shit.

Nancy walked out of the bathroom, towel-drying her hair. Her gaze was fixed on her husband. "Stephen? Did I hear the telephone?"

He nodded, fully aware of what she was really asking. "Yeah." Time for a partial truth. "It was someone from my staff telling me about this." He pointed at the screen. "Albert's car was stolen tonight. Actually, the car belonged to his son, Jeff. Al borrowed it for the day. It was taken right from his lot at work."

His wife's attention shifted to the TV, and her brows

knit. “That’s terrible. It’s also been happening a lot these past few months. One of my clerks had her car stolen while she was shopping. Are these professional jobs, or do you think it’s kids?”

Stephen shrugged. “Except for tonight, it screamed professional. But a classic Chevy? That’s not exactly an easy car to unload. I don’t know who’s doing it, but it can’t continue. We need to get some decent security at the Leaf Brook municipal lots. It’s one of the major issues on my plate right now.”

Nancy nodded, a wave of relief sweeping over her face—relief that had nothing to do with the car thefts. Stephen could read her mind as if she’d spoken. *That’s the Stephen I know,* she was thinking. *Maybe he’s coming back to himself after all.*

Well, he wasn’t there yet.

But he would be.

11

April 7

It rained all day Saturday.

That meant no baseball practice for Brian.

Usually, that would be cause for major dejection. Today, it only resulted in minor disappointment, since Uncle Connor was there to pal around with.

The whole family had breakfast together, after which Stephen closeted himself in his home office, Connor went to his room to catch up on a few important business calls, and Nancy and Brian sprawled on the family-room floor, going head to head in three games of Battleship.

Connor emerged before noon. He patiently answered his nephew's barrage of questions about why he had to work on weekends when he wasn't even the mayor, then made up for his absence by taking Brian out for a burger and an afternoon movie.

Stephen remained behind closed doors, and the light to his office line remained steadily lit.

Somewhere around three o'clock, the doorbell rang.

From her chair in the downstairs den, Nancy looked up, wondering who it could be. Doubtless one of Stephen's colleagues or one of his campaign workers. They saw more of her husband than she did these days.

Certainly more of him in a positive functioning state—like when he wasn't drinking or gambling.

Stop feeling sorry for yourself, she lectured herself sternly. *No one's forcing you to stay in this marriage. You're here because you want to be. Because you love Stephen, because he's Brian's father, and because you remember how it was, how it can be, between you. Everyone has problems. We're no exception. We'll get through this. We have to.*

She sighed, massaged her throbbing temples. If only she didn't feel so utterly depleted, physically and emotionally. And if only she could restore Brian to being the happy-go-lucky kid he'd been a few months ago. Having Connor here helped, but still there were times when Brian seemed far away and withdrawn. . . .

The doorbell rang again, yanking Nancy away from her thoughts.

With a start, she came to her feet. She'd completely forgotten there was someone at the door. Blinking away the moisture that had gathered on her lashes, she set aside her paperwork and padded down the hall to the entranceway.

"Who is it?"

"Me, Nance." It was Cliff Henderson's voice.

She took a deep breath and opened the door. "Hi," she greeted her friend, forcing a practiced smile.

"Hi, yourself." He stepped inside, tapping the file that was tucked beneath his arm. "Stephen and I have a meeting. We've got a ton of paperwork to review." Abruptly, he paused, studying Nancy's face and frowning. "What's wrong?"

Now, *that* was a first. As a politician's wife, Nancy had learned never to let her feelings show. Over the years, she'd developed one hell of a public face, if she had to say so herself. Even Cliff, who was closer to them than anyone, had never seen through her carefully maintained veneer. If her distress was transparent enough to change that, she must be slipping.

She had to try harder.

"Nancy?" Cliff pressed, shutting the door and moving toward her. "What is it?"

"Why? Do I look that lousy?" Despite her attempts to sound normal, she could hear the odd, strained quality to her voice.

"No. You look stressed out. Like you've got the weight of the world on your shoulders. Anything I can do?"

Funny, she remembered the days when it was Stephen who gave her this kind of emotional support.

Then again, there had been other days when he'd been the cause of her needing it.

"Thanks, Cliff," she replied, squeezing his arm. "You're an amazing friend. I don't know what I'd do without you. I can't understand why some incredible woman hasn't snapped you up yet."

A corner of his mouth lifted. "Because Stephen got the last one of those. I'm spoiled. I'm waiting for another you."

Maybe the me of ten years ago, Nancy reflected sadly. *But not the me of today. I feel like a tired old woman.*

"Thanks for the compliment," she said aloud. "As for the offer to help, I really appreciate it. But, truly, there's nothing's wrong. Nothing but exhaustion. The boutique's been a zoo, the campaign is picking up speed, and Brian's practices are exploding into high gear. Oh, and Connor's here for a visit. So I'm running around like a chicken without a head. I was just winding down last night, when Stephen got that call about Albert Kirson's car being stolen. I guess it was too much in one day. I didn't shut an eye all night."

Operating on autopilot, she gestured for Cliff to take off his raincoat. "Why don't you give me that, and go have your meeting? Stephen's in his office. He's been buried in phone calls all morning."

"That doesn't surprise me," Cliff murmured, shaking out his damp trenchcoat before giving it to Nancy with a nod of thanks. "Albert Kirson's car being stolen probably instigated more debates over security at the Leaf Brook municipal lots."

"Exactly."

This conversation Nancy could handle. The issues. The dilemmas of the city. Even the campaign. She was programmed to address all that on the same autopilot.

"I know Stephen's very concerned about the number of car thefts the city's been having," she offered. "I hope the council and the police can come up with a solution that works all the way around."

"Yeah, me, too." Cliff paused, again scrutinizing Nancy's face, this time coming to some kind of decision. "Where's Brian?"

"Connor took him to a movie. They should be home around five."

"Then why don't you use this time to take a nap? You're beat. And with Tornado Brian whirling back into the house in no time, there'll be no relaxing until eight-thirty or nine."

True enough. And, God, the thought of a nap sounded wonderful. "You're right," she acknowledged, mentally relegating her paperwork to the back burner. "I shouldn't look a gift horse in the mouth. I'll go upstairs right now and catch a few Zs." She was already heading for the stairs. "You go ahead and have your meeting with Stephen. I hope it's productive."

Her final words were swallowed by a yawn.

Cliff watched her go, contemplating her bone-weary ascent with a worried scowl. He was torn between a rock and a hard place. And he wasn't sure there was any way to squirm free.

Deeply troubled, he made his way down to Stephen's office.

4:35 P.M.

Greg had awakened that morning to a blaring alarm clock. He'd punched the sleep button, only to have the blast of loud music replaced by the pelting of raindrops against his window.

So much for teeing off.

He'd called the golf course, confirmed that the game had been canceled.

Great, just great.

Now, not only did he have to pump an entire city council for information, but he had to do it all by telephone. And finagling information that way was a real pain in the ass, because he couldn't fully gauge the guys' reactions without seeing—and reading—each of their expressions.

On the flip side, there was a positive edge to all this, an edge that did much to improve his humor. Instead of whipping into action at six A.M., he could do his fact-finding much later in the day, which meant that Stephen Stratford would have all that time to make his own calls.

Whatever support he managed to drum up, Greg would learn about in his late-afternoon conversations. As a result, he'd have a much more comprehensive understanding of the situation to report.

Bearing that in mind, he'd waited until three to begin his game of six-way political tag. What he'd found out had been enlightening, although not surprising, in light of Friday night's high-profile car theft.

There had been two converts to the mayor's cause. As of now, two council members, including Kirson, were eager to give Philip Walker the contract he sought. The other four, however, were not. Their preference was to institute the less expensive, city-run program and step up local police surveillance in the municipal lots.

That meant that even with the mayor's vote, he was one vote short.

Close but no cigar.

Greg poured himself a glass of wine and sat down on his couch, crossing his legs at the ankles. Funny thing about that car theft, he mused, sipping at his wine. Albert Kirson's car, of all things. Quite a coincidence.

6:30 P.M.

Connor yanked on a dark blue turtleneck sweater, ran a comb through his hair, and glanced at the clock. He had to be out of there in ten minutes, or he'd be late picking up Julia. Which he had no intentions of being, given his plans for the evening. However, he was determined to speak with Stephen before he went.

He hadn't seen his brother since breakfast. Nor, for that matter, had Brian. Stephen had still been closeted in that damned office when they got back from the movie.

What the hell was going on?

As far as Connor knew, Stephen had restored the five hundred thousand dollars he'd given him to his campaign account. So why was he still so uptight? Had the hole he'd dug himself been even deeper? Could he possibly owe more than he'd admitted?

Time to find out.

Slinging his sport coat over his shoulder, Connor left his room and headed straight for Stephen's office. As he reached the closed door, he could hear the muffled sound of voices raised in anger. Stephen and Cliff. They were obviously having a disagreement—a big one. That was rare. It was also damned inconvenient. But it wasn't going to stop him.

He knocked.

"Can't it wait?" Stephen barked.

"No, it can't." Connor walked in, nodding at Cliff. "Hi, Cliff. Good to see you."

"Hey, Connor." Cliff looked unusually flushed.

"Sorry to barge in, but I need a minute with my brother, and I'm about to head out for the evening."

"No problem." Cliff scooped up his papers. "It's late. And I've got dinner plans myself." He shot Stephen a look. "Think about what I said."

"Right." A muscle was working in Stephen's jaw. "See you."

Connor waited until Cliff had gone, then shut the door carefully behind him. "What was that all about?"

"Nothing."

"It didn't look like nothing to me. It also didn't look like business. It looked personal. Cliff didn't figure out what was going on with the missing money, did he?"

"No." Stephen slapped his hands on the desk, pushing

himself to his feet and pacing around. "If you must know, Cliff's worried about Nancy. He thinks she's depressed. He just doesn't know why."

"But we do." Connor gripped the back of a heavy leather chair, leaning forward to brace himself. "Stephen, your home life's falling apart. Why? I gave you the half-million dollars. So why are you still so freaked out?"

Stephen paused, shoving his hands in his pockets and gazing at Connor. He looked like hell—drawn and haggard, as if he'd aged ten years. And there were dark circles under his eyes, the kind that aren't caused by lack of sleep alone.

"I'm freaked out about a deadlock in the city council that I can't break. I'm freaked out about the increase in car thefts that won't do a whole lot for my credibility as mayor or for my chances at a senate seat. And I'm freaked out because I'm expecting Dad to barge in sometime later this week for one of his periodic checks on my campaign progress. Is that enough?"

Knowing Harrison Stratford? More than enough.

Connor studied his brother, sensing the frazzled state his nerves were in, wondering for the hundredth time if all this was worth it. He doubted that even Stephen himself knew what he wanted at this point or if a career in politics was truly the right path for him to be taking. If he was this stressed out from a finite campaign, what would happen to his emotional state when their father aimed him at Washington and lit the fuse?

Now wasn't the time for that particular heart-to-heart. Not when Stephen was this close to the edge. Connor wasn't sure when the right time would be. Maybe after this election was over and Stephen's mind was free of the burdens of campaigning. Maybe then he could assess if the current track he was heading on—their father's track—would make him happy on a long-term basis.

In the meantime, at least what he was freaking out about wasn't more gambling debts. Connor was grateful for that much.

"Yeah," he told his brother quietly. "That's enough. Especially the part about Dad." He inclined his head quizzically. "Anything I can do?"

"You can start by not lecturing me, which I'm sure is why you barged in here. I'll beat you to the punch. Yes, I realize I've neglected my family today. What am I going to do about it? I'm going to have a stiff drink, wash up, and head for the kitchen, where I intend to spend the rest of the evening with all of you. Okay?"

Connor nodded. "Except I won't be there. I've got a date." He glanced at his watch. "Which I'm going to be late for if I don't get a move on. I'm supposed to pick her up at seven."

That diverted Stephen. His brows rose in surprise. "Someone local? I didn't know you were seeing anyone in Leaf Brook."

"I wasn't. I'm still not. It's our first date."

"Do I know her?"

"You sure do." Connor's expression never changed. "Julia Talbot."

Stephen's jaw dropped. "Julia . . . when the hell did that happen?"

"Yesterday when I picked Brian up. I asked. She said yes. We're having dinner."

"Does Greg know?"

Connor shrugged. "I didn't get the feeling they were too involved—at least, not from Julia's perspective."

"So much for your thinking she was too good to be

true for your taste." A shadow of a grin. "Then again, I never really believed you. You couldn't keep your eyes off her at any of Brian's games."

"Brian's the reason I'm seeing her."

"Brian is." Stephen sounded as if he'd just been told the earth was flat. "Right."

"I'm not joking."

"Really? What did my son do, set you two up?" Stephen looked genuinely amused. "Actually, now that I think about it, that's not so unlikely. You two are his greatest heroes. So, is that it? Did Brian push you together on the playground?"

"Cute." Connor didn't smile. "No, it was my idea. Julia's fixated on Brian's state of mind. She's worried that he's hurting emotionally—and she's right. She's also damned close to figuring out why." He paused, then went on with the more upsetting news. "When I got to school to pick Brian up, guess which slimy journalist was cornering Julia, asking for her perspective on why you were so uptight when she grilled you at the game last week?"

All the color drained from Stephen's face. "Shit."

"Yeah, you could call her that."

"Did Julia talk to her?"

"Nope. She pretty much told Ms. Lager to go to hell. I did the rest. She won't be around for a while, not until she's had some time to rethink her strategy. I threatened her with a lawsuit."

"Son of a bitch." Stephen rubbed his forehead vigorously, as if whatever hurt was buried too deep to reach. "You obviously spoke alone with Julia. What did she say?"

"She fired questions at me. She's not stupid, Stephen. She knows something's not right. She assumes it's the pressure of the campaign or, at worst, that you're feeling guilty because Dad and I are bankrolling you. But she flat-out told me she's not going to leave this alone. Not unless she sees some improvement in Brian."

Stephen's arm dropped to his side, and he looked as if he'd been punched. "So what is it you plan to do?"

"Two things. Stick around here until things get back to normal and Brian *is* better. And keep Julia Talbot's free time filled with something other than worrying about her students, particularly Brian."

"I see." A slow, painful breath. "Connor, I don't know what to say. I've been a real prick to you lately. I just feel like a cornered rat and . . ." He broke off. "It doesn't matter. That's no excuse. You've really come through for me, and I don't just mean financially. I realize you're doing a lot of this for Brian, but I want you to know how much I . . ."

"Hey," Connor interrupted, waving away his brother's thanks. The last thing he wanted was to bring Stephen down another notch. That shaky self-esteem was what had started this downhill spiral. "Don't thank me. First of all, you're my brother, and Brian's my nephew. Second, I know Dad as well as you do. I know the part he's played in screwing up your life. And third . . ." He strove for a light note. "You're right. I can't take my eyes off Julia Talbot. So let's not make this out to be such a sacrifice, okay?"

"Yeah, okay." Stephen shot his brother a speculative look. "I'm not sure how much of what you just said was to make me feel better and how much was true."

"Me, either. Guess it's time to find out." Connor headed for the door. "You guys have a good night. And don't wait up."

12

7:50 P.M.

Julia glanced around the restaurant, wishing she could lose herself in its understated charm. The wood-paneled room was warm and cozy, its ambience that of an Italian bistro. Soft music played in the background, and the waiters moved about in an unhurried fashion, as if inviting their patrons to savor the meal and the company.

She and Connor had been escorted to a private table tucked away in an alcove that was banked by windows overlooking the Hudson River. In the distance, a hazy glow illuminated the Tappan Zee Bridge, enhancing but not intruding upon the leisurely pace of the dining experience.

Turning her attention to her wine glass, Julia sipped at the chardonnay, wishing it would calm her nerves. She'd been nervous all day—changing her clothes three times before settling on brown wool slacks and a cream-colored sweater. She'd never been this jittery on a date, not even a first one. Then again, she'd never been so blindly drawn to a man before—a man she wasn't sure she had a single thing in common with, other than their mutual affection for his nephew.

"You look far away," Connor noted, fingering the stem of his own wine glass. "Is this place not what you expected?"

"The restaurant is lovely." Julia set down her glass. "If I look far away, it's probably because I'm wondering whether you and I will have anything to talk about once we wear out the subject of Brian."

"I think we'll manage." That unsettling stare delved deep inside her. "But look on the bright side. You won't have to wonder for long."

"I suppose not." She tried to ignore the butterflies that were having a field day in her stomach.

"Finish your appetizer," Connor suggested, pointing at the stuffed portobella mushroom that was nestled, half-eaten, on her plate. "It's the chef's pride and joy. He'll be crushed if you leave any."

Julia gave him a rueful smile. "Then maybe you should take half of what's left." She gestured for him to do so. "Much as I love portobella mushrooms, I can't eat this whole thing and save room for a main course *and* that tiramisu you raved about."

"Sounds good." Connor polished off the last of his mussels. Then he helped Julia transfer a portion of her mushroom to his plate.

For a brief instant, their fingers brushed, and Julia felt a jolt of heat shoot through her. She did the best she could to hide her reaction, keeping her gaze on the plate in front of her. She had no idea how successful she was, nor did she intend to look at Connor to find out. Instead, she concentrated on finishing her appetizer and getting her heightened senses back under control.

By the time their plates were cleared and their wine glasses refilled, she'd succeeded.

"How's Brian today?" she asked, folding her hands on the table.

Connor ripped off a piece of warm bread. "Fine, other

than hating the fact that baseball practice was rained out. We went to a movie instead."

"Just the two of you?"

One dark brow rose. "Um-hum. Is that a problem?"

"Of course not. I'm sure the mayor was bogged down."

"Fishing, are we?" Connor drizzled some olive oil onto his plate to dip his bread in. "As it happens, Stephen was dealing with the aftermath of that car theft last night. I'm sure you caught the story in the paper and saw that the victim was a city councilman."

"I didn't have to catch it in the paper. I saw it on the eleven o'clock news." Julia ignored her own bread. "I knew something serious had happened in that municipal lot last night. I got stuck in the traffic jam there on my way home from Poughkeepsie. I flicked on the news as soon as I walked in. When I saw that a car had been stolen and that it had belonged to Councilman Kirson, I realized Mayor Stratford would have his hands full this weekend. So, no, I wasn't fishing; I was stating a fact. I'm glad you were there to spend time with Brian."

Her chin came up a notch. "Not everything I say is meant as an attack. Nor am I big on ulterior motives. If I had something to say, I'd say it. I teach elementary school, remember? I lack one of those personal agendas you were spouting about."

"True." Connor ripped off an edge of his bread and dipped it in olive oil, his manner deceptively calm. "You don't have an agenda, at least not a hidden one. But you did threaten to bypass me in this matter with Brian."

"If I remember right, it was *you* who threatened *me*. You told me to stay out of it. I told you I can't. I also said I'd try handling things your way first. If Brian responds to your being here, if you can give him the stability he needs to bring back the old Brian, I'll be thrilled to leave it at that." Julia leaned forward. "I'm not Cheryl Lager. She's a vulture who feeds off people. I'm not. I'm a teacher, one of the good guys. I want only Brian's well-being."

"I know that." Connor resumed munching. His tone and expression were guarded, the same way they always were when this subject came up. "As for Cheryl Lager, I'd hardly put you two in the same category. She's a self-serving bitch. You're anything but."

"I can't believe that woman was actually thinking of approaching Brian directly," Julia muttered, remembering the speculative glint in Ms. Lager's eyes when she'd glanced Brian's way.

"That's not going to happen."

"No, it's not. She'd have to come through me first."

A hint of amusement curved Connor's lips. "That sounds intimidating, if a bit far-fetched. I can't imagine you as the fistfighting type."

"I'm normally not. With Cheryl Lager, I'd make an exception."

"You mean that, don't you?"

"For Brian, yes."

Connor propped his elbow on the arm of his chair, regarding Julia intently, as if he wasn't sure if she was just venting or really serious about her threat. "I admire your loyalty. But I wouldn't suggest taking a swing at Cheryl Lager. First of all, you'd end up getting hurt. You're slight. She's solid. She outweighs you by at least twenty pounds. Second, you'd be smacked with a whopper of a lawsuit. So would your school. And third, what kind of example would you be setting for your students if you pounded Cheryl Lager into the ground?"

"You've got me with your second and third arguments. But you'd lose with your first. Solid or not, I doubt Ms. Lager could hold a candle to me in a fistfight. I had great trainers."

"Trainers—you mean martial arts instructors?"

"Better. The town of Poughkeepsie's Little League. They taught me to fight when I was eight. I had lots of lessons and lots of practice. I spent every free minute of my childhood with them."

This time, Connor's amusement was genuine. "So *that's* where you perfected your curve ball. And here I thought you accomplished that during softball practice."

Julia made a face. "My dad taught me to throw when I was younger than Brian. I couldn't wait to start school so I could join the Little League. I was crushed when I found out there was no girls' baseball team. Softball always seemed like a wimpy substitute. Oh, I played it, right through high school. But every chance I got, I went to the park and joined in with the boys."

"I'm surprised they let you."

"They more than let me. They were thrilled. I kept their skills sharp. I threw better than their star pitcher." An impish grin. "Of course, I had to promise them I'd shove every strand of hair under my cap so anyone watching would think I was a boy."

"A boy?" Connor's gaze wandered leisurely over her, after which he shot her a skeptical look. "I can't imagine you pulling that one off."

She flushed. "Well, I did. At the time, I was a skinny little tomboy. So the masquerade wasn't all that tough to manage. Of course, once in a while, someone figured me out and gave the boys a hard time. That's where my fighting skills came in. I'm small, but I pack a powerful punch."

"I'll try to remember that, in case I overstep my bounds." A deliberate pause. "Whatever bounds you intend to hold me to."

There was something disturbingly intimate about that comment, or maybe it was just the way Julia took it. Not likely, though. Not with the tone of Connor's voice or the look in his eyes. No, he knew just what he was saying and how she was hearing it.

She swallowed, wishing she had a clever comeback to dispel the tension.

Her dilemma was resolved by the arrival of their entrees, and she turned her full attention to sampling her shrimp marechiara.

"This is wonderful," she declared. "You were right about the food."

"I'm right about a lot of things."

He wasn't about to let her off the hook.

Well, she was going to free herself, then, by steering this conversation back to safe ground.

"You and Brian have a very special bond. Was it always like that?"

The subtle lift of Connor's brows said he saw through her obvious change of subject. But he answered her question nonetheless. "Yup, right from the start. I was in the Far East on a business trip when Brian was born. I flew home as soon as I could break away and went straight to Stephen's house. Brian was two weeks old. I was scared to death that if I touched him, I'd break him. Nancy just put him in my arms, showed me how to support his head, and backed away. He and I stared at each other for a while. I think he was trying to figure me out. Whatever he decided must have made him happy, because he started pumping his arms and legs, and then he gave me a big toothless smile. I was hooked."

Julia smiled, wondering if Connor knew how much of himself he revealed when he spoke about Brian. "What about your parents?"

"What about them?"

"Brian's their first, their only, grandchild. They must have been ecstatic when he was born."

An offhanded shrug. "My mother was delighted. That's as close to ecstatic as she gets. And my father was pleased. That's over the top for him."

Julia toyed with her food, trying to decide how to respond. Not that she was stunned by Connor's reply. She'd had a pretty good idea that Harrison Stratford hadn't made his billions by attending PTA meetings. But her own values were so different, her home life so much the opposite of Connor's. Still, she had no right to judge his father and certainly no right to condemn him.

"The mayor and his wife are amazing parents," she said instead.

"And coming from a household like mine, that's quite a coup," Connor correctly interpreted.

"I didn't mean . . ."

"Yes, you did. And based on your view of what parents should be, you're right." He laid down his fork. "Look, Julia, it doesn't take a genius to guess your opinion of my upbringing. The name Stratford is a regular on the business and political scenes. We probably seem like aliens to you. But to Stephen and me, growing up in that environment was business as usual. Our lifestyle seemed as normal to us as Little League did to you."

"That's obvious. It's also obvious that you have a

strong sense of family. You're very protective—of your family and your family name."

"Both of those go with the territory. And just for the record, I was hardly a deprived child. Neither was Stephen. We had the best of everything, including opportunities that other people would kill for. As for personal attention, we had that, too. Okay, our house wasn't *Leave it to Beaver.* But it also wasn't the classic case of an absentee father and a socialite mother who didn't give a damn. My parents were involved in our lives. They just placed their emphasis in areas other than the ones you're used to. Their efforts went toward securing our futures. They didn't spend much time on psychological stroking. As a father, Stephen's philosophy is different. He's a much more hands-on dad."

"I can't say I don't applaud that. I do. It's good for your brother—and for Brian."

"I agree." One dark brow rose. "Now, are we finished psychoanalyzing my family?"

Thoughtfully, Julia nodded. She had the distinct feeling she'd just been given a party-line speech, one that Connor had perfected over the years. It wasn't so much what he'd said, but what he *hadn't* said that struck her. As if the sketchy description of his upbringing could be filled in with a lot more impactful details than he'd chosen to provide. "Yes," she replied, taking his cue. "We're finished."

"Good. Because there's nothing much else to tell, nothing that wouldn't bore you to tears. I could go on with lengthy discussions of investments, acquisitions, cash flow—you know, the stuff financial empires are made of. From there, I could branch out into how we rally behind a political candidate, one who's destined for greatness. That's the Stratfords, in a nutshell." He propped his chin on his hand. "On the other hand, we could talk about you. You could tell me exactly what your relationship with Greg Matthews is."

Julia's fork clattered to the table. "Where did that question come from?"

"Are you going to answer it?"

She fiddled with her napkin. "I could say it's none of your business."

"You could. But we both know that wouldn't be true."

God, this conversation was getting *way* out of hand. And this time, Connor had swerved it there abruptly, giving her no time to prepare.

Well, prepared or not, she wasn't going to lie.

"Greg and I have gone out a handful of times. There isn't much else to say."

"I think you just said it."

Julia swallowed, hard. "Connor . . ."

"You're not sleeping with him."

Her chin shot up, hot color flooding her cheeks as she met his gaze. "That's *definitely* none of your business."

"If you say so."

"I do."

Julia attacked her shrimp with a vengeance, devoting her full attention to eating. She needed a reprieve, badly.

Connor didn't intend to give it to her. "Would he mind that you were out with me?"

Slowly, Julia's head came up. "Probably. But I didn't ask his permission."

"Will you tell him?"

"If the subject comes up, yes."

"When?"

"When . . . what?"

"When might the subject come up? Do you have another date with him planned?"

"As a matter of fact, we're having brunch tomorrow."

"Will you enjoy it as much as you're enjoying dinner?"

"I don't know," she answered in a quiet, frank tone. "I'll let you know when I can think straight."

"That might not be for some time. Not if I can help it."

Julia's mouth went dry. She was still reeling when the waiter came over to take their dessert order.

Numbly, she shook her head, protesting that she couldn't manage another bite.

The waiter wouldn't hear of it. "Please, *signora,* our desserts are all homemade," he coaxed.

She shot Connor a pleading look.

He didn't help.

"I did promise you a tiramisu that would straighten your curve ball," he reminded her.

The waiter beamed. "A perfect choice. I have a suggestion, if I may. Our portions of tiramisu are very generous. Why don't the two of you share a piece?"

"Good idea," Connor agreed. "We'll wait on coffee. If we run out of room, that's what we'll do without." He ignored Julia's weak protest. "You'll thank me for this later—you'll see."

"If you say so."

"I do."

The creamy slice of heaven that arrived minutes later wasn't generous. It was huge.

The waiter set the plate in the center of the table, handed each of them a spoon, and left.

"Dig in," Connor urged.

There was something about slicing off creamy spoonfuls of dessert from the same plate, then bringing them to your lips, that screamed intimacy. Especially on the heels of their very unsettling conversation.

Connor felt it, too. He watched her intently, his gaze fixed on her mouth. "Well?" he asked after her fourth bite.

"Well what?"

"Isn't it everything I promised?"

The dessert. He was talking about the dessert.

"Oh, yes. It's fabulous."

"Good." He savored another bite, and Julia found herself staring just as blatantly as he, unable to look away from his mouth as he chewed and swallowed, his tongue capturing the final bits of marscapone cheese from his lips.

"Let's skip coffee," he said abruptly, pushing back his chair.

Julia nearly bolted from her seat. "What?"

"I'm not thirsty. Are you?"

"No." What in God's name was she doing? She was letting this man think she was ready to go to bed with him.

She wasn't entirely sure she wasn't.

"I'll get the check." Connor signaled the waiter.

Ten minutes later, the check was paid, Julia's coat was reclaimed, and Connor was leading her out of the restaurant.

The rain had stopped, leaving the night cooler, with droplets of moisture clinging to the trees and the grass. The air smelled fresh, rife with that just-having-rained scent.

Their shoes crunched on the gravel as they made their way through the parking lot. Other than the light pressure of his palm against her back, Connor didn't touch her. Yet Julia was more acutely aware of him than she'd ever been of a man before in her life.

Connor pressed his electronic key button, unlocking the silver Mercedes. He opened the passenger door, waiting until Julia had slid in before shutting the door and going around to the driver's side.

He climbed in, started the car, and eased out of the parking lot, while Julia searched frantically for a topic of conversation. Anything to break this charged silence. Especially with a half-hour drive ahead and a decision she didn't want to think about waiting at the other end.

"Tell me what a venture capitalist does," she blurted out. "Not only what he does but why he does it."

Connor slanted her a measured look. "Why?"

"Because, as you aptly pointed out, I don't know any venture capitalists. I can't form an opinion without some facts."

"Ah. You want to know if we fit into the same vulture category as Cheryl Lager."

"Very funny. No, I'd hardly describe you as a vulture. What I meant is, what motivates you? Is it really all about money? Or is it the power?"

"If you're asking if there's a rush involved in picking a long shot, getting behind it, and seeing it soar—sure. Why do I do it? Because it fascinates me. Because I like to see fledgling companies I believe in grow. Because it challenges my mind. Because I want to have a stake in the future of industry and technology. Because I'm good at it." He gave an offhanded shrug as he stopped at a light. "The money's more of a success indicator than anything else. It means I'm doing my job well. As for being rich, well, that alone doesn't float my boat. I've had money all my life. It comes in handy, but it's not the be-all and end-all of existence. Then again, that's easy for me to say. I've never been poor."

Julia blinked. She hadn't expected such self-effacing honesty.

Connor's lips curved ever so slightly. "Don't look so shocked. I'm not always evasive. On occasion, I've been known to tell the truth."

"It's not just your honesty that surprises me. It's your insight."

"I've been known to be insightful, too. I read people well; it's a gift I developed early. It was one of the benefits of being a loner. I cultivated great powers of observation. They've come in handy in my profession."

"Were you always a loner?"

"I was pretty independent, if that's what you mean. Another Stratford trait."

"What about your brother? You're close in age—didn't you hang out together?"

"We're a year apart, and no, Stephen was a lot more outgoing and social than I was. He had tons of friends. I preferred my own company. That still holds true. What about you? Any siblings?"

Julia shook her head. "No, there's just me, although I often wished for a brother or sister. I guess I romanticized the whole idea just like every other only kid does. Anyway, now that I look back on it, I was—and am—very fortunate. I have two amazing, loving parents. By example, they taught me the importance of caring, of giving something of myself to everything I do, and of following my instincts, even if it means walking a rockier path. I'm still learning from them, corny as that might sound."

Connor didn't comment on that. On the other hand, he didn't look mocking. If anything, he looked pensive.

He veered off the highway at the Leaf Brook exit and made a left turn at the end of the ramp. "Those workshops you mentioned giving, you said something about doing them with your mother."

"Yes. My mom's an RN. She's also one of the most selfless, compassionate human beings I've ever met. She started offering these pro bono workshops five years ago, in conjunction with the American Professional Society on the Abuse of Children. I joined her when I finished graduate school."

"Where do you hold them?"

"At hospitals in Poughkeepsie and a couple of other Dutchess County towns. We deal with topics that involve children's emotional well-being. Our attendees are health-care providers—prenatal, pediatric, and obstetric. Our goal is to help identify potentially neglectful families and take preventive actions before potentiality becomes reality."

"I see." Connor processed that information with the same pensive expression. "Now I see why you're so attuned to your students. And why you're qualified to spot any signs that they're hurting."

"Kids internalize a lot," Julia explained. "That fools many adults, even well-meaning ones. They don't see any outward change in their child, so they convince themselves all is well. But internalizing takes its toll. It's up to trained observers, like teachers, to point that out. Bringing the parents around is the hard part. They balk at the need for outside help. They view the situation as a failure on their part. But it's not. It's an important, courageous step. It can make all the difference to a child's emotional well-being."

"Your knowledge is impressive. So's the fact that you're willing to share it by giving those workshops." Connor shot her a look. "And before you question my sincerity, I mean that. Your mother sounds like a remarkable woman. The two of you are making a major contribution."

"We hope so."

"What about your father? I assume he doesn't teach curve-ball throwing for a living?"

Julia smiled. "He's a professor at Vassar. He teaches philosophy and literature. I grew up on a college campus, surrounded by the world of academia. In that way, I was very sheltered. In other ways, I wasn't." A shadow flickered across Julia's face. "Anyway, my dad and I argue literary interpretation and ideology to this day."

"I'm sure you hold your own nicely." Connor cast another quick glance in her direction. "In what ways weren't you sheltered?"

Obviously, her brief comment hadn't gone unnoticed.

She turned her head and gazed out the window. "Let's just say I've seen my share of ugliness. It's made me realize that there's very little of life that's within our control. The few things that are—principles, ideals—those need to be clung to like life preservers."

"That's a nice thought but a pretty simplistic view. Being principled is great. But what if something unexpected comes along, something that throws a major monkey wrench into your ideals? Shouldn't you reassess things?"

Julia stared at the rows of trees they were passing. Was he referring to his own experiences or reading into hers? "I suppose. It depends on how deep the ideal in question runs and how significant the monkey wrench is."

Connor slowed down the car, turned onto Julia's

street. "Fair enough." He eased into a parking space and turned off the ignition. "Enough heavy conversation for now. We can pick it up again later." A heartbeat of silence. "Much later."

The sexual tension that had accompanied them from the restaurant slammed back to the forefront with a vengeance.

Julia blinked, thrown abruptly off balance. She gazed about, wondering when they'd reached her apartment. She'd been so caught up in their conversation, she'd stopped concentrating on the road.

Well, they were here. And she was no more prepared for what would happen next than she'd been thirty minutes ago.

There was no chance of simply saying good night and bolting. Connor was already out of the car, walking around to help her.

She climbed out, opening her pocketbook and rummaging for her keys. Her hand was shaking as she gripped them, and she purposely avoided Connor's gaze as she led the way into her building.

Three minutes later, they were standing in front of her apartment door.

"I . . ." She cleared her throat, staring at a corner of the hall carpet. "Thank you for dinner. It was . . ."

"Julia." Connor's voice was low and intense, and for the first time he touched her—*really* touched her—his hands curving around her shoulders, smoothing down the soft wool of her sweater. "Invite me in."

The electric charges that shot through her at his touch were so acute, she jumped. Her chin jerked up, and she met his heated gaze, seeing her own stunned awareness reflected in his eyes.

"No," she whispered.

One hand shifted, his knuckles caressing her cheek. "Why not?"

"You know why not."

"I also know you're not ready."

"Then why are you asking to come in?"

"Because I want to kiss you good night." His thumb traced her lower lip.

"And you can't do that out here?" she managed, barely able to speak.

"No, I can't."

Julia didn't question him further. She groped behind her, unlocking the front door and shoving it open.

They stepped inside, and Connor pushed the door closed behind them. The apartment was pitch dark. Neither of them made a move to turn on a light.

Backing her against the wall, Connor braced his arms on either side of her. He waited until she raised her head, then lowered his mouth to hers.

No kiss she'd ever experienced had prepared her for this.

Connor's mouth simply took hers. No preliminaries, no gradual onset. His lips just opened hers, molded them to his. His tongue sank inside, rubbing against hers in a blatantly carnal motion that quickly became an unbearable rhythm of plunge and retreat.

Liquid heat shot through her.

Without thinking, Julia reacted. She reached for him, her fingers digging into his sweater, anchoring her, pulling him closer to deepen the kiss.

It was all the encouragement he needed.

His hands dropped to her waist, clamped down, and lifted her up and into him. His body pinned hers to the wall, holding her there as his mouth continued to eat at hers.

Julia's senses were on overload. The woodsy scent of Connor's cologne, the incredible taste of his mouth—she'd never wanted anything so much. Her breasts were flattened against the solid wall of his chest, and her nipples were tight, throbbing inside her bra. Connor's muscles were taut beneath the deceptively soft texture of his sweater, and she could feel the rigid outline of his erection as he moved against her. His breath, like hers, was coming in fast, shallow pants. His hands drifted restlessly down the sides of her breasts, then up again, gliding forward, moving closer and closer to where she needed him.

She was frantic for him to give in and take her in that full caress. She squirmed, waiting for him to shift that small distance.

It happened, but only for an instant.

Connor's palms whispered over the hard points of her nipples—once, twice. Julia heard herself whimper, felt the shudder that ran through Connor's body.

Abruptly, he stopped. His hands dropped to her waist and gripped her tightly, and he tore his mouth away from hers in what was obviously a painful gesture.

"Julia," he demanded, his voice a low, grating rasp. "Is this what you want?"

She felt as if she were drugged. Yes, this was what she wanted. Her body was screaming for it.

"This is about to become a helluva lot more than a kiss," he managed. "So if you don't want me inside you, you'd better say so now. Because that's where I'm going to be in about two minutes."

Think. She had to think.

Their eyes had become accustomed to the darkness,

and Connor read the indecision on her face. Slowly, he lowered her feet to the floor. "I guess that answers my question."

"No, it doesn't," she whispered. "You can't know what I want. Because *I* don't know what I want."

"Oh, yes, you do. You're just scared to death of it."

Scared? She was terrified. She didn't even know this man. And at the moment, she didn't know herself.

"It's too soon. We're so different. I can't just . . ." She broke off.

"Coward," he breathed against her lips. "What happened to those instincts your parents taught you to follow? Shouldn't you be listening to those?"

"Only when I'm clearheaded. Right now, I'm not."

"Neither am I." He tugged lightly at her lower lip, then paused to lose himself in another deep, drugging kiss. "Next time will be our second date," he muttered thickly. "Will that be too soon?"

"Connor, it's not just about how many times we see each other. It's about . . ."

"Ideals. Principles," he finished for her. "I'm not sure how those factor into what's happening between us. But it looks like you're up against that major monkey wrench we talked about."

"Big time," she agreed, still gripping his forearms for support.

"Work through it by next weekend."

"Next weekend?"

"Um-hum. You'll be saving the weekend—*all* of it—to spend with me. Other than your workshop night."

A hard swallow. "I'll try."

"Do better than try. And in the meantime, expect some impromptu weeknight get-togethers. Drinks, dinner, coffee—I don't care which. You decide. But I'm going to see you."

"I want that, too."

"Good." His fingers threaded through her hair, and his gaze lowered, lingered on her mouth. "I'd better go now," he murmured reluctantly. "While I still can. But Julia, just so we understand each other, next weekend when you invite me in, I won't be leaving until morning." His thumbs traced the sides of her breasts again, shifting to circle her nipples slowly. "Hurry up and get past whatever rules you've invented to keep us apart," he commanded, his voice thick. He swallowed her soft moan of pleasure, kissing her as she trembled in his arms. "Sleep tight."

11:45 P.M.

Stephen heard Connor come in.

Wide awake, he leaned back against his pillow, folding his arms behind his head and staring at the ceiling, as Nancy tossed fitfully beside him.

He hoped that Connor's date had been a success and Julia Talbot would now be distracted from her crusade to be Brian's guardian angel.

But she was the least of his problems.

He hadn't managed to bring around enough of the council members. He'd spent all day trying. He was still one vote short. Philip Walker wasn't interested in his efforts; he was interested in results. Unfortunately, he wasn't going to get any—not the ones he wanted. Which meant he'd follow through on his threat. He'd slash Stephen's career to ribbons, maybe even make sure he wound up in jail.

Stephen could just imagine the headlines—and his father's reaction to them.

Well, it wasn't going to happen. Not in this lifetime.

He'd tried to do this the easy way, but it wasn't meant to be. He couldn't finagle the contract the way Walker wanted it. So an alliance was out.

He'd have to gain leverage another way. He'd launch a subtle counterattack. It was risky, but he needed insurance. And he had a pretty good idea how to get it.

He'd have to work fast. He'd make a few phone calls tomorrow, arrange a meeting for first thing Monday morning.

Time to fight fire with fire.

13

April 8
1:05 P.M.

Two men in two days.

Robin would be so pleased with her improved social life, Julia thought wryly, watching Greg take a bite of his omelette. Well, she herself wasn't pleased. She was exhausted and confused, and her insides were twisted around like a pretzel.

The restaurant was lovely, the food ample and well prepared, but she was no more in the mood for brunch than she was in the mood for skydiving.

She'd gotten three hours of sleep max, and her head was pounding like a hammer. Worse, she was no closer to figuring out what to say or do than she'd been last night. She'd stared at her bedroom ceiling all night, trying to sort out what had happened between her and Connor. No, that wasn't true. She *knew* what had happened. What she didn't know was what it meant or how she was going to handle it.

And what should she say to Greg? *By the way, I went out with another guy last night, and I'm so damned attracted to him that if he hadn't had the self-control to stop, I probably would have had sex with him right there against my foyer wall even though it was only our first date*? That would go over well, especially since Greg had been fervently courting her for more than a month now and she'd scarcely let him kiss her good night.

But even if she left out the graphic details, how could she explain what was going on between her and Connor when she herself didn't know?

She had to tell Greg something. Not only because she felt it was the right thing to do but because Connor was the mayor's brother and Greg would inevitably find out she was seeing him.

If she kept seeing him. That was a whole other can of worms. Connor had been blunt about his expectations. And the point was moot, because she wanted him as much as he wanted her. If she went through with next weekend's date, they'd end up in bed. Was she ready for that? She'd promised herself she wouldn't compromise, that when she slept with a man it would be out of mutual caring and commitment, not just sexual attraction. Then again, that had been an easy decision to make before she'd wanted someone the way she wanted Connor. The question was, what did a night in bed mean to him? And was she equipped to handle whatever that answer might be?

God, she was a mess.

Sitting across from her, Greg was charming as always, regaling her with the antics of his next-door neighbor's cat, who insisted on howling loudly for his breakfast each morning at five A.M. "It's like living with a rooster," he claimed, rolling his eyes. "I might as well throw out my alarm clock."

She gave an automatic smile, although her mind was only half on what he was saying.

"Julia?" He gave up the one-sided chat, propping his elbows on the table and leaning forward to study her.

"Are you all right? You haven't said ten sentences in the last hour."

She sighed, laying down her fork. "I'm sorry, Greg. I'm having a hard time concentrating."

"Is it me?"

The question was almost ironic. "No, it's not you, it's me. I slept horribly last night."

His brows knit in concern. "Any particular reason?"

That was the two-million-dollar question. "Actually, yes. I was confused, and I wanted to talk to you about it."

Greg misinterpreted that, looking thoroughly self-satisfied as he took a healthy swallow of orange juice. "I'm flattered. And I'm pleased. Very pleased. I want you to come to me with your problems."

"I hope you'll feel that way after you hear what my problem is." She took a deep breath, suddenly realizing she should have done this last week, rather than leave things hanging. "Greg, I like you. You're a great guy. We have fun together. But I have a feeling your take on this relationship is different from mine. I can't let you think . . ."

"Julia," he interrupted, now looking edgy rather than pleased. "I thought we went through this last week. I'm sorry I pushed you. It won't happen again—not until you're ready."

"That's just it. I don't think I'm going to be ready." Julia gripped her napkin tightly in her lap. She hated doing this. But it had to be done, no matter what ended up happening between her and Connor. The fact was, she'd never want more than friendship with Greg. She'd sensed that from the start, but now, after experiencing last night's blind rush of passion, she was sure of it. And it was unfair to keep Greg dangling.

"Greg, I meant what I said. It's not you, it's me. I can't help it—it's just not in the cards for us."

"I see." He shot her a wary look. "And what brought you to this conclusion?"

She sighed. "I think we both sensed this might be coming. I've tried to change the way I feel, but I can't. And you deserve better."

"Is there someone else?" he demanded bluntly.

She didn't avert her gaze. "I don't know. There might be. But, either way, that's not the issue."

Greg interlaced his fingers, rested his chin on them. "I didn't realize you were seeing anyone else."

"I wasn't. I'm not sure I am." She waved away her explanation in frustration. "I sound like a babbling idiot. The fact is, I went out to dinner with someone last night. The whole thing was very spontaneous. It was just a date."

"It must have been some date if it made you realize you and I are wrong for each other."

Julia felt hot color flood her face, color that broadcasted its confirmation of Greg's statement. She wished the floor could swallow her up. Why didn't she just hang up a sign announcing what had happened between her and Connor last night?

"Wow." Obviously, Greg didn't miss her reaction. His features tightened, but he kept a firm hold on his composure. "Tell me, where did you meet this guy? At your Friday night workshop?"

This was going to be the most awkward part of all.

"No, actually through Brian Stratford."

Greg blinked. "The mayor's son?"

"Yes. The guy I went out with is his uncle."

Slowly, Greg sank back in his chair. "You're seeing Connor Stratford?"

"I *saw* him," she corrected. "Once. I mean, we've met before, a bunch of times, but nothing ever came of it."

"Until now." Greg pursed his lips thoughtfully. "And now he asked you out. For dinner, you said. It's quite a hefty drive from Manhattan just to spend a few short hours in a restaurant."

Julia got Greg's meaning, loud and clear. Normally, she'd be offended at his implication and his audacity at prying into what was none of his business. But under the circumstances, he deserved an explanation. "It *was* just for dinner. As for driving up from the city, he didn't. He's staying with the mayor and his family."

"Really? Since when?"

"Since Friday. Mayor Stratford is swamped these days. I don't need to tell you that. And now he has the additional headache of whatever fallout arises from Councilman Kirson's auto theft. Brian's feeling a little low; he's used to spending lots of time with his dad. So Connor's filling in, devoting his time and attention to Brian."

"And to you, apparently."

She flushed again. "I told you, I don't know if that's going anywhere. Regardless, I apologize. I should have been honest with you—with both of us. I should have resolved things definitively a week ago. But I kept thinking something might develop . . ."

"You don't need to explain." Greg surprised her by reaching out, wrapping her fingers in his. "Julia, it's no secret that I have feelings for you. I'd be lying if I said otherwise. But I can't fault you for not sharing them. What I can do is hope you change your mind. I know you're saying otherwise, but fate works in strange ways. You've stated your case. I've accepted it. You're also still uncommitted to any new relationship. So, is there any reason we can't continue seeing each other—not romantically but as friends? No expectations, I promise."

Now, *that* reaction came out of left field, Julia thought, nearly gaping in surprise. She'd braced herself for a number of reactions—all unpleasant—but she'd never imagined that Greg would be so magnanimous. It just didn't fit. He was an ambitious man, one who was unwilling to settle for anything short of winning. What she'd expected was his anger at a perceived rejection. She figured he'd shoot her down, toss some bills on the table, and cut their brunch short. Yet here he was, taking the news right in his stride, actually suggesting they continue on as friends.

She didn't know what had prompted his amenable response, but she wasn't about to look a gift horse in the mouth.

Feeling as if a huge weight had been lifted from her shoulders, she gave Greg's hand a quick squeeze. "I'd like that. Thanks for being so understanding."

"My pleasure." He brushed her fingers lightly before releasing them. "That's what friends are for."

1:45 P.M.

Understanding? Friends? Yeah, right.

Greg watched Julia pull out of the parking lot, flashing her an automatic smile and waving his good-byes. His smile vanished as soon as she turned onto the main road and disappeared from view.

Taut with annoyance, he climbed into his own car and slammed the door. He sat quietly for a long time, calming himself down, then evaluating what had just occurred and its ramifications.

His decision had been spontaneous. But it had been the right one, the only one.

Okay, so he'd eaten his pride. He didn't do it often, but there were times when it was necessary. This was one of those times. He had to keep a relationship with Julia going—on whatever terms he could. Oh, he didn't plan on giving her up. Not by a long shot. And in the end, he wouldn't have to. Connor Stratford would go back to New York and his thriving business, and Julia would find herself seeking a constant, someone she could count on. Well, he was that constant. And if he had to prove it by playing the role of her friend, he'd do it.

In the meantime, he had to stay plugged in. Today's turn of events might make that job even easier. Much as he hated the idea of Julia with another man, if that man was Connor Stratford, it could mean getting more information than ever.

Speaking of which . . .

Greg pulled out his cell phone and punched up a number.

"Yes?" Philip Walker answered.

"It's me."

"Good. Where do things stand? And be careful what you say. I don't like cell phones. They bring out my sense of paranoia. Too many cross-connections."

"Okay. You know yesterday's golf game was rained out. But I touched base with all six players. So did the mayor, incidentally. He worked on them for a good part of yesterday. It didn't help. They're still divided."

"How divided?"

"The mayor's one vote short. Most of the players are sticking with their belief that security should be separate from parking fees and that the taxpayers shouldn't bear the brunt of a few thefts. I'm sure he plans to keep working on them, especially after Friday night." A pause. "Which I assume was your doing? It had your trademark stamped all over it."

Walker's response was chilly. "I'm not sure what you mean."

"Yeah, right. Anyway, it was a smart move. I'm sure it scared the right people shitless." Realizing that Walker didn't intend to reply, he continued. "Let's get to Julia. I just left her. It seems that the mayor's brother is in town for a long stint. He's staying with the mayor and his family."

"Really? Now, that's interesting." There was a pause as Walker digested what he'd just been told. "My guess is he's here to bail his brother out—if he hasn't already. That will take care of the mayor's immediate problem. But not the long-term one." Walker's wheels were turning. "Let's see where he goes from here. I'll be in touch."

A definitive click.

7:45 P.M.

Julia was curled up in her living-room chair, reading Jimmy Thomas's "What I Wish For" essay. Typically, his wish was for a longer recess and less homework. Not a surprise, Julia noted with a twinkle of amusement. As bright as Jimmy was, he had the attention span of an active puppy.

She corrected one or two grammar mistakes, wrote "Good job" at the top of the page, and set his essay aside.

The pile of essays was now down to two. Julia massaged her temples. She was mentally shot, much too tired to be doing this now. She should have gotten to these earlier, but her weekend had been one colossal soap opera.

She turned to the next essay. Brian's. A grin tugged at her lips. No doubt, she was about to read two paragraphs on his aspiration to pitch for the Yanks in the next World Series.

An instant later, her grin vanished.

Brian's essay began:

I wish I could live with Uncle Connor. Just for a while. He's busy, too. But that doesn't make him so mad. We could play baseball in a big park. And it would be just him and me. I wouldn't be in the way. And he wouldn't yell or cry. Then I could go home later.

The next paragraph was about how Connor had been coming over a lot lately to keep him company, but it would easier if he kept him company in "Manhatin" until his mom and dad said to come home.

Julia's heart dropped to her feet.

She slapped down the sheet of paper and grabbed her purse, rummaging around for the telephone number Connor had given her. It was Sunday night. He was probably hanging out with his family—including Brian. That would make this conversation hard to orchestrate. Well, that was tough. Connor had insisted on being kept in the loop if a red flag went up. And this red flag couldn't wait.

She found his number and snatched up her phone.

Connor answered on the second ring. "Connor Stratford."

"It's Julia," she said tersely.

"Hi." His tone was measured, as if he wasn't at liberty to talk.

The blare of a TV set in the background, along with the familiar sound of Brian's voice, explained why.

"Don't tell Brian it's me," Julia said quickly. "I need to talk to you alone. Can you excuse yourself?"

"Hang on." He cleared his throat. "Hey, ace," he called out over the TV show Brian was watching. "I've gotta take this call in my room. I'll be back in a few minutes."

"Okay" was Brian's magnanimous reply.

"I'll be right with you," Connor said in a low tone. Muffled movements, followed by the quiet click of a door. "Okay, we're alone. What's wrong?"

Julia didn't mince words. "I know the timing's lousy, but this is important. I gave my students an essay to write called 'What I Wish For.' I just read Brian's. Usually, he writes about baseball. This time, he wrote about how he wants to live with you because then he wouldn't be in the way. He wrote that you don't get mad or yell or cry. Connor, he's upset and confused. Whatever's going on is affecting him badly."

Connor swore under his breath.

"I can't just sit here and do nothing," Julia informed him. "I've got to . . ."

"No, you don't." The Stratford in Connor kicked in. "Julia, remember that Brian wrote that essay before I moved in. I'm here now, for as long as he needs me. His state of mind will improve."

"Maybe. Maybe not. He's still living in a tense environment, an environment he counts on for security."

"I'll make sure he gets that security."

Carefully, Julia considered the situation and weighed

her options. "You've got a point. But so do I. So here's the way I'll handle things. Tomorrow, when I give Brian back his essay, I'll talk to him. That's nothing unusual; I always chat with the kids about their work. In this case, I'll take the opportunity to assess his state of mind. I hope I'll see an improvement. If not, you'll hear from me again. And Connor, I won't be intimidated. If I think it's necessary to bypass you and call your sister-in-law, I will."

A prolonged silence.

"Did you hear me?"

"I heard you," he replied. "But I don't think it'll be necessary."

"I hope not." She blew out her breath. "Anyway, I'll let you get back to Brian now. I said I'd call you about anything concerning him, and I did."

"I appreciate that." A brief pause. "How was brunch?"

Julia blinked at the sudden shift in gears. "Fattening."

"You know what I mean."

"It was very pleasant."

"Very pleasant," Connor repeated. "Not the way you'd describe last night's dinner, now, is it?"

"I'm not answering that."

"You don't have to. I was there. Did you tell him?"

Why did he manage to throw her off balance so easily? "Connor, I didn't call you to discuss Greg. I called to discuss Brian."

"And we discussed Brian. He's as much my priority as he is yours. In fact, I think we should discuss him again tomorrow, after you two talk. Meet me at Starbucks, around eight o'clock."

"For whose benefit, Brian's or yours?"

"Both," he returned flatly. "I want to make sure my

nephew is okay. And I want to see you. I'm not playing games, if that's what you're implying. Nor am I using Brian's emotional state as bait. I told you we'd be getting together this week. In fact, I was going to call you after Brian went to sleep tonight. You just beat me to it."

"Starbucks," she murmured. "Do I get a scone or just a measly cup of coffee?"

"Whatever you want. I wish I could buy you dinner, but Stephen and Nancy are both working late, and I promised to split a pizza with Brian. So I'll have to settle for coffee. I'll meet you right outside Starbucks." Connor's voice dropped to a husky pitch. "I'd offer to pick you up at your apartment, but then you might feel compelled to invite me in. And I promised to give you till Saturday for that."

"Good night, Connor," she interjected hastily.

He chuckled. "Starbucks at eight?"

"Starbucks at eight," she agreed.

"In that case, good night, Julia."

14

April 9
10:15 A.M.

Stephen pressed the intercom on his phone. "Celeste, hold all my calls during this meeting."

"Yes, sir."

He leaned forward in his chair, folding his hands and facing the three men who sat across from him. He had to play this very carefully, to avoid arousing suspicions.

And he had to pull this off.

"I appreciate all of you being here on such short notice," he began.

Martin Hart, Leaf Brook's chief of police, took a gulp of coffee and set the cup down on the edge of the desk. "Not a problem. It sounded important."

Stephen nodded. "It might be, depending on how the city reacts and how the council votes. I want to get a jump start, just in case public anxiety influences what we do."

Greg Matthews frowned. "What exactly are we talking about?"

"The question of who gets the municipal parking contract." Stephen kept his tone even. "Last week, the council was leaning away from a private company handling things. But after Friday night and Albert's car being stolen, I'm not sure how they'll feel. Or how public opinion will sway them, to be frank. There's been a real increase in auto thefts. And to have a city councilman as one of the victims makes people feel nervous and vulnerable."

Hart shifted uncomfortably. "We've doubled the number of patrol cars that cruise the municipal lots. But we don't have the resources to . . ."

Stephen waved away his explanation. "You're doing a great job, Marty. This isn't about you."

"It's about Philip Walker," Cliff assessed, speaking up for the first time.

"Right. He's offered us security as part of his contract proposal. With what's going on, there's every possibility that the council will vote to accept his bid." Stephen took a healthy swallow of coffee. "I think we should start the due diligence process, do a thorough background check on Walker Development. Cliff, do a full legal search. Greg, conduct a financial rundown. And Marty, run a criminal check. It's all routine, but it'll save us a helluva lot of time and avoid a major roadblock if the council suddenly jumps on Walker's bid."

"It makes sense," the police chief agreed. "Enough of these auto thefts, and the whole damn city will panic. It'll be much easier for us if we have a ready-made solution, one that won't cost the taxpayers thousands more."

"Exactly." Stephen took another gulp of coffee, grateful that he'd asked Celeste for decaf. He was having enough trouble keeping his hands from shaking. "I need you to do this ASAP. Judging from the calls I got over the weekend, this is about to become a front-burner issue."

"You got it." Hart was already coming to his feet. "Anything else?"

"No, that's it." Stephen rose, too. "Just keep me posted."

Hart went directly back to police headquarters.

Cliff headed off to the legal records department.

Greg went straight into his office.

Five minutes later, Philip Walker got a phone call. He hung up, livid. So Stratford wanted to play dirty. Well, he had no idea what dirty meant.

But he was about to find out.

10:50 A.M.

Julia wasn't happy.

Her classroom was quiet. It was also empty, except for her and Brian. The rest of the kids had gone on to art. Julia had timed things that way, asking Brian to stay behind for a few minutes so they could go over his essay. This way, there'd be no distractions, and she'd be able to devote all her energies to assessing his reactions and figuring out where his head was.

Well, she'd been doing just that. She'd watched him the entire time they spoke, listened to what he was saying *and* what he wasn't saying. He was quieter than usual, less animated. And, in contrast to his usual attentiveness, he was restless, shifting in his seat and swinging his legs around as if he couldn't sit still. Julia tried all the usual things to put him at ease, from complimenting his writing to asking about his Little League team's chances this year. He gave her terse answers, his gaze darting around the room, a gaze that was heavy-lidded with fatigue.

"Brian," she said at last, placing a gentle hand on his shoulder. "Your essay is really good. I'm especially impressed that you wrote about your family rather than the Yankees."

A nod.

"In a way, your wish came true. I mean, I realize you're not staying with your Uncle Connor, but you don't need to. He's staying with you."

"I know."

"It must be neat having him at your house."

"It is." A pause. "But it would've been neater staying at his apartment."

"Why? Because it's in a really tall building?"

"Nah. It's tall, but not as tall as the Empire State Building. Uncle Connor took me there once. It was cool. His apartment's cool, too. But that's not why I want to stay there. I want to stay there because Uncle Connor isn't sad or cranky, and he wouldn't mind . . ." Brian broke off, averting his gaze.

"Wouldn't mind what, Brian?"

No answer.

Julia chose her words carefully. "Sweetie, everyone gets sad and cranky sometimes. It usually means they're tired or have too much work to do. It's not about anyone else."

"I guess. But what if it is?"

The worry in Brian's voice made her heart ache. "You don't really feel like you're in the way at home, do you?"

A shrug. "I guess not. I just wish things could be like they used to be. Even with Uncle Connor there . . . it's different."

"Different how?"

"I don't know—weird, I guess. Uncle Connor tries to make me think about other stuff, so I won't see Mom cry. She does that a lot. Especially the night before Uncle

Connor came. She thought I was asleep. But I wasn't. She cried until really late. Then Dad came home. He didn't sound like him. His voice was weird. And he was mad. He yelled at Mom."

Julia ruffled Brian's hair, feeling a tight knot form in her gut. "Were you scared?"

"Kind of, yeah. I didn't tell them I was up." His head jerked around, and he gave Julia an anxious look. "You're not going to tell them, are you? I don't want to make things worse. They'd feel bad."

"No, sweetie, I won't tell them. Not if you don't want me to." Julia's mind was already racing, as she formulated the way she'd phrase things when she called Nancy Stratford. She wouldn't break Brian's confidence. But she wouldn't close her eyes to this situation. Not anymore. No matter what Connor said, this problem wasn't going away. And it was time Brian's parents knew it.

It was lunchtime when Julia got her first opportunity to break away. The lunch aide had taken over her class and was supervising the noontime meal and playground time.

Julia went into a private office in the school and called Nancy Stratford at home. Voice mail. She hung up and tried Mrs. Stratford's boutique. Voice mail again. This time, Julia left a message. It was better to do that at the boutique than at home. Brian would be less likely to hear the message.

Just the same, she kept it vague. All she said was that she had a quick but important matter to discuss, one that warranted an immediate response.

She hung up, knowing she had one other commitment to fulfill.

She punched up Connor's cell-phone number.

When he answered, she said simply, "Things are worse than you thought. I left a message for your sister-in-law. I'm talking to her as soon as possible. No arguments, Connor," she added quickly as he started to speak. "Under the circumstances, I think we should cancel tonight. I want to be available in case your sister-in-law calls. Besides, I don't want to argue with you. You won't change my mind. If you still want to see me after I see this problem through, let me know."

Without giving him a chance to reply, she hung up.

Outside on the playground, Brian went straight to the fence and tossed his jacket and baseball cap in the usual spot, the one that had been assigned to his class. The rules were that any personal items not being worn or used during recess were supposed to be left in those assigned areas. His jacket and baseball cap went there every day. He never wore either one when he played. If he did, he got too sweaty.

He shuffled over to the other side of the playground. Sitting down by himself, he picked up a stick and started drawing in the dirt with it. He had a bad feeling in his stomach, even though he hadn't eaten his turkey sandwich or his Yodel. Maybe he shouldn't have told those things to Miss Talbot. Maybe he should have kept them to himself. But if anyone would know how to make things better, it was her. Her and Uncle Connor.

He sat like that for the whole twenty-minute recess period. He didn't feel much like playing.

Finally, Mrs. Parkins, the lunch aide, signaled the class that lunchtime recess was over.

Brian got up and went over to the fence to get his stuff.

It took him a minute to realize that his baseball cap was missing. He searched everywhere. He even fumbled around in his friends' stuff. But the cap was gone.

He swallowed hard, fighting back tears and feeling worse than ever. That was his Little League cap, the one he wore every time he was on the mound. It brought him good luck. He could get a new one, but it wouldn't be the same.

A car horn sounded from the parking lot.

He looked up in time to see a black car drive slowly by. The driver rolled down his window. Most of his face was hidden by a cap, one that was pulled way forward and was too small to cover his whole head.

It was Brian's baseball cap.

Beneath the rim, the man's lips curled in an ugly smile. He tipped the cap in Brian's direction.

Then he drove off.

7:35 P.M.

Stephen Stratford left the municipal building even later than usual that night. He'd hoped to get a report from Marty or Cliff cluing him in on some illegal deal Walker Development was involved in. Anything that would give him ammunition to use against Philip Walker. A man as dirty as that had to have some skeleton in the closet that could be uncovered in record time.

Connor had left him two messages, neither of which he'd returned. Partly because he was too busy, partly because he had a pretty good idea what the messages were about—and he wasn't ready to deal with it. Connor probably knew when their father was planning to show up in Leaf Brook. Well, he didn't want to hear about it. All he could do was pray that it wasn't going to happen for a few days. He needed that time. He had to get things under control before his father descended on him like a ton of bricks.

Feeling unbearably weary, Stephen trudged through the parking lot, his heels echoing on the concrete. The lot was deserted, since everyone had gone home hours ago.

He reached his car and was just inserting the key in the lock when he heard the screech of a car rounding the corner of the lot. It sounded as if it was roaring right at him.

He jerked around, just as the black coupe slammed to a stop beside him.

Two men jumped out.

He caught a brief glimpse of them as they lunged forward, one hefty, the other tall and muscular. The tall one's fist connected with his jaw, sending him reeling backward, crashing into his car.

"A gift, Stratford," the hefty guy grated out, slamming his fist into Stephen's gut. "From Walker Development."

Ten minutes later, they walked away, leaving Stephen crumpled and bleeding on the concrete floor.

"Due diligence is over," the hefty guy muttered. "And you will be, too, if you pull something stupid like that again." He jumped back into the car.

"So long," his counterpart added. "Mr. Walker will be in touch. Oh, and Stratford . . ." He strode back long enough to drop a ten-dollar bill beside Stephen's head. "That'll cover what I owe your kid. Next time, what I take will be worth a whole lot more."

8:30 P.M.

Nancy's insides were twisted into knots.

She shifted restlessly on the family-room sofa, easing the blinds aside and checking, for the dozenth time, to see if Stephen's headlights were visible on the winding driveway.

Nothing.

Where the hell was he?

She twisted back around, watching as Connor and Brian finished Brian's arithmetic homework on the floor. Connor glanced up and met her gaze, attempting a reassuring look.

She didn't buy his façade for a minute. Connor was as worried as she was. She could see it on his face. Just as she'd heard it in his voice when he called her at the boutique this afternoon and demanded, "Nancy, have you checked your answering machine?"

"No," she'd replied, slipping off her coat. "I just got back from lunch. Why?"

"Because you have a message from Julia Talbot. She didn't leave it at the house, so it must be at the boutique."

Her heart had dropped to the floor. "Julia Talbot? Oh, God, is Brian . . . ?"

"He's fine. It's nothing like that. Nancy, listen to me. Julia's worried about Brian's emotional state. Don't return the call. Not yet. Not until after we've talked to Stephen."

She got it then. She more than got it.

"Have you reached Stephen?" she'd asked woodenly.

"I've tried. He's in meetings."

"I should come home."

"No. Brian's expecting me to pick him up and you to

work late. Do that. I'll have him call you when we get in, so you can hear for yourself that he's okay. Nance, let's not make things worse by upsetting him. Stephen won't be home until seven-thirty or eight. There's nothing we can do until then. Brian and I will have our pizza, as planned. Come home at seven, like you said you would. We'll save you a slice. When Stephen comes home, we'll get Brian off to bed. We'll keep things as normal as possible. Then we'll talk this through. And, Nancy . . ." He paused. "We'll work everything out."

"I hope so, Connor. Because this isn't *my* life we're talking about anymore. It's my son's."

With a quiet click, she'd dropped the telephone receiver back into its cradle.

The boutique was busy, but she'd played Julia Talbot's message through three times anyway. God, she'd been so tempted to call the woman back. But she owed it to Stephen to wait. She didn't know how much Julia Talbot suspected. And she had to know what she was up against before speaking out.

Brian had called the boutique at a quarter to four, just as Connor promised. He'd sounded fine, other than being upset about losing his baseball cap.

Fine. That was an interesting choice of words. By other people's standards, Brian did sound fine. But she knew better. So, apparently, did Julia Talbot. Compared with his usual exuberant self, Brian was hardly fine these days.

Then again, how could he be?

She squeezed her eyes shut, feeling a surge of guilt as painful as any physical injury. Maybe she should have done something sooner. But what? Leave Stephen? That would have broken Brian's heart and destroyed Stephen.

She couldn't do that. So she'd turned to Connor, who'd dropped everything to be there. And Brian did seem better with his uncle around.

Obviously, not better enough.

Over the course of the afternoon, she'd tried Stephen's office twice. But, just as Connor said, he'd been tied up in meetings. She hadn't left a message. This wasn't something she could just blurt out. They had to talk—tonight. As for her rushing home, Connor was right. That would have been a mistake. It would only have made Brian's qualms worse and ruined the "guys' night" he had planned with his uncle. Besides, there was nothing to be done until Stephen got home and she could lay out all the facts, determine what was at stake and how it should be handled.

She'd almost called Cliff.

But she leaned on him too much these days as it was. He had a life of his own, and that didn't include fixing hers.

She'd walked in the door at five of seven, hurrying straight to the kitchen to assure herself that Brian was all right.

He'd been sitting at the table, stuffing his face with pizza, and he'd given her a mozzarella grin as he finished his last bite. "Hi, Mom."

"Hi, yourself." She'd glanced at the pizza box and shuddered. "What did you guys get on that thing?"

"The works," Connor had informed her cheerfully. "Meatballs, sausage, green peppers, mushrooms, onions . . ."

"Enough." Nancy had held up her palm, bending over to kiss the top of Brian's head. At times like this, she wished he was still little enough for her to hug as tightly as she wanted to without his getting all embarrassed. "How was your day?"

"I lost my baseball cap." His entire face had fallen. "I looked everywhere for it, but it was gone. I think some guy took it."

"Why do you think that?" Nancy had asked in surprise.

Brian had shrugged. "I saw a man drive away wearing a red cap. It looked kinda like my baseball cap. But I guess that's pretty dumb. Why would a man want my cap? How am I gonna pitch without it?"

"Honey, I doubt you'll have to. It'll probably turn up in a day or two in the school's lost and found. But, if not, we'll get you a new one."

"Yeah, ace," Connor had agreed. "That cap was getting kind of shabby. Too much wear and tear. A new one would be a good idea. Then, if you find the old one, you can change off."

"I guess." Brian hadn't sounded convinced. But he'd brightened up when Nancy reminded him that his dad would be home soon. He'd shot off to get his bookbag so he could finish his homework.

For a three-minute span, Nancy and Connor had been alone.

"Was Julia's message at the boutique?" he'd demanded.

"Yes. I did as you asked. Did you get hold of Stephen?"

"Nope. He never called me back."

"How has Brian been acting?"

"Not great." Connor hadn't lied. "He's been pretty down. I'm not sure how much of that's based on what we're worrying about and how much on the fact that he lost his baseball cap."

"Dammit." Nancy had run both hands through her hair, feeling as if the world was closing in on her.

"Hang in, Nance. Stephen will be home soon."

She'd raised her head and met Connor's gaze with growing trepidation. "And then what?"

She was still asking herself that, only now it was an hour and a half later, and there was still no sign of Stephen.

"Where's Dad?" Brian asked, looking up from his math problems. "It's late."

Nancy opened her mouth to reassure him, for the third time, that they'd be hearing from Stephen any minute.

Connor's cell phone rang.

He looked up, meeting Nancy's uneasy stare. "Business," he predicted, tugging the phone out of his pocket. "Remember that it's morning in places like Australia."

She nodded.

"Connor Stratford." A long pause. "Yeah. Everyone's fine. I'm positive. Right here. Okay. Where?" Another pause. "I'm on my way."

He punched the end button and unfolded to a standing position. "That was your dad," he told Brian. "He's having car trouble, which explains why he isn't here. I'm going to run over and help him out."

Brian scrambled to his feet. "How come he called on your cell phone?"

An offhanded shrug. "He had trouble getting through on your home line, so he called me."

"That's a lot of trouble, Connor," Nancy noted quietly. "Car trouble. Phone trouble."

Connor looked at her and gave an almost imperceptible shake of his head. "That's the digital age," was all he said aloud. "Filled with glitches." He turned to Brian. "Listen, ace, let Mom help you with that last problem. Then get ready for bed. That way, you'll be able to spend more time with Dad when he gets home. Okay?"

"Yeah, okay," Brian agreed.

"I'm on my way, then."

Nancy followed Connor into the hall. "What is it? What's happened?"

"I don't know," Connor replied in a tense, worried, tone. "Whatever it is, it's not good." He grabbed his jacket, keeping his voice low. "Nancy, get Brian into bed. Stephen doesn't want his son to see him—not right away. I'll drive him here. We'll leave his car in the lot."

Nancy watched as Connor dashed out the door. She wrapped her arms around herself as if to ward off the all too obvious truth. *Stephen doesn't want Brian to see him in his current state*, she thought numbly. *Just like the other night. He's drunk. That's his 'car trouble.'*

Feeling half-dead inside, she turned and walked back to the family room.

She had to be there for her son.

15

Connor's Mercedes tore into the parking lot and came to a hard stop beside Stephen's Explorer. The drive had been emotional hell. His mind was racing, trying to figure out why Stephen had demanded that he come alone and that he explain it away as car trouble to Nancy and Brian. He was protecting them, but from what? He wasn't drunk. That would be the logical conclusion, the one Nancy had undoubtedly drawn. But Connor had heard the pained sound of his brother's voice. Stephen was hurt, physically hurt. His speech had been forced, as if every word was costing him. And he was scared. He'd insisted on knowing if Brian was okay—he'd asked Connor that twice—before pressing Connor to drive down to the municipal building and get him before a patrol car cruised by and spotted him.

Whatever the hell was going on had come to a head.

Connor sprang out of his car and over to Stephen's, peering through the passenger window. Stephen was sprawled in the driver's seat, which had been pushed back into a reclining position. His head, propped against the headrest, was turned away from Connor, hiding his face from view.

Connor rapped on the window. "Stephen, it's me."

His brother swiveled his head stiffly in Connor's direction. Even through the tinted glass, Connor could see that Stephen's face was puffy and caked with blood.

Bile rushed to his throat. "Open the door," he commanded.

Stephen nodded, fumbling beside him until he found the button that opened the power door locks.

Connor leaped in on the passenger side, assessing his brother's physical state as he did. "Shit." His gaze shifted from Stephen's face to his rumpled clothing and stiff posture. "I've got to get you to a doctor."

"No." Stephen shook his head, wincing as he did. "It looks worse than it is. Nothing's broken. Just a few bruised ribs and a messed-up face." He drew a slow, painful breath. "But Brian would freak if he saw me like this. I can't go home, not till we get me cleaned up." A frightened, searching look. "You're sure Brian's okay? You were with him when I called?"

"We were sitting on the family-room floor doing math. He's fine." Connor bit back his myriad questions. First things first. They had to get Stephen fixed up and out of there.

He spotted a half-empty bottle of water perched in the cup holder between them and a pile of bloodstained tissues lying on the floor. Clearly, Stephen had already begun the cleanup process.

"I've got more water in my car," Connor said tersely. "I'll get it."

"Good." Stephen jerked his thumb toward the rear of the Explorer. "There's a roll of paper towels back there and a first aid kit. Nancy keeps it there for Brian. I tried to get at it, but it's buried under a ton of stuff. And it hurts so damned much when I try to lift things . . ."

"Then don't. Don't even move. Just sit still." Connor sprang out of the car, dashed around back, and got what they needed.

"Hurry," Stephen urged as he returned. "A patrol car's bound to make its rounds soon, especially with the escalation in auto thefts. I can't let them see me."

"Yeah, right." Connor fell silent, concentrating on mopping the blood off Stephen's face. He treated the deeper cuts, then helped him straighten his clothes, trying to keep them from pressing against his bruised ribs.

When the job was finished, Stephen still looked somewhat swollen and pained, but he was a lot closer to presentable. "Good enough for now," Connor declared. "The rest we'll take care of at home." He peered around, relieved that there were no patrol cars in the area. "You can't drive, that's for sure. We'll leave your car here. You supposedly had car trouble, so the story we'll use—not only for Brian but for the public in general—is that you hurt yourself climbing around under the car. I'll drive you home and get you back here tomorrow."

He shoved open the door, then came around and helped Stephen out. Draping Stephen's arm around his shoulders, he slowly guided his brother to the passenger side of the Mercedes and eased him in. He tossed the bloody tissues and paper towels into the trash and was just about to scribble a note to leave on the dashboard of the Explorer when a patrol car rounded the bend and rolled up to them.

"Is there a problem?" the officer at the wheel asked, glancing over at the mayor's car, then at Connor. There was no suspicion in his eyes, only curiosity and a firm resolve to display top-notch performance. He recognized the mayor's vehicle, and the resemblance between the

Stratford brothers was too strong for him not to realize who Connor was.

"Actually, yes," Connor answered smoothly. "I was just about to put a note on the windshield explaining. The mayor's car was giving him some trouble, and he banged himself up pretty badly trying to fix it. I came over to give him a lift home." A questioning look. "I'm not thrilled about leaving the car here overnight, especially since my brother fixed the loose wires, making the car fully operational for wannabe thieves. But I don't want him driving; he's in a fair amount of pain. Would you guys mind keeping an eye on the car overnight? I'd really appreciate it."

"Yeah, sure, no problem." The other cop, a middle-aged guy with a worried expression, climbed out and crossed halfway over to the Mercedes. "You okay, sir?" he called out to Stephen.

Thank God for tinted glass, Connor thought. Without it, there'd be no way to mask Stephen's half-closed eye and swollen lip and no way, even at this distance, that they'd be able to convince trained police officers that the wounds they were seeing were the result of Stephen's tinkering under a car.

No one knew that better than Stephen. And pained or not, he managed to summon up the consummate politician that was so much a part of him. Forcing a wave, he gave the officer one of those charming, charismatic smiles that were his trademark. "I feel like I've been in a brawl," he called back. "When the car companies say SUVs have punch, they mean it. I won't be crawling under one of those again any time soon."

The officer chuckled. "I know what you mean. Anyway, you and your brother go on home. We'll send for an extra patrol car. Between us, we'll keep an overnight watch on your vehicle."

"Thanks. Thanks a lot." Stephen held the smile until Connor had offered his good-byes, climbed in, flipped on the ignition, and zoomed off.

Then he sagged back against the seat. "Damn, it hurts."

"No kidding." Connor handed Stephen the remaining contents of the bottled water. "Drink the rest of this. Then tell me what the hell's going on. Who did this to you, and why?"

"I'm assuming you heard from Dad. When's he coming?" Stephen asked instead.

Connor slanted him a look. "Not till Thursday. More than enough time for the swelling to go down. You'll be able to pull off the car-fixing story."

"Good." In agonizing relief, Stephen's eyes slid shut. He put the bottle to his lips and gulped.

"Forget Dad. He's not the issue—other than keeping him in the dark. You're not ducking this one, Stephen," Connor warned, turning the car onto Main Street and heading toward home. "Not from me or your wife. Nancy knows something major is wrong. And not just because of your bizarre behavior. Julia called her today. She's worried about Brian. *Really* worried. There've been new developments. Forget my chances of sidetracking her. They're not going to cut it anymore. This problem isn't going away. You can't stick your head in the sand."

Stephen had tensed beside him. "What new developments? What happened to make Julia more worried about Brian? Did someone do something to him?"

"No." Connor offered the requisite taut reassurance. "She just talked to him about an essay he wrote. Clearly, he's a mess about his home life." His jaw clenched, the sinking feeling in the pit of his stomach intensifying. "Who do you think might have done something to Brian? The same son of a bitch who did this to you?"

"Yeah. Not 'done something' in the sense of hurting him, but maybe paying him a visit. I'm probably being paranoid. It's just that the way they talked about him, it was like they'd seen him, like they'd taken something that belonged to him. It scared the hell out of me."

"His baseball cap." Connor's knuckles whitened on the steering wheel. "That's why Brian said what he did."

"His baseball cap? What about it?"

"It's missing. Brian put it by the fence with his coat during recess, and when he went back, it was gone. He said something about seeing a guy drive by wearing it. We all dismissed it as a coincidence, a red cap that just looked like his. Obviously, we were wrong. Whoever that guy was, he was leaving you a message."

All the color drained from Stephen's face. "Christ."

"I'm going to ask you one more time," Connor bit out. "And you'd better answer me before I lose it. What's going on? Who's after you? Some high-powered goon you owe money to? Is that what this is all about? More gambling? Even after you swore to me that you wouldn't . . ."

"No." Stephen gripped his head with both hands, wincing at the resulting throb. "I haven't bet a dime since you gave me the five hundred thousand. This isn't about money. Not anymore. I wish to God it were."

"Go on."

A weighted pause. "Connor, I don't think you should get involved in this. It would make you an accessory. That's the last thing I want. And I can't go to the police with this. It would be the end of everything—and I don't just mean me. I mean our entire family, everything we've built."

"You mean everything Dad's built."

"Not just Dad. You, Nancy, and Brian—my son's life would never be the same. I can't let that happen."

"I'm already an accessory, Stephen. I became one the minute I bailed you out by giving you that five hundred thousand dollars, knowing full well you'd borrowed campaign funds for personal use. That's a criminal act. So, unless you've embezzled money outright or murdered someone and want me to hide the body, I won't be getting in any deeper than I already am."

Stephen released a weary breath. "Fine. What I told you about the money I owed, that was only part of the story. The rest of it is about the man I owed most of it to."

"Who is?"

"Philip Walker."

"Philip Walker." Connor's brows drew together in thought. "That name sounds familiar."

"He's a pretty big commercial real estate developer. He's also a lot dirtier and more cold-blooded than I realized." Quietly, Stephen filled Connor in on the details of what had taken place from the time Walker gave him the hundred-thousand-dollar campaign donation to his current attempt to blackmail Stephen into getting him the municipal parking contract. "I have no idea how he found out about my gambling," he concluded. "But he's got enough details to ruin our family and put me in prison."

"And you didn't bother mentioning this to me? Not even the night he first put the squeeze on you, when I came to Leaf Brook to find you stinking drunk and passed out?"

"I'm responsible for this nightmare; I wanted to be the one to end it. I really thought I could do that alone. But I never realized the lengths Walker would go to to get what he wanted."

Connor frowned, trying to assimilate everything he'd just been told. Something was nagging at him. He just couldn't figure out what. "Is Walker behind all the car thefts, or just Kirson's?"

"Good question. I don't know."

"It's worth finding out. Especially in the cases where the stolen cars were parked in independently owned lots—lots with corporate owners who could be scared into turning over their contracts to Walker, since he offers security as well as management. If that's the case, he's an even shrewder bastard than we realize. He's offering quite an incentive for companies to switch over."

"Yeah, I know." Stephen paused to regather his strength. "Connor, there's something else bothering me. Obviously, the guys who beat the crap out of me are Walker's response to my checking out his company. He could have found out I was doing that in any number of ways, I guess. But how did he find out so fast? I just got the process going this morning when I met with Cliff, Greg, and Marty."

"You're sure that's what prompted the beating?"

"Uh-huh. When my attackers walked away, they made sure to say, 'Due diligence is over.' Which means they're clued in to how I'd planned to play this. And *that* means Walker's network is widespread."

"It certainly seems that way." Connor's frown deepened. "Well, Cliff's loyalty's a given. What about Greg and Marty—do you trust them?"

A shrug and a wince. "I have no reason not to. Greg's

done a great job as city manager since I took office, and Marty's been chief of police for twenty years."

"What about their contacts? Who did they speak to after leaving your office today?"

"My guess is that Cliff went over to legal records, Greg went to his office to pull whatever files we have on Walker Development from our previous dealings with them, and Marty went back to headquarters and started a criminal background check. But I plan to ask each of them that very question first thing tomorrow. Especially Marty. He's got a lot of territory to cover, even by computer. So he probably got some help."

Connor pursed his lips. "You think someone at police headquarters could be on the take?"

"It occurred to me, yes."

"Dealing with that could be very sticky."

"That's putting it mildly. But I can't stop now. Walker wants that contract in his pocket by the end of this week. I can't give it to him. I wouldn't even if I could—not at this point. The man's more than a dirty businessman. He's a goddamn mobster who hires goons to beat and threaten people. God knows what else he's capable of. I'm not about to commit Leaf Brook to doing business with him. No way. So I need to get something on him—fast. I've got to be discreet, but I've got to do it. The problem is figuring out who I can trust."

"You're playing with fire."

"What choice do I have? I've got to get the goods on this guy if I want to protect Brian." Stephen finished off his water.

"And how do you protect him in the meantime?"

A grim look. "By making sure he's never alone. It'll be home to school, school to home, period. We'll hand him over to Julia Talbot and pick him up at the end of the day. I'll take him to practice myself and wait there while he plays. We're only talking about a couple of days."

"And Nancy? Where does she fit into all this?"

"The same way she always fits in—by being an incredible mom. If you're asking about my marriage, I don't know where things stand. My guess is, my wife's on the verge of choking me. Right now, she probably assumes I'm drunk."

"Yeah, I'm sure she does." Connor slowed the car as he turned onto Stephen's street. "Nancy's pretty strung out," he admitted. "Go easy on her."

"I get the message. Right now, it's not Nancy I'm worried about. She's a survivor. She'll weather this in the same stoic way she weathers everything. Either that, or she'll cry on Cliff's shoulder."

Connor heard the tinge of bitterness underlying his brother's tone. "Cut it out, Stephen. There's nothing between Nancy and Cliff but friendship. You know that as well as I do."

"Do I? Cliff's a great guy. He's also my best friend. And, yeah, I know him. Too well, maybe. I trust him never to overstep his bounds. Not in actions. As for feelings, that's another matter entirely. Ever wonder why he still dates incessantly with no inclination to get serious? Why no woman's ever held his attention for more than six months? And, most of all, why he's so protective of Nancy? If not, let me fill you in. It's because he's in love with her."

"Has he actually told you that?"

"Of course not. He'd never insult our friendship or undermine my marriage by saying the words out loud. But we both know they're true."

"If they are, they're one-sided."

"Maybe, maybe not. At one time, I'd agree with you. Now? Who knows? Nancy leans on Cliff more and more these days. I guess I can't blame her. I'm not in the running for Husband of the Year." Stephen fell silent, watching as Connor rounded the drive and the house loomed into view. "The truth?" he muttered finally, assessing his home and his life with the same utter resignation. "Even if what Nancy's feeling for Cliff is starting to become more than friendship, I'm too worn out to do a damn thing about it."

Connor and Stephen were scarcely in the door when a scuffle of footsteps sounded from overhead. An instant later, Brian came racing down.

"Dad!" He stopped short when he saw his father. "What happened to you?"

Stephen managed a grin. "I tried fixing the car. I'm not really good at crawling around under those things. I scraped myself to pieces, slammed my head twice, and when I crawled out, the tailpipe butted me in the eye. I guess I look pretty grim, huh?"

Nancy had come up quietly behind her son. She was staring at Stephen, a haunted look in her eyes.

"Hi," Stephen greeted her gently. "Don't look so worried. I'm fine."

"Right." She cleared her throat, turned to Brian. "Okay, our deal starts now. Ten minutes with Dad. Then it's bedtime. We'll get that ear looked at in the morning."

"His ear's bothering him?" Stephen wasn't usually this jumpy. Then again, he wasn't usually on alert for his son's safety. Given how on edge he was, even a minor earache threw him for a loop.

Nancy scrutinized him intently, then nodded. "He started complaining right after Connor left."

"Yeah," Brian confirmed. "It's kind of like there's a tunnel in my ear. I hear an echo when I talk. When you talk, too. And it stings. I'll probably need some of that bubblegum medicine."

"Probably," Nancy agreed. "I'll make an appointment with the pediatrician first thing tomorrow. We can rent a video on the way home. It'll be a rest-in-bed day."

Connor and Stephen exchanged a quick, relieved look. They didn't want Brian sick, but having him home, safe and sound, was a big plus.

Brian wasn't at all pleased. "I'll miss practice."

"Pitchers need a few days off between games to rest their arms," Connor reminded him.

"Yeah, I guess. But what about my baseball cap?" he asked. "How will I know if they find it at school?"

Connor could actually feel Stephen tense at the mention of the cap, and warning bells went off in his head. The worst thing would be if Brian picked up on his father's tension and questioned it. Walker's veiled threat about Brian's safety was something Stephen needed to talk to Nancy about alone.

Abruptly, he came up with an idea, a way to kill two birds with one stone: divert Brian and Nancy from picking up on Stephen's reaction, and get at someone he was more than eager to speak with, for several reasons.

"I tell you what, ace," he interceded. "I'll go to your school first thing tomorrow. I'll get your homework from Miss Talbot and see if your baseball cap's turned up in the lost and found."

That appeased Brian. "Okay. But you'll tell her how important it is, right?"

A corner of Connor's mouth lifted. "I won't need to. We're talking about Miss Talbot. She's as committed to your pitching as you are."

Relief flooded Brian's face. "You're right. She'll find my cap. Or you will." He squirmed a little, rubbing his right ear with the palm of his hand.

"That's it. It's Tylenol and bedtime," Nancy announced. Her voice sounded unnaturally high, and Connor studied her as she stepped into the downstairs bathroom, emerging a minute later with Tylenol and water. Her hand shook as she gave the medicine to Brian, and Connor wondered if she was on the verge of losing it.

"But Dad just got home," Brian protested, after dutifully swallowing down the pills.

"Dad looks worse than you. I'm going to give him some dinner, then send him to bed, too."

Reluctantly, Brian nodded. "Okay. G'night." He headed toward the steps, then paused, turning to face his father. "Dad, will you be here for breakfast?"

"Sure will." Wincing a little, Stephen walked stiffly over to his son, placing both hands on his shoulders and gazing down at him with a pained expression that Connor knew had little to do with his injuries. "How about waffles? They work wonders on ear infections and banged-up faces."

A glimmer of hope flickered in Brian's eyes, as if his father's gesture were a lifeline, an indication that everything just might be okay. "Waffles would be great." He eyed his father. "Our car really messed your face up. Donny Simms looked like that after he put red ants in Mitch Pratt and Krissy Halpern's sandwiches and they beat him up. Mitch only gave him a bloody lip, but

Krissy punched him till his whole face swelled up. I guess cars hurt even more." He patted Stephen's hand sympathetically. "Ice helps."

"Thanks."

"G'night, Dad."

" 'Night, Brian." Stephen leaned heavily against the banister, staring after Brian until he disappeared from view.

The phone rang.

"I'll get it," Nancy said. She headed toward the kitchen, darting a jittery glance at Stephen as she did. She looked as close to collapse as her husband. "After I get rid of whoever that is, we'll talk."

Stephen sank onto the bottom step, resting his head against the wall.

"I'll go to my room. You two need time alone," Connor assessed quietly.

"Fine." Stephen sighed. "It's good that Brian will be home with Nancy tomorrow. It'll give me time to do some digging without having to worry about repercussions."

"For a day," Connor agreed. He rubbed his palms together, gazing solemnly toward the kitchen. "Nancy's a mess."

"No kidding." With great effort, Stephen pushed himself into an upright position. "I'm not telling her about the threat to Brian. The rest, yes, but not that."

Connor's jaw dropped. "What?"

"She'll fall apart, Connor. I don't have the emotional reserves for that. Not right now. I've got to focus on protecting Brian and getting something on Walker. Once I'm in the driver's seat, then I'll tell her."

"She's Brian's mother."

"And I'm his father. I'll handle this."

"You keep saying that," Connor ground out, trying to keep his voice low so Brian wouldn't overhear. "The truth is, you're not handling a goddamn thing."

"I am. I will." That familiar defiance was back in Stephen's eyes, the defensiveness that surfaced whenever he was called on the carpet and he knew damned well he was at fault, that his gambling had, once again, screwed things up. His life was spinning out of control, and he was thrashing around trying to stabilize it. "I just need a couple of days. In the meantime, telling Nancy wouldn't do either of us any good. She can't help me. No one can. I got myself into this. I'll get myself out. I'll keep my wife and son safe. I'll protect the family name. I'll do it all. Just back off. Cut me some fucking slack."

Before Connor could respond, Nancy returned to the hallway. She looked positively ashen. "That was Julia Talbot. She's seriously worried about Brian. He's showing signs of depression. He's isolating himself and blaming himself for whatever problems are going on at home. She says it's getting worse."

Stephen rose unsteadily, defensiveness escalating into panic. "What did you tell her?"

"Tell her?" Nancy dragged a shaking hand through her hair. "I didn't tell her anything. I don't know anything. I made up something about it being a bad time to talk. I told her Brian was sick and needed me. I practically hung up on her." Hysteria crept into her voice. "Stephen, what the hell is going on? Who beat you up? What kind of trouble are you in?"

Connor saw the irrational anger erupt on his brother's face, and he inserted himself, determined to nip the oncoming battle in the bud.

"Stephen, don't," he ordered tersely, his fingers digging into his brother's arm. "Brian's still awake. According to Julia, he's already an emotional wreck. Don't make things worse. Whatever you and Nancy have to thrash out, do it quietly. Poor Brian's absorbing too much of this as it is. Please, think about your son."

It was the only appeal that would work. Connor knew it, so he wasn't surprised when some of the blind rage on Stephen's face drained away. "Yeah, you're right."

Connor turned, glancing briefly at Nancy. "Go easy," he murmured. "For everyone's sake."

She nodded, and Connor walked off, heading for his room. He'd done everything he could.

But hearing their tightly controlled, biting voices as he retreated down the hall—Stephen's providing a fabrication about a political adversary to whom he owed a huge chunk of money and who was blackmailing him, then Nancy's snapping back a shocked, bitter reply about Stephen's gambling ruining their lives—he wondered if anything he said or did would be enough.

Not just enough to save his brother's marriage. Enough to keep the walls from crashing down on the Stratfords.

16

~

April 10
8:25 A.M.

Julia was at her desk early, just as Connor expected.

He stood in the open classroom doorway for a moment, watching her grade papers. Her dark head was bent over her work, her features fixed in concentration as she read the material. A smile curved her mouth, and she caught her lower lip between her teeth as she reread whatever had amused her. Unaware that she was being watched, she fiddled with her necklace, her fingers sliding across the delicate chain, taking with them the tiny heart that dangled there.

He found himself staring, watching her fingers glide back and forth across her bare skin just above where the scoop neck of her sweater ended, over her collarbone, down to the upper swell of her breasts.

Damn, he wanted her. And not only because sidetracking her was crucial to protecting his family secrets but because the fascination he'd had for her from the start had grown into a full-blown obsession.

He was still burning from that kiss they'd shared in her apartment. Memories of it had kept him awake the past three nights. And now? Hell, he was hard just from watching her play with a necklace.

Julia must have sensed his scrutiny, because, abruptly, her head came up, and she met his gaze.

"Connor." She lowered the papers, rising slowly to her feet behind her desk. "What can I do for you?"

He walked over. "I need to see you."

"I'm working."

"Your class isn't due in for at least fifteen minutes. Besides, this is work-related. It concerns Brian."

The look she gave him was wary. "What about Brian?"

"He's sick. I came to get his homework, his class work, whatever assignments he has to make up."

Julia's palms flattened on the desk. "Is he really sick?"

"Of course. His mother told you so last night."

"I know what she told me. I'm not sure I believed her."

Connor's brows rose. "Why would she lie?"

"You tell me. She sounded strained. *Very* strained. As if she'd say anything to get me off the line."

"She was with Brian when you called," Connor answered smoothly. "His ear was stinging. He's got an appointment with the pediatrician this morning. I'm sure he'll be as good as new in no time. Ear infections are painful but easily fixed with some bubblegum medicine."

"Right." Julia didn't smile. Instead, she scrutinized Connor with keen perception and gave one pointed clap of her hands. "You're very good, do you know that? Maybe *you're* the one who should be in politics."

"What's that supposed to mean?"

"It means you're a very glib speaker. You have an amazing way of relaying information—the information you choose to, that is."

"I'm telling you the truth."

"Part of it." She cleared her throat. "In any case, you're here to get Brian's work. I'll get it for you."

She crossed over to Brian's desk, tugged out a reading workbook, a spelling list, and a looseleaf binder. She tore a blank sheet of paper out of the binder and jotted down some instructions. "Here you go." She handed the entire pile to Connor. "This should be everything Brian needs. He already has his math text at home. Tell him to do only as much as he feels up to. And tell him to get well soon."

"Thanks. I will." Connor took the stack of books but made no move to leave.

"Was there something else?" Julia prompted.

"Yes. I promised Brian I'd look for his baseball cap. He misplaced it yesterday afternoon. He's more upset about that than he is about his ear."

Julia frowned. "He didn't mention losing his baseball cap."

"It happened during afternoon recess." Connor's brows rose in tacit challenge. "Maybe that's why he seemed so out of sorts yesterday. That cap is his lucky charm."

"I know. But I doubt it." She gestured toward the door. "Let's go check the lost and found. It's probably there."

Connor caught her arm as she passed. "There's a third reason I'm here. I wanted to see you."

Julia tensed. But she didn't yank her arm away. "Why?"

"You canceled our date. Without giving me a chance to react, by the way. I want to reschedule."

"Connor . . ."

"What's happening between us has nothing to do with Brian," he stated flatly. "You know that, and so do I. Don't build walls that aren't there."

This time, she did tug out of his grasp. "Maybe you

can separate things into neat little compartments. I can't. My emotions overlap."

"Meaning?"

Julia glanced swiftly at the door to make sure they were still alone. "What's happening between us is sexual attraction. Okay, maybe it's more," she added swiftly, seeing the dubious look in his eyes. "I don't know. What I *do* know is that I don't completely trust you. And I'm not even sure that I like you."

The very frankness he'd found so implausible was now starting to turn him on. "Fine. Let's get together and talk about that." He wasn't going to give up. "Have dinner with me tonight."

At first, he thought she meant to refuse. Especially after what she'd just said. Not to mention that ambivalence was written all over her face.

"We're very different," she hedged, engaged in her own internal conflict. "Right down to our priorities."

"Maybe, maybe not. We won't know if we don't explore those priorities. Oh, and our principles. We still have to discuss those, remember?"

He could feel her resolve slip. "I remember."

"Do you also remember our plan to get together for several evenings during this week?"

A measured look. "That was *your* plan, if I remember right."

"Fine. *My* plan, then." He took a step closer, held her gaze with his. "Have dinner with me."

The pull between them was winning. Connor could feel it.

"What about Brian?" she murmured. "Won't he miss you?"

"He'll be with his parents. And I'll be with you." Connor leaned forward until their faces were just inches apart, yet he made no further move to touch her. "We can talk, learn more about each other. Surely that would appeal to your overlapping emotions?"

Julia wet her lips with the tip of her tongue. "It might."

"Good. It's a weeknight, so we won't make it late. How about if I pick you up at six?" A corner of his mouth lifted. "I realize it isn't Saturday yet. So I'll come up to your apartment, but I won't cross the threshold. I'll wait outside in the hall, okay?"

"Okay."

Laughter and voices interrupted them as the students burst through the front doors of the school and scurried toward their classrooms to begin their day.

Julia stepped away from Connor. Glancing at the clock, she headed back to her desk. "It's late. I don't have time to go to the lost and found."

"Not a problem. I can find it on my own. Brian gave me great directions. He's pretty eager to get that cap back." Connor tucked the books under his arm. "See you tonight."

"Connor, wait." Julia reached for her purse. Rummaging through it, she yanked out what she was looking for. She walked over and handed it to him. "Here."

Connor felt the brush of fur against his skin. Puzzled, he glanced down and saw the bright red rabbit's foot she'd pressed into his palm.

"That was *my* lucky charm on the mound," she explained. "My dad gave it to me when I was nine. I went twelve-and-three that season. Tell Brian it's his for as long as he needs it. It's got his team color and my dad's good luck. I'm passing that luck on to him." A soft smile.

"The truth is, Brian doesn't need a lucky charm. He has talent, heart, and a ton of people who think he's the best. Still, with this baby, he can't miss. So he'd better take his medicine and get well fast. Tell him that."

Connor turned the rabbit's foot over in his hand, knowing damned well the lift this would give Brian's spirits. If Julia Talbot *was* too good to be true, she had a hell of a lot to teach the world. "Thanks," he replied, more touched by her gesture than he could remember being in a very long time. "I'll tell him."

11:50 A.M.

Nancy pushed open the front door, her temples throbbing as she scooted Brian into the house.

The wait in the pediatrician's office had been endless. So had the wait in the drugstore while the pharmacist attempted to fill Brian's prescription. In his haste, the poor man had spilled the last bottle of amoxyl. Apologizing profusely, he'd given Nancy the remainder of the liquid antibiotic—which he'd assured her would last two days—and promised to have the rest delivered to her house first thing tomorrow. She'd readily agreed, thrilled to get out of there. She had another stop to make, and she wanted to get home before the lunchtime traffic started jamming the streets.

An eon later, armed with the partially filled bottle of medicine, a new superhero videotape, and an extra large box of malted milkballs, they were home.

She was a mess. Not from the trauma of an ear infection—she'd been through a half dozen of those in Brian's life—but from last night. First, the shock of seeing Stephen, not drunk but beaten and bruised. Next, the phone call from Julia Talbot, which only fed the fear gripping her gut. And last, the argument with Stephen. It was the ugliest fight they'd ever had. Oh, they'd kept their voices down, retained their control, and behaved in a remarkably civilized manner. But the rage was there, brimming beneath the surface as they bit out accusations.

She was on the verge of snapping. And Stephen, rather than being conciliatory about the mess he'd gotten them into, was defensive, nasty, ordering her to back off and give him room to fix things, accusing her of not trusting him, snarling that he had everything under control.

For the first time, she wondered if their marriage would survive.

"Mom, can I watch the video in my room?" Brian interrupted her thoughts to ask. He looked pale and tired, much worse than an ear infection would cause.

Nancy bent down and gave him a hard hug. "Of course, honey. I'll make you a bowl of soup and a sandwich and bring it upstairs."

"I'm not real hungry."

She frowned. "You should be. You didn't eat much of your waffle this morning."

"Neither did Dad. And he's bigger than me and felt much worse."

Nancy's chest tightened. "Dad looked a lot better this morning. His face was hardly swollen at all."

"Yeah, but he must still have been hurting, because he was in a really bad mood. He yelled at Uncle Connor. And I heard him walking around all night."

"What were you doing up?"

"My ear hurt." Brian stared at the floor for a minute,

and Nancy had the distinct feeling it was more than Brian's ear that had kept him awake.

His next question confirmed that. "Are you mad at Dad?"

A hard swallow. "No, Brian, I'm not mad."

"You look mad. You sound mad, too. So does Dad."

She had to say something to make it better. On the other hand, she couldn't lie. So she settled for a partial truth. "Dad is working very hard these days. He's tired. So am I. Maybe that's making us less patient than usual. I'm sorry if our moods are upsetting you." She tipped up Brian's chin, desperate to erase the pain he was feeling. "Sweetheart, none of this has anything to do with you. You're the greatest joy in our lives. Dad and I both love you very, very much. You do know that, don't you?"

Brian nodded, but the sad look was still there. "Yeah, Mom, I know."

1:15 P.M.

Stephen paced around his office, feeling like a hamster in a wheel. He was running as frantically as he could but getting nowhere fast.

Neither Cliff, Marty, nor Greg had turned up anything on Walker Development. Not yet. Then again, none of them had been instructed to make this a top priority. They didn't know the real reason he was conducting a background check on Philip Walker. And he couldn't risk telling them. Not without getting into messy explanations. Plus, he didn't know where the breach in security had come from, who'd told Walker he was conducting due diligence. The worst thing would be if whoever that was found out he was still pursuing the matter—with increased urgency—despite the beating they'd provided as a warning.

No, the problem and the pressure were his. On his own, he had to find something on Walker. Now.

He went over to the window, rested his forehead against the cool glass. Unlike his colleagues, he wasn't investigating Walker Development. He was checking out Philip Walker himself, making a few subtle calls to see what the man was about. If there was any angle to take that might result in nabbing the son of a bitch, this would be it. Scum like Walker showed their true colors in some aspect of their lives. And whatever that aspect was, they didn't want it made public.

A tidbit of dirt would be all the ammunition he needed. Some nasty little skeleton Walker wanted kept in the closet. If he uncovered that, he'd have grounds for a swap. His silence for Walker's.

The whole scenario made him sick. Philip Walker belonged in prison, not out there victimizing local officials and businessmen. But if Stephen tried to put him there, it would be his own life, and the lives of his family, that would blow up in his face.

He couldn't let that happen. He had to follow through with his plan to put the brakes on Walker, to get him out of their lives, and to sever whatever business ties he had with Leaf Brook.

But how? He had to move fast. At the same time, he had to keep a low profile. Walker was keeping a close eye on his actions. He needed someone else to do his dirty work, to go after Walker without involving him in the investigation. He needed a professional.

As if in answer to his thoughts, a brief knock sounded

at the door, and Cliff poked his head into the office. "Good, you're in. Celeste wasn't at her desk, and . . ." He stopped, staring at his friend's face. "What the hell happened to you?"

"Car trouble." Stephen had perfected this explanation after giving it a dozen times. He now gave it again, from soup to nuts, ending with: "Remind me never to become a mechanic."

Frowning, Cliff walked over, still studying Stephen's cuts. "Are you sure you're all right? You really sliced yourself up."

"I'm sure. Although last night I wasn't feeling so cavalier. If it weren't for Connor, I'd probably have spent the night on the parking-lot floor. He got me home. Nancy got me fixed up. So I'm on the mend."

"Good." Like everyone else, Cliff seemed to accept Stephen's accounting of the incident. He took a gulp of coffee. "I dropped in on my way back from court. I wanted to make sure you knew your father was driving in from Connecticut on Thursday. I didn't know if Connor had mentioned it to you."

"He mentioned it. Did you speak with my father directly?"

A nod. "He didn't want to break in on your meetings yesterday. He figured that between Connor and me, one of us would get the news to you." A tactful pause as Cliff inspected his cup. "I wouldn't be too concerned about this visit. Your dad's pretty high on the current polls. It should be smooth sailing."

Stephen arched a brow. "Yeah, right."

Cliff cleared his throat. "Do you want me here when he comes?"

"It would probably be useful. You know, you and

Connor, flanking me on either side. A united front against a formidable adversary."

"It's not quite that bad." Cliff chuckled, but there was understanding in his eyes. He'd known Harrison Stratford for too many years, both personally and professionally, long enough to learn never to minimize his imperious presence. And he was well aware of Harrison's expectations for Stephen. "Besides, you've got one foot in the door of the state senate. That'll put him in a good mood for sure."

"Don't bet on it." Stephen rubbed the back of his neck, eager to get to his agenda. "Cliff, you didn't happen to dig up anything on Walker's company, did you?"

"Nothing out of the ordinary." Cliff shot him a quizzical look. "Why? Were you expecting something?"

A nonchalant shrug. "Not really. There's just something about the guy . . . I don't know."

"He's a little pushy, I'll give you that. And, yeah, he's rough around the edges. But that's not news. You've dealt with him in the past."

"True, but not on anything as big as this." Stephen debated whether to give Cliff more to go on before he asked for a name, then realized he had to. Cliff was too smart to take this request at face value. He had to be offered some reason for Stephen to want Walker investigated.

"It's not just a question of being rough around the edges," he clarified. "I get the feeling Walker's a real street fighter. Which could be nothing more than a veneer. On the other hand, it could mean his character is less than stellar. I just don't know. What I do know is that for Leaf Brook to give him this municipal parking contract would mean entrusting a significant source of city money to a private individual. And while the idea has merit, I have a fiduciary responsibility to Leaf Brook to check out Walker thoroughly, just to be on the safe side."

"I see your point."

"Good." Having gotten this far, Stephen negotiated the next step. "Do you have the name and number of that private investigator my father used when we checked out Braxton's background? I liked the guy; he was quick, thorough, and discreet."

Cliff nodded. "I've got his information on file." He reached into his jacket pocket and pulled out his PalmPilot. Flipping it open, he pressed a few buttons. "Here it is. Harry Shaw. He's on the Post Road in White Plains. I'll write down his address and phone number for you." Grabbing a notepad from Stephen's desk, he scribbled the information.

"Thanks." That took care of the biggest obstacle. But there was another. Someone had to speak to the attorneys involved in Walker's out-of-area business transactions, just in case the bit of dirt he needed was a legal indiscretion that a lawyer wouldn't offer up to a PI. Cliff was the logical choice for the job. He was sharp and trustworthy and had the necessary legal credentials.

Careful, Stephen cautioned himself. *Say as little as possible.*

He sank back into his chair, wincing as his ribs protested the motion. "The other avenue I want to pursue is contacting attorneys outside Westchester County who've been involved in Walker's commercial projects—either those he developed or those he managed. I want to make sure they have only positive things to say about him."

Cliff shot him a puzzled look. "Okay, Steve, I don't

get it. Why the sudden reticence? You were satisfied with your past dealings with the guy. Enough to make you pretty gung-ho about his taking on this contract. At least, you were at first. Did something happen to change that?"

Stephen had his answer prepared. "I'm getting pressure from the city council. That's what happened."

"Enough pressure to launch a full-scale background check? I'm sure you've done some due diligence on Walker in the past."

"Some, yes. But the city council is squeamish about this deal. I'm anticipating a big-time interrogation. I need to be ready to answer anything they might throw my way. I want all the facts. That means broadening due diligence to cover areas outside Westchester County. Harry Shaw can't make attorney-to-attorney inquiries. You can."

Cliff lowered his cup to the desk. "So can you. Last I remember, you passed the bar. Why not just call and ask the questions yourself?"

It was time to call a halt to this interrogation.

"Because I'm the mayor," Stephen replied, keeping his gaze fixed steadily on his friend. "If I made those phone calls myself, it would make the background check look like a big deal. Like I didn't trust Walker. That's what I'm trying to avoid. I'm asking you a favor, Cliff. I'll give you the names. You make a few discreet phone calls—today, if possible. And stop grilling me. I know you're a good lawyer. But I'm not on the witness stand. So cool it."

Cliff heard the finality in Stephen's tone loud and clear. "All right," he agreed, stifling whatever questions he still had. "If it makes you feel better, give me the names. I'll check things out."

4:30 P.M.

Nancy peeked into Brian's room, relieved to see that he'd dozed off. He was exhausted. With the ear infection, the stress, and the lack of sleep, he really needed a nap.

Not that he'd overexerted himself today. To the contrary, he'd been uncharacteristically subdued. He'd spent most of the day in his room, playing with his action figures, glancing disinterestedly at the videotape they'd rented. He'd perked up a little when Connor dropped by with his homework, only to become even more depressed when his uncle reported having no luck finding the baseball cap at the school lost and found. The only time Nancy had seen glimpses of the old Brian was when Connor gave him Miss Talbot's rabbit's foot. Then he'd beamed, firing questions about when Miss Talbot's father had given it to her, wanting to know the number of wins and losses she'd had that season.

Following that brief resurgence of exuberance, Brian had taken the rabbit's foot and gone back to his room.

He hadn't eaten at all. Even with Connor's coaxing, he'd only nibbled at his sandwich and popped one or two malted milkballs into his mouth. He'd asked about Stephen twice. Hearing his father was doing much better, he'd curled up on his bed—with the rabbit's foot—and waited for him to come home.

Damn Stephen for not calling, Nancy thought bitterly. It would have meant the world to their son.

She tucked a blanket around him, bending to press her lips to his forehead. No fever. And the fact that he wasn't fitful meant the medicine was doing its job. As for parenting, that job was apparently being left up to her. Fine.

She was getting more accustomed to flying solo since Stephen had started fighting his demons once again.

Downstairs, the doorbell rang.

Quickly, Nancy scooted out of Brian's room, easing his door shut behind her. Whoever was there, she didn't want them to disturb her son.

She hurried down the steps, through the hall, and to the front door.

"Who is it?"

No answer.

She peeked through the peephole and saw no one. That was weird.

She was just about to go back upstairs when she heard the sound of a van pulling away. She glanced through the peephole again. A delivery truck. That explained it. A package must have been dropped off. Maybe their pharmacist had gotten hold of the antibiotic sooner than expected.

She opened the front door. There was no prescription tucked between it and the screen. She stepped outside and glanced at the front step. There was a small box sitting there. It was addressed to her. Oddly, there was no return address.

Studying the package, she went back inside, pushing the door shut behind her. *Who could this be from?* she wondered. She hadn't ordered anything. Nor was Stephen in a frame of mind to send her gifts.

In the kitchen, she set the box on the table, got out a letter opener, and sliced through the tape. She folded back the sides of the package. The first thing she saw was a flash of red. Lying on top of that object was an envelope, presumably with a card.

She pulled out both things—and froze.

The flash of red was Brian's baseball cap.

For a long moment, she stared at it, turning it over in her hands as an ugly sense of foreboding gripped her. Abruptly, she tossed the cap onto the table and snatched up the envelope. On it was typed "Mrs. Stratford." She ripped it open, yanked out the note inside, and unfolded it.

Dear Mrs. Stratford,

I believe your son accidentally misplaced his cap. I'm returning it. Sometimes I think kids would lose not only their hats but their heads if parents didn't make smart choices for them. I hope your husband makes smart choices for Brian. It will ensure he grows up strong and healthy. Urge the mayor to do so. Urge him not to take unnecessary risks. Gambling with your son's safety would be a stupid and dangerous thing to do. It could result in future accidents and lead to untold heartache. Don't let that happen.

Very truly yours,
A Friend

Nancy didn't remember sinking into the kitchen chair. She didn't remember much of anything. Her hands were shaking, and her vision was blurred by tears. She read the note through twice, her entire body quaking as she did.

Someone was threatening Brian's life. The same someone who had Stephen over a financial barrel and who'd had him roughed up last night. That someone knew Stephen was gambling. And he was blackmailing him with it. Only it wasn't just Stephen who was at risk anymore. It was their seven-and-a-half-year-old son.

She crossed over and snatched the phone from the cradle, punching up Stephen's private number.

Celeste answered. "Mayor Stratford's office."

"I need to speak with him, Celeste." Nancy wasn't asking, she was telling.

A surprised pause. The mayor's wife was always cordial. "I'm sorry, Mrs. Stratford, but he's behind closed doors and asked not to be disturbed."

"Is he alone?"

"Well, yes, but . . ."

"Then put him on. This is an emergency."

Another pause. "Of course. Just a minute."

Mere seconds passed before Stephen picked up. "Nance? What's the matter? Is Brian okay?"

"You bastard," she managed, tears clogging her throat. "No wonder you're worried about Brian. How could you let this happen? How could you endanger your own son? And how could you keep it from me?"

Stephen sucked in his breath. "What happened? Goddammit, Nancy, is Brian all right?"

"For now, yes." She hardly knew what she was saying, she was so hysterical. "He's asleep. That's after waiting for you to call all day. But that's not what you're asking, is it?"

"Nancy, calm down. Calm down, and tell me what's going on."

"Tell *you* what's going on? You have it backward. *I'm* not the one being blackmailed. *I'm* not the one causing my son's life to be threatened."

"Threatened? Who threatened Brian?"

"A friend," she said sarcastically. "The one who dropped off Brian's baseball cap with a note telling you to be a good boy or else."

"Shit." Stephen's insides gave a violent twist. "He was there?"

"A delivery truck did the dirty deed. It brought Brian's cap and this message." She read the note aloud, her voice cracking three times as she did. "God damn you, Stephen," she ended, sobs choking her. "God damn you to hell."

"Nancy, listen to me. I've got this under control."

"Under control?" she countered shrilly. "You call what's happened these past few days having things under control?"

"I call it a fight to survive," Stephen shot back. "I call it racing the clock to protect my son. And to protect you. Why do you think I didn't tell you anything? I knew you'd go to pieces like this."

Nancy's head was hammering so loudly she could scarcely think. "Who's behind this?" she demanded. "The truth, Stephen. Who's blackmailing you, and why?"

Stephen sucked in his breath. "Fine," he fired in that tone that meant he was about to lose it and blow a gasket. "You want to know? Here it is. I'm being held over a barrel by a real estate developer who wants a big city contract and won't stop until he gets it. He knows about my gambling. I've got two days to get him the contract, or he'll tip off the media and the cops—not to mention what he'll do to Brian."

"Oh, God." Nancy wiped the perspiration off her brow. "Okay, then. Just give him the contract."

"It's not that easy. Number one, the city council isn't behind me on this. So we won't get enough votes. Number two, Walker's scum. I can't commit Leaf Brook to a deal as big as this—not with him on the other side."

Hysterical laughter bubbled up in Nancy's throat.

"You're being honorable *now?* You've destroyed yourself and your whole family, and now you're concerned about morality?"

"It's not about morality!" he blasted. "It's about getting rid of this bastard for good. I'm digging around. I've got to be careful. Walker's got a mole somewhere. That's why I came home looking like I did last night. But that's not going to stop me. I hired a private investigator. He'll dig up some dirt on the SOB. Something that could ruin him. And then . . ."

"*If* he digs up dirt. A man like that might be too clever to leave any skeletons around." Nancy's mind was racing, searching for possible solutions. The FBI. She could call the FBI—after all, this involved a physical threat to a child. But the threat was only implied, which meant there was no guarantee they could do anything. In the meantime, the story would leak out, Stephen's whole sordid secret would become public, and Brian's life would be ruined. Worse, he still wouldn't be safe. If the authorities couldn't act, or if they did act but couldn't capture every single creep involved, one of them could still go after Brian.

She was his mother. It was up to her to do something.

Abruptly, her hysteria passed, transforming into that calm center at the eye of a hurricane. "I can't let you do this to Brian and me, Stephen. Not anymore."

"Goddammit, Nancy, you're supposed to be my wife!" he exploded. "I need your support. It's just a few days. Keep Brian home. That way, no one can get to him. After Thursday, it'll be over."

"It's over now," she said quietly.

She replaced the phone in its cradle, driven by blind maternal protectiveness. Her marriage was secondary. Brian came first.

She picked up the receiver again, pressed the familiar number.

Cliff was driving back toward Leaf Brook when his cell phone rang. "Hello," he answered, expecting to hear Stephen's voice.

"Cliff, it's me."

His hands tightened on the wheel. "Nancy, what's wrong?" She was obviously crying.

"I can't talk about it. I've just got to get out of here. Now. Today. I need a favor. A few favors, actually. Can you meet me?"

"Wherever and whenever you want."

"Where are you now?"

"On the Taconic. Three exits north of Leaf Brook."

"Good. Can you come straight to the house? Brian's sick, and I won't leave him alone. Besides, I need every minute of time I can get. I've got to pack for him and for me."

"Pack? Pack for where?"

"I'll tell you when you get here."

Twenty minutes later, Cliff was sitting in Nancy's kitchen, his mouth hanging open as he reread the note she'd received.

"Christ. This certainly explains why Stephen's been so freaked out about this guy." He lifted his gaze. "What does Walker have on Stephen—or do I need to ask?"

"No, you don't need to ask." Nancy didn't elaborate. This was one subject they never broached, even though Cliff was well aware of its existence. "I don't have details. Nor do I want them. It's the same old dance. I've got to get away—for Brian's sake. I'm scared to death for him." She dashed her hands across her tear-streaked face. "Cliff, the keys to your ski lodge in Stowe, do you have them with you?"

Slowly, Cliff nodded. "Yeah, I have them."

"Would you let me use the place for a while?"

"You know I will."

She swallowed, her jaw set in an uncompromising position. "Now comes the hard part. You've got to promise you won't tell anyone where I am."

"Anyone?" he repeated woodenly. "What about Stephen?"

A choked pause. "Especially Stephen."

Cliff's conflicting loyalties were evident in the torn look on his face. "Do you understand what you're asking me? Stephen's my best friend. When he realizes you and Brian are gone, he's going to be frantic."

"And Brian's my son. He comes first. Look, I won't scare Stephen. I'll leave him a note, explaining what I've done and why."

"Just not where."

"Right. Cliff, if you feel you can't do this, just say so. I won't hold it against you. I have no desire to put you in an untenable position."

"But if I say no, you'll drop out of sight somewhere else. Only then no one will know where you are."

"Exactly."

Blowing out his breath, Cliff rose. He jabbed his hand in his pocket, pulled out the keys. "Take them," he said, stuffing them in her palm. He frowned, feeling how icy her hand was. "Nance, maybe you shouldn't drive. I can take you and Brian up . . ."

"No." She cut him off with a wave of her arm. "It's late. You have a life. Besides, you've done enough already." A tentative pause. "Actually, that sounds a lot more magnanimous than it is. Because I'm about to ask you to drive up tomorrow. Brian's got an ear infection. He's taking an antibiotic. The pharmacist spilled some of the medicine when he was making up the prescription. So he gave me what he had, which was a few days' worth. He's having the rest delivered tomorrow." She stared at the keys in her hand. "I hate to ask this of you . . . I know how busy you are . . ."

"I'll clear my morning calendar. As soon as the prescription's ready, I'll pick it up and drive it to you at the ski lodge."

Relief coursed through Nancy in wide rivers. "Thank you so much." She went to Cliff, hugged him tightly.

For a brief instant, his arms closed around her, and he held her against him. Abruptly, he released her and stepped away.

A current of communication passed between them.

"Will you be all right?" Cliff asked in a ragged voice.

"Yes." Nancy stared at him for a long moment. "At least, I think so."

"You'll stay in touch?"

"I'll call on your cell phone. Late at night, when I know you're not with Stephen. I won't stay away for long. When this crisis is over . . ." Tears filled her eyes. "Who am I kidding? There'll be another one to take its place. And another after that, if Stephen doesn't jump off this merry-go-round and get some help. Cliff, I can't live this way. Not anymore."

"Nancy . . ." He swallowed, hard. "Now's not the time to make any rash decisions."

"You're right." She averted her gaze, turning and heading toward the stairs. "I've got to wake Brian. I want to be on the road before dark."

17

6:05 P.M.

Connor had a late-day meeting in midtown Manhattan. From there, he drove straight to Julia's.

He'd tried to reach Stephen twice, but both times Celeste said he was behind closed doors. No doubt, he was trying to deal with the catastrophe he'd created. He'd better be. For everyone's sake.

Entering the lobby of Julia's building, Connor punched the buzzer, announced himself, and turned his attention to the evening ahead. If Julia's earlier reticence was any indication, he had his work cut out for him. Well, that was fine. Challenge or not, he had no intention of leaving things hanging. Not when he had a very definite ending in mind.

He gripped the door handle and waited impatiently for the responding buzzer to sound.

It did.

He yanked open the door, strode through the inside lobby, and headed upstairs.

Inside her apartment, Julia gave herself a once-over in the full-length hall mirror. Her silk blouse was a warm blue and mauve print. Her slacks were a deep midnight blue. Her makeup was light, and her hair was loose, curving softly around her shoulders. The overall effect was pretty much what she'd wanted. Simple but flattering. Not too fussy, not too casual. Attire that would work with anything.

Which was good, since she had no idea where tonight was heading. All she knew was that she and Connor had a great deal to work through if they were going to continue seeing each other.

She turned away from the mirror just as Connor's knock sounded.

Slinging a jacket over her arm, she took a deep breath, walked over, and opened the door.

"Hi," she greeted him.

"Hi, yourself." His gaze flickered over her, and he made no move to disguise his approval. "All set?"

"Um-hum." She stepped into the hall, locked the door behind her. "Where are we having dinner?"

"Actually, I thought we'd go to that little French place by the lake. They've got great quiche, great bread, and great wine. After that, maybe we'll take a walk. It's a beautiful night—not too chilly. And we have a lot to talk about."

Julia nodded. "That sounds like a good idea." She glanced at his suit, gave him a quizzical look. "Am I underdressed?"

"Not a bit. I just came straight from a meeting." He took her jacket, held it as she slipped into it. "Let's go."

The car ride was quiet. *Very* quiet, with an underlying tension that was palpable. Only a few polite comments were passed, and those pertained to nondescript things like the weather and the day's headlines. Fortunately, the drive was short, so the lapses didn't become unbearable.

Dinner was more conversational. But the strain was

still there, stemming from a host of things that needed discussion. Until that discussion happened, the strain wasn't going away.

Connor took on the challenge first. Over coffee, he leaned forward, propped his elbows on the table, and tackled the fundamental issue—or, at least, the one blocking them from moving on to the others.

"Look, Julia, you're dying to bring up Brian and see where things stand," he said. "There isn't going to be any right moment to do so. Let's just grab the bull by the horns and confront the subject, so we can get past it and get on with our evening. Fair enough?"

A flicker of surprise crossed Julia's face. "Fair enough."

"Good. And don't look so astonished. I told you, I can be very direct. I figured you'd noticed that the other night in your apartment."

Just the memory of what he was alluding to made heat shimmer through her. "I noticed. I also remember being pretty direct myself."

"Direct but ambivalent," Connor modified.

"With reason." Julia didn't deny it. "That kiss—whatever it was a prelude to—overwhelmed me. I don't expect you to understand. As I pointed out, we're very different."

"In some ways. Not in others. Don't kid yourself—I was as blown away by that kiss as you were. The difference is, I wasn't afraid."

"Fine. I stand corrected."

Connor's jaw set, and Julia could almost see his wheels turning as he decided whether or not to push the matter further.

She took the decision out of his hands. "I think we're

getting ahead of ourselves. We've got some basics to cover before we start analyzing the chemistry between us."

"Are you so sure of that?"

"Connor . . ."

"Okay." He waved away her protest. "We'll do it your way. Let's get back to the original subject, Brian." Connor's demeanor altered slightly, became less intimate, more businesslike. "I do understand what's going on in your head, Julia. You care about my nephew. He's a very special kid. You're worried because you see him going through a rough time. Worried enough to alert his parents. You assumed I'd be furious at you for doing that. You were wrong. True, I asked you not to go to Stephen and Nancy. But you made it quite clear to me that if things got out of hand, you planned to do just that. You were honest. You even gave me a heads-up before you called. So, contrary to what you believed, I wasn't angry. You would have found that out if you'd asked. Next time, be sure of your facts before you break a date with me, okay?"

Julia set down her cup, nodding slowly. "That sounds fair."

"It is. Getting back to your commitment to Brian, I find it admirable. More than admirable. I think it's rare and touching. I mean that." One dark brow rose in question. "Any doubts about what I've said so far?"

"No—at least, not yet."

"Fine, then let's move on to the sticky part. Yeah, your telephone call caught Nancy at a bad time last night, but let me assure you, she took your message very seriously. So did Stephen. They plan to do whatever's necessary to help their son. Brian's happiness comes first. It always has, and it always will. Things will work out. In the meantime, the poor kid's got an ear infection. When I saw him earlier, he looked washed out. But he's on an antibiotic, so he'll be better soon. Physically *and* emotionally. His parents will make sure of it." Connor leaned closer, met Julia's gaze, and held it. "Is that aboveboard enough? Or are you still convinced I'm lying?"

Julia's forehead creased in a frown. "I never accused you of lying, Connor. Only of speaking in partial truths. And not about Brian. Only about how whatever pressure his father's under is affecting his life. I realize you think I'm a busybody . . ."

"That's another thing," he interrupted. "You're constantly telling me what I think of you. And you're usually wrong." He reached across the table, capturing her hand and slowly, deliberately, interlacing their fingers. "I don't think you're a busybody. I think you're complicated. There are layers you keep carefully concealed. The rest is an open book—one with a cover that's so beautiful you have half the men in the bleachers at Little League games staring at you. Trust me, I'm one of them. I think you're frank, dedicated, and caring, and it drives you crazy when others aren't. I also think you're passionate—and I don't mean only in your work. Teaching just happens to be a safe outlet for your passion. There are other outlets that aren't nearly as safe. Me, for example. Or, rather, us. What happens between us scares you to death."

"Wow." Julia sucked in her breath. "That's quite an analysis. Are you sure *you're* not the one with the degree in psych?"

A slow grin. "Nope, I'm the cold-blooded venture capitalist who devotes all his energies to making money."

"Not *all* your energies, apparently."

He chuckled. "No, not all of them." His thumb caressed her palm. "So, now that we've cleared the air, are you still not sure if you like me? Or trust me?"

Julia couldn't ignore the frisson of pleasure that shot through her at his touch. She just wished she could separate her involuntary responses to him from her more rational thought processes. She knew that his explanation about Brian had just brushed the tip of the iceberg. But so what? Sketchy or not, his words were sincere. As for the rest, well, when it came down to it, she had no right to expect him to open up to her about his family's inner workings. And more to the point, was it his decision to be close-mouthed that was freaking her out, or was it something more fundamental, like the fear he'd described moments ago?

"Julia?" he prompted.

She drew a slow, shaky breath. "At this particular moment, I'm not sure of anything—which seems to be becoming a habit when I'm around you."

"I like the sound of that."

"I'm not sure I do."

Connor's thumb stilled, and his fingers tightened around hers. "Take that walk with me."

It might just as well have been an invitation to bed, it sounded so intimate. And Julia was far from immune. But she wanted to take this walk for more than just romantic reasons. She needed to talk to Connor, to see what made him tick, and to see if he could understand what made her tick.

Nodding, she pushed back her chair and rose. "I'm ready."

They left the restaurant as quietly as they'd arrived

and with the same underlying tension, although this time the tension was rooted in anticipation rather than strain.

The lake was quiet, moonlight glistening off it in a golden haze. A narrow path ran the full perimeter, close to the water's edge, and newly budding trees lined the path on either side.

Connor took Julia's arm and led her away from the restaurant. He released her when they reached the path, and they strolled along, side by side, acutely aware of each other, though they made no further move to touch.

This time, it was Julia who broke the silence. "You were right. I am scared to death."

"I know." He slowed the pace of their walk, concentrating on the essence of the conversation. "What I don't know is why. We're different. Okay, fine. Why is that such a deterrent? Have all the guys in your life been so much like you? Greg Matthews sure as hell isn't."

"Greg was never really *in* my life, so it didn't matter. Besides, I wouldn't exactly put you two in the same category."

"Meaning?"

"You're a Stratford."

"So's Brian. You're not afraid of him."

Julia shot him a look. "Very funny."

"I'm not being funny."

"Nor am I. I'm being honest. You come with a whole persona, not just a high-powered career. It's foreign to me—and it's daunting."

Without warning, Connor came to a dead stop, pivoting around and gripping her shoulders. "You're afraid of me because of my name? Because I'm written up in the newspapers as a chip off the old block? Because my father built a financial dynasty?"

Julia hadn't expected such a vehement response. Connor looked furious, as he had when Cheryl Lager challenged his integrity.

"You've built quite a dynasty of your own," she reminded him.

"Your point being?"

"Connor, it isn't your name or your money. It's all of it—who you are, how you were raised, the way you view life. You think idealism is a stupid waste of time. I think it's the only salvation we've got."

"Maybe you're right. Maybe it is. Maybe I've been around the wrong people for too long. Maybe meeting you has changed that." His fingers tunneled through her hair, and he urged her closer, tipped her face up to his. "Dammit, Julia, life doesn't come in neat little packages. Surprises happen. We're one of those surprises. So stop putting up walls to stop this from happening. Because you can't. Neither of us can."

He lowered his head, his mouth covering hers, taking it with the same utter lack of preliminaries as last time. His lips parted hers, and his tongue pressed deep, stroking hers in a hot caress that ended all conversation.

This moment had been building since Saturday, and suddenly it was all that mattered—not only to Connor but to Julia, too. She heard herself moan, and then she was kissing him back, her mouth just as frantic as his, her hands gripping his jacket, knotting in the lapels to anchor herself. Connor wasn't satisfied with that. He caught her arms, lifted them around his neck, bringing her against him as he did.

The kiss exploded. Julia was a mass of nerve endings, her lips wild under his, her entire body shaking as she strained for more. Dimly, she felt Connor back her against a tree, pin her there with the powerful weight of his body. His palm cupped her breast, his thumb rubbing her nipple in dizzying circles. His muscles were taut, his breath coming in hard rasps, and, through the confines of their clothes, his erection throbbed against her belly. The pressure felt wonderful—but it wasn't enough. She needed to be closer, to feel more.

With a broken, frustrated cry, she began struggling, trying to move higher, to shift their bodies into just the right position. Connor made a strangled sound that was part laugh, part groan, and he gripped her bottom, lifted her up, and fitted her against him.

The world stood still.

Julia's breath caught, live currents vibrating through her. Blindly, she tugged Connor's mouth to hers, arching even closer and raising her knees to hug his hips. All that mattered was the throbbing inside her, the spiraling need Connor had to fill.

He moved against her—once, twice—then abruptly stopped, tearing his mouth away to stare down at her with eyes that glittered with passion. "Julia." He sounded hoarse, as if uttering that one word was more than he could muster. "Julia!"

Her eyes cracked open. She didn't know why he'd chosen this moment to talk, nor did she care. Her body was screaming its protest. "Don't," she managed. "Don't stop."

"I don't plan to." Connor pressed his forehead to hers. "Let's get out of here."

"What?" She was having trouble focusing.

"We're at a restaurant. By a lake. Remember?"

Suddenly, she did. She blinked, glancing around, trying to regain her bearings. They were outside, in public. And she'd completely lost her mind.

She had no desire to regain it.

"No one saw us," Connor murmured, interpreting her silence as embarrassment. "The restaurant's way behind those trees. We're alone." He swallowed hard, his body still rigid against hers. "Don't change your mind." It was part order, part plea. "For God's sake, don't."

Everything inside her was tight and trembling. Her limbs felt watery. She wondered if she could walk. Change her mind? Impossible. "I won't," she said unsteadily. "I can't."

Connor searched her face for one long, restless moment. He must have seen whatever he needed to convince him, because he loosened his grip just enough for her legs to slide down and her feet to touch the ground. Then he locked an arm around her waist, anchoring her against his side. "Let's go."

The drive home was a blur. Julia had no second thoughts. She had no thoughts at all, other than anticipation. Connor cut the drive time in half by going twenty miles over the speed limit and running two traffic lights. He swerved his Mercedes into the parking lot of her building and was out of the car almost before he cut the engine. Julia scrambled out of the passenger seat just as fast, her keys already in her hand.

It was the second time they'd tumbled into her apartment without turning on the light. Only this time, Connor flipped the lock behind him, watching her with a hot, predatory look. "I know I said I'd wait till Saturday. I can't."

Julia's heart was slamming against her ribs. "Neither can I."

In one motion, Connor shrugged off his jacket, flung it aside, and went to her. "Where's the bedroom?" he asked in a heated voice.

She tipped her head toward the rear of the apartment. "Back there."

"Too far. I'm not sure I can last." He kissed her, a blatantly carnal kiss that reawakened all their earlier urgency, brought it screaming back to life.

"There's a couch in the living room," Julia managed, pointing to their left and shivering as Connor began unbuttoning her blouse. "That's a lot closer."

His lips burned a path from her collarbone to her throat. "Which is bigger, the couch or the bed?"

"The bed."

"Then I'll last." Connor was pulling her down the hall. "Barely."

Julia's blouse was gone by the time they reached the bedroom, and Connor's tie and shirt were half off. He got rid of them in a few quick tugs, his hot stare devouring Julia as she stood there in her slacks and bra. His gaze darkened as she reached around, unhooked the lacy bra, and let it drift to the floor. He stepped closer, his palms gliding down her shoulders, shifting around to cup her breasts.

"You make me crazy," he muttered, absorbing her tiny quivers of pleasure. He pressed his lips to the side of her neck, his thumbs grazing her nipples, feeling them harden beneath his touch. She arched, the inadvertent action forcing her breasts against him, her nipples skimming the hair-roughened surface of his chest.

They both froze.

"God." Connor sucked in his breath, locking an arm around her to bring her closer. "Maybe you were right." He rubbed his torso against hers, shuddering at the resulting pleasure. "Maybe we should be scared to death."

"Ummm," Julia murmured, lost in sensation. She

mimicked Connor's motion, only very slowly, dragging her breasts across his chest in a way that accentuated each shimmering nuance. "Maybe we should."

Something inside Connor seemed to snap. A hard shudder racked his body, and he gripped her arms, forcibly shoving himself away. "You've got thirty seconds to get into that bed."

"I only need twenty." Julia tugged at the button of her slacks. She had no idea who this woman was, but she knew what she wanted. And if she didn't have it, she'd die.

Connor was naked first, and he toppled Julia to the bed, hooking his fingers inside her panties and shimmying them down her legs and off. "Finally," he rasped, already nudging her thighs apart. He moved, covering her body with his. "Julia, this isn't going to be slow. Not this time. I've got to get inside you."

Julia nodded, feeling as frantic as he. She didn't want slow. She wanted Connor. Her breath caught in her throat as his hand glided up the inside of her thigh, his fingers opening her, slipping inside, exploring her wetness, and making her cry out. She was still reeling from the impact when he spread her legs wider and settled himself between them.

His penis probed at the entrance to her body, then pushed inside. She was more than ready for him, and he glided slowly forward, stretching and filling her. Julia acted on pure instinct, arching to take him deeper, lifting her legs to cradle his hips. She gave a choked, aroused cry, her head tossing from side to side as she tried to hurry his motions.

"You're tight," he said thickly, tremors of restraint rippling through his biceps. "I don't . . . want to hurt you."

"I don't care." Julia's hands balled into fists at the

base of his spine. "Connor, please." She undulated against him.

It worked.

His hands went under her, angling her to receive him, and he thrust all the way in. She felt him tense, felt her own body give, but none of that mattered. All that mattered was putting out the fire.

Connor murmured something unintelligible, his tone harsh, guttural, as he fought to slow himself. But he couldn't, and Julia refused to let him. She writhed beneath him, and his resistance shattered. He began moving, hard and fast, his fingers biting into her skin as he anchored her to take more and more of him.

The pleasure ignited, burst into flames, and Julia met him, thrust for thrust, her body finding his rhythm and matching it. There was a clawing ache inside her that intensified with each thrust, coiled tighter and tighter until she thought she'd die.

Connor must have sensed her urgency—and shared it—because he grabbed the headboard, hoisted himself up higher, and drove deep, penetrating her completely and rubbing against a spot so exquisitely sensitive that she moaned. He withdrew and did it again, and Julia heard herself cry out, her body arching like a bowstring as it struggled for release. She couldn't bear this, not anymore. Neither could Connor, if his ragged breathing and frenzied motions were any indication.

He thrust into her again, and, abruptly, she shattered, all her nerve endings splintering into fragments as her body unraveled, pulsed around Connor's rigid penis. He gave a hoarse shout, burying himself in her climax, pushing deep, and holding himself there as her contractions milked him, hurled him over the edge.

He came violently, his body jerking under the impact as he jetted into her in powerful spasms of completion. He crushed their lower bodies together, totally lost in sheer physical sensation. His hips were still moving when he collapsed on top of her, tiny aftershocks of his orgasm—and hers—rippling through them.

Julia sank into the bed, her limbs quivering with reaction. Her mind was blissfully numb, her body sated, and she could easily have stayed like that for ages.

Connor had other ideas. Julia was still floating when he propped himself on his elbows and gazed down at her. "Are you okay?" When she didn't answer, he caressed her cheek, his touch gentle. "Julia, look at me."

She forced her lids up.

He looked sweaty and exhausted, as if he'd run a marathon. But his expression was intent, and his brows were knit in concern. "Are you okay?"

"Fine," she managed in a thin voice.

Sucking in his breath, Connor gathered his strength and lifted himself away from her. Cool air brushed Julia's overheated skin, and she shivered, groping for the blanket.

Connor found it for her, yanking it up, then pausing a moment before he pulled it over them. His gaze raked her, his features set in harsh lines, illuminated by moonlight. "You're so damned beautiful," he muttered with husky male satisfaction. "You deserve to be lingered over for hours. Next time . . ."

His own words brought back to mind his original concern, and he frowned, draping the blanket around them, then propping himself on one elbow, leaning over her to watch her face. "Why didn't you tell me?"

She smiled faintly, not even pretending to misunderstand what he was asking. "Because it wouldn't have changed anything."

"It damned well would have. I would have taken more time . . ."

"In that case, I'm glad I didn't tell you. I was as frantic as you were. Any more time, and I would have died."

He was still frowning. "I hurt you."

"No, you didn't," she replied with utter candor. "You were amazing."

His expression softened, an intimate light glinting in his eyes. "So were you." He brushed damp strands of hair off her cheek. "Care to tell me why?"

"Why I was amazing or why I was a virgin?"

A corner of his mouth lifted. "The first part's innate. I was asking about the second. Is it more of your idealism or something else?"

She shrugged, feeling somehow more exposed, more vulnerable, than when their bodies had been joined. Having this conversation when they were strolling around a lake was one thing. Having it when they were lying together naked, having just made love, was entirely another. "A little of both. To begin with, my virginity never was an issue before tonight."

He stared at her as if she'd lost her mind. "Julia, you're a knockout. No, it's more than that. You've got a natural, unaffected kind of beauty that I've never seen any other woman pull off. It makes me hard just watching you cheer at a Little League game. What the hell do you mean, your virginity never was an issue—are the guys you know all eunuchs?"

Despite the significance of what she was about to get into with him, she had to laugh. "Thank you—I think. As for the guys I know, no, they're not eunuchs. It wasn't them, it was me. I was a late bloomer. I told you, I was a skinny, plain kid. I grew into a skinny, plain teenager, far from a knockout. I also told you I was a tomboy. I lived for my pitching and my schoolwork. Except summers, when I was a camp counselor. I loved working with kids. I can't remember a time when I didn't want to teach. In college, I zeroed in on child psych and elementary ed. My studying became even more focused and intensive. Then came graduate school, and, well, you know the rest." She interlaced her fingers on the blanket, stared down at them. "On top of that, I was always kind of a private person."

"You're telling me you didn't have much of a social life."

"Right. I was on the varsity softball team, and I could have hung out with that crowd—if I'd wanted to. But I didn't really fit in. I was too shy and too much of a bookworm." A wry grin. "I'm sure my going to Vassar didn't give my social life much of a boost. Not with my dad a professor there."

Connor inclined his head quizzically. "Is your father really menacing, or is he just the protective type?"

"Menacing?" Julia chuckled. "Not even close. As for protective, yes, I guess he is—except when he's teaching a class. Then he wouldn't know if I was abducted by aliens right in front of him. He's lost in his work. Either way, he's not the violent type. So he didn't scare guys off with a shotgun. They balked on their own."

"Why?"

"Academic prudence. To begin with, I knew a lot of the professors on campus since I was a kid. That made anyone I hung out with feel like they were living in a fishbowl. Then there was the conflict of interests when it came to the waiting list."

"You lost me."

"I'll explain." Julia found herself wishing the rest of this discussion would be as uncomplicated as this part. "My dad's an animated guy who breathes life into his teaching. Every semester, there's a run on his philosophy and lit courses and a waiting list to get in. Most of the guys figured that hitting on Professor Talbot's only daughter didn't seem like the best way to get into his good graces." Again, she shrugged. "It didn't matter. I never thought of the outcome as a sacrifice. Like I said, I was a quiet little bookworm, not exactly hot dating material."

Connor was watching her with probing intensity. "You're leaving something out," he stated flatly. "Something that's at the heart of all this and that's responsible for your being so determined to cling to your idealism. What is it?"

Julia started. Connor had told her he was good at reading people, but she hadn't expected him to be quite this perceptive.

"I'm impressed," she said, striving for a light tone. "You're pretty astute for someone without training."

"Julia." He wasn't about to be deterred. "You said there were some ways in which you weren't sheltered. Like what?"

She was beginning to see how he'd made his millions. He had a gut feel for spotting red flags, sifting through them, and coming up with bottom-line approaches. And he knew just what to look for to yield the most profitable results.

Maybe venture capitalists and early-childhood educators had a lot more in common than she realized.

Regardless, this was going to be the hard part for her

to get into. Not that the story was a secret. Most of it was a matter of public record. It was just that it was something she rarely talked about, and, when she did, it was only to her mother. Meredith Talbot understood better than anyone. She'd been right in the thick of things—first as a confidant, then as a nurse—no, more than a nurse, a proverbial Florence Nightingale who'd seen the signs and taken the necessary steps to end the crisis and start the healing.

"Julia?" Connor prompted. "Tell me what you're thinking."

She twisted around so she could meet his gaze. "I'm thinking about how to answer your question."

"As frankly as you've answered all the others."

She nodded, determined to relay the details while keeping a firm lid on her emotions. "I had a best friend when I was a kid. Franny. She was a sweet, gentle little girl. When I wasn't tossing a baseball around, she and I were inseparable. Near the end of third grade, she started acting different—moody and withdrawn. My mom noticed it even before I did. Or maybe I noticed but didn't understand enough to give it a name. I don't know. Either way, the symptoms got worse. She became sullen, jumpy, even angry."

Connor's features had hardened, and his expression told Julia he sensed what was coming.

She told him anyway. "To make a long story short, it turned out that Franny's stepfather was abusing her. And not just emotionally. He threatened her with all kinds of horrible things. Sometimes he hit her. And near the end . . ." Julia swallowed, feeling sickened by what she was about to say. "Near the end, his attacks became sexual. He threatened to kill her if she dared say a word to anyone. Not that she had anyone to turn to. Her mother was in some kind of self-protective denial. Her real father was in Europe with his twenty-year-old secretary. Franny was terrified, and she was alone."

Julia faltered for a moment, thinking that the reality was even more horrible to her now, as an adult, when she could fully comprehend the enormity of what her friend must have endured. "Thank God for my mom. She recognized the signs from her days as a pediatric nurse. She got Franny to open up to her. Then she contacted child services. There was a hearing, a divorce, and lots of counseling. Franny's stepfather ended up in jail, and Franny ended up staying with her mother. But she was never the same. She took off when she was in her teens, severed all ties with home. I don't blame her."

"Christ." Connor looked physically ill. "I can't even imagine . . ." He drew a slow breath, studying Julia with new understanding. "That explains a lot about you."

"I'm sure it does." Julia sighed. "Like why I'm so attuned to my students. Like why I want to preserve whatever idealism I can. Like why my principles matter so much to me. I've seen life's ugliness, Connor. It's not always fair about who it strikes. So whatever beauty is out there, we've got to grab it. And whatever dreams are within our control, we've got to hold tight to them and not compromise unless we absolutely must."

"With regard to things like relationships."

"Yes, with regard to things like relationships." Julia couldn't tell what Connor was thinking. Obviously, he was getting her point. How he would react to that point was another matter entirely.

"Did your friend's experience scare you off men?" he asked.

"Sexually, you mean? No." Julia shook her head. "I didn't even realize the full extent of what had happened to Franny until I was old enough to deal with it. Besides, I had a great role model at home. My dad's a devoted husband and father. So, no, I never lumped all men together with Franny's stepfather. He was vile and sick. But he's one person. This isn't about my being afraid of men."

"It's about not selling yourself short," Connor supplied. "You want to have a full-blown relationship rather than just sex. You want to trust and like the person you're sleeping with. And you want to have a meeting of the minds and the emotions, as well as the bodies."

"Corny as it sounds, yes." Julia searched his face. He didn't seem to be mocking her. Still, she wished they'd had this conversation earlier—when they hadn't yet slept together and the idealistic principles she was spouting would still have sounded believable. "Like I said, there are very few things left to dream about. Making love with a man I cared about was one of those dreams for me. I didn't want to compromise, experience just the sex and not the emotions. It might sound ridiculous, especially since I just fell into bed with you after two dates, but it's the truth. I didn't plan on the profound attraction between us. I thought it would be minds and hearts first, passion second. I guess I was a fool."

"And now you're sorry?"

"No, I'm not sorry, I'm just . . . changed. Like you said, monkey wrenches do that to you. I just didn't anticipate this one. Not just the pull between us but how incredible it would be when we . . ." Her voice trailed off, the aura between them taking on that charged quality.

"Made love," Connor finished for her. His expression

was no longer unreadable. It was tender, and there was a heated look in his eyes. His fingertip traced her cheekbones, caressed her lower lip. "Go ahead and call it that, because that's what it was. We didn't just fall into bed, Julia, we wanted to be here. It might have happened faster than you planned, but there's nothing casual about what's happening between us. As for the order of things, I'd say it all happened together, like an avalanche."

He lowered his head, kissed the hollow at the base of her throat. "For the record, I think you're amazing." He moved to kiss her collarbone. "You're also the most honest, genuine human being I've ever met." A trail of kisses down the side of her neck. "You're intelligent and sensitive, and I have a pretty good idea what makes you tick." He shifted, his lips gliding down, brushing the upper swell of her breasts, then lower, tracing the delicate expanse of cleavage. "That takes care of the liking and trusting, as well as the meeting of the minds and emotions, right?"

Julia's breath was coming faster. The awkwardness of their heavy conversation was vanishing beneath the sensations Connor was wreaking on her with his touch. And everything he was saying rang true. "Right," she managed.

"As for the passion . . ." Connor tugged the blanket out of her unresisting hands, flung it aside. "I've never wanted anyone like this, to the point where it consumes me." He shifted to his knees, bent over her breast, and wet her nipple with the tip of his tongue. "I get hard every time I think about you—and I think about you at the most inopportune times, like in the middle of a business meeting." His lips surrounded her nipple, tugged at it, sending tiny jolts of pleasure darting through her.

She whimpered, arching against him.

"I took a cold shower Saturday night," Connor muttered thickly, shifting to her other breast, nuzzling it with his lips. "I'm thirty-five years old, and I took a cold shower. Worse, I've taken one every night since. Tonight, I could barely get my clothes off in time. And when I finally got inside that beautiful body of yours . . ." His tongue lashed across her nipple, tugged the hardened peak into his mouth. He paused, savored her cry of pleasure. "It was more than incredible. It was explosive, like hurtling into the sun. I felt it as much as you did. But Julia . . ." He raised his head, met her dazed stare. "This time's going to be even better."

"Is it?" Julia's body was screaming to life, and she could hardly speak.

"Um-hum." He raised himself up, tangling his hands in her hair and tugging her mouth up to his. "Remember I said you deserved to be lingered over for hours? Those hours are about to start."

"Now?" she whispered, her palms gliding down his chest, exploring his muscled torso, then slipping lower.

Connor's breath hissed out between his teeth as her fingers closed around his erection. "*Definitely* now."

18

~

Julia was sound asleep when Connor eased out of bed and began pulling on his clothes. He glanced down at her, feeling an odd tangle of emotions in his chest. She looked like a sleeping angel, her expression serene, her hair a disheveled waterfall on the pillow. He was half tempted to chuck his clothes aside and climb back into bed, make love to her again, and go to sleep with her in his arms.

But common sense prevailed, reminding him that it would be ill advised, at least this time. The reality was, it was almost two A.M., and he had to get back to Stephen's house. He hadn't spoken with his brother all day. That made him uneasy. Not to mention that he didn't want Brian waking up in the morning and finding him gone, probably assuming he'd returned to Manhattan. That was the last thing the poor kid needed. He had enough instability to deal with. To top that off, once Brian saw for himself that his uncle hadn't left but had spent the night elsewhere, he'd have a million questions—questions Connor wasn't remotely equipped to answer.

Besides, Julia had to be fit to teach in the morning. As it was, he'd worn her out. If he stayed, she wouldn't get any sleep. He couldn't keep his hands off her.

His gaze returned to the bed as he finished buttoning his shirt, and he stood quietly, watching Julia sleep. The night had yielded a hell of a lot more than he'd expected. Things had spun completely out of control. *He'd* spun completely out of control. For someone accustomed to being in the driver's seat, that was an uneasy first. Talk about being thrown for a loop.

Then there was another issue, one that had inserted itself in his mind more than once since he'd realized Julia's sexual experience wasn't limited, it was nil. And that was the issue of protection. He hadn't used any, not once during their long hours in bed. Another uneasy first. He'd been stupid and careless, and, what was worse, he hadn't done a damned thing to correct it.

They'd have to talk about this. Right away, tomorrow, before another night arrived and they lost their minds again.

He leaned over the bed, brushing a gentle kiss against the side of Julia's mouth. She made a soft sound and rolled onto her back. He kissed her again, more deeply this time.

Her lashes fluttered and lifted. "Connor?" She looked dazed, confused.

"It's late," he murmured against her parted lips. "I've got to go. Otherwise, you'll have to explain to Brian where his uncle spent the night."

She smiled, returning his kiss with a reluctant sigh. "You're right. What time is it?"

"A little before two." He tucked the blanket around her, more as a self-imposed barrier for himself than for her. All he wanted was to climb back into that bed, bury himself inside her, and damn the world to hell. "Go back to sleep. I'll call you tomorrow."

"Um-m-m . . ." Her eyelids drooped. "Would you set my alarm?" she mumbled.

He reached over to the clock radio on her night table and flipped the alarm switch on. "Done. And I'll close the door behind me. Anything else?"

No answer.

A corner of Connor's mouth lifted. She was already asleep.

He left the bedroom, scooped up his jacket, and headed for the door.

It wasn't until he was in his car that he pulled his cell phone out of his pocket, turned it back on, and checked it for messages.

There were five. All from Stephen. All frantic.

He was still listening to his brother's strung-out pleas to call when he zoomed out of the parking lot and headed off.

The house was eerily silent when Connor walked in. Not two-thirty in the morning silent, but weird silent, as if the household was in crisis rather than asleep. The upstairs was pitch dark, which meant Stephen was somewhere on the first level.

Connor moved from room to room, peering through the darkness to find his brother. He didn't want to call out and wake Brian, but he was getting more antsy by the minute.

He reached the family room and stopped. A single table lamp was on. And by its limited amount of light, he could see that Stephen was sprawled on the sofa, one arm thrown over his eyes as if he'd fallen into a reluctant, troubled, and most probably drunken sleep.

"Stephen."

His brother started awake the minute Connor said his name. He struggled to a sitting position, rubbing his eyes. "Connor, what time is it?"

"Two-thirty."

"Where've you been? And what's wrong with your cell phone?"

"I was tied up. And I turned it off." Connor flipped on another light. Then he headed toward the sofa, fully intending to shake away the alcohol effects clouding his brother's head. "What happened? Is Brian okay?"

"That depends on what you mean by okay." Stephen rose, waving Connor off. "I'm dead sober. I haven't touched a drink all night. I've been too out of my mind to think of liquor."

An icy premonition shot up Connor's spine. "Why?"

"They're gone." Stephen's expression was tortured. "Nancy took Brian and left."

"Left, as in left *you?*" Connor's jaw dropped. "That's impossible. I saw them around lunchtime. Nancy had taken Brian to the doctor's. She wasn't planning on doing anything all day but spooning doses of antibiotic down your son's throat and watching videos with him."

"That was then." Stephen raked a hand through his hair. "A lot happened after that."

"I called your office twice. Celeste said you were tied up."

"I was. I was trying to figure out a way to get to Philip Walker. Unfortunately, he got to me first." Stephen filled Connor in on the afternoon's events—the note and package Nancy had received, her urgent phone call to him, and the biting argument that had ensued.

"Damn," Connor muttered. "Walker is one twisted bastard. Delivering Brian's cap to your door and freaking the hell out of Nancy as a way to get to you—that's pretty extreme. As for her reaction, that couldn't have come as a surprise. You should have told her the whole story last night."

"I should have done a lot of things, but I didn't." Stephen blew out his breath. "Anyway, when she called me, she was a total wreck. At first, she shouted accusations—all justifiable. After that, she got very quiet. Too quiet. She told me it was over. Then she hung up. It should have dawned on me that she might do something like this. But my entire focus was on finding a way to protect Brian. I spent the next few hours on the phone with the PI I hired. He's busting his ass to get me information on Walker—yesterday, if possible. He also has a colleague who used to be in police surveillance. I got hold of him around dinnertime and hired him to keep an eye on Brian. After that, I came home. I found this." He handed Connor a sheet of paper.

Connor took Nancy's note and scanned it. It said that she and Brian were fine but that she'd reached the end of her rope, in terms of both her tolerance for Stephen's compulsion and her fear for Brian's life. She said she'd taken Brian somewhere safe, that she'd be in touch, and that she and Stephen would work out the details of their respective futures *after* Walker was dealt with and Brian was no longer in danger.

With a hard sigh, Connor handed back the note. "Looking for them would be a lousy idea. You'd open up a can of worms, alerting too many people, including Walker. That would put Brian at an even greater risk. Besides, Nancy doesn't want to be found. The threat to Brian came out of left field. It pushed her over the edge."

"Yeah." Stephen didn't dispute his brother's words.

He looked pretty much over the edge himself. "But Nancy's state of mind isn't what kept me from going after them. My first reaction was to call up every person we know, every relative Nancy has, until I got a lead on her whereabouts. But what you said about the can of worms I'd be opening, that's what stopped me. If I initiate a search, the press will get hold of this, and so will Walker. I can't let that happen. I've got to protect my family, even if it means going crazy in the process. Which is what I've been doing—pacing around the house, doing nothing but wracking my brain for another alternative. And calling you. I wanted your input. Maybe I just wanted to hear another human voice, one I could trust. I've got nowhere else to turn. Christ, Connor, everything is unraveling . . ." Stephen's voice broke. "I've never heard Nancy sound like that. Like a haunted stranger. It scared the hell out of me. And when I got home and she and Brian were gone . . ." He swallowed hard. "No matter how bad things got, I never really believed she'd leave me. I guess I was a stupid, insensitive jerk."

"I wouldn't go that far." Connor's mind was racing, worrying about Stephen, worrying about Brian and Nancy, worrying about the situation with Walker. "Sometimes it takes having a bucket of ice water dumped on our heads before we open our eyes. You love your wife. You lost sight of that. Now you've regained it. Once she's back here, you'll have to show her. It's not going to be easy. You'll need professional help—for your gambling problem and your marriage. If you get it, I really think you can fix things. But, Stephen, no matter how your marriage plays out, Nancy would never keep you and Brian apart. Not once she's sure he's safe. You're his father, and a damned good one. Nancy knows that. She'll bring him back."

Stephen nodded, staring at the carpet. Abruptly, he raised his head and met Connor's gaze. His eyes were damp. "I'd chuck it all, you know," he said quietly. "If it meant keeping Nancy and Brian safe, I'd call the police, implicate myself, and screw my whole political future. But I have no proof that Brian's in any danger or that it's Walker who sent that package. All I have is my word that he's blackmailing me. That's enough for an investigation and a scandal. But it's not enough for a conviction. We know Walker has men out there; they're the ones who pounded me. What if he gets ticked off and sends his goons after Brian just to punish me? It's too great a risk."

Connor stared at his brother, hearing a different Stephen, a man who was actually willing to own up to his weaknesses and pay the price. A man who'd sacrifice it all for his family.

Maybe there was hope after all.

"I agree," Connor replied. "Involving the police at this time would be a mistake. We've got nothing concrete to report, and we might piss off Walker. At best, the scandal would eat our family alive. No. It seems to me that Nancy plucked Brian out of the line of fire by dropping out of sight. Let's use this time to bring Walker down."

"Time? What time? Walker expects me to come through by Thursday," Stephen reminded him bitterly.

"I know." Connor could actually feel the minutes ticking by. "Is there anything you can say to stall him? Anything he'd buy?"

"Walker understands one language: blackmail."

"Fine. Then use it."

Stephen shot his brother an irritated look. "What do you think I spent the past two days trying to do?"

"I'm not talking about getting something on Walker. I'm talking about telling him you're trying to get something on others—like two of your city councilmen."

Irritation transformed to comprehension. "You're saying I should tell him I'm digging into those councilmen's backgrounds and that I'm on the verge of uncovering a few skeletons they'd like to keep hidden."

"Um-hum. Badly enough to throw their votes your way. That's a technique Walker can relate to."

Stephen nodded slowly. "It might work. At least long enough to buy me a few more days."

"With any luck, that's all we'll need." Connor ran a hand over his jaw. "You said you hired a PI. Who?"

"The same guy Dad used to check out Braxton. I didn't give him too many background details, just in case his loyalties are with Dad rather than me. Just the basics, more than enough to go on. As for the surveillance guy, he knows only that someone's sent a threat or two my way, pointedly mentioning my son. Again, I didn't get into specifics."

"Smart move. In the meantime, I'll access my own network of contacts the minute the sun comes up. They're discreet. They'll check out Walker's company." Connor frowned. "Speaking of Dad, he'll be here in about thirty hours. We've got to decide how to handle him."

"I don't want him knowing anything about Walker," Stephen said adamantly.

"I realize that. But you know Dad; he's got the instincts of a fox. He'll pick up on the tension the minute he walks in the door. Plus, you've got to explain where

Nancy and Brian are." Connor thought for a minute. "We'll come up with something. A vacation, maybe, or a trip to visit one of Nancy's relatives. That story will work for everyone, including the press. No one knows Brian's sick, so they won't think it's weird that Nancy took him away . . ." Connor's voice trailed off as a realization struck. "Shit."

Stephen's head shot up. "What is it?"

"Julia. What do we tell her? She knows Brian's got an earache. She's expecting him to be home recuperating, then back at school in a day or two."

"Great." Stephen shook his head in frustration. "Now I've got Julia Talbot to worry about. Fine. I'll go see her tomorrow, tell her the earache was a false alarm, not an infection after all. I'll tell her the vacation story. I'll say Nancy took Brian away to ease the tension he's been feeling from the election campaign. That should please her, since she's so worried about him."

"It won't work."

"Why the hell not?"

"Because Julia *knows* Brian's earache was an infection."

"How? You saw her this morning. Nancy hadn't taken him to the doctor yet . . ."

"I saw her again tonight."

"Tonight? When? I thought you just came from some business meeting that ran half the night."

"I never said that. All I said was that I was tied up and that I'd turned off my cell phone."

Connor's words sank in, and for the first time, Stephen took a good, hard look at his brother. "Wow," he commented, noting Connor's rumpled appearance. "You're in a lot deeper than I realized."

"Yeah, a lot deeper than I realized, too." Connor didn't mince words. His brother wasn't a fool. Besides, his wheels were turning again. "Julia's going to be worried sick when she hears Brian's gone. I won't add insult to injury by lying to her about the reasons behind his disappearance. I'll just tell her it's a personal matter and ask for her cooperation. That'll have to do."

"But will she go along with it? If she voices any suspicions to her principal, or if Cheryl Lager shows up on her doorstep again, pushes her too hard . . ."

"Julia won't say anything."

Stephen shot his brother a questioning look. "Because of her feelings for you?"

"No, because of her feelings for Brian. Me?" Connor gave a humorless laugh. "When I lay this one on her, she'll probably punch me out."

19

April 11
6:55 A.M.

The diner was a dump. Indeed, *diner* was a misnomer, because what the place really was was a broken-down truck stop, used primarily by the drivers of eighteen-wheelers when they needed a caffeine fix. They'd stop off to refill their thermoses with coffee strong enough to carry them for a couple of hundred miles. The mud this place served filled the bill.

It also served Cliff's purpose. It was directly off the highway, just ten miles south of Leaf Brook. And he would bet his bottom dollar that he wouldn't run into a familiar face, not in this dive.

He held out his cup so the frazzled waitress could refill it. It was his third round of mud so far. Worse, he'd probably down the whole thing before his seven o'clock meeting got under way.

He set down the cup, rubbing the back of his neck and trying to stay calm. He'd never dreamed things would go this far. The blackmail they'd used to secure his help had been a vile fabrication. They'd gone right for his Achilles heel. And they'd exploited it—successfully. The pictures had hit too close to home for him to slough off. They'd damned well have hit too close to home for Stephen to slough off. Their friendship would have been shattered,

Harrison Stratford would have written him off, and Nancy's life would have become a living hell.

He'd given in for all those reasons. Mostly for Nancy and because he was weak. But now . . . A vein throbbed at his temple. Violent assaults? Threatening a child's life?

Christ, what had he set in motion?

The front door swung open, and Greg Matthews walked in. He scanned the diner, spotted Cliff, and headed over.

"What is it?" Greg glanced disdainfully at the torn chair before sitting down. "Why did you need to see me so early? And why did you sound like a time bomb about to go off?"

"Because I feel like one." Cliff's entire head was throbbing, and he leaned forward, pressing both fists to the table. "Stephen's face was all torn up yesterday."

"Yeah, I know. He said something about cutting it when he was trying to fix his car."

"Bullshit." Cliff wasn't playing this game. "His lip was swollen, and he winced every time he moved. Someone beat the crap out of him. I told myself to look the other way. I tried to believe he was telling the truth and that anything more sinister was all in my mind. But it wasn't, was it? Any more than it was all in my mind that Brian's baseball cap was delivered to Nancy's door yesterday. Which, by the way, scared her to death. Just as you and Walker planned."

Greg's eyes narrowed. "I'd be careful about the accusations you throw around, counselor."

"Or what? You'll show those doctored photos to Stephen? Make him believe I was in bed with his wife? You played that card already, Matthews. It won't work again."

One brow rose. "It worked pretty well the first time, if I remember right. It got you to tell me about the mayor's little gambling problem." Greg's expression hardened. "It's not my fault if the women you take to bed are all dead ringers for Nancy Stratford. It didn't take much to dummy up those shots or to get you worried. If you didn't have the hots for the mayor's wife, you wouldn't have gone so nuts. You just would have blown me off, gone to Stratford, and told him the truth. But you didn't. Because you know there's a chance he wouldn't believe you. Hell, even *I* don't believe you, and I know the shots are phony. So it's not a question of my needing a new incentive for you. The old one works fine." A tight smile. "Look at the bright side. If the tension at home gets too much and the mayor's marriage breaks up, you'll get a chance at the real thing."

"Stay the hell away from Nancy. And Brian. He's a kid, Matthews. For God's sake, is Walker desperate enough about getting his parking contract to hurt a seven-year-old?"

Greg shrugged. "You'll have to ask him. I'm just the city manager."

"Yeah, right. A city manager who gets huge kickbacks from a gangster." Cliff took another gulp of coffee. "You and Walker have finagled him into exactly the position he wants. Stephen will make sure he gets that contract, especially now. And I'll keep my mouth shut—as long as Walker backs off the threats and violence. If he doesn't, all bets are off. I won't stand by and see people get hurt, especially a little boy."

"Now, *that* sounds like a threat." Greg folded his hands on the table. "And if it is, I'd reconsider. Especially when it comes to Philip Walker. I hear he has quite a temper." A probing look. "So, will the mayor be coming into the office today? Or is he staying home, guarding his family?"

"He's got no one to guard, thanks to Walker's scare tactics. Nancy took Brian and bolted. That's the other thing you should know. Tell Walker he's got one less way to yank Stephen's chain. Nancy and Brian left Leaf Brook."

"Really?" Greg looked intrigued. "And who told you this?"

Silence.

"Ah, the good Mrs. Stratford herself. So, tell me, where did she take her son?"

"Do you honestly believe I'd tell you that, even if I knew?"

"Probably not." Greg shrugged. "Never mind. Wherever they are, their taking off is a good thing. It'll give Stratford the incentive he needs to kick some of those councilmen's butts and get Walker his deal. Once that happens, you're off the hook."

"It's not me I'm worried about."

"Isn't it?"

Cliff glanced at the grimy clock on the diner wall. He'd made his point, given Matthews the facts he wanted passed on to Walker. It should shift Walker's focus off using Nancy and Brian's safety as bait to twist Stephen's arm.

Either way, he had to leave. Now. The pharmacy opened at eight, and he wanted to pick up Brian's amoxyl and head up to Stowe ASAP.

He pushed back his chair and rose. "I've got to get going."

"A client?"

"An errand." Cliff's stare was icy. "Just give Walker my message. He'll get his contract. But no more violence. And leave Nancy and Brian alone."

Greg waited until Cliff had left. Then he punched up Walker's number.

"Henderson just left," he announced. "According to him, Nancy Stratford packed up her son and took off yesterday, right after the package arrived."

"Interesting," Walker murmured. "That explains why she didn't come home last night. The guy I've got watching the house said she drove away with her kid at around a quarter to six and hasn't been back. Henderson was with her up to the last minute. He drove away right before she did." A pensive pause. "Now, the question is, was she just running away, or was she leaving her husband for good? Where did Henderson say she was headed?"

"He didn't. Or, rather, wouldn't."

"Wouldn't," Walker clarified flatly. Another pause. "You say he insisted on meeting you first thing this morning?"

"Yup. He actually wanted to meet earlier than this. I told him no."

"I see. And where was he was going next that he had to meet at such an ungodly hour?"

"To run an errand."

"That's what I figured. He's probably on his way to check up on Mrs. Stratford. Follow him. See where the lady's hiding. The knowledge might come in handy."

"Okay." Greg had had that very thought himself. He was already heading for the door.

Walker gave a triumphant chuckle, as if he were playing some challenging game of cat and mouse—and winning. "In the meantime, I'll check in with the good mayor, remind him that tomorrow's Thursday. I'll make sure to ask how his little boy's doing. That should light a fire under his ass."

"Are you going to hold him to the deadline?"

"That depends on how close he is to coming through for me. I might give him a few more days. I can't lose sight of what I want. And the fact that it's potentially mine until the final vote's over. Besides, it's fun to watch Stratford squirm."

"I'm sure it is." Greg was only half listening. Hovering inside the diner's front door, he watched as Cliff got into his car. "Just so you know, Henderson was making noise about telling Stratford the truth if there was any more violence."

Walker grunted, clearly unruffled by that news. "I admire a man with loyalties. But Henderson doesn't pose any threat, except to himself. Let him tell Stratford whatever he wants. The only news flash he can offer the mayor that he doesn't already know is who blabbed about his gambling and why. And that would shoot only one person in the foot: Henderson himself."

"I agree. Just wanted to keep you posted." Greg tensed as Cliff's backup lights went on and his car zipped into reverse, then zoomed out of the lot onto the highway. "Henderson just left. I'm on my way. I'll check in later."

8:17 A.M.

Julia was late.

Connor propped his hip against her car, glancing at

his watch, then back at her apartment building. The drive from her place to school was about fifteen minutes. So even if she left right now, she wouldn't get to her desk until after eight-thirty. She'd obviously overslept.

And he was the reason why.

He raked a hand through his hair, wishing like hell that he didn't have to tell her about this latest development. The conversation he'd planned as a followup to last night was a far cry from the one they were about to have.

The light in her apartment window was still on. She was awake but not ready. He could go across the street, buzz, and go up, but he didn't want to demean last night's memories by walking into the intimacy he'd left just six hours earlier and laying this bombshell on her.

Instead, he'd wait out here until she came out and then lay the bombshell on her.

Dammit.

He yanked the morning paper out from beneath his arm, scanning the pages to pass the time. Automatically, he flipped to the political section, grimacing as he saw that the most frequent byline belonged to Cheryl Lager. That woman had an opinion on everything and no qualms about sharing it.

A piece of hers at the bottom of the page caught his eye. She'd reported on the municipal parking contract proposal that was under consideration and would be voted on next week at the city council meeting. She cited reliable sources as claiming that the council was wrestling with a major decision about whether to keep the contract under city control or allocate it to a private contractor who offered security as part of his proposal. She made a few pointed comments about the recent increased number of car thefts in city-run lots, implying that perhaps a private source would do a better job of protecting the residents' property than the city had. In three paragraphs, she managed to insult government officials, parking lot attendants, and the Leaf Brook police department.

Typical Cheryl Lager.

With a snort of disgust, Connor crumpled the newspaper and tossed it in the nearest trash can. Great. Just what Stephen needed. Publicity that would generate more pressure and more public opinion. Reliable source—yeah, right. Connor would bet his last dollar that Philip Walker had been the little voice whispering in Cheryl Lager's ear.

The slamming of a door and the sound of hurried footsteps interrupted his thoughts. Connor looked up in time to see Julia sprinting toward her car, shoving papers under her arm as she did.

She came to an abrupt halt when she saw him, a look of surprise darting across her face. "Connor." She walked over to him. "What are you doing here?" A tiny smile curved her lips. "I'd think you slept in my parking lot, except you've obviously showered and changed."

He wanted to drag her into his arms and kiss her. Instead, he forced himself just to brush her cheek with his knuckles. She looked fresh and beautiful, even with the shadows of fatigue beneath her eyes.

"I have to talk to you," he said without preamble. "I wanted to catch you before you left for school, partly because I wanted some privacy for what I have to say and partly because I didn't want you to be blindsided."

Julia heard the gravity of his tone, and her smile vanished. "What is it?"

"It's Brian. Nancy's taken him away for a while. Until they return, he won't be in school."

Her eyes widened in shock. "Taken him away—why? Where? Is he sicker than we originally thought?"

This was even harder than he'd expected. "Nothing like that. The story we're giving the press is that Nancy's sister in California took a bad fall and will be incapacitated for a few weeks. Nancy and Brian flew out there to help and so Brian could spend some time with his cousins."

Julia shook her head, as if she couldn't process what Connor was saying. "You must be wrong. California? That doesn't make sense. Brian has an ear infection. Flying would be painful *and* dangerous. Mrs. Stratford would never . . ." Suddenly, Connor's choice of words sank in. "The story you're *giving* the press?" She leaned against her car. "In other words, the lie you're supplying."

Connor didn't deny it. "Julia, listen to me. I need your help. You're the only person outside the family who knows Brian has an ear infection, except for his pediatrician and pharmacist, and they're bound by confidentiality. I know he missed a day of school, but we can explain that away by saying his earache was a false alarm and that when the phone call came from Nancy's sister, she packed him up and went. I'm asking you please to go along with this story and not to make waves."

"Why?" She bit out the word.

"For Brian's sake. That's all I can say. This involves a family crisis, one I can't discuss. You've got to trust me."

"Trust you?" Julia looked torn between fury and tears. "You told me Brian was okay, that his parents were completely committed to his emotional well-being. You led

me to believe that there'd been a turning point in whatever was going on. Just last night, you sat across the table from me and claimed . . ." She broke off, sucking in her breath as if she'd been struck. "Tell me something, Connor," she said in a cold, distant tone. "Just when did Mrs. Stratford and Brian leave for their cross-country trip?"

A heartbeat of silence.

"When?" she demanded.

Connor swallowed, but he didn't avert his gaze. "Last night."

"Last night. While you were in my bed. Diverting me so I wouldn't mess things up by trying to see or speak with Nancy Stratford."

"Goddammit, no!" Connor grabbed Julia's arm, gripping it tightly as she tried to pull away. "That's not the way it was. I had no idea Nancy was leaving. I'd never use you like that."

"Right." Tears glistened on her lashes, and she fought for control, managing to free her arm and fumble with her keys until she unlocked her car. "Yet another lie. You Stratfords know every move the others make. Whatever's going on must be a real whopper of a scandal. Did your brother send his wife and son away, or did they take off on their own?"

It was a rhetorical question, one they both knew Connor wasn't going to answer. Nor did Julia wait for his response.

She groped for the handle of the car door, yanking at it—futilely, since Connor was holding the door shut. "As for me, I was your fly in the ointment, a potential obstacle you had to divert. Well, you certainly did that effectively. Congratulations. Mission accomplished. Now, get out of my way so I can go to school."

Connor refused to budge. "Not until you listen to me."

"I've listened to you enough," she snapped, shoving at him. "Don't worry. I won't upset your little scheme. I wouldn't do that to Brian. Whatever's going on, he's safer wherever his mother's taken him. And if she's smart, she'll keep him there. Now, get out of my way! We have nothing to say to each other."

Whipping her around, Connor jerked up her chin. "You're not writing me off."

"Watch me."

"Julia . . ."

"Don't try to convince me I mean something to you. It would be an even bigger lie than the one you just told me. *And* an insult. I mean as little to you as you do to me."

His teeth clenched with frustration. "*Now* who's lying?"

Naked pain flashed across her face. "You bastard. Whatever I felt for you, you just killed. Now, get away from me. I want nothing to do with you again, ever."

"What if you're pregnant?" He blurted out the words in desperation.

And wished he could recall them the minute he saw Julia's reaction.

She went sheet-white, and he could feel her start to tremble. "I'm not," she refuted.

"Are you sure?" He was fighting for something that meant more to him than even he'd realized. "I climaxed inside you three times last night. I wasn't wearing a condom. I doubt you're on the pill."

Carefully, she schooled her features. "You're right, I'm not. But you don't have to worry. I may be inexperienced, but I'm not uneducated. I just finished my period. Pregnancy is out."

"Unlikely, maybe, but not out." Connor held her gaze. "If you are pregnant, that child is mine."

"Fine." She jerked open her car door. "In that unlikely event, I'll send you a birth announcement. And don't expect to see the name Stratford on it. Good-bye, Connor."

She jumped into the car, turning the key in the ignition even before the door was shut. She threw the car into reverse, and Connor had to leap out of the way to avoid being hit as she shifted into drive, floored the gas, and tore out of the lot.

20

Later, Julia wondered how she'd made it through the school day.

She operated on autopilot, handing out papers, teaching the number seven multiplication tables, supervising recess. The kids seemed to sense that she was upset, because they were unusually well behaved, right down to curtailing their usual fight over who got to erase the blackboard.

Even Robin kept her distance. She approached Julia at recess and asked about her date with Connor.

"It's over," Julia bit out. "In every sense of the word. End of subject."

Seeing the dark circles beneath her friend's eyes, the tight line of her mouth, Robin frowned. "Julia, are you okay?"

"No, but I will be." Julia turned and walked away.

It didn't get better as the day progressed. The fabricated story about Brian's long-term visit to his aunt trickled through the school. Near the end of the day, Jack Billard, Julia's oh-so-accommodating principal who loved the fact that the mayor's son attended his school—and the publicity that generated—visited her classroom to suggest that she put together a pile of work for Brian.

He "urged" her to write down the assignments she'd be covering for the rest of that week, clip the assignment sheet to the necessary textbooks, and deliver the whole package to the mayor, so he could send it on to Brian.

"Did the mayor request this?" Julia asked.

Jack frowned his displeasure. "Not yet. But he's very committed to Brian's education. So I'd like to anticipate his request."

Slowly, Julia blew out her breath. "All right, but I'll need some time to go through my lesson plans and print out all the worksheets that'll be supplementing my textbook assignments. Is tomorrow too late to drop everything off? I doubt Brian will be diving into his schoolwork the minute he steps off the plane." She almost choked on the last, knowing how phony it was.

Definitely placated, Jack nodded. "Great. You can take everything over to the municipal building first thing in the morning. I'll arrange for your class to be covered until you get in."

"Fine." Julia leaned back in her chair. "Wouldn't you rather take the material over there yourself?"

"Too obvious," he answered. "I don't want the mayor to think I'm brown-nosing."

Even though you are, Julia thought silently.

She spent a half hour after school printing out worksheets and getting Brian's books together. She decided to write up the assignment sheet at home, since her head was pounding so badly she could scarcely think. She needed a hot bath, two Tylenol, and a few quiet hours by herself to think. It wouldn't erase the pain that was wrenching her heart like a vise, but it might at least give her some perspective. And maybe a shred of peace.

Peace was, apparently, not yet to be had.

As if she hadn't already endured enough torment for one day, Julia walked out of the building at four P.M. to find Cheryl Lager waiting beside her car.

"Ah, Ms. Talbot," she said brightly. "I've been hoping to get a word with you."

The end of her rope was fast approaching, and Julia was about to snap. "I'm very tired, Ms. Lager. And I can't imagine what we have to discuss."

"Brian Stratford, of course. Did you know his mother was taking him on this trip?"

Ice glittered in Julia's eyes. "Mrs. Stratford doesn't have to run her parental decisions or her travel plans by me. Besides, from what I understand, there was a family emergency. So I doubt Mrs. Stratford herself knew she'd be going." Leaning past Cheryl Lager, she unlocked her car, thinking that this was the second time today she'd had to bypass someone physically to get into her vehicle.

It hurt too much to think about the first time.

"Don't you think the timing of this trip is a little too coincidental?" Ms. Lager persisted.

"Emergencies don't happen on cue. That's why they call them emergencies. And what I think is that you should stick to the facts and avoid innuendo. Now, if you'll excuse me . . ." Julia jumped into her car.

Cheryl Lager wedged a hip against the open door. "If you don't want to talk about Brian Stratford, perhaps we can chat about his uncle. Rumor has it you're seeing Connor Stratford. Is that true? It would certainly explain why you're so eager to protect their family."

Julia felt bile rise in her throat. She raised her head, forcing herself to mask all emotions but outrage. "I resent your accusation," she replied in a tone of controlled rage. "In fact, I'd say it constitutes slander. Now, get out of my way, or I'll file charges." She tugged at her door until she shook Cheryl Lager loose.

Thirty seconds later, she was out of the school parking lot and on her way home.

It was a good thing Cheryl Lager didn't try to follow her. The way Julia felt, she might have run her off the road. The woman's nasty intimations were beyond slimy journalism. Slimy would be questioning Julia about her relationship with Connor, poking around like some tabloid columnist looking for a juicy piece of gossip. But implying that Julia was part of some Stratford conspiracy? Now, that was over the top. Julia had had just about enough of Cheryl Lager. One more interrogation like that, and she *would* press charges.

She turned onto the main road, thinking about the dark irony of Cheryl Lager's question. Seeing Connor Stratford, she mused bitterly. Now, *that* was an oxymoron if ever there was one. She doubted anyone ever really saw Connor. He was such a polished enigma, she doubted anyone knew him at all.

Flashes of last night stabbed at her brain with each throb of her head. Flashes that she'd cherished just hours ago and now seemed mocking and dirty.

Liking. Trusting.

Well, they'd certainly touched on those subjects, she remembered, tears stinging her eyes. The problem was that all they'd discussed was *his* liking, *his* trusting. They'd never actually gotten around to talking about *her* gnawing doubts about *him*. So not only was the man an enigma, he was a master at manipulation. Not to mention a master at seduction. She'd fallen like a stone.

Talk about casting a sinister light on a beautiful night.

Here she'd been, throwing herself into whatever magic she thought was happening between them, and Connor had just been keeping her busy while Brian was ushered away. Which, by his definition of what mattered, made a world of sense. Given her concerns about Brian's state of mind, her persistence about contacting his mother, she was a loose cannon. The Stratfords couldn't risk her showing up on their doorstep, screwing up their well-planned vanishing act, now, could they?

Julia arrived home with a headache that had erupted into a full-scale migraine. She stumbled into her apartment, tossing her mail onto the kitchen table. Then she swallowed two Tylenol and went into the bathroom to run the water. She passed by the answering machine and saw that she had three messages. Great. Now what?

The first message, left around two o'clock, was from her mother, letting her know that Friday night's workshop had to be canceled because their scheduled speaker, FBI Special Agent Patricia Avalon, expert in crimes against children, had been called away on an emergency. Normally, Julia would have been disappointed. This particular time, she was relieved. She wasn't up for the atrocities Special Agent Avalon would undoubtedly be discussing. Nor was she up for having coffee with her mother afterward. The woman had a way of seeing right through her. And she was not ready to discuss Connor.

The next message had come in at two-forty-five. It was from Greg. The faraway quality of his voice and the background road noise told her he was calling from the car. All he said was that he realized he wouldn't catch her at home yet, but he'd love to hear from her tonight or tomorrow so they could make plans to get a drink or catch a movie together sometime over the weekend.

Now, *that* sounded uncomplicated enough—friendship and light conversation. She might very well take Greg up on it. But she wouldn't call him back tonight. Tonight she needed her space.

The third message, left five minutes ago, was from Connor.

"Julia, pick up," he commanded. A long pause. "Goddammit, are you there? If you are, pick up. I have to talk to you." He sucked in his breath. "Okay, maybe you're not home yet. You didn't leave school until late. I know because I came by to see you, but that vulture was waiting at your car. I don't want to give her any more to exploit us with, so I left. But you and I need to talk." Another pause. "I'm not going away. Not until you listen to me. So call my cell phone as soon as you get in. Or I'll call you, all night if I have to."

Click.

Julia stared at the answering machine, tears dampening her lashes. Then she pressed ERASE and headed for the bathroom.

True to his word, Connor called every hour on the hour, leaving terse messages that escalated in anger and frustration as the evening wore on.

Julia ignored them, going through the motions of taking her bath, nibbling on a sandwich, organizing Brian's work to give to his father tomorrow.

She wondered where Brian was, where Nancy Stratford had taken him, and, yes, why. Whatever was pressuring Mayor Stratford was obviously a lot more serious than she'd realized. She prayed that Brian would be better off with this temporary change in environment, that whatever was wrong would be quickly fixed, and that the solution would bring Brian back home soon. She missed him already.

That led to another line of thought, one she'd desperately tried to avoid but no longer could.

Her palm strayed to her abdomen, resting there a moment. She could still hear Connor's voice, bluntly reminding her that she might be pregnant.

It wasn't as if she hadn't considered the possibility herself. Several times during the predawn hours, when she'd lain awake, staring at the ceiling and reflecting on the hours she and Connor had spent in bed, she'd found herself wondering if the unlikely had happened and she'd conceived.

Would the baby resemble Brian? Would he or she have Brian's quick mind and lovable nature? Would baseball be in his genes, the way it was in Brian's and in hers? Would he have Connor's probing intensity, his ability to read people?

Dammit, no. She wasn't going to think this way.

She yanked away her hand as if she'd been burned. Last night was over, leaving today's reality. It was unlikely that she was pregnant. But if she was, well, she loved children. She'd share all that love with her own baby. Period. End of subject.

Dismissing that line of thought, she turned to the task of finishing up her organization of Brian's assignments. Then she drank a cup of chamomile tea in the hopes of quieting her nerves and headed off to bed.

The ringing of the phone woke her.

Before she was clear-headed enough to process her actions, she groped for the receiver and picked it up. "Hello?"

Connor released his breath in a hiss. "Finally. What

happened? Did you get sick of dealing with a ringing phone, or were you so groggy you forgot not to answer it?"

Julia came fully and abruptly awake. Her gaze fell on the clock. "Connor, it's after midnight."

"I know what time it is. My next call was jacked up for one-fifteen."

The emotions that had been building inside Julia all day burst out in a rush. "Can't you take a hint? I don't want to talk to you. I don't want to listen to you. I'm not interested in anything you have to say. You used me. You lied to me. Those aren't things that can be explained away. Good night."

"Don't you dare hang up," he ordered. "I never used you. Last night was real. You felt it. I know you did. Stop being so goddamn stubborn and accept that."

"Okay, it was real," Julia managed, sitting up in her bed, wishing she could erase the memories of him lying beside her. "For me, anyway. For you, I don't know what it was. I don't know what *you* are." She fought for control. "I notice you didn't deny lying to me. Care to do that?"

"I shaded truths. I never lied."

"Fine. I stand corrected. You shaded truths. And all to protect the glorious Stratford name. By the way, in case you're worrying about it, I didn't tell Cheryl Lager anything. She grilled me about Brian's trip. She even grilled me about us. I blew her off on both counts. Satisfied?"

"She grilled you about *us?*" He was clearly incensed. "What the hell did she want to know?"

"If I was protecting your family because of our personal involvement."

"Shit." Connor ground out the word. He sounded as if

he wanted to punch Cheryl Lager's lights out. "I'm sorry you had to take that. You don't deserve it."

"No, I don't. Then again, we don't always get what we deserve. Like poor Brian, who was whisked away for God knows what reason. He's probably bewildered as hell. My guess is, so's his mother. Are his parents splitting up? Is he going to have to deal with a broken home on top of everything else?"

"Julia, I didn't call to talk about Brian. Or about Nancy and Stephen. I called to talk about us."

"Ah, another of your evasive answers. Well, here's my direct one. There is no us. Therefore, we have nothing to talk about."

"Because you think I was using you last night." Connor's voice was filled with anger and incredulity.

Julia swallowed past the lump in her throat. "Even if you weren't, it doesn't matter. My first instinct was to doubt you. I think that says it all."

"All it says is you were wrong."

"Maybe this time. But there would be others. As I told you, I don't trust you. I doubt I ever will." Abruptly, an even more profound truth struck Julia. "But you know what? This isn't just about *my* trust. It's about *yours*. You don't trust anyone, Connor. You never learned how."

Quietly, she replaced the receiver in its cradle.

21

April 12
8:45 A.M.

Connor refilled his coffee cup, then strode over to Stephen's panoramic office window, staring out at nothing. "So Walker called yesterday?"

"Uh-huh. Late last night. He called the house. You'd already gone to bed."

"I heard the phone. I hoped maybe it was Nancy."

Stephen dropped into his desk chair, feeling as if he'd aged ten years this week. "No such luck. I haven't heard a word from her."

"She'll call. Give her time." Connor inclined his head. "What did Walker say?"

"Pretty much what we expected. He reminded me that Thursday was just a few hours away. Then he asked how Brian's pitching was coming along." A pained swallow. "He wanted to know if Brian really held up under pressure. Or if he eventually wore down and needed to have relief sent in."

"Sick bastard. He's taunting you. A little reminder about the package he sent with Brian's baseball cap."

"Yeah, but the good news is, it was just a taunt. He wasn't interested in focusing on Nancy and Brian. It's obvious he knows they're gone. He must have men watching the place. He said something about lending me a bunch of hot videos to keep me occupied while I'm home alone at night during this dry spell, for however long it lasts. Then he got right back to business."

"*Very* sick bastard." Connor took a gulp of coffee. "But I'm glad his attention's off your family. How did you play his reminder about the Thursday deadline?"

"In true Stratford style," Stephen replied bitterly. "I hid my fear. I told him I'd resolve the municipal parking contract in his favor but that I needed a few more days."

"You used our story about the skeletons you're about to dig out of councilmen's closets?"

"Yup." Stephen's tone was derisive. "He actually sounded intrigued by the whole idea. He said he admired my initiative. And he gave me an extension. I've got till Tuesday."

"That's all we need." Connor raked a hand through his hair. "I should have some preliminary answers from my business contacts this afternoon. I could have pressured them to come through this morning, but I didn't think getting calls like that would fly. Not with Dad due to walk in here in fifteen minutes."

"Definitely not. We don't want Dad getting wind of anything. Let's get this tête-à-tête over with. Then we'll concentrate on Walker."

"Agreed." Connor turned to face his brother. "Dad might not have men watching you, but he has a thousand eyes. By now, I'm sure he knows about Nancy and Brian's trip. It was mentioned in this morning's paper."

Stephen gave a humorless laugh. "I never doubted Dad would know. I'm sure he's read every story that concerns me—and there have been many, thanks to our friend Cheryl Lager. He'll have pages of notes to grill me on." Stephen fiddled with a pen. "As for what I tell him about Nancy and Brian, I'll start with the statement we gave the press. Then I'll improvise, depending on his questions and reaction. Just follow my lead."

Connor nodded. "By the way, when this is over, I'm suing Cheryl Lager's ass."

"Feel free." Stephen made a grand sweep with his arm. "You have my blessing."

"She's not just going after us, she's going after Julia. She pounced on her outside the school yesterday, actually accused her of keeping quiet about whatever she knows about Brian's trip because of her personal involvement with me. The vicious bitch. I wouldn't dare try to see Julia at school now, not with Brian away and no justifiable reason for me to be there. Lager's probably lurking in the bushes with a photographer, waiting to snap some shots that would confirm Julia's and my relationship and lend credibility to her conspiracy theory." A frustrated pause. "Not that Julia would speak to me, anyway."

Stephen arched a quizzical brow. "She was pretty pissed off by Cheryl Lager's implications, I take it."

"Among other things, yes."

"She blames you for what's going on?"

"Big time. She thinks I was a decoy sent to distract her while Nancy took off."

"You're kidding."

"Do I look like I'm kidding?"

Stephen studied his brother. "No, you look like you're hurting. You really care about her, don't you?"

Connor blew out his breath. "Let's have this conversation another time, okay? I haven't slept in days, I'm pretty on edge, and I want this meeting with Dad to go well. When's Cliff coming?"

A quick glance at his watch. "Any minute now."

Stephen grimaced. "With any luck, he and Dad have business to go over at lunch. That'll keep this get-together to a minimum."

"Did you tell Cliff the truth about Nancy?"

Stephen shook his head. "He was tied up with some out-of-town client most of the day yesterday. Besides, I don't want to put him in the middle of Nancy and me. He's too damned involved in her life as it is."

"You think it's possible he knows where she is?"

"Maybe." The hard set of Stephen's jaw told Connor he'd thought of this long before now. "But if by some chance she told him, he'd never breach her trust. What's more, if she did tell him, I don't want to know."

There was a brief knock, and Cliff walked in. "Celeste said I should just come in. Are you all set?" he asked, shutting the door behind him.

"As set as I'll ever be." Stephen's gaze was sober as he watched his friend cross over to get some coffee. "I assume you've spoken with my father this morning?"

"Not ten minutes ago. His driver just turned off the parkway at the Leaf Brook exit. He should be here by nine."

Connor was also studying Cliff intently. "You look as lousy as we do. Everything okay?"

Cliff rubbed the back of his neck, weariness etched on his features. "Yeah, I'm just beat. I guess I need some time off."

"Well, you're not getting it today." Stephen realized he'd come off more abruptly than he intended. "Sorry. I'm beat, too. What kind of mood is my father in?"

Cliff shrugged. "It's hard to read him, especially on the phone. We talked for about three minutes. He wanted to finalize details on an acquisition we're working on. He didn't want to waste time doing that while he's here. He sounded pensive and rushed."

"The usual," Stephen muttered.

There was another knock, and the three men exchanged glances.

"Since when does Dad knock?" Connor voiced aloud the thought they were all having.

"Never," Stephen responded. "He just blows by Celeste and walks in. Yes?" he called out.

Celeste poked her head in, her nose wrinkled in apology. "Forgive me, sir, but I completely forgot to mention to you that Ms. Talbot would be stopping by before nine. She said she didn't need to see you, that she could leave Brian's work with me. But since she is Brian's teacher, I thought you should know that she's here, and . . ."

"Send her in," Connor interrupted.

Celeste started, then glanced at the mayor for corroboration.

Stephen gave it with a nod. "Go ahead, Celeste."

He waited until she left, then sent a sidelong look at Connor. "This should be an interesting soap opera. Julia and you, slugging it out. Then Dad will arrive. All that's missing is the popcorn."

"Cute." Connor was scowling. "Did you expect her?"

"No. I didn't ask for Brian's work. I thought I'd wait till he and Nancy were settled. Does Julia know you're here?"

"Hell no." Connor rubbed a palm across his chin. "Or she'd never have come."

A corner of Stephen's mouth lifted. "You really have it bad, don't you?"

Connor wasn't even listening. His eyes were on the door.

An instant later, it opened, and Julia walked in, a shopping bag draped on her arm. "Excuse me for interrupting, Mayor Stratford, but . . ." She saw Connor and stopped, a glimmer of pain flashing in her eyes. "Oh, I didn't realize there was anyone in here with you."

"No problem," Stephen assured her, coming to his feet. "This is my attorney, Cliff Henderson. And you know Connor."

"Yes." Her tone was clipped, and she averted her gaze from Connor's as she shook hands with Cliff.

"My secretary said you brought Brian's work?" Stephen asked, puzzled.

"Yes, a week's assignments." Still ignoring Connor, Julia walked over and handed Stephen the shopping bag. "Mr. Billard thought you might want to send it to Brian in California." She looked as if she might choke on the lie. "That way, he won't be behind when he gets home."

Stephen took the bag, genuine gratitude flickering across his face. "Thanks. To you and Jack. I'm sure Brian will appreciate it."

"How is he?" Julia blurted out, as if she couldn't help herself. "We miss him. Class isn't the same without him. And the baseball team is hurting."

"I miss him, too," Stephen replied. "A lot."

The sentiment had barely been uttered when the door flew open, and an imposing man with graying temples, a custom-designed suit, and an implacable expression strode in. "Good morning, gentlemen." A slightly surprised glance at Julia as he tossed a leather briefcase on the desk. "And ladies."

Julia was already easing away. "I'm interrupting a meeting. I apologize, Mayor Stratford. I'll be on my way."

"I'll see you out." Connor moved so quickly that there was no time for Julia to refuse. He reached her side, gripping her arm tightly enough so the only way for her to shake it free was to make a scene—something he knew she wouldn't do. "Hi, Dad," he greeted Harrison Stratford. "Good to see you. This is Julia Talbot, Brian's teacher."

"Really." A glint of interest flashed in the ice-blue eyes. "It's a pleasure to meet you, Ms. Talbot."

"Thank you, Mr. Stratford. It's nice meeting you, too." A cordial nod. "You have an exceptional grandson. I'm sure you're very proud of him."

"Indeed." He was still studying her, his gaze flickering to Connor's viselike grip on her arm. "Does your being here have anything to do with Brian?"

She hesitated, and Connor read her thoughts as clearly as if she'd spoken them aloud. She wanted to do what was best for Brian. At the same time, she had no idea how much his grandfather knew. And she had no desire to walk this minefield.

Connor let Stephen take the lead on this one.

"Ms. Talbot dropped off some of Brian's work," Stephen supplied briefly, keeping the explanation short and sweet. He rose from behind his desk. "Glad you could make it, Dad. Can I offer you something?"

"Just some black coffee." Harrison Stratford snapped open his briefcase, gave a curt nod to Cliff, then turned his full attention to Stephen. "We have a lot to discuss."

That was Connor's cue.

"I'll see Ms. Talbot to the elevator," he announced, leading Julia to the door. "I'll be right back."

The minute they were out in the hall, the door closed behind them, she yanked away her arm. "I know the way."

"I realize that." He blocked her path. "You have two choices. Either let me show you to the elevator, or scream rape. It's the only way you're going to get rid of me."

Julia's jaw dropped. "Are you insane?"

"Probably. Going without sleep long enough will do that to you." He folded his arms across his chest, awaiting her decision. "Well? Which is it going to be?"

"Fine." She threw up her arms. "Show me to the elevator. But no discussions. I'm not up for them."

"Fair enough." Connor gestured, and the two of them walked down the hall, weaving their way through the thin stream of city employees they passed.

They rounded the corner and reached the cluster of elevators.

As Connor had suspected, the corridor was bustling. No surprise. It was nine A.M.

He kept right on walking.

Julia stopped. "We're here," she said, keeping her voice low so as not to make a spectacle of herself.

"Wrong elevator." Connor took her arm again, knowing she wouldn't pull away in public. "Come on."

"Where are we going?"

"To an elevator that's more direct."

He led her to the back of the building and down the corridor that housed the service elevators. Excellent. Only two of the three were in use.

He headed toward the idle one.

When Julia realized what he was doing, she started trying to tug herself free. "Have you lost it entirely?" she bit out. "Let me go."

"In a minute." Connor pulled her into an empty elevator and jabbed the button that said SHUT.

The doors slid closed.

Connor angled his head toward her. "I didn't plan this, any more than I planned taking you to bed the other night. That was fate. So is this. I couldn't have plotted this elevator excursion. I didn't even know you were coming here today. Just like I didn't know Nancy was leaving. Sometimes things just happen. Other times, we seize the moment. Like I'm doing now."

He punched the big red button that brought the elevator to a grinding halt.

Immediately, the emergency bell started ringing shrilly.

"Connor." Julia was staring at him in shock. "What do you think . . ."

"Shhh. You said no discussions, remember?" He pulled her into his arms, tilting back her head and covering her mouth with his before she could catch her breath. "We've only got a minute," he murmured, savoring the feel and taste of her. "But I need you to know how wrong you are. To remember how right it was. Don't fight me, sweetheart." He caught Julia's arms, which were trying to shove him away, and brought them around his neck. "For the few seconds we've got before the mechanics show up to fix this thing, don't fight me. Don't fight either of us."

Julia opened her mouth to protest, and Connor took full advantage. His tongue slid inside, entwining with hers and stroking it in slow, sensual motions that made lust pound at his brain. He knew he was using her desire for him as a weapon, but he didn't care. Not if it brought her to her senses, shocked her into seeing what was real. Besides, having her back in his arms was like a jolt to his own established reality—at least, the reality he'd known for thirty-five years. He was in deep. Really deep. And he had no desire to get out.

He waited only until he felt Julia respond, sinking, almost against her will, into the kiss, before he backed her up to the elevator wall, lifting her until their bodies fit, then pinning her to the wall with his weight.

"You make me crazy," he muttered into her parted lips. "I lose my mind when I touch you. I could forget the whole damned world and make love to you right here, right now, even if the entire maintenance staff finds us." He worked up her skirt, wedging himself between her thighs and pressing his erection into the notch between them.

Julia whimpered, her reaction instant if involuntary. She arched to deepen the contact, her body softening against him in unmistakable need.

Connor had to fight the urge to tear off her panty hose and finish this. He wanted her so much he was shaking with it. But that's not why he'd brought her there. He'd brought her there to make her face the truth.

"Julia." His voice was a husky whisper, barely audible above the piercing emergency siren. He raised his head, his fingers tangling in her hair. "How can you doubt this is real?"

Tears glistened on her lashes. "I don't. But what does it prove? That we want each other? I knew that already."

"It proves more." His fingers tightened. "Tell me you believe I didn't use you."

She stared up at him, her features strained, dark circles of fatigue shadowing her eyes. "Fine. I believe you didn't use me. That doesn't mean I believe you *wouldn't* use me. Connor, please, let me go. What I need . . ." She swallowed hard. ". . . you're just not capable of giving."

He opened his mouth to reply but never got the chance.

From overhead, the sound of pounding footsteps intermingled with the blaring of the alarm.

"Hey!" a voice bellowed. "Is anybody down there?"

Connor reacted to the panic-stricken look on Julia's face. He stepped away, letting her feet slide to the floor. Then he walked over and punched the red button again.

The siren stopped.

The car continued its descent, moving away from the mechanics above.

"I'm all right," he called back, his voice easily heard now that it was quiet. "Sorry about the noise. I leaned against the button by mistake, and it jammed. I just unjammed it. I'm on my way down now." He purposely said nothing to contradict the impression that he was a delivery man with every right to be using the elevator.

Apparently, his ruse worked, because there was a brief silence, followed by: "Okay, but next time be more careful. You got the whole place in an uproar."

"Sure will." Connor turned to Julia, who was adjusting her skirt. "Are you all right?" he asked quietly.

She nodded, combing her fingers through her hair. "I'm fine. But I've got to get to school. And you've got to get back to whatever deal you're cooking up with your father and brother." A sad smile. "I guess that says it all, doesn't it?"

As if on cue, the elevator stopped on the ground floor, and the doors glided open. Julia poked her head out, relief sweeping her face as she saw the hallway was temporarily empty. She paused, turning to look back at Connor as if she had something more she wanted, needed, to say.

Whatever it was, she changed her mind. Straightening her shoulders—and, Connor suspected, her resolve—she walked away.

Tempted though he was, he didn't go after her. Not now. Not when she had a classroom of kids to see to and he had Stephen's ass to keep out of the fire.

But later—later would be different.

The timing might be wrong, but the two of them were right.

Connor knew it.

And by the time he was finished, so would Julia.

22

The tension in Stephen's office was so thick you could cut it with a knife.

Connor walked in and shut the door behind him, sizing up the situation. Cliff was pacing around, thumbing through some papers as if he were looking for data to report. Stephen was seated behind his desk, the essence of a calm and commanding leader. His posture was straight, his expression was confident, and his fingers were steepled in front of him, as if he were about to issue a proclamation of some sort. It was a look he had long since perfected, a look their father expected of his political prodigy.

As for Harrison Stratford, he was in his usual confrontational stance—poised at the edge of his seat, inching forward one impatient, aggressive increment at a time. Like a damned German shepherd crouched in the attack position.

"So what did I miss?" Connor asked lightly, crossing over to pour himself some coffee.

"Nothing much," Stephen assured him. "Just going over the latest polls."

That was odd. Connor would have bet his bottom dollar that their father would go straight for the jugular: the issue of Nancy and Brian. He made split-second eye contact with his brother and saw that the same question was on Stephen's mind.

"How are the numbers looking?" Connor sipped at his coffee, wondering when their father was going in for the kill and what was stopping him.

He soon found out.

"The numbers are strong," Harrison announced, swiveling around to pin Connor with an icy stare. "Up through yesterday, that is. I can't vouch for what will happen after the press has a chance to put some spin on the fact that Nancy's gone cross-country for God knows how long. Nice of you to join us, by the way."

Ah, so that was it. He wanted Connor present for the inquisition.

That meant that today's agenda involved either big money or a big issue.

A family issue.

Given everything that was going on, it didn't take much to guess it was the latter.

Connor steeled himself for a bigger boom than expected to be lowered. "I had some elevator trouble," he replied. "Besides, I'm not good at second-guessing the press about potential spin. So I wouldn't have been much help."

"Elevator trouble?" That raised Stephen's brows. "The racket down the hall was you?"

"Yup." Connor's expression remained unreadable. "A jammed emergency button. No harm done. Sorry about the noise."

Stephen's lips twitched, an obvious sign that he'd read between the lines and that what he'd deduced had supplied welcome comic relief. However, out of respect for Connor's privacy, he didn't pursue the subject.

Their father harbored no such reservations. "What about Ms. Talbot?"

"What about her?"

"Was she in this elevator trouble with you?"

Connor's jaw set. He wasn't going down this path. He knew his father's mind and how it worked. The son of a bitch was trying to figure out where best to use Julia as a pawn in his power game. He wanted to know her opinions and relationships with their family, what she might or might not know about Brian's absence, and how her image as Brian's lovely, wholesome teacher could be exploited so the Stratfords appeared in the best possible light.

Connor could already smell the apple pie baking in his father's manipulative mind.

"Yes, Dad, she was there," he supplied in clipped tones. "Now she's on her way to school. And I'm here. So let's get back to business."

"She *is* business," Harrison countered. "She's my grandson's teacher. And she didn't look too happy about this sudden trip his mother took him on. He's missing school. That can't be going over well."

"Not to worry," Connor assured him, a biting edge to his words. "Julia's dedication to her teaching has no impact on her opinion of Stephen. She told me herself that she voted for him for mayor, and she plans to vote for him for senator. So no holes to plug up there."

Harrison gave a hard nod of approval. "You're sleeping with this woman," he concluded. "Good. That'll stop her from spouting negative publicity. On the other hand, keep it low-profile. The last thing we need is for the press to take this and run, making it out to be some kind of incestuous affair. You know, 'The mayor's son's teacher beds down with his brother,' that kind of thing."

Connor had never been closer to telling his father to go to hell.

Before he could do so, Stephen jumped in to do damage control. "Relax, Dad. Julia's fine with Brian's trip. She was just dropping off his work. As for her and Connor, that's their business. Besides, they're both single, well respected, and squeaky clean. That might sound appealing to you, but it's too boring for the media to do much with."

From across the room, Cliff cleared his throat. He looked decidedly uncomfortable, although Connor wasn't sure whether his discomfort stemmed from the conversation or from whatever information he'd just found. "I don't know if news of Nancy's trip leaked out before today's paper came out. It's possible, but I don't have any feedback, negative or otherwise. That could be because there is none. Or it could be because I was at client meetings most of yesterday and didn't check. Do you want me to?"

"No." Harrison rose. "I want you to excuse the three of us for a few minutes. Take a time-out from your watchdog duties. I need to speak with my sons in private."

A startled nod. "All right." Cliff gathered up his file and headed for the door.

"Don't go far," Harrison advised. "I have a few things to go over with you before I leave."

The door clicked quietly shut.

"That was tactful," Connor observed dryly.

"It wasn't meant to be. Now, suppose we dispense with the bullshit." Harrison slapped his palms on the desk. He leaned forward, his stare lethal, fixed on Stephen. "Where did Nancy really go and why? Is she leaving you?"

Not a flicker of reaction marred Stephen's political face. "What makes you think she's not in California?"

"Because I called her sister in LA. She's a lousy liar, by the way. You prepped her well enough for the press but not for me. She fumferred her ass off. Nancy's no more there than I am. So where is she?"

So this was the bomb their father had been waiting to drop, Connor mused. Okay, now the ball was in Stephen's court.

He eyed his brother, waiting to see how he chose to play this. That would decide the particular backup that was needed.

Unblinking, Stephen made a casual sweep with his arm. "Fine. Nancy and I are having a few problems. She needed time to think. I'm not sure where she is. She said she'd call. I didn't think you'd want that published in the papers. Was I wrong?"

Harrison ignored the sarcasm. "And has she called?"

"Not yet."

"Great. Who did you hire to track her down?"

"No one. Nor do I intend to." Now Stephen was angry. He came to his feet, glaring at his father across the desk. "She's my wife, not an escaped con. I'm not going to hunt her down and drag her home. When she's ready, she'll come back on her own."

"And what about your son?" Harrison fired back. "Where does he fit into all this?"

"He's with his mother."

"How touching. In case you've forgotten, Nancy's not the one running for senator. You are. You need Brian here with you. And Nancy, too, for that matter. She can disappear for a few days if she has to, but no more. Not with the election less than six months away."

A muscle worked in Stephen's jaw. "It always comes back to that, doesn't it?"

"You're damned right it does. What do you think we've been working for all these years? Your political future. So tell me, how do you expect to win on your platform as a loving family man when your family walked out on you?"

"Dad, you're overreacting," Connor interceded. "Nancy didn't walk out. She's under an unusual amount of pressure. Some of it's her own personal stuff." A bit of an exaggeration but a necessary one. "Things she's going through. And, yeah, some of it's political strain, campaign and otherwise. Cut her some slack. She'll be back."

Harrison pivoted, leveling his icy stare on Connor. "Ah, the voice of reason. Funny, a moment ago, I could have sworn you wanted to tear my head off for prying into your personal life. Yet now you're calmly trying to pacify me. All because I'm asking Stephen to account for his actions." He made a disgusted sound. "You and Henderson stand on either side of your brother like two goddamn bookends. Like if you move aside, he might collapse. Well, he won't." Pursing his lips, Harrison turned back to Stephen. "What political strain?"

"I run the city, Dad. Things come up."

"And more things will come up when you're in the state senate. You'll have to cope with that. So will Nancy." Harrison's brows drew together, as if he were trying to determine what issues might be pulling at Stephen's marriage. "Your popularity rating's never been higher. Leaf Brook is thriving. As for your visibility, it's ideal. Between that huge mall opening and the upcoming vote on that municipal parking contract you're haggling over, you've got it made."

A flash of irony glittered in Stephen's eyes. "I take it we're talking about the power of the press again."

"Damned right we are. They're the ones who are going to send you to the senate. And they love controversy. Issues like a divided city council—they gobble those up. They also love heroes. Which is just what you'll be after you make the right fiduciary decision for your constituents. The articles will be glowing."

"Glad to oblige." Stephen snapped off a mock salute. "Although I had the crazy idea it was voters who elected their senators. I guess I was off base on that one."

Harrison's gaze narrowed. "Is it the press that's causing problems in your marriage?"

"I can handle the press."

"Good. Now handle your wife."

Connor snorted. This whole inquisition was becoming extreme, even for their father. "You're in rare form today, Dad. What's got you so pissed off—the fact that Nancy's hiatus might hurt the election or the fact that something's happened that's outside your control?"

"Both." Harrison didn't look the slightest bit put off by his son's barb. "That high-visibility mall opening, it's this Saturday."

"I'm aware of that," Stephen responded. "I'm also aware that Nancy and Brian are normally with me at those kinds of events. That's why I came up with a family crisis as Nancy's excuse for being away. The public can empathize with a woman who wants to be there for her injured sister. It sure takes precedence over making a token appearance at your husband's side."

"Maybe, maybe not." Harrison waved away the sentiment. "The public might feel compassion for Nancy's situation, but they still want to see the all-American family you three represent. Your showing up solo won't make them happy."

"I agree," Connor said, cluing their father in on a decision he and Stephen had made last night. "Which is why I'm going to be there. I'm not as pretty as Nancy, but I am Stephen's brother. Family support will be the pitch of the day."

"No," Harrison corrected swiftly. "Family rallying will. Because I'll be there, too. The media will applaud the Stratford unity, our show of strength." A pleased nod. "Your idea was good. Mine's better."

If he was expecting an argument, he didn't get one.

"Yeah, it is." Connor's wheels were turning. "What's more, why stop with just us? If we're going for the whole family unity thing, Mom should be there, too." Picturing his stylish, diplomatic mother—a seasoned vet when it came to playing the corporate wife—Connor knew this was the right move. "She'd make the whole thing feel more natural, sort of balance out the overabundance of testosterone. And just like that . . ." Connor snapped his fingers. "We'd have a different version of the all-American family. Not a wife and child but a brother and parents."

"Not bad," Stephen murmured, rubbing his chin. "It would make a strong show of family unity, and it would sure as hell take everyone's mind off Nancy and Brian not being there. Is Mom free?"

"For this? She'll make herself free." Harrison dismissed what he knew to be a nonissue. Lynette Stratford was as eager as he for their son to reach the White House. "My driver's bringing her down to Manhattan on Friday evening for a command-performance cocktail party we've been invited to. She was planning on spending Saturday visiting the new exhibit at the Met. She'll change her plans. I'll arrange for my driver to take us to Leaf Brook first thing Saturday morning."

"You're staying in the city till then?" Stephen asked. Their parents had an enormous penthouse suite on Central Park West, in addition to their estate in Connecticut.

"Yes. I've got back-to-back meetings there this afternoon and all day tomorrow. No point going home just to sleep. This works out well. The mall's grand opening is ten A.M. on Saturday. We'll all drive over there together, make a big showing." A hard stare at Stephen. "In the meantime, I expect you'll have heard from your wife and that she and your son will be on their way home. And whatever the hell your problems are, fix them. Now."

Stephen looked as if he was biting back a few choice words. But, under the circumstances, it was better they remained unsaid. The sooner this confrontation ended, the better. With Harrison due for an afternoon meeting in Manhattan, he'd have to blow out of there soon. After which, Stephen and Connor could get back to digging up dirt on Walker.

As if on cue, Harrison glanced at his watch. "Let's get Henderson back in here. We've got some campaign strategizing to do, and I want to look over the most recent contributions. I've got to be on the road by noon." He lowered himself back into the chair, his body language proclaiming this portion of the meeting over.

"I'll have Celeste send Cliff in." Stephen reached for the phone.

His father leaned forward, gripping Stephen's wrist firmly. "I won't say this again, certainly not in front of Henderson, but for the sake of your senate seat, get your wife and son back under your roof."

11:45 A.M.

Stephen peered out the window, heaving a sigh of relief as he watched his father's town car roll out of the parking lot and onto the main road. "Thank God that's over."

"Not terribly pleasant, was it?" Connor returned dryly. He unfolded himself from the chair, standing up and stretching. "No wonder my clients don't faze me. A morning with Dad makes the average CEO look like a newborn kitten."

"One that's declawed," Stephen amended, rubbing the back of his neck. He slanted a look at Cliff. "Sorry about that abrupt dismissal earlier on. My father's not known for his tact."

Sliding the last of his campaign files away, Cliff gave an offhanded shrug. "To tell you the truth, I barely noticed. And I wasn't offended. That's your father. You either accept him or you don't. It wasn't a personal slap. He had something on his mind that related to family. He wanted to talk to you alone. That's his prerogative."

A corner of Stephen's mouth lifted. "Maybe you're the real politician here."

"Well, I've known you for almost twenty years. So I guess some of it must have rubbed off." Cliff gave a tired smile. "If it's okay with you guys, I'm going to cut out. I've been burning the candle at every end, and I'm beat. I had no idea how long your father planned on staying, so I cleared my entire afternoon calendar. Which gives me a block of much-needed time for myself. So I think I'll take advantage of the situation, go home, and get some rest."

"No problem." Stephen was watching Cliff with quiet

intensity. "Anything special making you run on overdrive? You usually thrive when your workload's heavy. A new woman, maybe?"

"Nope." If Stephen's question made Cliff squirm, he hid it well. Then again, his poker face was as good as Stephen's.

He snapped his briefcase shut and swung it off the desk. "No new woman. Just a lot of crucial things coming to a head at once."

"Anything you can talk about?"

"Unfortunately, no. The details are privileged. Most of it's the usual—two major litigations, a corporate merger, and that acquisition I'm working on for your father. Just a lot of balls to juggle at once. I'll handle it, with a little rest." Cliff headed for the door. "I'll be home if you need to reach me. If you get my machine, just leave a message. That means I turned off the ringer so I could sleep."

"Right," Stephen muttered once the door had shut behind Cliff. "Or it means you took off to be with my wife."

Connor's brows rose. "My, isn't our imagination working overtime? The guy looks like hell, he's going home to bed, and you assume he's shacking up with Nancy somewhere. That sounds likely. Especially with my miss-nothing-and-report-all nephew there. Yup. Sounds like a plan."

"Okay, fine, I'm overreacting," Stephen snapped, running both hands through his hair. "But I'm losing my mind. Why doesn't Nancy call, even if it's just to say she and Brian are all right?"

"Because she needs to regain perspective and get her emotions under control. That package freaked her out. She's in shock. She'll come around. She'll call." Connor stared thoughtfully at the door. "And I don't think you're losing your mind. Overreacting, yes, but not completely off base."

Stephen's head snapped around. "What does that mean?"

"It means I don't believe Cliff and Nancy are, or ever have been, lovers. But they are tight. And my gut tells me Cliff knows where she is. He's a mess. Cliff doesn't get that way from overwork. My guess is, he feels caught in the middle of two people he cares about. If he tells you anything, he's betraying Nancy and risking pushing her over the edge to the point where she really will take Brian and vanish. On the other hand, you're his best friend. Keeping this from you, especially knowing what you're probably going through, I'd say he's torn in half."

"And I'd say you're right." Stephen's laugh was humorless. "I don't know whether to choke him until he tells me where Nancy and Brian are, then beat the crap out of him for loving my wife, or thank him for being there for Nancy when I wasn't, then heave a sigh of relief that he'll make sure she and my son stay safe."

"Don't do anything. If you force Cliff's hand, it'll only antagonize the situation and alienate Nancy even more. She already feels betrayed and manipulated. Don't add to it. That's not the way to get her to come home. She'll make that decision on her own, after you've eliminated the threat to Brian's safety." Connor was still gazing at the door, his eyes narrowed pensively. "If Nancy asked for Cliff's help, she must have told him about the baseball cap and about Walker's threats."

"And about my gambling, you mean." Stephen sounded more weary than angry. "Maybe. It doesn't matter. If she did confide in Cliff, I doubt it would come as a surprise. The guy's been my friend since college. He's not an idiot." A hard swallow. *"I'm* the idiot. Connor, what the hell have I done to my life?"

Connor walked over, clapped a hard hand on his brother's shoulder. "Just the fact that you can ask that question means you've turned a corner. You'll get your life back. You finally want it badly enough to fight for it. And one thing I know for sure: the Stratfords might be screwed up in lots of ways, but we're damn good fighters. We don't give up until we win. The problem is, we've spent too much time fighting for the wrong things. But all that's about to change. We're about to get it right."

Stephen eyed his brother. *"We?* Why don't I think we're just talking about Nancy and me?"

"Because we're not."

Stephen's intercom buzzed, and he walked over and pressed the button. "Yes, Celeste?"

"Mr. Henderson said your meeting was over. I know you said to hold your messages. Did you want them before I leave for lunch?"

"Anything pressing?"

A rustling sound as Celeste shuffled through the messages. "Two of them. The chief of police called. He wants to discuss how much added security you want at the mall opening on Saturday. I told him you'd get back to him this afternoon. And a Mr. Harry Shaw called. He said it was important and that you were expecting to hear from him."

Stephen had tensed at the mention of his PI's name. "I was. What's the message?"

"He said he's got some of the information you requested. He's out of cell range until this afternoon. He wants to meet you for a drink around four. If that works, leave the specifics on his voice mail. He'll pick it up when he's back in range."

"Thanks, Celeste. Go ahead to lunch." Stephen punched the button again, raising his head to look at Connor. "He must have something on Walker."

Connor's lips tightened into a grim line. "I hope so."

23

3:35 P.M.

Julia let herself into her apartment. She'd waited all day long for this solitude, and now that it was here, she felt too out of sorts to enjoy it and too restless to sit still.

Inadvertently, her gaze fell on the answering machine. The unblinking light told her no one had called.

Damn the surge of disappointment she felt.

She dropped onto a stool in the kitchen, folding her arms on the counter and resting her head on them.

All day long, she'd relived those moments in the elevator. Her body still burned with the memory and ached with unfulfilled desire. Worse, her heart ached for all the things she knew she couldn't have with Connor but wanted nonetheless.

Damn, damn, damn—why did it have to be Connor Stratford she'd fallen in love with? Why couldn't it have been an uncomplicated man with a normal family, a man with values she could understand, who was capable of trusting and being trusted in return?

And why did she still want to believe Connor could be that man?

She raised her head, determined not to think about Connor for at least a few minutes. A distraction. That's what she needed. Someone with whom she could discuss something, anything, that didn't end in the name Stratford.

Someone who'd offered to be her friend and nothing more.

She dialed Greg's office number.

"Greg Matthews." He answered the phone himself, sounding busy and distracted.

"Greg? It's Julia. I'm sorry. I obviously called at a bad time."

"Hmm? No, I'm just swamped, and my secretary's out sick." He blew out his breath, then laughed awkwardly. "Let's start again. Hi, Julia, good to hear from you."

Uncomplicated. Thank God. "It's good to talk to you." Julia felt herself relax a bit. "I got your message, but yesterday was crazy, and I had a killer migraine. I'd really enjoy getting together with you."

"Me, too. But tonight's out. I'll probably be working until midnight." A pause. "How about tomorrow night? I know you've got a workshop, but we could meet afterward. Even if it's only for a drink."

"I can do better than that. My workshop was canceled. I'll buy you dinner. But only if you promise we won't talk about work."

"Fine with me." Greg was quiet for another moment. "You sound really stressed yourself. You okay?"

"I'll be better after a glass of wine and some light conversation."

"Done." Rustling papers indicated he was ready to hang up and get back to whatever he'd been doing. "How about the steak house on Maple Street? Does that work?"

"Perfect." Julia felt more relief than pleasure. An enjoyable night out. It might not be the cure, but maybe it would be medicine enough to mask the symptoms. "How's seven o'clock?"

"Make it seven-thirty. I'd pick you up, but, unfortunately, I'll be slaving away on this budget right up till the last minute. In fact, the way it looks, I'll be in here on Saturday finishing up. Would it be okay if we met at the restaurant?"

"Of course. Are you sure you can take the time for dinner?"

"Very sure. See you then."

4:15 P.M.

Stephen had just left the office to meet his PI for a drink—and, he hoped, to get some damning facts on Walker.

Connor was seated at his brother's desk, cell phone in hand, catching up on some business calls with clients he'd neglected all week.

The intercom buzzed.

Connor glanced over at the phone in surprise. Obviously, Celeste didn't know Stephen was gone. Either that, or it was Connor she was looking for.

Only one way to find out.

Putting down his cell phone, Connor leaned across Stephen's desk and punched the button. "Yes, Celeste?"

A brief pause before Celeste replied, "I'm sorry, Mr. Stratford, I was looking for the mayor."

"You just missed him. He must have walked by your cubicle five minutes ago."

"Oh, I was in with Mr. Matthews. His secretary's out sick, and he needed a few files. Five minutes ago, you said? That means he's probably in the parking lot. Okay,

I'll tell the chief of police to wait a few minutes and then try him in the car."

"Wait." Connor spoke up quickly. Stephen had been tight as a drum when he'd left. He was totally focused on getting to that meeting, praying that Shaw would give him something he could nail Walker with. The last thing he needed was to chat with Martin Hart about extra security at the mall opening.

"Pardon me?" Celeste was waiting for clarification.

"Stephen's been playing phone tag with Marty all afternoon," Connor explained. That was a gross exaggeration. Stephen had returned the police chief's call once and was told he was taking a late lunch. Hardly enough to constitute an afternoon-long game of phone tag.

Fine. Connor would take full responsibility for his actions. He realized he was overstepping his bounds. He also realized it was necessary. He'd hold the police chief at bay for a few hours, until Stephen could think straight. Their security arrangements could wait that long.

"I know he wants to touch base with Marty right away," Connor continued. "That way, the police can get started on the additional security for Saturday. Put him through. I'll give him the updated information he needs. By that time, Stephen will be reachable on his cell. So, if Marty has any questions, he can call Stephen directly."

"Great. Hang on, and I'll forward the call."

Connor scooped up the phone when it rang. "Hi, Marty."

"Connor." The police chief sounded puzzled. While he and Connor were certainly acquainted through Stephen, they were hardly drinking buddies. "I was surprised when Celeste said I'd be talking to you. Is everything okay?"

"Absolutely. It's just that Stephen's out of cell range, and I know you two have been trying to touch base about security at the mall opening."

An uncomfortable silence. "Well, yes, but that's not why I'm calling now. He'd asked me to check into something for him. City business. I'm following up." Another awkward pause. "Any idea when he'll be reachable? I know he's anxious for my report."

Connor did next what he did best: he followed his instincts and took a risk. "Is this about Walker Development?"

Hart's silence told him he'd guessed right.

"Marty, I'm helping my brother check this company out. I'm doing some financial investigating to supplement Greg's, and I know you're doing a criminal background check. Did you turn up anything?"

"Not in the way you mean, no. But I did run through the entire list of cars that have been stolen from Leaf Brook municipal lots in the past six months. Funny, but not one of those cars was stolen from a lot maintained by Walker Development."

"Interesting coincidence."

"I've been a cop for a long time, Connor. I don't believe in coincidences. I believe in instincts. And mine are bugged by this."

Connor pursed his lips thoughtfully. "Maybe Walker's security staff is so good they scare off potential thieves."

A snort of disbelief. "He doesn't exactly hire the secret service. And, not to toot my own horn, but my department is damned good. I'd buy it if fewer cars were stolen from Walker's lots than from ours. But none? It doesn't wash. So, yeah, maybe Walker's security makes his lots the safest ones in Leaf Brook. Or maybe he's just doing something to convince people of that."

Exactly what Connor was thinking.

"Connor, is there more to this than Mayor Stratford's telling me? Does he have reason to believe Walker's doing something illegal?"

Connor didn't miss a beat. "The truth is, there's not a shred of proof that Walker's anything but on the level. Stephen's just being cautious. Exactly like you are. I'll pass this on to him. And I'll have him call you back."

"You do that."

Bingo, Connor thought, replacing the phone. They were onto something. Time to follow it through, to get some proof. Or at least enough pseudo-proof to counter-blackmail Walker with.

He was pondering ways to do that when his cell phone rang.

He punched TALK. "Connor Stratford."

"Hi, Connor." It was Tom Roderman, his own primary contact. Tom was a renowned corporate attorney who specialized in high-level mergers and acquisitions. His connections ran the gamut, from manufacturing giants to rapidly developing technology companies to corporations that were solid household names. And that included banks, insurance companies, and a host of other corporations that would have access to more sensitive, inside information on Walker Development.

"Tom. Excellent. Do you have anything for me?"

His friend blew out his breath. "Nothing as incriminating as you were looking for. I made a few discreet phone calls. And, yeah, this Philip Walker is definitely a borderline operator. He's pushed the boundaries in a lot of his business dealings. The problem is, nothing illegal has ever been pinned on him."

"Why doesn't that surprise me?" Connor crossed one

leg over the other. "He's smart, and he's careful. Okay, so a blatant illegality is not going to cut it. I'm going to have to get to someone he's done business with, someone who feels Walker screwed him. Can you get me some names?"

"Most of it's a matter of public record, so, yeah, I can put together a list." A slight hesitation. "Look, Connor, I have no idea why you need this, but if it's so important to you, why not start with your father? I know he's not your first choice when it comes to sources, but in this case he might be the easiest. Especially since time is of the essence, and . . ."

"My father?" Connor interrupted. "Why would I go to him with this?"

"He and Walker did a couple of real estate development deals together. I don't have the details—it was a number of years ago, and, frankly, I assumed you knew. Now that I think about it, I don't know why I'd assume that. You were pretty young, maybe even still in grad school. Let's see, they joint-ventured on a strip mall in Danbury and an office complex in Stamford. Both of those were shrewd investments. The populations in those areas have grown by leaps and bounds. So have the profits."

"Damn," Connor muttered. His mind was racing, remembering the vague sense of familiarity he'd experienced when Stephen first mentioned Walker's name. So that's what had been nagging at him that night. He hadn't tried to decipher it then—he'd been concentrating on patching Stephen up and getting him home, and everything had been too hectic. But now . . . yeah, he did remember.

Next question: was it a coincidence?

Like Marty, Connor didn't believe in coincidences.

Not in business. And *definitely* not when they involved his father.

"Connor?" Tom prodded.

"You're right, I do remember them co-investing." Connor gripped the phone more tightly, recalling that earlier that day his father had brought up—albeit in passing—the municipal contract dispute and the good press it would result in. Another coincidence? Doubtful.

"Do me a favor, Tom." Connor was suddenly very eager to wrap things up. "Start compiling that list of names for me. In the meantime, I'll touch base with my father. I'll get back to you first thing tomorrow about where things stand."

"You've got it."

"Thanks. I owe you one."

6:30 P.M.
Central Park West

Harrison Stratford strode through his apartment, tossing his coat onto a chair and unknotting his tie as he headed for the living-room bar. It had been a damn long day. Too long. In his twenties and thirties, he'd thrived on these meeting marathons. But at sixty-one, it was getting old. Or maybe *he* was getting old—although he doubted it. Not one of these cocky Generation X hot shots could hold a candle to him for brains. Not for ambition or insight, either. In fact, most of them were so wrapped up in making a million overnight, they missed the big picture entirely, tripping on their own egos and landing flat on their faces.

Which was why his empire kept flourishing and his millions kept multiplying.

He splashed some Makers Mark into a glass, taking a deep, appreciative swallow. The upcoming generation was, by and large, quite pathetic. Then again, so were their parents. They were the ones who'd raised a bunch of weak, spoiled brats with zero grit and zero ingenuity.

He, on the other hand, had done it right.

Refilling his glass, he turned to cross over and sit down—and started as he saw Connor perched on the edge of the sofa, watching him.

"Hello, Dad. I figured you'd be wrapping things up around now. Hope you don't mind my letting myself in."

Harrison's eyes narrowed, assessing his son. Connor's tone was even, his expression bland. But that didn't fool him. His son was ripping mad about something.

"Next time, mention that you're here," he retorted. "Unless your goal is to give me a heart attack so you can inherit early." He gestured toward the bar. "Do you want a drink?"

"No." Connor shook his head. "I want to talk."

"I was under the impression that we did that, all morning." Harrison remained standing. It gave him the advantage, which he intended to keep until he knew the basis for this impromptu get-together.

"That wasn't talking. That was interrogating," Connor corrected. "And *you* did all that." He leaned back, stretching his arms across the back of the sofa and meeting his father's gaze head-on, letting him know that sitting could wield as much authority as standing. "Now it's my turn."

A corner of Harrison's mouth lifted. He was damned proud of Connor. In so many ways, he was his father's son.

Nursing his drink, he propped an elbow on back of the leather chair. "Shoot."

"I want to discuss Philip Walker."

"What about him?"

"You two ever work together?"

"If you're asking, I'm sure you already have the answer." Tired or not, Harrison felt his adrenaline kick in. He was going to enjoy this sparring match. Further, he was intrigued as hell about where it was leading. "But if you want clarification, here it is. Yes, Walker and I have partnered on a couple of deals. A few of them were years back; a few others were more recently. Do you want details?"

"Only as they relate to Stephen." Connor eased forward slightly. "This morning, you brought up the subject of the debate over the municipal parking contract. That wasn't a random example, was it?"

"You tell me. Obviously, that's what you came here to do."

"How do you factor into Walker's bid for the contract? Did you know about it before the fact?"

Harrison took a swallow of bourbon. "It was my idea."

Connor's jaw tightened. "That's a new low, even for you. What were you doing, drumming up good press for Stephen's election campaign?"

"Bingo."

"Do you have any idea what kind of scum Walker is? How far he'd go to get what he wants?"

A shrug. "I know he grew up a street kid. He's used to fighting dirty to get ahead. If that's what you call scum, so be it. I call it ambition."

Connor rose slowly to his feet. "His ambition is what's choking the life out of Stephen's marriage."

"Really? How's that? By putting pressure on him? By adding a little challenge to his job?" Harrison made a harsh sound of disgust. "If so, it's about time. Being mayor of Leaf Brook has become entirely too cushy for your brother. As far as his constituents are concerned, he walks on water. Well, he's going to have to win bigger and tougher popularity contests than that. He's got to learn to deal with pressure, to rise above it and come up with creative solutions, if he wants that senate seat—and all the other seats to come. And if he wants the White House, he's going to have to learn not just to deal with pressure but to thrive on it."

"In other words, to become a son of a bitch like you." Connor said it as calmly as if he were making polite conversation.

"I think that's a bit optimistic where your brother's concerned. I'd settle for a close second."

A brittle glare. "What about his marriage? His family?"

Again, Harrison shrugged. "Nancy knew what she was getting into. The night Stephen slid that engagement ring on her finger, I pulled her aside and told her exactly what kind of future she should expect. She welcomed the idea of being in the political limelight. If she's suddenly decided otherwise, that's tough. She said her I do's. She'll stand by them. Even if it's for Brian sake."

Disbelief flashed across Connor's face. "This whole thing's like a game of chess to you. Every step's a calculated move; every person's a pawn to exploit."

"If you're waiting for an apology, you're not getting one. I raised my sons to succeed. That's just what they're doing. Take a look at yourself—I'd say I did a damned good job."

Connor ignored the accolades. "Speaking of pawns, what about Cheryl Lager? Was she your idea, too?"

Harrison's brows drew together. "Who? Oh, that obnoxious journalist. No, she just jumped in on her own. But her little digs and innuendos do add some spice to the local paper." A tight smile. "Although I *am* glad she got diverted by the contract debate. Her recent cracks about my bankrolling your brother to the senate were beginning to get on my nerves."

Connor drew a sharp breath, and Harrison got the feeling he was choosing his words carefully. Whether he was hoping to go for a shock effect or mentally confirming that whatever he said, or didn't say, would protect Stephen, that remained to be seen.

"Let's get back to Walker," was what Connor finally settled on. "How would you react if I told you he arranged for cars to be stolen from municipal lots *not* maintained by Walker Development in order to cast himself in a more favorable light?"

Harrison inclined his head with interest. "Did he?"

"I think so. I have no proof—yet."

"Then I'd say it was a shrewd idea, as long as he covered all his tracks and doesn't get caught."

That got his son's attention. Lightning flashed in Connor's eyes. "You really don't have any scruples, do you? Not a single, goddamn one."

"Business is business." Harrison polished off his drink. "You do what you have to to succeed. I'm not a crook myself, but if I were one, I'd make damned sure no one realized it. So my answer to you is this: If you find proof, then Walker's an ass. If you don't, he's either innocent or clever as hell. And if it's the last, I'd want him on my team—under my watchful eye, of course."

Connor walked away, heading for the door. "I'm getting out of here before I lose it." He turned and shot his father a hard look. "I hope to God you don't end up paying dearly for this one. But you know those keen instincts I inherited from you? Well, they're screaming otherwise."

7:05 P.M.
Leaf Brook

Philip Walker swiveled around in his desk chair, peering out the window of his office suite. Sunset in the suburbs. It looked a lot nicer from up here than it did from the gutter.

He grinned, thinking about the fact that Harrison Stratford was in town, wondering what his reaction would be when he heard about the events that had taken place over the past few weeks.

He'd be impressed by some of the ingenuity Philip had displayed, especially since the son of a bitch thought he had the cornerstone on brilliance.

On the flip side, some of what he'd done would piss Stratford off, big time.

As for what he had planned, *that* would give the mayor's daddy a coronary.

7:15 P.M.
Central Park West

Connor was still breathing hard when he swerved his Mercedes out of the parking garage, heading for Leaf Brook. He wasn't sure what he'd expected, but if he'd hoped for a shred of compassion, then he was a jerk. His father was a cold-hearted bastard. Meeting with him had done nothing but confirm that. Okay, fine. That was bad enough. But his reaction to Walker's actions, to the fact that he might be an out-and-out criminal? Christ, the man had all but applauded his initiative.

That in itself made Connor sick. But more important, it worried the hell out of him. It raised some really ugly questions about how much his father knew. Was he aware of the lengths Walker had gone to to secure that contract? Had Harrison turned a blind eye to it or, even worse, agreed to it? He'd made it indisputably clear that he wanted to toughen Stephen up. Was this part of that toughening-up campaign? Would he really go so far as to let Walker beat the crap out of his son and threaten his grandson?

Connor was no longer certain.

But if his father *did* know about Walker's violent tactics, then he also knew what had provoked them. Which meant he knew about Walker's campaign contribution and about the fact that he was blackmailing Stephen.

As well as what ammunition he was using to blackmail him with.

That was the most disturbing prospect of all. Despite the great lengths Connor and Stephen had gone to to keep their father in the dark, did he know about Stephen's gambling? Had he kept that knowledge from them since whenever the hell he'd figured it out? If so, why? Why hadn't he shoved it in Stephen's face, demanded that he clean up his act for the sake of his future? It didn't make sense.

But someone had tipped Walker off to Stephen's gambling. Could that someone have been Harrison Stratford?

No way. That's where this line of reasoning reached an irrefutable dead end. To give Walker information like that would risk undoing everything their father was working for. It would give Walker the power to blow Stephen's political career to bits and to drag the Stratford name through the mud. Neither of which Harrison Stratford would allow.

So it was doubtful he knew about Stephen's Achilles heel. If he did, he'd be concealing it and battling to eliminate it all at once.

But how much *did* he know?

Connor gritted his teeth. He wished he could have tested his father by dropping the entire two-week scenario in his lap—sans the gambling issue. But it was just too big a risk. If he breathed a word about Walker's blackmail, and if Harrison wasn't aware of Stephen's compulsion, Connor would be throwing open Pandora's box.

So his hands were tied.

Cursing under his breath, Connor whipped out his cell phone and snapped it into place. It beeped, indicating that it was recharging. He'd shut it off during his time in the penthouse. If nothing else, he'd been determined to confront his father without interruption.

Another beep, announcing that the phone was all juiced up and ready to go. The LCD announced that he had a voice-mail message.

He retrieved it. The message, left a half hour ago, was from Stephen, asking him to call him at home right away.

He punched up the number as he turned the car onto the highway.

Stephen answered on the second ring, his voice strained. "Where have you been?" he demanded.

"At a meeting." Connor ducked the question. "I'm on my way back. Did the PI give you anything?"

"Yeah, but before I get into that, when I walked in here, there was a message from Nancy. She called a few hours ago, when she was sure I'd be at work. Anyway, she said she and Brian are fine. His ear's doing better. She said that if they're not home soon, she'll let him call and talk to me."

"Did she say where she was?"

"No." An audible swallow. "But she sounded really weird and on edge. Like she wanted to say more but didn't. Or couldn't. Who knows, maybe she had company."

"Then she would have waited until later to call," Connor retorted.

"Right. Anyway, at least I know they're all right and that Brian's feeling better." Stephen cleared his throat roughly. "Did you hear from your contact?"

"Yes." Connor told Stephen what Tom had said about Walker being on the borderline in his business dealings, as well as the fact that nothing definite could be pinned on him. He didn't mention their father's part in all this—not yet. Not until he sorted out the various possibilities where Harrison was concerned and what effect they'd have on Stephen.

Right now, Stephen sounded too strung out to deal with even one more thing.

"I also got an interesting call from Marty," Connor continued. "Or, rather, *you* did. I intercepted it because you'd just left for your meeting with Harry Shaw. I figured it had something to do with mall security. As it turned out, it didn't. I hope you don't mind my stepping in."

"Hardly. Was it about Walker?"

"Um-hum." Connor relayed that piece of the puzzle to his brother.

"So it looks like our suspicions were right," Stephen murmured.

"It's not just our suspicions anymore," Connor warned. "Be prepared. Marty's going to grill you. His instincts are on red alert." Connor accelerated the car, zoomed up the left lane. "What happened with Shaw?"

"He did some personal digging. Apparently, Walker's been seeing a new woman, frequently, and out of the blue. She's young enough to be his daughter."

Connor shrugged. "So what? He's rich. That's a turn-on to women of all ages. Why did it push Shaw's button?"

"It's *who* he's seeing that made Shaw leery."

"Who is it?"

"Robin Haley."

Connor's brows went up. "The computer teacher at Brian's school?"

"You know her?"

"We've met. She's a friend of Julia's. How did Walker get involved with her? And why now? You think he started seeing her to gain access to Brian's school—and Brian?"

"The same questions I asked. Shaw hadn't pursued the answers yet. He wanted the okay from me. He was more than willing to question Robin. It's my call." Stephen drew in a breath. "I told him to wait. I think there's a better way, one that's less obvious. I know things are rocky between you and Julia, but do you think she'd tell you anything?"

"If she can and it would help Brian, yes." Connor's mind was racing a mile a minute. "I'll call her right now. But I'm telling you up front that she's going to ask questions. And I'm going to give her answers. I trust her. You're going to have to trust her, too."

Stephen gave a tired sigh. "At this point, I don't think we have a choice. Do whatever you need to. Just find out if there's a connection here."

"I will. I'll give you an update when I get home. Figure forty minutes or so."

Connor punched the END button, steeled himself, and pressed the digits of Julia's number.

One ring. Two.

On the third ring, she picked up. "Hello?"

"It's me."

She made a distressed sound. "Connor, I don't want to . . ."

"Don't hang up, Julia, please. I need your help."

A heartbeat of silence. "Is it Brian?" she asked at last.

"Indirectly, yes."

"I'm listening."

"Your friend Robin Haley, do you know the guy she's dating?"

"Excuse me?"

Connor gritted his teeth. "I asked if you knew . . ."

"I heard your question. What has that got to do with Brian?"

"Maybe a lot. I'll explain in a minute."

Julia's laugh was hollow. "I doubt it. But to answer your question, no, I've never met the man. I know she's seeing someone special these past few weeks. But that's all she said."

"So you wouldn't know if this guy ever came to the school—maybe to see her or drive her home?"

"I've never seen Robin talking to any guy, other than the ones she works with, on school grounds."

"Damn." Connor slammed his fist against the steering wheel. "Is there any way you can ask her some questions, get her to talk about him, without making her suspicious?"

"I don't see why not. Robin loves talking about her social life." Julia paused, clearly perceiving the urgency in his tersely fired questions. "Connor, what is it?"

"Your instincts were right," he replied without a second thought. "There is something serious going on, something that could hurt Brian. I'd rather relay as little as possible right now—not because I don't trust you but because I don't trust cell phones. Suffice it to say that Stephen's under the gun. Brian's being shoved into the cross-fire. And the man I'm asking you about might be the one with his finger on the trigger. Is that enough for you to help me?"

"Oh, my God." Julia's voice shook. "Is Brian all right?"

"Yes." This much, at least, he could give her. "Nancy called today. They're both fine."

"But she's keeping him away." Julia swallowed. "Okay, I won't push you for details. As for Robin, I'll see her during afternoon recess. She doesn't have a class then, so she always comes out to shoot the breeze. I'll find out everything I can about this man." A weighted pause. "You think he's dating Robin to get close to Brian?"

"I don't know. But Stephen's a wreck. Frankly, so am I." Connor heard the apprehension in his own voice, and he found himself wishing like hell that Julia were there beside him. He needed to hold her, to comfort her and himself.

"I'll call you the minute I can break away from my class. Or, at the very latest, when I get home."

"Good." Connor stared at the phone. "Julia?"

"Yes?"

"I really appreciate your doing this."

"I know." A long pause. "I'm glad you called me."

There was a quiet click as she hung up.

24

April 13
10:45 A.M.
Stowe, Vermont

Nancy sat at the rustic kitchen counter, nursing her third cup of coffee. She'd been at the ski lodge since the middle of the night when Tuesday had become Wednesday, and she'd scarcely slept five hours total. She felt detached from everything, as if she were falling in slow motion and had no idea when she'd land.

Or maybe she'd stopped caring.

From the other room, she heard Brian changing the channels as he watched TV. That's all he'd done since they got there. He'd gone from bewildered to unsettled to depressed and downright listless. Seeing Cliff had upset him even more, triggering the understandable slew of questions about where Stephen was and why he couldn't have been the one to bring up his medicine.

Nancy hadn't had any answers. But she had told Cliff to stay away.

Cliff hadn't argued. Part of him probably had been relieved. He cared about her, deeply, but Stephen was his best friend. This whole situation had to be tearing him apart. He'd called her twice since then, making sure she and Brian were okay, adding how worried about them Stephen was.

In some ways, it would be so much easier if she were

in love with Cliff. He was solid, stable, free of emotional baggage. And he loved her, with an all-encompassing kind of intensity. She'd be the center of his world, not a valued facet.

But she didn't love Cliff. She loved Stephen. Even now, when he'd put his life, and the life of their son, at risk. She probably should have her head examined for feeling that way. The thing was, she knew Stephen—the real Stephen—in a way he didn't even know himself. He was so much more than he believed he was, so much more than Harrison Stratford had trained him to believe. He was a good man, a caring, compassionate man, a man with noble convictions—convictions he transformed into reality. He was a man who made a difference, who inspired people just by being himself, even though he insisted—to her and to himself—that it was all a political façade. He was the man she'd fallen in love with the first time they'd met, during the first conversation they'd shared, at that first instant he'd flashed her his charismatic smile. And, yes, he was Brian's father—a wonderful, loving father whom Brian adored.

Becoming a Stratford hadn't been easy for her. Dealing with Stephen's demons had been harder still. But she loved him, and he loved her. Not in the uncomplicated and absolute way Cliff did, but then, Stephen wasn't an uncomplicated man. And marriage wasn't a starry-eyed romance. It was hard work, a lifetime commitment.

So she'd committed herself to it with a fervor that had been tested time and again, by forces that had bent but somehow never broken the bond between her and Stephen.

She'd tried so hard to be all he needed, praying it would be enough to give him the strength to overcome his self-doubts, to fill his psychological voids.

Maybe the time had come to admit that she'd failed. Or maybe she was just too damned tired to keep fighting.

So where did that leave them? Where did they go from here?

Tears filled Nancy's eyes, slid down her cheeks.

A faint noise from the front doorway caught her attention, and she swiveled around on the kitchen stool to check it out.

The rest happened in a heartbeat.

A man wearing black clothes and a ski mask lunged at her, dragging her off the stool and forcing back her head. She opened her mouth to scream, but he crammed a cloth into it, covering her nose in the process. She struggled, inhaling the medicinal smell despite her attempts to evade it. Black filaments of dizziness crept into her brain like spiders, weakening her struggles and crowding out consciousness.

Reality slipped away in rapidly accelerating increments, until there was nothing but blackness and one terrifying fear.

Brian. He'd come for Brian.

2:45 P.M.

Julia was practically jumping out of her skin.

Naturally, there'd been a fire drill that day, which had screwed up the entire afternoon schedule. Regular recess had been canceled, and instead the kids were being given a late-day outdoor play break before the buses arrived.

The minute her class scattered to their respective playground spots, Julia began scanning the area for an aide she could impose upon to watch her kids so she could go find Robin.

As it turned out, it wasn't necessary. Robin found her.

"Hey, you," she greeted Julia, strolling up beside her. "I haven't seen you all day."

"I know." Julia warned herself to stay calm. "The fire drill blew my whole schedule to bits."

"I've been worried about you. Deny it all you want, but you've got it bad for Connor Stratford. And since the night you went out with him, you've been a mess. You look like hell—and it's not all because you're worried about Brian, either. What did Connor do to throw you so badly?"

Julia swallowed. This was the last thing she wanted to talk about, partly because she was too damned confused right now and partly because she had a mission to accomplish—for the very man Robin was asking about. "You're right, Rob. I'm a mess. My feelings about Connor are very intense and very mixed. I've got to work it through before I talk about it. But once I do, you'll be the first one I come to, okay?"

Robin nodded, understanding glinting in her eyes. "Okay."

Time to get to the crucial subject. "So how are you doing?" Julia tried to sound casual. "Are you in your usual, bouncy weekend mood?"

An offhanded shrug. "Not really."

Julia's brows rose. "Aren't you seeing your mystery guy?"

"Yes, but I think I'm going to put an end to it. The whole relationship's getting a little weird for me."

"Weird?" Julia's antenna went up. "What do you mean? I thought the guy was a winner."

"So did I, at first. He's older, he's very sexy and successful, and he literally swept me off my feet. But I'm beginning to get the distinct feeling that the whole thing's a sham, that he's using me for his own ends. Being used is bad enough. But I have a hunch that his ends are not something I want to be a part of."

Chills rippled up Julia's spine. "How so?"

"Like I said, he's successful. He owns a real estate development company, a big one. Well, a few nights ago, he started talking about hiring me to write a special software program for him. I thought that was strange. To begin with, I'd never mentioned to him that I do that."

"Did you ask him how he knew?"

"Um-hum. He claimed he heard about my expertise from a colleague. That's possible, I suppose. But, Julia, the guy's company has a fully staffed IT department. Why would he need me to write a program for him?"

"You're a computer whiz, Robin. Maybe no one on his staff is up to your level."

"Or maybe he doesn't want them knowing what he has in mind."

"What do you mean?"

Robin chewed her lip. "I could be way off base. But I keep reading about that municipal parking lot contract he's bidding on, the one Mayor Stratford and the city council are debating over."

"That's apparently a hot issue," Julia agreed, her wheels spinning rapidly as she recalled the articles she'd read and tried to fit the puzzle pieces together. "There's friction over whether or not the contract should be allocated to a private company." A quizzical look. "The guy you're dating is Philip Walker?"

"Right. And maybe his bid for the contract and his wanting to hire me are completely unrelated. But if they're not, well, the program he wants me to write sounds a lot like something that could be used to automate kickbacks from the lots he'd be maintaining. If he wins the contract, of course. The council's still divided. But Philip is determined. He wants that contract badly. And he's not the type of guy who takes no for an answer."

Julia's stomach turned over. So that was it. Walker was pressuring the mayor. And whatever he was pressuring him with involved a threat to Brian.

"When he talks about the contract, does he bring up the mayor?" she asked, somehow managing to sound normal.

"Constantly. Oh, he's subtle about it. First, he brings up Brian, since he knows I teach him. He asks how he's doing, how his pitching arm is this year—that kind of stuff. He always makes sure to tell me how proud Mayor Stratford is of his son. Then he segues into how tight he and the mayor are, how many projects they've done together. And that leads to his resolve over the municipal parking contract. It's becoming a pattern."

Julia was feeling sicker by the minute. "What else does he say about Brian?"

"About Brian?" Robin looked surprised. "Nothing much. Just what a cute kid he is, how great it must be to have him in class, how hard it must be for him to sit still when he'd rather be out playing ball. Once he asked how often Brian has recess and what he likes to do when he's on the playground. Truthfully, I think he's just acting interested in Brian because he knows I love kids and he wants to charm me. That way, I won't notice when he jumps to the subject of the contract."

Walker's interest in Brian meant something entirely different to Julia, and the implications were almost too much for her to bear. "You said he's much older than you," she verified, trying to keep her voice steady. "I don't think I've ever seen him around. Has he been to the school?"

"Nope. You know me better than that. I don't invite my dates to school. He picks me up at home. And, yeah, he's older, somewhere in his mid-fifties, I guess. I know that sounds really old, but he's one of those guys age looks great on. He's in incredible shape, he's sexy in a rugged kind of way, and he's rich and charming. Too charming, maybe. My guess is, he's a real operator. And I fell for it, hook, line, and sinker. If I'm right about his motives, then he really played me. Right from the beginning. That kind of deviousness isn't something I want to mess with. It gives me the creeps."

Robin turned to her friend and frowned. "Julia? You're white as a sheet. Did I upset you?"

"What?" Julia had to struggle to compose herself. "Actually, yes. I want you to stop seeing this guy right away. He sounds like trouble."

A grin. "Okay, Mom."

"I mean it, Rob." Julia had to make sure she kept her friend away from Philip Walker. He was obviously scum, and maybe a whole lot worse. "You're a wonderful person. You deserve so much more than a jerk who's using you."

"You got it." Robin's smile gentled. "Thanks for caring. I'll break it off with him tonight, on the phone. That way, I'll avoid having to get into any long-winded explanations. I don't want to make him suspicious. I'll just use the excuse of the age gap. That should do it."

She gave Julia's arm a warm squeeze. "Let's both straighten out our lives. I'll find a fabulous new guy, and you work things out with Connor Stratford. You're in love with him, sweetie. It's written all over your face. And being that you're the one-man-forever type, I'd suggest you snag this guy, pronto."

3:35 P.M.

Snagging Connor was exactly what Julia had in mind when she burst into her apartment that afternoon, although her reasons for doing so, at least for the moment, were a far cry from the romantic ones Robin had intended.

She slammed her apartment door shut and grabbed the phone. Her fingers were shaking as she dialed Connor's cell number.

"Connor Stratford."

"Hi," she responded. "I'm not on my cell phone, because you said you were uneasy about using cell phones to discuss the grittier details. But I had to call on yours. I didn't know where you were. And I didn't want to waste time finding out."

"I'm in Stephen's office. Are you home?"

"Yes."

"Hang up, and I'll call you right back."

Julia snatched up the phone before it had completed its first ring. "Connor?"

"Yes, it's me."

"You were right. Philip Walker zeroed in on Robin for a reason. More than one reason, I think. She's onto him about one, but the other . . ." Julia's voice choked.

"Sweetheart, calm down. Talk to me. What did Robin say?"

Taking a deep breath, Julia relayed the entire conversation to Connor.

"Christ," Connor muttered.

"So Robin is suspicious of Walker's business ethics. She knows he's using her, which I'm sure he is. But the rest . . . Connor, he talked about Brian too much. Why would he want to know what he did at recess or when he had it scheduled? Do you think he meant to hurt him? Robin said he's never been at the school, but that doesn't mean he didn't show up without her realizing it. Could he have . . ." Julia's words trailed off as a sudden memory struck. "Brian's baseball cap," she breathed. "Remember you said it vanished during afternoon recess? He'd never lose that cap. It means everything to him."

"Walker took it," Connor responded without preamble. "Then he sent it to Nancy with a threatening note. That's why she packed up Brian and left." He rushed on, as Julia started to interrupt. "No more questions, not now. Just know that Brian is with his mother. She'll keep him safe. I've got to hang up now. I need to pass your information on to Stephen."

"Okay," she accepted quietly.

A pause. "Julia, you've helped more than you know. I can't thank you enough. I'll call you later."

It wasn't until after they'd hung up that Julia remembered that later she'd be out with Greg.

6:40 P.M.

The wooden sign that said "Walker Development" was propped up against a tree in front of the construction site. Unlike the other Leaf Brook projects that Walker Development was currently involved in building, this one was stalled. The steel girders lay dormant, the concrete foundation was only half filled. The crew hadn't been there in two weeks, since a hold-up with the architect had delayed submission of the updated plans to the building department. No plans meant no permit. As a result, construction had stopped in its tracks.

And the site was deserted. That's why he'd chosen it. It was the perfect hiding place, for more reasons than one.

He parked behind the trailer and climbed out of his car. At the passenger side, he eased Brian Stratford to a sitting position. The boy was still a little groggy, although the chloroform he'd readministered was starting to wear off. Just to be on the safe side, he yanked his ski mask on before carrying Brian out of the car. Later it wouldn't matter, but right now he preferred to remain anonymous.

He couldn't wait for this whole damn thing to be over. He wanted to unload Stephen Stratford's son, get the ball rolling, and reap his reward.

Scooping Brian up, he headed quickly for the trailer. He climbed inside the dark, cluttered compartment, just as Brian picked up his head and gazed around. At first, he looked bleary and confused. Then memory returned, and his eyes widened with fear. He began struggling, crying out as he did. His attacker ignored his protests and plopped him into a chair.

"Don't bother howling," he muttered, yanking Brian's wrists behind him, then binding both his ankles and his wrists. "No one can hear you. But just to be on the safe side . . ." He pulled a handkerchief out of his pocket, crammed a portion of it into Brian's mouth. "There. That should keep you nice and quiet."

He squatted down, peering at Brian's terrified face through the slits in his mask. "You're gonna be here for a couple of days. So take it easy. I'll be back to check on you. If you're good, I'll bring food and water. And if your father's good, you'll be home on Monday. Understand?"

Tears glistened in Brian's eyes, but he nodded.

"Good. See you tomorrow." He left the trailer and drove off.

7:20 P.M.
Leaf Brook Police Headquarters

Martin Hart leaned a hip against his desk. Folding his arms across his chest, he frowned at Connor and Stephen.

"Let's get to the pressing issue and leave the mall details for later," he stated flatly. "Philip Walker. I'm even antsier about him now than I was when I spoke to Connor yesterday."

Stephen leaned forward in his chair. "Why? Did you find something else on him?"

"Something concrete, you mean?" Marty's frown deepened. "No, but the idea of a coincidence is sure looking more unlikely by the minute. Get this. I did some more extensive digging into auto thefts that took place in Leaf Brook. I expanded my search to cover the last two years. And guess what?"

He let his question hang for an instant before answering it himself.

"As it turns out, there were a bunch of thefts that occurred in privately owned and maintained lots. The incidents were spread out over a period of time, which is why they didn't raise any red flags with my department. But these crimes had something in common with the more recent thefts, the ones in the city-run parking facilities. None of them took place in lots maintained by

Walker Development. Correction: they weren't maintained by Walker at the time of the thefts. *Afterward*, now, that's another story. Suddenly, all the small companies that owned the lots were eager as hell to turn their security over to Walker Development. It's like they needed convincing, and Walker conveniently provided it."

"More proof the guy's a crook," Stephen muttered, dragging a hand through his hair.

Marty's brows rose. "You don't sound too surprised, Mayor Stratford. Now, why is that? Could it be you're dealing with that same kind of arm twisting right now? Because it occurred to me that that's why Councilman Kirson's car might have been stolen. It happened right at a time when Kirson's vote could make a difference to Philip Walker. So tell me, was that Walker's way of winning the city council over to the idea of giving him the municipal parking contract? Has he been strongly encouraging you to help him do the same?"

Stephen met Marty's gaze head-on, without a trace of evasiveness. "Yes. The problem is, I have no tangible evidence, other than some dicey conversations and a few ugly actions I can't actually pin on him. Plus, there's a lot more on the line here than money or contracts, a lot I can't get into with you yet. We've been friends a long time, Marty. I'm asking for your understanding. And, of course, for your cooperation. By all means, keep investigating Walker. But do it discreetly. The minute you get something on the guy, we'll jump all over it. You have my word on that."

Marty had been a cop too long not to recognize what Stephen was really saying. His eyes narrowed in anger. "If he's threatening you . . ."

"As I said, I have no proof. But I intend to get it."

Connor listened to this exchange with a mixture of surprise and pride. He hadn't expected Stephen to be so frank. But maybe he should have, based on their last few conversations. Stephen loved his family. He wanted to turn his life around, to reclaim his principles. That took a hell of a lot of courage, especially since it meant putting his own neck on the line.

Well, if Stephen was marching into battle, he wasn't going to do it alone.

"Just give us a little time, Marty," Connor inserted, throwing his weight behind his brother's. "We're leaving no stone unturned. Stephen's working on it. I'm working on it. I've also got some private business contacts working on it. They're in constant touch with me. We're checking out everyone Walker's done business with over the past decade, even longer if necessary. If there's something to find on this guy, we'll find it."

"Greg's turned up nothing yet?" Marty asked.

"No," Stephen replied. "But he's been harried with other work, and he has no idea how critical this is. So I can't blame him."

Marty cleared his throat. "Will Walker be at the opening tomorrow? He was a big investor in the building of this mall."

"I'm sure he will."

A stiff nod. "Then so will I. Nothing like the personal touch of a police chief to strike fear in the wrong hearts. Just in case Walker feels like carrying out whatever threats he might or might not be issuing."

Stephen understood. "Thanks, Marty. I appreciate it."

"No problem." A corner of his mouth lifted wryly. "The good news is, the mall's parking lot should be safe.

With Walker having such a big investment in the place, I doubt we'll have to worry about any thefts taking place in that twelve-story monstrosity tomorrow."

9:05 P.M.

This dinner had definitely been a mistake.

Julia shifted in her chair, taking another sip of wine in the hopes that it would calm her nerves. So far, it hadn't. Neither had the conversation, although Greg had tried everything to relax her. It wasn't his fault. It wasn't even her feelings for Connor that were interfering with her evening or causing her steak to lie like lead in her stomach. It was her worry over Brian.

My God, this involved more than family tension or discord. This involved physical danger. Or the threat of it, at least. It was a good thing Nancy Stratford had whisked Brian away in time.

Still, the questions kept crowding her brain.

Why hadn't Stephen Stratford called the police? Why were he and Connor keeping Walker's threat so hush-hush and doing all the investigating on their own? What was it she was missing that would keep them from blowing the whistle on Walker? Lack of proof? The police could help find it. Political fallout? The city could only applaud Mayor Stratford for exposing a criminal. Then what?

"Earth to Julia." Greg was leaning across the table, tapping her wine glass. "Are you making telepathic contact with that thing?"

She gave him a rueful smile. "Sorry. Actually, I was wishing I could drink more. Being totally smashed might make me forget what a miserable week it's been.

The problem is, I drove myself here. So getting drunk is out."

Greg chuckled. "That bad, huh?" He took a sip of his own wine. "Is this all school-related?"

"More or less," she hedged. "It's been like a circus there since Brian went with his mom to California. Jack has me dancing over to the mayor's office with homework. The press is huddled outside my door. I guess I'm not used to the political scene like you are."

A snort of disgust. "Maybe I'm around it a lot more than you, but you never get used to it. Especially when it comes to the media. They're like leeches." Greg's brows lifted quizzically. "Speaking of Brian, how are things with you and Connor Stratford—still progressing?"

Julia felt color tinge her cheeks. It wasn't that the question was unfair—after all, her relationship with Connor was why she'd shut things down with Greg. It just felt weird discussing such a personal subject with a guy she knew had feelings for her.

"Too personal?" Greg guessed, letting her off the hook.

"Partly. Also, I'm not even sure how to answer you. I wouldn't say things are progressing. I'd say they're fermenting."

Greg's lips curved at her choice of words. "Into a fine wine or a sour pickle?"

"Ah, now, that's the question," she said, striving for as much honesty as she felt comfortable with. "My relationship with Connor is one big paradox. Like I said, I'm not into the political scene. And I'm not into money. Well, the name Stratford is synonymous with both. So I feel a little like Dorothy Gale from Kansas. I'm in Emerald City, but I'm not sure I want to stay there."

"There's no place like home, huh?" Greg commiserated gently.

"Something like that, yes." Julia studied his face. He didn't seem to be bothered by what she'd said. But he did seem strained and tired. "I hope I haven't upset you."

"You didn't. I asked. Besides, I've been regaling you with my problems all night. And you've been a trouper, listening to me. Even after I promised we wouldn't talk about work." Greg rubbed his eyes. "Sorry. I don't mean to be rude. It's no reflection on your company, believe me. I'm just beat. The mayor's been tied up in meetings all week, my secretary's out sick, and I've still got a bunch of figures to go through before I can finalize this budget."

"Are you still planning on going in tomorrow?"

"Yup." Greg yawned. "It'll be nice and quiet. Everyone's going to the mall opening, so there'll be no interruptions. I'll get an early start. I should be through by the end of the day."

Julia picked up her purse. "Why don't we call it a night?" she suggested, pulling out her wallet. "It's almost ten o'clock. We're both exhausted. We've had a great meal and a nice talk. Now it's time for a good night's sleep, especially for you."

Greg shot her a rueful look. "You don't mind?"

"Not a bit." Truthfully, Julia couldn't wait to get home. She wanted to try to reach Connor, see what else he could tell her. "My treat, as promised," she said firmly, waving away Greg's offer to pay. "You saved me from cold pizza and boring TV reruns."

"That sounds almost as bad as preparing my budget," Greg said dryly. He stood, stretching. "Come on. I parked right next to you. I can at least walk you to your car."

They strolled across the parking lot, stopping when they reached their vehicles, which were parked beneath a bright overhead light. Greg's Audi was to the left of Julia's Beetle, and he headed around to his driver's side, waiting for her to slide between the two cars and unlock her door.

"Thanks for dinner," he called as she slid her key into the lock.

"Any time." Julia turned, flashing him a smile.

Inadvertently, her gaze flitted across his car's interior as she turned back.

With a flash of surprise, she jerked around again, staring at the bright red object lying on the side of his passenger seat.

"What's the matter?" Greg asked, seeing the stunned expression on her face.

"That rabbit's foot," she replied, pointing.

Brows knit, Greg unlocked his car, reached in, and pulled out the scrap of fur. "This?"

"Yes." She took it, checked it out carefully. "It's mine."

"You're kidding."

"No. I gave it to Connor the day Brian left town. It was meant as a good luck charm. It used to be mine. I wanted Brian to have it."

"That's odd." Greg glanced at the rabbit's foot, clearly perplexed. "The only thing I can think is that Connor didn't have a chance to give it to Brian before he and his mom left for the airport. He must have planned to send it to him instead. It probably got mixed in with all the other stuff Celeste has been packing up for Brian's care package. The poor woman's crazed. With my secretary out sick, she's been pinch hitting for me, running around like a chicken without a head. Let's see, yesterday alone she made two trips down to my car to grab some files. As a matter of fact, Cliff Henderson was down there, too. He had to get some material I brought on a due diligence matter we're conducting for the mayor." A rueful grin. "So, as you can see, my car is like Grand Central Station. Someone must have dropped your good luck charm in transit."

"Oh." Julia nodded, still clutching the rabbit's foot. She didn't know why, but for some reason it made her feel closer to Brian.

"I tell you what," Greg promised. "I'll leave it on the mayor's desk tomorrow, with a note. He can send it out Monday."

"That's fine." Julia handed it back, feeling strangely uneasy, although she had no idea why. The explanation made perfect sense. Greg had no way of knowing that Brian wasn't in California. He, like everyone else, believed Brian was with his aunt and her family. He couldn't know that Brian's well-being was being threatened. And he couldn't know how empty she felt knowing that Brian didn't have that rabbit's foot.

"Julia?" Greg prompted. "I'm sorry about the mix-up."

"It's okay. It's not your fault." She massaged her temples. "I'm just overtired. I'd better get home to bed." She patted Greg's forearm. "Thanks for a nice evening. Good night."

"Good night." He waited until her motor was on before he climbed into his car.

Then he watched her drive off, a pensive expression on his face.

10:15 P.M.

Cliff was bone-weary.

He stared down at the negatives he'd plucked out of Greg's car the day before, wondering how things had deteriorated to the point where he'd be reduced to doing what he'd done.

Who was he kidding? He knew the answer to that. The cause and the defense were the same: his love for Nancy.

For thirteen years, he'd stayed on the sidelines, watching Nancy build a life with another man—his best friend, no less—watching them marry, watching her have and raise Stephen's child. He'd stood by her side as a friend and confidant, helping her through Stephen's most trying emotional hurdles, never saying a bad word about his best friend, even though he resented the hell out of him for his weakness and how that weakness affected Nancy.

The fact was, Stephen didn't deserve her. And, no matter how he'd tried to pretend otherwise, Cliff had always secretly hoped that one day Nancy would see that for herself and walk away from the marriage.

This past Wednesday, for the first time, he had realized that wasn't going to happen—ever.

It had hit him like a ton of bricks when he drove up to Stowe, brought Brian his medicine, and, with Nancy at her breaking point, waited for her to turn to him, not as her friend but as her future.

Instead, she'd wept to him about Stephen, admitting that after hours of soul-searching, she'd faced the inevitable and had to be honest with him. She would never stop loving her husband, no matter how much easier it would be if she could. Further, to spare Cliff undue pain, she'd decided that the only fair thing was to pull away from him—or, in Cliff's mind, to shut him out.

She'd announced that he shouldn't come up to the ski lodge again while she was staying there. Not just for his sake but for Brian's. It seemed that Brian had freaked out when he heard Cliff, and not Stephen, would be delivering his medicine and checking up on them. He interpreted it to mean that Cliff was assuming the role of a father figure, when it was Stephen he wanted and missed.

Bottom line? She had to consider her son first. So Cliff had to stay away.

Talk about a reality check.

He'd spent all Wednesday night digesting it. Then, yesterday, at the meeting with Harrison, Cliff had watched Stephen. The man was so caught up in his own hell, he didn't even know anyone else's existed.

That's when he'd made his decision.

Stephen's focus was about to change. He'd see someone else's hell, all right.

And in the process, his own hell would get that much worse.

10:25 P.M.

Julia saw the flashing red light on her answering machine the minute she walked in. She ran over and pressed the PLAY button.

"One message," the machine announced.

"Julia? I was hoping to catch you before you left for your workshop." It was Connor, sounding very troubled. "It's the only chance I'll get to call you tonight. Stephen and I are meeting with the chief of police about added security at tomorrow's huge mall opening—among other things. Under the circumstances, we can't be too careful." He paused, as if he had a lot to say but didn't want to risk saying it to an answering machine. "We *will* talk," he continued. "Soon. I'll be at the mall hoopla most of tomorrow, for Stephen's sake. If I can get cell reception there, I'll call you. Otherwise, I'll call the minute I'm out. I've got to see you, right away. We've got major issues to resolve."

A click, followed by the machine announcing, "Friday, six forty-five P.M.."

That was less than five minutes after she'd walked out the door to meet Greg. She'd just missed Connor's call.

Sinking down on the sofa, Julia rested her head against the cushioned arm. She was still plagued by her earlier uneasiness, now coupled with the tight ache that resulted from listening to Connor's message. She wished she could talk to him now. And not only because she wanted to know what those major issues were—whether they dealt solely with Brian or spilled over onto the two of them—but because she still felt so out of sorts, just as she had since getting his phone call the night before. Maybe if he filled her in on some more of the details, her apprehension would subside.

Then again, maybe not.

25

April 14
7:35 A.M.
Stowe, Vermont

Nancy's head lolled about, and she fought to grab hold of consciousness. It hovered just out of reach, crawling into her head in increments, only to slip away just as quickly. During that time, day faded into night, and night somehow transformed into day.

What time is it? she wondered groggily, again battling the effects of the drug.

Remember. Try to remember.

She was tied to a chair. Her arms were bound tightly behind her, and her muscles were cramped from being forced into that position. Her legs were also bound, a thick piece of rope twined around them to anchor them to the legs of the chair. And she was gagged, the cloth strip tied around the back of her head, the material biting into the sides of her mouth.

Why was she so weak and out of it that she couldn't even try to free herself?

A flash of memory. The man in the ski mask, the one who'd attacked her, he'd given her something. She remembered him shaking her awake long enough to command her to drink. Whatever she'd drunk, combined with the stuff she'd inhaled when he first grabbed her, was strong.

God. Brian.

For the dozenth time, she tried to call his name, her voice emerging in a hoarse croak from beneath the gag. Still, the sound was audible enough. Brian would have answered her if he were there—and if he could. Maybe he was tied and gagged in the other room.

Her maternal instincts told her otherwise. Brian wasn't in the ski lodge. Whoever had drugged her had also kidnapped her son.

With a surge of fear and adrenaline, she began struggling at her bonds, desperate to free herself. She had to get out of there. To call for help. To find Brian.

The bonds wouldn't budge.

Whimpering, Nancy collapsed against the back of the chair. Tears welled up in her eyes, slid down her cheeks.

Where was Brian? What had they done to him? He was obviously terrified. Was he also hurt? Had they contacted Stephen so he could give them whatever they wanted for the safe return of his son?

They. That son of a bitch Walker and whoever he had working for him. Those filthy bastards had taken her child.

The drug was doing its job again, dragging her into mental oblivion. Her body was too damned weak to fight it. Her eyelids drooped, and her head sagged forward.

A flash of the man in the ski mask darted through her mind. The whole thing had happened so fast. She'd scarcely had time to glance up before he grabbed her.

But in that brief instant . . .

His eyes. She knew those eyes.

She'd seen them many times before.

8:30 A.M.

Brian heard the crunching sound of tires on gravel, followed by the slamming of a car door.

The man in the mask was coming.

His entire body tensed, and he began shaking.

He knew he should be brave, not act like a wimp, but he couldn't help it. He was scared. The trailer was dark and creepy. It had gotten darker and creepier as the night wore on, and he'd heard weird noises coming from outside. He told himself it was just animals, but it sounded more like monsters. Or aliens.

He'd gladly have taken on both if it meant getting away from that man.

Footsteps plodded through the mud, neared the trailer.

Brian stared at the door, his eyes wide with dread.

Was the man coming to bring him food or to hurt him? Why had he taken him to begin with? And why had he tied up his mom? Not just tied her up, made her drink some stuff that had put her to sleep?

The ropes hurt a lot. His whole pitching arm was fuzzy, as if there were pieces of sand stuck in it. His legs felt the same way. And his mouth was sore from the handkerchief he'd managed to spit partway out.

He felt tears seep out of the corners of his eyes. He missed his parents. He wanted to go home.

The door to the trailer swung open. The man in the ski mask walked in.

"Hey, Brian." He walked over, squatted down beside the chair, a no-nonsense look in his slitted eyes. "This is going to be quick. I've got someplace I have to be. So be a good kid and don't fight me." He reached into his pocket, and Brian froze, waiting for him to pull out a gun. This was the part where the victim got whacked. Just like in his new computer game.

He braced himself for the bullet.

Instead, the man whipped out a bottle of Gatorade and a snack-pack box of Frosted Flakes. "Breakfast time." He reached for Brian's gag. "No yelling. Just eat, drink, and stay put. Okay?"

Brian nodded. He was too thirsty, too hungry, and too scared to disobey.

He just silently followed instructions.

The man's voice was low and kind of hoarse, as if he were trying to disguise it. But Brian recognized it anyway. He'd heard it before, a whole bunch of times.

He knew just who it belonged to.

10:15 A.M

Julia hadn't slept a wink.

All night long, she'd tossed and turned, troubled by the elusive feeling that something wasn't quite right.

Over her second cup of coffee, she realized what it was.

The timing. It just didn't ring true.

She'd given Connor her rabbit's foot at eight-thirty Tuesday morning. He'd clearly been touched by the gesture. Like Julia, he knew it would lift Brian's spirits tremendously. By the time she'd had dinner with him ten hours later, he'd seen Brian. He'd specifically said so. In fact, he'd gone on to say how bad he felt that Brian looked so washed out, that he had an ear infection and was on an antibiotic.

So why hadn't he given him the rabbit's foot? Why would he hold on to it for a day, even if he didn't know that Brian was going away, when it would definitely have brought a smile to his nephew's lips?

He wouldn't have.

And there was another thing that was bugging her. Something Greg had said. She hadn't given it much thought last night. She'd been too upset over Brian not having her good luck charm. But now, it struck her as she replayed the conversation she'd had with Greg. He'd said something about Cliff Henderson needing to get something out of his car relating to a due diligence matter they were conducting for the mayor.

Could that matter involve Philip Walker? He was certainly the most pressing due diligence matter on the mayor's plate. Was Greg privy to more confidential details than he'd been able to discuss? It made sense. He was the city manager, and he'd worked with Mayor Stratford for years. And Cliff Henderson was the mayor's attorney. Why wouldn't Stephen Stratford elicit their help?

Julia shoved aside her coffee cup. She had to do something. Connor was at the mall opening. She couldn't speak to him about this until tonight. There was no way she could leave it alone till then. She was too worked up.

Greg, on the other hand, was in his office working. Presumably on the budget, although she was beginning to wonder if he was really doing a background check for the mayor.

There was only one way to find out.

She'd invent a plausible excuse for dropping by the mayor's office. That way, if she was wrong and Greg was buried in his budget numbers, totally oblivious to what was going on with Brian, she could make a graceful exit, and no harm would be done. But if she was right, then maybe they could put their heads together and come up with something concrete on Walker while the mayor made his requisite political appearance at the mall.

Now for the excuse.

She went over to her binder, pulled out the couple of reading and spelling tests that belonged to the kids who were absent when she'd graded them. Let's see—Jennifer's science sheet, Randy's reading quiz. There. Brian's spelling test from Monday. He'd gotten a 97. A nice surprise to pass on to his father. A nice excuse in case she needed one.

She grabbed her purse and left the apartment.

10:45 A.M.
Municipal Building

Julia had a hell of a time getting into the building. Not only was it locked, but it was manned by a security attendant who grilled her as if she were a terrorist. Even the spelling test she'd brought as her alibi wouldn't have been enough to get her upstairs.

Luck helped out on that score.

The security officer was about to buzz Greg in his office and verify that Ms. Talbot was expected, when the front door blew open and Celeste dashed out.

"Ms. Talbot—hello." She halted in her tracks, a surprised expression on her face. "What are you doing here?"

Relief swept through Julia. She hadn't wanted Greg to know she was coming. Advance warning would give him time to hide any confidential material he was working on and whip out his budget, fabricating a "normal" scene for her to walk in on. This way, he'd be caught off guard.

"Hi, Celeste." With a sheepish look, Julia waved

Brian's spelling test in the air. "I wanted to leave this on the mayor's desk so he could send it to Brian. Greg mentioned to me that a package would be going out to him on Monday. And since Mayor Stratford is tied up all day at the mall, I thought I'd drop it off here. I had no idea it would be such a big deal to get in." She held up her other arm, giving the Dunkin' Donuts bag she clutched a light shake. "Also, Greg mentioned to me that he'd be working all day. I thought I'd say hi, bring him a cup of coffee and a doughnut to make working on a Saturday easier to bear."

Celeste grinned. "I'm sure he'd appreciate that." She turned to the guard and nodded. "It's okay, Joe. Ms. Talbot can go up."

"Okay." Joe shot Julia an apologetic look. "Sorry, Ms. Talbot, just doing my job." He scratched his head, angling it at Celeste. "Boy, today's been busy," he commented. "You, Mr. Matthews, Mr. Henderson, and now Ms. Talbot. Saturdays are normally real quiet. And I thought today would be even more so, with everyone going to the mall opening. Guess I was wrong."

"Not completely," Celeste assured him. "I'm off to the mall right now." She waved good-bye to Julia.

"Celeste, one quick question," Julia interjected.

"Sure."

"In that package you're putting together for Brian, did either the mayor or Connor Stratford give you a red rabbit's foot to include?"

With a puzzled shrug, Celeste replied, "You've lost me. I'm not putting together any package for Brian. The mayor is taking care of all that himself. As for the rabbit's foot, I haven't seen it. That doesn't mean it isn't there." She smiled. "It's a gift from you, I take it?"

Julia nodded, processing that piece of information. "Okay, well, thanks anyway. Enjoy the grand opening."

She waited while the guard held open the door and let her pass. Then she made her way through the lobby to the elevator. So Greg had been wrong about Celeste handling Brian's package. Either wrong or lying. If he was wrong, then the mayor was keeping him in the dark about whatever was going on. But if he was lying, that gave her hunch even more credibility. Especially since Cliff Henderson either was, or had been, there that morning. If he and Greg were collaborating, working privately with the mayor on Brian's situation, what better time to do it than today, when the office was quiet and the rest of the city was at the mall opening?

Time to stop speculating. Time to find out.

Julia took the elevator up to the executive level and made her way toward Greg's office, which was just around the bend from the mayor's.

The mayor's office door was shut. But it swung open as she passed, and Cliff Henderson strode out, his jaw clenched as he skimmed through what looked to be sheets of stationery and some photographs. He was so absorbed in his thoughts that he nearly collided with her.

"Oh, excuse me." He blinked, clearly surprised to see her. He stuck his right hand behind his back, but not before Julia saw the Walker Development letterhead on the stationery he was gripping and the photo stapled on top of it.

It was a snapshot of Brian standing on the pitcher's mound.

"Ms. Talbot, right?" he asked, waiting for her nod. "If you're looking for Stephen or Connor, they're both at the mall."

"I assumed as much," Julia replied. She was wracking her brain to think of why a picture of Brian would be stapled to Walker's stationery and why Cliff Henderson would be holding them. Also, what were the other photos of? "Actually, I'm dropping in on Greg. I brought him a cup of coffee. Is he in there with you or in his own office?"

A shrug. "His own office, I assume. I haven't seen him in the past half hour or so."

"Fine. I'll head down there." Julia inclined her head. "Are you on your way out?"

A brief pause. "Soon. I have a few legal matters to tie up for the mayor. Then I'll join him at the grand opening. But don't let me keep you. Bring Greg his coffee while it's hot."

He was clearly dying to get rid of her. Why?

Julia's insides knotted.

Cliff Henderson wasn't acting like an attorney handling a confidential matter. He was acting like a criminal trying to conceal his guilt.

Keeping the photos firmly hidden, Cliff glanced at his watch, and Julia saw beads of perspiration gathering on his brow. "Forgive me, Ms. Talbot. I don't mean to be rude. But I have to finish up my work."

"No problem." She forced a smile. "Good-bye." Turning, she continued down the corridor, purposely keeping her steps slow and even in case Cliff Henderson was watching.

Indeed, he was watching. From outside Stephen's office door, he stared after her, his lips drawn in a grim line.

Julia reached Greg's office, praying that she could glean something from him, *anything* that could help her. She was feeling more uneasy by the minute.

The door was slightly ajar, and Julia was just about to knock when she heard Greg's voice on the phone.

"According to my notes, Mr. Walker will be leaving the country around noon on Monday," he was saying.

Startled, Julia leaned closer. She eased the door open a bit farther, glancing cautiously inside. Greg's back was to her, so she grew bolder, wedging herself in the open doorway to hear better.

"I'm just verifying that the flight plan to Switzerland has been filed and that the company jet will be fueled and ready." Greg paused, nodding. "Um-hum. I know it's short notice. I have no idea what the trip's for. Make something up if you have to. One passenger and a large attaché case. No luggage. I know, but you need to keep this low-profile, Jerry. Um-hum. Pay whatever it takes. A thousand's not a problem. You'll get the money Monday. Yeah, that's what they say. Secret banks and great chocolate—a perfect place for the rich to disappear forever. I already told you, no return plans." A chuckle. "Excellent. Thanks."

He hung up, turning before Julia could duck out and digest what she'd just heard, maybe make some sense out of it.

"Julia." His greeting was surprised and anything but pleased, and his eyes narrowed on her face. "What are you doing here?"

"I c-came to see you." She tried desperately not to stammer. "I brought you a doughtnut and coffee." She stepped inside, set the bag down on the nearest end table. She couldn't look Greg in the eye, not until she'd figured out why he'd been making phone calls on Walker's behalf. And, more important, why those phone calls implied that Walker was leaving the country—for good.

What in God's name was going on?

She had to get hold of herself. "Actually, the real reason I'm here is to put this with the rabbit's foot you left for Brian on the mayor's desk." She fluttered the spelling test in the air for the umpteenth time that day. "A 97. Definitely worth including in his care package."

"I haven't had a chance to put the rabbit's foot on Mayor Stratford's desk." Greg's gaze was steady. "But I will. In case you doubted it."

"Of course not. I know you'll take care of it before you go home." Julia retreated to the doorway, intent on acting as normal as possible. "I didn't expect it to be the first thing on your mind. You're swamped with work. Truthfully, I'm on overdrive myself. I've got a ton of errands to run and some lesson plans to catch up on. I promised myself I'd just pop in, drop off my goodies, and take off. So I'm on my way. Enjoy the breakfast. I'll talk to you next week."

With a little wave, she withdrew back into the hallway, then made a beeline for the elevator.

Greg followed her into the hall. He noticed she didn't stop to take a detour into the mayor's office to leave the spelling test for Brian.

12:10 P.M.
Leaf Brook Mall

The twelve-level parking lot was packed like a giant can of sardines.

Julia drove around and around in one long, spiral ascent until she finally saw the tiny parking spot on the eleventh floor. Her Beetle just barely managed to squeeze in.

She flipped off the ignition, taking a deep breath to steady her nerves.

She had to find Connor.

All the way there, she'd mulled over what she'd seen and heard, mentally reviewing the facts, over and over. And over and over, her gut told her something was wrong.

Brian's picture, stapled to a letter from Walker. Plans for Walker to leave the country, comfortably and permanently.

When she fit the puzzle pieces together, they formed a pretty heinous picture.

She had to be wrong. There had to be some logical explanation for this.

She needed reassurances. And she needed them from the Stratfords.

She jumped out of her car, hurried off, and grabbed a down elevator just as its doors were about to shut. She took it down to the mall's main level.

They opened to mayhem.

Mobs of people had come either to shop or to enjoy the opening-day amusements and exhibits the city had provided. Jugglers, face painters, performing mimes, and a popular deejay were some of the main attractions. In the dead center of the complex, a huge Ferris wheel was situated, its cheerful lights and carnival music beckoning children and adults alike.

Julia plowed her way over there, scanning every which way to try to spot Mayor Stratford.

All she saw was a sea of humanity.

Precious time wasted. She could almost feel it slipping away inside her. The scene that was unfolding around her—the activity, the laughter, the noise—took on a kind of surrealistic quality.

Where was the mayor?

She wouldn't give up until she found him.

It took an eternity, but finally, nearly forty-five minutes later, she caught sight of some members of the press crammed near the eastern corner of the mall. At the head of the bunch was Cheryl Lager, deliberately blocking her competitors. And that could mean only one thing: the mayor was nearby. That vulture Cheryl Lager was, no doubt, first in line for the exposé du jour.

Julia shoved her way forward. Sure enough, there was Stephen Stratford, a hundred feet away from her. It might as well have been a hundred miles, for all the good it did. She could see him, yes, but she couldn't get through to him.

Beside the mayor, Julia spotted Harrison Stratford and a regal-looking woman who had to be his wife. On the mayor's other side, she could make out the back of Connor's head. She cupped her hands over her mouth, shouted his name, but she might as well have been in Yankee Stadium, trying to be heard over the din following a grand slam.

She was buffeted by the crowd, shoved this way and that, practically stampeded into the ground.

The mayor and his entourage moved on.

The press followed, like a swarm of bees, maintaining a traveling wall between her and the Stratfords.

This was pointless.

Julia peeled off to one side, ran a frustrated hand through her hair.

There were tons of police officers in the vicinity. She could stop any one of them, tell them it was an emergency and she had to see the mayor. But that would immediately incite the very scandal Connor and Stephen were desperately trying to avoid. She couldn't do that to them, especially since she had no absolute proof that Brian was in danger.

It was already one-thirty. Connor had promised to call her the minute he got out of there, to see her right away. Walker wasn't scheduled to jet off to Switzerland until Monday. Which meant that if there was an ugly plan in the works, Julia had all weekend to prevent it. For now, Brian was safe. He was with his mother. Nancy Stratford would have notified her husband if anyone had tried to hurt their son.

Calm down, Julia cautioned herself. *Don't overreact.* The best thing to do was to go back to her apartment, sit tight, and wait for Connor's call.

And then they would get to the bottom of this, if they had to drag Greg, Cliff, and Walker all in by their necks and interrogate the hell out of them.

She jostled her way to the stairwell, climbed as quickly as she could to the eleventh floor, and stepped out. The parking level was still wall-to-wall cars, not one of them having pulled out since she arrived. Apparently, everyone was staying for the entire day's festivities.

She headed to her car, reaching for her ignition key as she did. Her mind was deeply troubled, and she glanced down at the spelling test she still clutched in her hand—her ostensible reason for catching up to the mayor.

The screech of tires alerted her.

Her head shot up, and she jerked around.

It all happened in a split second. The silver Mercedes careened around the corner, bearing down on her with terrifying speed and purpose.

She was right. Something horrible was happening.

And now she'd never be able to stop it.

The car struck her even as she lunged out of the way, and she felt the impact, saw the concrete rushing up at her. Shards of pain shot up her arm, through her head.

Brian, she thought dazedly, agony giving way to unconsciousness. *Who's going to save Brian?*

2:35 P.M.

Connor was beginning to fidget. He'd tried to get cellphone reception six times already. Not once could he get enough signal to call Julia.

Damn.

He had to talk to her. To connect. To share his fears with her and count on her support. To show her some of that trust she was convinced he'd never learned.

He wanted to make plans for tonight—and for all the nights to follow.

He'd turned off his cell phone in frustration when Martin Hart came up quietly beside him. "Connor? I need to see you and the mayor right away. Pretend it's a security check, and step away from your parents and the press."

The urgency of Marty's tone wasn't lost on Connor. He shot the police chief a look. "Okay."

Casually, he leaned forward, murmured something to Stephen.

Stephen's head came up, but he maintained his cool. Tactfully, he excused himself, explaining that he had to run through a routine security check with the chief of police. Then he moved away from the crowd and joined Connor and Marty to one side.

"There was a hit-and-run in the municipal lot about twenty minutes ago," Marty announced in a low voice.

"The victim was run down as she approached her parked car."

"My God. Is she all right?" Stephen asked.

"I don't know. She was unconscious when the ambulance left here with her. Listen, there's more. She had a piece of paper with her. It had Brian's name on it."

Stephen went rigid. "What do you mean, it had Brian's name on it?"

"It was his. A spelling test or something. It had some of the victim's blood splattered on it, but you could definitely make out Brian's name, written in a kid's handwriting. My men took it as evidence."

All the color had drained from Connor's face. "A spelling test?" he repeated. "Do you know the identity of this woman?"

"According to her driver's license, her name's Julia Talbot. She's twenty-seven, slight, reddish-brown hair . . ."

"What hospital did they take her to?" Connor demanded, grabbing Marty's arm.

The police chief's gaze narrowed. "I take it you know her."

"Yes. Now, where is she?"

"Leaf Brook Memorial. Connor, wait." He held out a detaining hand.

"Let him go, Marty," Stephen said quietly. "I'll answer the rest of your questions."

"Yeah, you will—later, when we can talk alone. But this wasn't a question. Connor, the car that hit Ms. Talbot—it was yours."

26

6:25 P.M.
Leaf Brook Memorial

Connor was saying something, but his voice was far away. Julia couldn't make out his words. The throbbing in her head was too loud.

She shifted slightly, trying to hear him better. She winced at the slivers of pain that shot through her arm and side.

Where was she and why did she hurt so much?

"Lie still," Connor was saying. "Don't try to move. Just open your eyes and look at me. Please, Julia."

He sounded awful.

She cracked open her eyes, waiting for his face to stop swimming around and come into focus.

He looked even worse.

"Connor?" Her voice was a weak croak.

Stark relief swept his features. "Thank God." He leaned over, brushed her lips gently with his. "Yes, it's me. You're all right. Everything's going to be fine now."

"I'm in the hospital," she observed, recognizing the antiseptic smells. She felt disoriented, the pounding in her head standing between her and lucidness.

"Um-hum." Connor took her left hand and tenderly wrapped her fingers in his. "Does that hurt?"

She started shaking her head, then thought better of it. "No. Should it?"

"Not this hand. But the other one might."

She glanced down, surprised to see that much of her right hand and arm were bandaged. "Are they broken?"

"I don't think so. Frankly, I don't remember. I couldn't focus on anything except your waking up. After that, the rest will heal." He brought her palm to his lips, and Julia was stunned to feel his hands tremble. "You scared the hell out of me," he said roughly. "I've been waiting all day to tell you I love you, and I was afraid I'd never get the chance."

Julia wondered if she'd heard right. "What did you say?"

He swallowed hard, and when he spoke, his voice was filled with raw emotion. "I said I love you. I'm going to keep saying it, now and for the next hundred years, if you'll let me. I need to hear that you feel the same way, but that's going to wait until I'm damned sure you're clear-headed enough to know exactly what you're saying." A poignant pause. "Back to me. Not only do I love you, I also trust you. I'd planned to prove that tonight by telling you everything. You certainly put a damper on my plans. But I'm adaptable. I'll still follow through, *if* the doctor says it's okay."

Another pause, this one longer, and a muscle worked in Connor's jaw. "God, I was so scared. I just found you. The thought of losing you . . ." He broke off, rose to his feet, and headed toward the door.

"I've got to let the doctor know you're awake," he announced, his words clipped, his body language taut. "Louis Tillerman—you'll like him. He's an old family friend and a top-notch neurologist. Fortunately, he's affiliated with Leaf Brook Memorial as well as Columbia Presbyterian. We got him up here right away. He'll keep your condition quiet until we get to the bottom of this. He gave me strict instructions to find him the minute you opened your eyes. I want him to check you out. I'll be right back."

"Connor?" Julia stopped him, her voice weak but clear.

He turned.

"You're babbling," she observed, not really processing much over the throbbing in her skull. Except his declaration of love—*that* she'd processed. "I've never heard you babble."

"That's because I never have. See what you've reduced me to?"

Her eyes grew damp. "I love you, too," she whispered. "Waiting till later won't change that. But I'll repeat it then, and for the next hundred years, if you'll let me."

He walked back, braced his arms on either side of her, and covered her mouth with his for one brief, fervent kiss. "Let's get you well and put this nightmare behind us," he murmured. "Then we'll make plans—the forever kind." He stood, his knuckles drifting over her cheek. "Now, let me get Louis."

The door shut behind him, and Julia sank back against the pillows, feeling a soft inner glow.

Which was overshadowed by an anxiety she couldn't put her finger on and physical pain that seemed to envelop her entire body. Especially her head.

She reached up, surprised to feel a bandage across her forehead. What had happened to her?

Two minutes later, Connor returned, joined by a stocky man in a white hospital coat. He was about forty, with pleasant features and an authoritative air. "Good morning, Julia," he said, his manner calm and reassuring.

"My name's Dr. Tillerman. You had us a little worried there. How do you feel?"

She frowned. "I hurt everywhere. Especially my head and my right side. And my mind's a little jumbled." She paused, regathering her strength. "I can't remember why I'm here. Also, I know there was something I had to do—but I can't recall what."

"You will. Don't push yourself. That blow you took was pretty nasty. Let me take a look."

Blow? What blow? Julia wanted to ask. Why couldn't she think past the wall in her mind?

Dr. Tillerman did a few routine tests, checking her eyes, her reflexes, her speech, and her cognitive responses.

Dutifully, Julia answered his questions, telling him her name, her birthday, and the school she taught in.

"Good," he praised. "Are you experiencing any nausea?"

"Not really. Mostly, my head just aches."

"I know it does. I'll give you something for the pain. I'm also ordering a few more neurological tests, just to be on the safe side. I don't expect any complications. Your CT scan came back a few minutes ago. Everything looks fine—no bleeding, no fractures. Still, you were unconscious for a long time. So, I'll want to keep an eye on you, just to be sure."

"What's wrong with me?"

"You have a concussion," he explained. "That's the reason for the pain and the mental confusion. You also have a nasty gash on your forehead, which we stitched up. As for the rest, you have lacerations on your right side and arm, a few bruised ribs, and some pretty impressive cuts on your right hand. The good news is, there are no internal injuries and, I'm fairly confident now that you're awake and I've examined you, no permanent damage to the brain. You'll be just fine, which is a blessing, considering the severity of the impact."

"The impact." Julia swallowed hard. "Where did I fall?"

Dr. Tillerman glanced at Connor.

"You didn't fall, sweetheart," Connor replied, gazing steadily at her. "You were hit by a car. In the mall parking lot. Do you remember?"

A flash of recall. "The Mercedes. It looked like yours."

"It *was* mine." Connor turned to the doctor. "Louis, if you're finished with the physical exam, I'd like to speak with Julia alone."

"All right," Dr. Tillerman agreed. "But Connor, don't wear her out. I want her to rest. The easier she takes it, the faster she'll heal."

"You have my word. In the meantime, remember, not a word of Julia's condition is to be released to *anyone*—not until we know who did this."

"Understood." The doctor patted Julia's uninjured arm. "I'll order that painkiller. You rest."

"All right." Julia barely managed to answer. And not because she was in pain. Because she was remembering. Throughout Dr. Tillerman and Connor's exchange, pieces had begun falling into place, taking shape like monstrous faces.

As the door shut behind the doctor, Julia jerked to a sitting position, moaning at the resulting pain in her skull.

"Shh." Connor caught her shoulders, gently easing her back. "Go easy on your poor head. It's been through quite an ordeal." He waited until she was resettled, and the agonized look had left her face. "It's coming back to you, isn't it?"

"Yes." Julia's breath was coming fast. "I drove straight from the municipal building to the mall. I tried to get through to you. But the crowd wouldn't let me. So I thought I'd go home and wait. The car came out of nowhere."

"Did you see who was driving it?"

"No. It happened too fast." Her forehead creased. "The Mercedes was yours?"

A nod. "Stolen right out of the mall parking lot. A dozen people saw it tearing through there and gave the police accurate descriptions. One couple actually saw you get hit. They scribbled down as much of the license plate as they could get. It was mine, all right. I'm sure we'll never see it again. It'll be stripped, the parts will be sold, and the world will think it was an accidental hit-and-run."

"We know better."

Connor's jaw set. "Yeah, we do. But Walker's a shrewd bastard. He figured you wouldn't be around to point any fingers. As for my car, it was the perfect choice. An expensive convertible owned by the mayor's brother who wouldn't be checking on it all day? Sounds like the ideal target for a pro. And we wouldn't have a shred of proof to say otherwise." His brows drew together. "Why did you go to the municipal building?"

"To get information." Julia gripped his sleeve. "Connor, the other day, did you give Brian my rabbit's foot?"

"Yes." Connor looked puzzled. "Why?"

"You're sure? You put it in his hand?"

"Of course I'm sure. I gave it to him the minute I saw

him. When I told him who it was from and what it meant to you, it made his day. It was the only smile I got out of him."

Tears filled Julia's eyes. "That's what I was afraid of. Brian's in trouble."

"What kind of trouble?"

Julia's grip tightened. "I'll tell you everything. But first, you've got to call Nancy Stratford. Make sure Brian's okay, that nothing's happened yet, that there's another explanation for that rabbit's foot not being with him now. *Please,*" she begged when Connor made no move toward the phone.

"I can't," he said quietly. "I don't know where she is. Neither does Stephen."

Everything inside Julia went cold. "Then how do you know they're all right?"

"Nancy called Stephen and said so."

"When?"

"Thursday."

"And since then, no one's spoken with them?" Julia demanded.

"Not to my knowledge, no."

She struggled to a sitting position. "We've got to find them." A moan of pain escaped her lips.

"Julia." Connor stopped her struggles. "Listen to me. Making your concussion worse isn't going to help Brian. Now, lie back and tell me what happened—calmly and without making any sharp movements."

She nodded, closing her eyes until the worst of the pain had subsided. "Okay." She took a few breaths, then opened her eyes again.

"Better?"

Another tentative nod. "I'm afraid Walker plans to

kidnap Brian. I pray he hasn't done so already." She waved away Connor's interruption. "He isn't doing it alone. Whoever's helping him is the reason I was almost killed. He knew I was onto him. He must have tipped off Walker, who sent the thug to run me down."

"Explain."

Slowly, resting a few seconds between sentences, Julia told Connor about how she'd spotted the rabbit's foot in Greg's car, about his explanation for how it might have gotten there, and about the telephone conversation she'd overheard him having that day regarding Walker leaving for Switzerland with a large attaché case and no plans to return.

"So Greg Matthews is working for Walker," Connor muttered in disbelief.

"Unless your brother got wind of Walker's plans and asked Greg to check them out by pretending he was doing so at Walker's instructions."

"Nope." Connor gave a hard shake of his head. "Stephen has no idea that Walker's taking off for Switzerland. He thinks he's still obsessed with being awarded the municipal contract."

"Then, yes, Greg's definitely involved. But there's another potential player."

"Who?"

"Cliff Henderson."

"What?"

Hearing the sharp disbelief in Connor's tone, Julia winced. "I know he's close to your family," she said, feeling like a cad. "I might be way off base. I hope so." She went on, explaining how she'd bumped into Cliff today and what he'd been holding—and hiding. "Even if Greg lied about Cliff and the rabbit's foot, I know what I saw in that office today. Cliff was nervous and edgy. He looked guilty as hell. And he was definitely hiding that photo of Brian stapled to Walker's letter. What would he be doing with what I'm praying isn't a ransom note?"

Connor scowled. "Why would Walker use his company stationery to write a ransom note? That doesn't make sense. It's downright stupid. He might as well hand over a written confession."

"That's what I thought." The conversation was beginning to take its toll. Julia's speech was slowing, and her skull felt as if it were going to split in two. "Okay, so it wasn't a ransom note. Maybe it was instructions. I don't know. If it was another threat for your brother, like the baseball cap . . ." She wet her lips, fighting for the strength to continue. "If so, and Walker had just delivered it, why wouldn't Cliff rush right off to the mall to give it to Stephen? Unless he has something to hide . . ." Julia squeezed her eyes shut as a sharp pain lanced through her head.

"Julia?" Connor gripped her hand. "Sweetheart, this is too much for you. We'll finish talking later."

Julia was about to answer when Dr. Tillerman returned with her painkiller. He helped her ease onto one side, then swiftly administered the injection. "That should start working almost immediately," he said, settling her back in. "It'll ease your pain considerably."

"Thank you," she said with a wan smile.

"I'll be checking on you throughout the night," Dr. Tillerman informed her. "Also, Connor's arranged for a private nurse. She should be arriving any time now. No one other than the two of us will be handling your case—or walking through those doors. With the exception of Connor, whom I can't seem to drag out." A glimmer of amusement lit his eyes, then quickly vanished as he saw the tight lines of pain on Julia's face.

"You're overdoing it," he informed Connor flatly. "I understand that time is of the essence. But she's got to rest. No more for now."

Connor nodded, worry creasing his forehead.

"I'm okay," Julia managed to reassure him.

"I just turned away the police," Louis added. "I told them Julia's condition still hadn't changed. They assumed I meant she hadn't regained consciousness. I didn't correct them. I said I'd call Martin Hart when she was up to being questioned."

"Thanks, Louis. Stephen and I will deal with Marty directly. Just not yet."

"Fine. In the meantime, no more talking. Julia, lie back and let the medication do its job. Rest. Connor can stay if he's quiet." A meaningful look at Connor. "I'll be close by until the nurse arrives. Then she'll be stationed right outside the door, to keep an eye on you and to shoo away any visitors. We'll change your bandage and your IV in a few hours. If there's anything you need in the meantime, Connor will come and get me."

"I appreciate that." Gratefully, Julia lay back. She felt as if she'd run a marathon.

She didn't speak until Dr. Tillerman had left the room.

"Connor," she said then. "What if Brian . . ."

"Stop." Connor pressed his finger to her lips. "Brian can't be in any immediate danger. Nancy hasn't called, and Stephen didn't receive a ransom note. I checked in with him a half hour ago, to update him on your condition. So whatever Walker's planning, he hasn't executed it yet."

"Thank God," Julia murmured.

"You get some sleep. I'll be right here when you wake up."

8:25 P.M.

Connor sat in the armchair in Julia's hospital room, his fingers steepled beneath his chin as he contemplated the prospects.

They were all pretty grim.

Regardless of how reassuring he'd sounded to Julia, he was worried sick about Brian. He prayed that whatever sleazy scheme Walker had struck pay dirt on, it was separate and apart from extorting Stephen.

He wished he could poke around and make sure.

But there were roadblocks every which way he turned.

If he gave the whole story to Marty, the police chief could pull Walker in for questioning. Walker, in turn, would deny all the allegations relating to the Stratfords and walk away a free man. And if by some chance the bastard did have Brian, Connor shuddered to think what the outcome might be.

Questioning Greg could be just as dangerous, if what happened to Julia today was any indication. As for Cliff . . .

Now, that was the most disturbing Catch-22 of all.

Cliff Henderson, Stephen's best friend and the only person who probably knew where Nancy and Brian were and could therefore put all their fears to rest, was now a suspect. And if Cliff was involved in this, well, God help them all. Nancy trusted him, Stephen trusted him, even Brian trusted him.

But visualizing Cliff in the role of Walker's accomplice seemed extremely far-fetched. What in God's name would his motivation be. Money? Hardly. Power? Nope. Jealousy? Maybe, but it was a stretch. Kidnapping Brian to pay Nancy back for marrying Stephen? Not unless he'd snapped completely.

And if he had?

The ramifications were too horrifying to consider.

This entire nightmare had snowballed far beyond a mere political and social scandal.

The stakes were now the lives of those he loved.

That brought Connor to the other life-or-death issue that was staring him in the face, the issue Julia clearly hadn't thought of.

The one involving her.

Walker had sent someone to kill her. Whoever that someone was undoubtedly had been instructed to stand by and see if he'd succeeded. And if not, to remedy that fact. Because if Julia survived, she could still mess up Walker's plan.

Connor had to keep her safe. No police, no PIs, no one who might inadvertently tip Walker off to the fact that Julia was alive and talking.

Just the opposite, in fact. Connor had to convince Walker that Julia was out of the picture, unable to interfere with his Houdini act when he zoomed off to Switzerland.

An ironic smile touched Connor's lips. He knew the ideal person to get that done.

27

April 15
8:05 A.M.

Sunshine danced across Julia's face, and she stirred and opened her eyes.

For the first time since yesterday, she felt fully alert, and her head wasn't pounding. She remembered awakening on and off during the night. She had vague recollections of Dr. Tillerman examining her twice, maybe three times, and a different pair of warm, gentle hands changing her bandage and helping her drink some juice. Whenever she'd opened her eyes, Connor had been there, looming over her like a protective guard dog.

He wasn't looming now.

She glanced over and smiled, seeing him in the armchair, asleep with his head propped on his hand and the newspaper crinkled up in his lap. He looked even worse than he had yesterday, his clothes rumpled, a day's stubble on his jaw. The poor man had been glued to this room for eighteen hours.

He must have sensed her scrutiny, because he blinked, jerking upright when he saw she was awake.

"Hi." He leaned over, studied her face. "You look better. How do you feel?"

"I should be asking you that question," she teased softly. "You look terrible."

A corner of his mouth lifted. "Get used to it. You're going to be waking up to me every morning for the rest of your life."

"I think I can manage that." Her fingers traced his jawline. "Stubble and all."

"Good." He turned his lips into her palm. "Because this is how I look after a sleepless night. And you and I are going to share a lot of those. Only they won't be spent in a hospital bed."

"I can't wait." Julia wriggled a bit and winced. "I hate this. I want to get well so I can get out of here."

"That sounds promising. You're irritable. That must mean you feel better."

"I do, but I'm worried. I kept having nightmares about Brian. Connor, we have to finish last night's talk."

"I agree. But first . . ." He whipped out the local section of the day's paper and indicated a substantial piece on the front page. "Take a look at this."

Julia scanned the article, her eyes widening in surprise.

Heralded by Cheryl Lager's byline, it was a comprehensive story about how tragedy had marred the previous day's grand mall opening when Julia Talbot, Brian Stratford's second-grade teacher, was struck by a hit-and-run driver during a car theft and now, according to this reporter's exclusive sources at Leaf Brook Memorial Hospital, remained in a coma. With her life hanging in the balance, Ms. Talbot's prognosis looked grim.

Julia blinked, staring at Connor. "This is a blatant lie."

He shrugged. "Actually, it's fairly accurate. Oh, she embellished it a little, but sensationalism is Cheryl Lager's trademark. On the whole, it's pretty much what I leaked to her last night."

"I don't understand."

Connor caressed Julia's cheek. "It was the only way I could keep you out of harm's way. Walker must have been waiting for word of your condition to get out. Now it has. He'll think you're at death's door. That'll keep him from trying again."

"Oh." A sudden new worry intruded. "Connor, my parents. If they should read this or hear about it from someone who has, they'll think . . ."

"No, they won't. I spoke to your dad myself. You were right; he's a great guy. By the way, he wants you to call him as soon as you feel up to it. As for your mother, I guess you were too out of it to recognize your private nurse."

Julia's jaw dropped. "My mother?"

"Um-hum." Connor gestured toward the door. "She's been right outside all night. Except when she was in here, taking care of you. When I went out to pick up the newspaper about a half hour ago, I told her to go grab a cup of coffee. I must have dozed off after that. I'll let her know you're awake as soon as we've talked."

The fact that he'd done this for her meant more than she could say. "Connor, thank you."

"My pleasure. I know how close you and your parents are. By the way, they're the only ones who know your true medical status, other than Louis and Stephen." Connor blew out his breath. "Which brings me to where things stand."

"Has there been any news?"

He shook his head. "We still have no hard facts to support our fear that Walker has Brian. Which is good and bad. It's good because it suggests that Walker's moneymaking scheme might have nothing to do with Brian.

It's bad because, until we know for sure, we can't tip our hand. If Walker finds out we're onto him and he does have Brian . . ." Connor's voice trailed off. "In any case, having him arrested right now would be futile. We have no proof. But we're on borrowed time. According to what you overheard from Greg, Walker's leaving the country tomorrow at noon. And we're sitting on that information. In the eyes of the authorities, that's withholding evidence. I can't ask you to do that."

Julia's chin came up. "You're not asking, I'm offering. If you think my talking to the police will jeopardize Brian, I won't talk to them. I'll stay in a coma, just like Cheryl Lager reported."

"Thank you," Connor said simply. He frowned. "It isn't just you. Louis is putting himself on the line for us, too. I can only ask him to cooperate for so long. Any way you look at it, I have to give Marty enough time to stake out Westchester County Airport and grab Walker before he gets on that plane. Which means I have to find Brian before then."

Slumping back, Connor dragged a hand through his hair. "It's risk-taking time. I've got to go with my instincts and pray you're wrong about Cliff. Because if anyone knows where Nancy is, he's it."

"Why do you assume that?"

"Because the two of them are very tight. She confides in him when she can't turn to Stephen." A look of pained resignation crossed Connor's face. "Here comes that trust you asked for. Are you sure you want it? The Stratfords are a pretty screwed-up bunch."

Clearly, this was going to be a heavy revelation. And Julia felt a stab of guilt that she'd put Connor in the position of having to spill his guts. Whatever was going on with Stephen Stratford, it was obviously both serious and personal.

Ignoring her own discomfort, Julia pushed herself to a sitting position and reached for Connor's hand. "You don't have to air your brother's dirty laundry to me—not if it hurts you or makes you feel disloyal."

"It does neither." Connor interlaced his fingers with hers. "The hurt I feel is for Stephen and the demons he's always fighting. As for the loyalty, he knows I'm telling you. We discussed it last night. He's very grateful to you, Julia. You put your life on the line for Brian. My brother's become a very different man these past few weeks. His priorities have changed. So have mine, for that matter. Until now—as I said, my family's pretty screwed up. Emotions were never even blips on our radar screens, much less prime motivators. Brian's birth changed that. But not enough. And now, well, I guess Stephen and I are both experiencing epiphanies at the same time. The fear of losing people you love will do that to you."

"People—in Stephen's case, are we talking about Brian or Nancy?"

"Both." Connor wasn't surprised by her perceptiveness. "The long and the short of it is this: Stephen's a compulsive gambler. Sports betting. He's been into it since high school. It ebbs and flow. Certain kinds of pressure instigate it. On the other hand, I've seen him keep it under control for long periods of time. You've got a degree in psych; I don't need to explain what lack of self-esteem can do. I can tell you that it's a perk of being Harrison Stratford's firstborn and having a father who's shoving you all the way to the White House. It's taken a huge toll on Stephen's marriage. Cliff's always been there for Nancy. I'm sure this was no exception."

"I see." Julia felt a huge wave of sympathy. "So Cliff knows about Stephen's gambling?"

"Cliff's a bright guy. He and Stephen go back almost twenty years. So, yeah, I'd say he knows. Other than that, the only people who know are Nancy and me. And now you." A bitter pause. "Oh, and Walker."

"Walker." More pieces fell into place. "So that's how he was pressuring Stephen into getting him that contract. He was blackmailing him."

"Right. He pushed Stephen to the wall. He had him beaten up, and he threatened Brian. That's where the baseball cap incident came in. When Nancy opened that package and read that note, she lost it. She couldn't take any more. She grabbed Brian and bolted."

"I don't blame her. She's terrified for her son. The next question is, how did Walker find out about Stephen's gambling problem? It had to be from Cliff."

"Maybe. It's funny, Stephen was racking his brain, trying to figure out who Walker's mole was. It never occurred to me that it might be Cliff. I was focused on an even uglier possibility."

"Who?"

"My father."

"Your father?" Julia gasped.

"His idea of motivation." With detached resignation, Connor told Julia about his father's connection to Walker and Harrison's reaction when Connor confronted him.

"No wonder your brother's got issues. With a father like that . . ." Julia broke off. "I'm sorry."

"Don't be. He's a hard-hearted bastard."

"Okay, but how could he be Walker's informant? From what you said, I assumed he wasn't aware of Stephen's gambling."

An on-the-fence shrug. "I've busted my ass trying to keep it from him. That doesn't mean I succeeded. He's a hell of a shrewd guy. Who knows what he's aware of, or what he'd do about it if he were?"

Julia felt a wave of nausea that had nothing to do with her concussion. "Let's get back to Cliff. He's Stephen's best friend. I can't think of any reason for him to betray him like that."

"I agree. Except for one thing: Cliff's in love with Nancy. He has been since the beginning. I thought he'd reconciled himself to the fact that she'd married his best friend, but there's always a chance that he didn't. That's the risk I was talking about. Cliff's our only answer. I've got to talk to him. I'll leave out what you saw and heard in the municipal building yesterday, because I don't want him to know you're conscious. Just in case he is on Walker's payroll."

A sickening silence.

"Would he really hurt Brian?" Julia whispered.

"I can't even imagine it. But there's still the unanswered question of how your rabbit's foot found its way into Greg's car. It's possible that Greg is telling the truth about that part. If so, and if Brian is safe with his mother, Cliff might have inadvertently picked up the rabbit's foot when he visited Nancy—if he knows where she is. If, if, and if. The truth is, we can't rule out anything. Or anyone. Not when Brian's life is at stake."

"Agreed." Julia didn't want to contemplate some of those ifs. They were simply too horrifying. "Stephen will want to be there when you question Cliff."

A tired nod. "He's not going to be happy about pumping Cliff for information. He's going to be sick when I explain why we're doing it. And he's going to hit the roof when I tell him about my father's relationship with Walker and what that might mean. But I can't keep anything from him. Not anymore. I've got to lay all the cards on the table. Finding Brian is the only thing that matters."

"Go." Julia waved him toward the door. "You can't have this conversation over the phone. Drive to Stephen's and fill him in. Then talk to Cliff. We've only got today. We've got to find Brian."

Connor hesitated, clearly torn about leaving Julia alone. A wave of relief swept his face as the door opened and Meredith Talbot walked in, her eyes lighting up as she saw her daughter sitting up and talking.

"It's okay, Connor," Julia said, gratefully beckoning her mother forward. "I'm in good hands."

10:25 A.M.

Philip Walker reread the newspaper report three times.

Julia Talbot was in a coma. She might never wake up. Connor Stratford was hovering by her bedside.

It was a scenario fit for Hollywood.

Figures it would be Cheryl Lager who got the exclusive story. She'd probably camped out in the hospital waiting room until the Stratfords were ready to explode. They probably gave her the scoop just to get rid of her.

Still, it bothered the hell out of him that no other newspaper had been given word one about Julia Talbot's accident. It wasn't as if the cops suspected foul play. They were busy looking for Connor Stratford's silver Mercedes, which they figured had been ripped off by professional car thieves. So why were the Stratfords keeping such a tight lid on all this?

Yeah, okay, so Connor Stratford was involved with

the schoolteacher who'd been hit. Big deal. Everything about the Stratfords made headlines. Why was this being treated so hush-hush? And whose idea was it to do so—the mayor's, his little brother's, or their father's?

Maybe he was making too much of this.

But right on the heels of Robin Haley blowing him off? That was too many coincidences for him.

He glanced at the phone.

Maybe he was waiting too long. Maybe he should accelerate things a bit, get his plan going before things snowballed out of control.

Good idea. He'd get his last few ducks in a row. Then he'd drop the bomb.

A hard smile curled his lips.

This was one call he wouldn't trust anyone else to make.

It was the ultimate power play.

And it was all his.

10:35 A.M.

Connor had intended to get Stephen alone.

It didn't happen that way.

When he strode into the family room, he saw that Stephen had another visitor: their father.

Harrison Stratford obviously had just arrived. He was flinging his coat onto the sofa when Connor crossed the threshold.

"Good," he greeted Connor, a muscle working in his jaw. "I've got you both together. Now maybe I'll get some straight answers." He paused, as if remembering the circumstances and how they were affecting Connor's life. "Brian's teacher—how is she?"

"The same," Connor said carefully. "It's touch-and-go."

"I'm sorry about that."

"Are you?"

Harrison's eyes narrowed. "What the hell does that mean?"

Connor took the plunge. "One of the reasons I'm here is to figure out why Julia was run down and by whom. Any ideas?"

"I assume you're referring to Walker."

Stephen's head jerked around, and he glared from his father to Connor and back. "What do you know about Walker?"

"You didn't fill your brother in," Harrison noted, shooting Connor a disgusted look. "Protecting him again?"

"Not anymore. He can handle it. The question is, can you? I think you're going to be surprised at the outcome."

"What are you two talking about?" Stephen demanded.

Connor turned to his brother. "Remember my Thursday-evening business meeting? Well, it was with Dad. I'd just found out he and Walker did some co-investing over the years. I went to get details. And lo and behold, I found out who put the bug in Walker's ear about the municipal parking contract."

"You're joking." Stephen didn't sound amused. He sounded furious.

"Nope. Seems it's good for drumming up publicity when your son's running for state office," Connor supplied. "And for building character, too. Go ahead, Dad. Explain to Stephen how you're strengthening his backbone for his political future."

"I don't need to. You just did it for me." Harrison glanced calmly around the room and, seeing a pot of coffee, went over and poured himself a cup. "You did leave out the part you threw at me just before you left—that theory about Walker being behind the car thefts. You said you had no proof. Did you confront Walker with it anyway? Because if you did, it was a bad move. Walker's just the kind of guy who'd get a kick out of rubbing your nose in it by ripping off your car. His idea of punishment. It's too bad Julia Talbot got caught in the cross-fire."

Connor bit back his anger. He was more interested in Stephen's.

His brother's entire body had gone rigid. "You knew about the car thefts?" he asked, his voice deadly quiet. "And about Walker? Did you know he was blackmailing me?"

One of Harrison's brows rose. "Really? And what would he have on you that would allow him to do that?"

Utter silence.

And in that instant, Connor had his answer.

So did Stephen. "You know," he stated flatly. "You know about Walker's campaign contribution. You know about my gambling it away, then soaking Connor to recoup it. You know exactly what Walker had on me."

"What *Walker* had on you?" Harrison set down his mug with a thud. "What the whole damned world would have on you if your brother didn't clean up your mess. Correction: *messes*. You've made twenty years' worth of them with your stupid gambling. Walker can be reined in. I'll manage that. But tell me, Stephen, isn't it about time you grew up and faced life instead of letting someone else make it go away for you?"

"You're right, Dad, it is." Stephen stared his father

down, a new kind of conviction emanating from him. It was as if he'd reached the edge of a huge abyss and leaped across. "I'm facing life right now. My wife walked out. My son is being threatened. A terrific woman whose only crime was to care about Brian's welfare is lying in a hospital bed. That's all I give a damn about. Not you. Not some meaningless election. Not all the plans you've made for my future that are never going to happen. I'm responsible for the nightmare we're living right now. And why? Because I've spent thirty-six years as a lump of clay waiting for you to mold me. Thirty-six years banging my head against a wall trying to live up to your expectations. Well, no more. It's time I took over the job; time I looked in the mirror, recognized who I really am. And if I'm lucky, maybe someday I'll actually like what I see."

Harrison didn't look impressed. Surprised but not impressed. "Really? And what would you like to see, a corporate attorney? They're a dime a dozen, even the bright ones. Look at your friend Cliff. He spends his life snatching up whatever crumbs are thrown his way, then waiting around patiently for leftovers. And I mean wives as well as legal cases—or did you think I didn't know about that, either?"

"I don't give a damn what you know."

"Fine, let's play it your way. You want to see yourself for what you are? You're weak. I made you. You've got the charm, the savvy, and the brains. But you haven't got the grit."

Stephen didn't even flinch. "Probably not. But I have a son who knows he can count on me, who knows I love him no matter what. That's a hell of a lot better than having a corporate empire, at least in my book." Hearing his own words, Stephen paused, a pleased glint flashing in his eyes. "Maybe I'm closer to getting my life together than I thought."

"I doubt it. Not with people like Walker pulling your chain."

"Speaking of which, just how did he get the ammo to do that, Dad?" Connor inserted in a steely tone. "Very few people know about Stephen's gambling. You're one of them, as we just found out. Did you happen to pass that information along to your colleague to help him strengthen Stephen's backbone? Is that the reason you're so sure you can rein him in?"

"Your accusations are beginning to piss me off," Harrison fired back.

"Then answer them."

"No."

"No, you didn't tell him, or no, you won't answer?"

"Take your pick."

Stephen made a rough sound, realization striking home full force. "You sick bastard," he ground out, advancing toward his father, eyes ablaze. "You actually gave Walker what he needed to tear my family apart. It's because of you that my son's life is in danger."

"No, Stephen, it's not." Cliff hovered in the doorway, guilt and regret twisting his features. "It's because of me."

They all turned to stare at him.

"The door was unlocked. I let myself in. As it turns out, I'm glad I did." He crossed over, a manila envelope marked "Confidential" in his hands. He stopped when he reached Stephen. "These will explain everything." He tossed the envelope onto the coffee table. "Before you open it, I have a few things to say. I'm asking you to listen. Then you can throw me out." A quick glance at Harrison. "In unison."

Stephen was still gaping. "*You* told Walker about me? Why? So he could get my ass thrown in jail, and you could have Nancy?"

Cliff winced. "No. Because I was a coward. And yes, because of my feelings for Nancy. But not so I could have her. So I could protect her."

Quietly, he told them how Walker had gotten intimate photos of him with a woman who looked enough like Nancy so that, with the right doctoring, she could pass for the real thing. In return for his silence, all Walker wanted was a tip—anything he could use as leverage against the mayor.

"I knew he wanted that municipal parking contract," Cliff said. "But that's all I knew. It never occurred to me . . ." He sucked in his breath. "I was so afraid that if those photos got out, Nancy would be destroyed. And it's not like I thought you'd be getting screwed by pushing Walker's proposal. I knew you'd think his bid for the contract had merit. Because it did, especially with the increased number of auto thefts Leaf Brook's been experiencing."

"Auto thefts that Walker orchestrated," Stephen qualified.

"I didn't know that then. I didn't know a lot of things. I was backed into a corner, and I grabbed the out Walker threw me. As it turned out, the whole situation blew up in my face. I'm not defending my actions. They were deplorable. I was a bastard and an idiot. I betrayed you. The important thing for you to know is that Nancy never did. Not in any way. Even when I thought—yeah, hoped—that your marriage was over, she stood by you. As for

Brian, when Nancy told me what Walker had done with that baseball cap, I went ballistic. I told Greg that if he ever . . ."

"Greg?" Stephen interrupted. There was an icy stillness about him. "Where does Greg fit into this?"

"He's Walker's contact. I don't know what their arrangement is or how deep he's in, but he's the one who blackmailed me with those pictures, and he's the one I called to tell Walker to back off. I thought my pressure had worked, because Greg delivered the negatives to me. I figured that was Walker's peace offering. I was wrong. When I went into the office yesterday, Greg handed me a letter. It was from Walker. It was cloaked in language that made it come off sounding like a pending legal matter in a development deal. He didn't write a word that could incriminate him. But the message came through loud and clear. I should stop rocking the boat, butt out, and let things be finalized to preclude damages to my party. There was a snapshot of Brian stapled to the letter. That made it very clear who the damages would be to."

Walker's veiled threat sent prickles of fear up Connor's spine.

But he forced himself to focus on Cliff and the explanation he'd just provided.

It elicited more relief than anger. Everything Cliff had said substantiated what Julia had recounted, which suggested that his guilt ran only as deep as he'd just admitted.

"Did Greg actually hand you the negatives?" Connor inquired, trying to get at the mystery behind the rabbit's foot.

"Hand them to me? No, but I knew they were from him, if that's what you're asking. He pulled me aside when I stepped out of Stephen's office on Thursday. He told me the negatives were in his car. I went down to the parking lot and got them myself."

Okay, so he'd been in Greg's car. That could be good news. It could mean that Brian was still with Nancy, safe and sound, and only the rabbit's foot had been taken—inadvertently.

Before Connor took the chance of asking him, point-blank, about Nancy's whereabouts, he had one more base to cover.

"Yesterday was Saturday," he prompted. "*And* grand opening day at the mall. You knew that was where Stephen would be. So why did you go to his office?"

Cliff pointed to the envelope on the coffee table. "I went to leave that. Look, Connor, I was like a wounded animal—angry at fate for putting me in this position, at Nancy for loving Stephen, at Stephen for abusing Nancy's love but having it anyway. I wanted to lash out, to shove my pain in Stephen's face. At the same time, I couldn't stand the guilt anymore. I'd duped my best friend, not to mention loving his wife and, for the first time, actively wishing she'd leave him for me. I couldn't look him in the eye. So I was going to take the coward's way out again, leave the photos and the negatives on Stephen's desk with a note of explanation. I started writing the note, then changed my mind. We'd been friends for almost twenty years. I owed it to him to tell him face to face. He deserved that much."

Cliff raked a hand through his hair. "After that, everything happened at once. Greg shoved Walker's letter at me. I'd barely finished reading it when Julia showed up. I was such a wreck, I hardly remember what she said. Something about dropping in to see Greg. I guess she went to the mall from there. That's when she must have been . . ." A flash of sympathy crossed his face. "I'm sorry, Connor. I hope she'll make it."

"She will." That was enough explanation for Connor. He took the plunge. "Cliff, do you know where Nancy is?"

An uncomfortable grimace. "I told Nancy from the beginning that Stephen deserved to know where she was, that he'd be frantic. But she swore me to secrecy. I can't . . ."

"Not even if I tell you that she and Brian are in danger? Because we have reason to believe they are. We think Walker's planning something really ugly. Like grabbing Brian."

"How can he do that?" Cliff demanded. "He doesn't know where they are. No one does."

"Except you."

For the first time, Cliff looked angry. "If there's one thing you can be dead sure of, it's that I'd never hurt Nancy. Or Brian, for that matter. I didn't tell a soul where they went."

"Did you visit them?"

A reluctant pause. "Yes. Once. I took Brian's antibiotic to them."

"Then you could have been followed."

A flash of memory and apprehension. "It's possible. I drove there Wednesday morning, right after my meeting with Greg. The only place I stopped was the pharmacy. He could have followed me."

"And reported to Walker." Connor leaned forward. "Tell me something, Cliff. And think carefully before you answer. During your one visit with Nancy, did you happen to see a red rabbit's foot lying around?"

"I don't have to think. Brian had it in his hand. He wouldn't put it down, not even to take his medicine. He said it was his good luck charm."

A tight knot formed in Connor's gut. "So there's no chance you accidentally took it when you left?"

"None." Cliff shook his head. "Brian spent the whole time I was there in his room. He was really upset that I'd been the one to deliver his medicine. He wanted Stephen. He didn't even come out to say good-bye."

"Shit," Connor muttered.

"Why are you asking?"

"Yeah, Connor, that's a good question," Stephen echoed, showing visible signs of panic. "Obviously, you're talking about the rabbit's foot that Julia asked you to give Brian. You told me you did that on Tuesday. So why is it an issue?"

"Because it's not with Brian now. As of Friday, it was in Greg's car."

"God . . . no." Stephen went sheet-white.

Cliff didn't look much better. "Are you sure?"

"Positive. Which means that whoever dropped that rabbit's foot had contact with Brian. Or worse, that Brian himself was in Greg's car."

Stephen crossed the room in three strides and grabbed Cliff by the shirt. "Where the hell did Nancy take Brian? Where are they?"

This time, there was no hesitation. "They went to my ski lodge in Stowe."

"You saw them Wednesday. Today's Sunday. Why haven't you gone back?" Stephen shook him. "You're the only one who knew where they were, the only one who could have protected them. If you love Nancy so damned much, why didn't you go back and check on them?"

"Because Nancy told me not to." Cliff made no attempt to free himself or to put up a fight. He looked ill. "She didn't want me holding out any hope of a future together. She's in love with you. And she saw how my visit affected Brian. He was already a mess about being away from you. My showing up made that worse."

"But you've called, right?" Stephen demanded in a pleading voice. "Surely, you've spoken with Nancy?"

Sweat broke out on Cliff's forehead. "The last time was Thursday night. Nancy told me not to call again. So I didn't. Then, yesterday, after Greg gave me Walker's threatening letter, I tried calling. I wanted to make sure that Brian was all right."

"And?"

"There was no answer. But that didn't surprise me. Nancy made it clear that she didn't want me interrupting her thinking time. And since no one else knew where she was, she'd assume it was me and not pick up."

"So you haven't spoken to her since Thursday night." Stephen was already on his way to the phone. "That means that Walker could be holding my wife and son for two and a half days now. What's the phone number at your ski lodge?"

Cliff supplied it.

Stephen punched the buttons and waited.

Three rings. Four. Five.

"There's no answer." He slammed down the phone. "I'm driving up there now."

"I'll go with you," Cliff said.

"The hell you will." Stephen whipped around, fire blazing in his eyes. "They're *my* wife and *my* son. If you ever forget that again, I'll break your jaw."

The telephone rang.

"Stephen," Connor said, staring at the flashing light. "It's your private line."

"Maybe it's Nancy." Stephen grabbed the receiver and held it to his ear. "Yes?"

He stood there silently for a long time, his color draining away, his features drawn with fear. "I heard you," he answered finally, his voice so tight it sounded as if it might snap. "How do I know he's all right?" Another agonizing pause. "What about my wife? You son of a bitch, if you've touched one hair on . . ." He forced himself under control, grabbed a pen and a pad. "Where and when?" Some scribbling. "You'll have it. No, no police. Now let me talk to Bri—"

He held the phone away from his ear, gazed vapidly at it. "He hung up."

Connor gripped his arm. "Walker has Brian?"

A nod. "He wants five million in cash. I'm supposed to put it in Brian's sports bag and leave it in some alcove he described, near one of the gates at Westchester County Airport. Tomorrow, eleven-thirty A.M."

"You're sure it was Walker?" Harrison Stratford spoke up for the first time since Cliff had arrived. He looked stunned and furious.

"What?" Stephen was clearly in shock. "Uh, yeah. He used one of those voice scramblers, just in case I was taping the call. But what he said—it was him."

"The time frame fits," Connor added quietly. "I got word that Walker's taking off for Switzerland at noon tomorrow. Now we know why."

"Christ." Stephen dragged both hands through his hair, trying to think straight. Abruptly, his head shot up. "Nancy. He said he doesn't have Nancy. That means he left her at Stowe. And no one's answering the phone up there. She could be . . ." He crossed the room in five strides. "I've got to get to her." He turned. "Connor . . ."

"I'll get the money," Connor assured him, a muscle working in his jaw. "You just get Nancy."

"And no police. Walker said if he sees a cop . . ." A choked sound. "He'll kill Brian."

28

Cliff turned to Connor the minute they were alone. "How can I help?"

The guy looked so devastated that Connor found himself pitying him. "I don't know, Cliff. Right now, I have my work cut out for me. Five million's a lot of money. Not to mention that today's Sunday, and the banks are closed. I'll have to call in a lot of favors to set the wheels in motion. I'd better get busy; we can't afford to waste a minute."

"I don't have your contacts. So I can't access my accounts until morning. But whatever I have is yours." Cliff shifted restlessly. "What about Greg? Do you think he's taken off? Because if Brian was in his car . . ."

"Good idea. Try to find him, although I'm sure he's long since dropped out of sight. He knows Walker's plan. And he knows you'd never sit by if Nancy and Brian were in physical danger. So he figures you'll give us his name. And we'll be on his trail like bounty hunters."

"Kidnapping is a federal offense. If he was involved, he's in for major jail time."

"Maybe he didn't do it. Maybe Walker hired one of his thugs to use Greg's car. They certainly helped themselves to mine. I don't know. Right now, all I want is to get Nancy and Brian back."

Cliff nodded. "I'll call you if I find anything."

"Do that. Oh, and Cliff?"

"Yes?" He turned.

"If by some miracle you do find Greg, don't mention the part about the rabbit's foot being spotted in his car. He doesn't know I have that piece of information. And I don't want him to. When the time comes, we'll use it—big time."

After Cliff had taken off, Connor spent the next three hours on the phone, tracking down the CEOs of several major financial institutions and making arrangements to liquidate his assets. He explained that it was an emergency, altering the nature of the crisis by saying it revolved around Julia's continuing comatose condition. He flat-out stated that although no official announcement would be made until she was out of the woods, Julia Talbot was his future wife, and her life was on the line. Drastic steps had to be taken. He would provide no further details—for everyone's protection against criminal prosecution.

The first part was the truth. The second was a manipulation of the facts.

The combination worked. That was all that mattered.

From a business perspective, Connor operated on autopilot, going through the motions, hoping that by dealing with the logistics, he could keep out the emotions. He was a man who made things happen. Now, more than ever, he had to rely on his sharp mind and problem-solving skills. If he stopped, let himself think about what Brian might be going through . . . He couldn't. He just couldn't.

That strategy worked until his cell phone rang.

It was Julia.

"I know I shouldn't call," she whispered. "Pretend it's someone else. I just had to find out if everything is okay."

The wall of reserve vanished, and the pain crashed in. Shaken by its intensity, Connor released a harsh breath. "No, it's not." He heard the tremor in his own voice. "Walker has Brian. He called with a ransom demand. I've been trying to get the cash together. Stephen went to find Nancy. She's in a ski lodge in Vermont. We don't know what Walker might have done to her. I'm terrified for them, Julia. What if . . . ?"

"Connor, don't." Julia's voice was choked with horrified tears, but her words were steady. "I want to know everything. But first, listen to me. Brian and Nancy are fine. They have to be. Stephen will find Nancy. As for Brian, you'll work with the police. They'll figure out where he is and bring him home."

"No. We can't call the police. Walker said he'll kill Brian if we do."

"Oh, God." White fear lanced through Julia. At the same time, her mind kicked into high gear. Connor wasn't thinking rationally. This was an area she knew more about than he did. And he was taking the wrong path.

It was up to her to fix it.

"Connor, I want you to come back to the hospital and fill me in on all the details. I need to share this with you—not just the pain but the planning. And if you'll trust me, I know I can help."

"How?"

It was the first test of Connor's faith in her, and Julia crossed her fingers until they ached. "Trust me," she repeated quietly. "Please."

"I'm on my way."

Thank God, she thought silently, *for Brian's sake.*

Hanging up, she turned to her mother, her gaze haunted.

Meredith didn't need to ask questions. Julia had brought her up to speed on the whole situation. Now, seeing her daughter's reaction, hearing her side of the conversation with Connor, she recognized the harsh reality. "Brian's been kidnapped," she stated grimly.

A sickened nod. "Mom, I need a phone number. Our speaker, the one who couldn't make it this past Friday night and who's an expert in crimes against children."

"FBI Special Agent Patricia Avalon," her mother supplied, already rummaging in her purse. "She's the CAC coordinator at the New York field office. She's a pro."

"I know. I've heard her speak several times." Julia gave her mother a questioning look. "You've done more than that. I remember your working with her."

"It was a parental kidnapping case," Meredith confirmed. "An abusive father who snatched his daughter and took off for parts unknown. I was familiar with the abuse that had led up to his losing his visitation rights and the impact it had on his daughter. So I was consulted during the investigation. Patricia and her team were astonishing. They had the child safely back with her mother in a day." She whipped out her address book. "I have her number in here."

"I need to talk to Connor before I make contact," Julia reflected aloud. "I need his permission and Stephen's." A shudder. "Philip Walker threatened to kill Brian if the Stratfords call the police."

"Agents like Patricia are trained to do their jobs without alerting the kidnappers. This Walker person won't even realize the FBI is involved." Meredith scribbled down the phone number on a scrap of paper. "Here."

Gratefully, Julia took it. "Now, pray that her emergency's resolved and she's available. Then pray that I can convince the Stratfords to follow my lead." Julia's voice broke. "Most of all, pray that I'm doing the right thing and that this will bring Brian home safe."

3:45 P.M.
Leaf Brook Memorial

Connor walked into Julia's hospital room and leaned back against the door. He looked positively haggard.

"Hi." His concerned gaze swept over her. "Louis says you're doing better. Is he telling me the truth or placating me?"

"He's telling you the truth. I'm much stronger, and my headache's down to a dull throb." Julia pushed herself into a sitting position.

Meredith rose from the chair beside the bed. "I think I'll grab another cup of coffee. If you two will excuse me . . ." She headed for the door.

"Thank you," Connor said quietly as she reached him. "You're a godsend."

Julia's mother laid a gentle hand on his arm. "I'm so sorry for what you're going through. But Brian will be fine. You'll see." She left the room.

Connor went to the bed, leaned over, and took Julia in his arms. She held him tightly, resting her cheek against his shoulder.

"It feels so good to hold you," he muttered, turning his lips into her hair. "I feel so damned helpless."

"We'll get through this," she promised. "So will Brian. My guy's a survivor."

"Which one?" Connor's dry question was suffused with pain.

"Both of you." Julia eased back until her weight was cushioned by the bed. "Now, sit down and tell me everything."

With a tired nod, Connor dropped into the armchair. He relayed the day's events, starting with the confrontation he and Stephen had had with their father, moving to Cliff's visit and subsequent admission, and concluding with the ransom call.

"Do you know where Walker called from?" Julia asked.

"Nope. Not from his house or his office, that's for sure. He used a voice scrambler. Clearly, he didn't want to be traced."

"Which means both he and Greg have probably dropped out of sight." Julia frowned. "Today's Sunday. Were you able to arrange for the money?"

"I've got a lot of contacts in the banking industry," Connor replied, rubbing his eyes. "That includes several CEOs. They're really trying to come through for me. I should have the full five million in cash by eleven o'-clock tomorrow morning."

Julia nodded. She reached out and took Connor's hand. "I love you. But I also love Brian. You know that, don't you?"

"Of course."

"Then keep it in mind. And hear me out." Julia took a deep breath, then launched into her pitch. "I realize I'm an educator, not a law enforcer. But you know how involved I am in efforts to prevent child abuse. Through the work my mom and I do with the APSAC, we've met professionals from all different fields. They come and speak at our workshops. One of those speakers is an FBI special agent who was trained at the National Center for the

Analysis of Violent Crime. Her name is Patricia Avalon, and she's a Crimes Against Children coordinator at the New York field office. My mom consulted on one of Special Agent Avalon's investigations, so she saw her in action. She thinks the world of her abilities. I want you to help persuade Stephen to let me call her."

Connor's mouth thinned into a grim line. "How can I do that? Walker said . . ."

"I know what he said. But think about it, Connor. You're handing him money; he's getting on a plane. How do you know he'll turn Brian over to you? How do you know Walker won't taxi down that runway before you find out where Brian is?"

She winced at the expression on Connor's face.

"Further, can you be sure that Walker won't take Brian with him, as insurance, when he flees the country?" Julia felt bile rise in her throat, but she swallowed it, forcing herself to speak the worst-case scenario aloud. "Last, did Walker give you any actual proof that Brian's still alive? Did he let Stephen talk to him?"

Mutely, Connor shook his head. "I assumed that was because wherever Walker was, Brian wasn't with him. You don't think . . ."

"No, I don't." Julia's fingers tightened in Connor's. "I know in my heart that Brian's alive. I do. Not to mention that I don't believe Walker's a killer. But I had to state all those possibilities so you'd see you're letting your fear cloud your reason. You and Stephen aren't professionals. You have no idea how to go about this. You think you'll just hand Walker his money, and he'll hand you Brian. Maybe that's exactly what will happen. But do you really want to take that chance? Does Stephen? Patricia Avalon is a federal agent. She's trained for this. So's the special unit that works with her. Let them help us. For Brian's sake."

Connor thought for a long, hard moment. Then he nodded. "Let's call Stephen on his cell phone. He must be coming up on Stowe by now."

4:35 P.M.

Stephen had sped past Burlington and was on U.S. 2 heading west for Stowe when his cell phone rang.

His hands were shaking so hard he could barely press the TALK button. "Hello?"

"It's me. No news," Connor added quickly.

"I'm almost there. God, Connor, she's got to be all right."

"She is." A muscle worked in Connor's jaw. "The money's being handled. It should be ready with an hour to spare."

"Thanks."

"Stephen, I'm in Julia's room at the hospital. I'm going to give her the phone. I know you're a mess, but listen carefully to what she has to say. It makes sense."

Frowning, Connor handed Julia the phone. Stephen sounded like a wreck. It was the worst possible time to do this. But time was the one thing they didn't have.

"Hello, Stephen," Julia said softly. A pause. "Yes, I'm fine. It's Brian I'm thinking about. We've only got nineteen hours to find him. And I don't think we can take on that responsibility ourselves and be sure we'll succeed."

She went on, calmly explaining to Stephen exactly what she'd explained to Connor.

"Special Agent Avalon will act as a link between the NCAVC, the FBI field office in New York, and the local

Leaf Brook authorities," she concluded. "Which brings me to Martin Hart. He already knows something's wrong. He's been waiting to question me since yesterday, and, according to Connor, he came by your house to question you, too. Connor says you trust him. Is that right?"

She listened, nodding. "Good. Then my suggestion is that we bring him in on this right from the beginning, at the same time as we contact Special Agent Avalon. It'll save precious time." Another pause. "I know you're frightened. You have a right to be. Brian's your son. But that's exactly why you have to do everything possible to bring him home quickly and safely. I'm sure he's fine, but he must be scared. Not to mention how much he must be missing you and his mom. I've listened to Special Agent Avalon describe their operational support and training. They're used to outsmarting serial offenders. And Walker's just a rank amateur. Trust me, these FBI agents are pros. They're not going to tip their hands, and they're not going to let Walker hurt Brian."

Another pause. "No. Catching Walker is secondary. So is recovering any ransom payment. The agents are trained to focus on the kidnapped victim first. Apprehending Walker would be a bonus but not a priority." With that, Julia waited for Stephen's decision.

She got it.

Her head sagged forward, and she squeezed her eyes shut, tears of relief seeping from beneath her lids. "Thank you. Yes, I understand. I'll call her right away. Here's Connor."

Exhausted, she handed Connor back the phone.

He took it. "Stephen?"

"I'm here." He sounded shaken but not as lost as he had a few minutes ago. "Julia's right."

"I know she is." Connor caressed the nape of Julia's neck as he spoke, soothing her emotional strain to the best of his ability. He wondered how he'd ever thought of her as naive and sheltered. She was strong and courageous, and he was lucky to have her. "We'll take care of things at this end."

"I've got about a twenty-minute drive to the ski lodge," Stephen replied. "I'm losing my mind anyway. So I'll use the time to call Marty, tell him what's going on. The next time he shows up at Julia's hospital room to follow up on her accident, let him in. I'll have him pretend it's you he's there to question, since we need to keep up the pretense that Julia's still in a coma. In the meantime, pray that Julia can reach this Special Agent Avalon."

Connor gave Julia a tender look. "She will. When Julia sets her mind to something, she makes it happen. Call us when you get to the lodge."

"I will. The minute I find Nancy and make sure she's all right . . ." Stephen broke off, struggling for control. "I'd better get on the phone to Marty. In the meantime, pray."

29

4:45 P.M.
Lake George, New York

Philip Walker had driven up to his cottage in the Adirondacks. It was the perfect place to lie in wait, since no one knew about it. So he was stunned when he heard a car tear into the driveway and screech around in front of the house.

A pounding at the door was followed by, "Walker, open this goddamn door. I know you're in there. I'll tear it off its hinges if I have to."

Walker's brows shot up. How the hell had Stratford found out about this place so fast? Amazing and gratifying. The ultimatum evidently had been even more jarring than he'd envisioned. Why, he'd never heard the cool, composed Harrison Stratford sound so unglued.

He walked over and opened the door. "Isn't this a nice surprise? You must have worked long and hard to uncover the location of this hideaway. I didn't buy it in my name or my company's."

"I know everything about you, you cocky bastard." Harrison strode in and shoved the door shut. "Except that you were stupid enough to try something like this. Did you honestly think you'd get away with hustling me?"

"Actually, yes. What's more, I must have succeeded, or you wouldn't be tracking me down like a bloodhound." Walker gestured toward the living room. "Do you want to come in, or should we slug it out in the hall?"

Harrison studied him through narrowed eyes, then blew by him and went into the living room.

"Drink?" Philip inquired, following him in.

"How much do you want?" Harrison demanded. "And don't tell me five million. That's absurd. Especially now that I know where you are. One phone call, and the cops will throw your ass in jail for so long that you'll be too old to walk when you get out."

Philip began to laugh. "Really. Then why didn't you call them before you burst in here? Or need I ask? You're a tough bastard, Stratford, but you have one weakness: your family. You'd go to the ends of the earth to protect them—or at least to protect their reputations and upward mobility. That's what started this ball rolling to begin with. And it's just what I'm counting on now. Don't you think I anticipated your finding me? I knew you would, sooner or later. I made provisions in case I'm taken out of commission. So go ahead, make your phone call. The minute you do, the ax will fall." He strolled over, lifted the receiver, and offered it to Harrison. "It's your funeral. Or, rather, the Stratfords'."

Stark amazement registered on Harrison's customarily unreadable features. "Christ," he muttered, making no move to touch the phone. "What kind of animal are you? We're not talking about dirty business practices or even illegal ones. We're talking about human life."

"That's being a little melodramatic, wouldn't you say?" Philip replaced the phone on the mantel, eyeing Harrison speculatively. He'd expected him to freak out over being blackmailed, but this reaction was bizarre.

Okay, so he was being beaten at his own game, but cat and mouse was nothing new to Stratford. It was certainly nothing he couldn't handle—and make go away, with the right incentive.

Speaking of incentives, why the hell had Stratford blurted out an obscene number like five million dollars? The man was a brilliant negotiator. He'd make a low-ball offer first, then sweeten the pot as needed, mostly with promises for the future. He wouldn't balk at the nature of this arrangement. Political favors for silence? Far from beneath him.

None of this made sense.

"Look, Walker." Harrison rubbed the back of his neck, contemplating his next move. "I promised you a quarter of a million dollars plus the hundred thousand you invested in Stephen's campaign for getting the newspapers to splash your municipal contract deal on their front pages. You pulled it off. I just found out the filthy tactics you used to make it happen. My first reaction was to destroy you and bankrupt your company. Instead, I'll pay you the full amount plus another million to start your new life. But I want proof that he's okay. Otherwise, the whole deal is off."

Ah. So Stratford had learned some of the details of the past weeks. Apparently, that's what was pissing him off. Although the imperious SOB had made it clear from the beginning that he wasn't worried about treading lightly when it came to getting the job done, even if it meant putting his son's neck in a vise and twisting. Maybe he'd changed his mind. Maybe he was getting soft in his old age.

"Who'd you talk to, Henderson?" Walker asked. "Or did one of your sons ante up?" A chuckle. "No pun intended."

"A million more, Walker. Yes or no?"

"Stick it," Walker replied calmly, resting his hip against the sofa. "This is about more than money. Your son is one screwed-up little boy. And a dishonest one, too. Let's see—he misappropriated funds, withheld information from the police, not to mention that gambling itself is illegal. He's hardly a role model for the New York State Senate, much less the White House. And I'm in a position to keep him from getting there."

Philip gave an offhanded shrug. "On the other hand, I could look the other way. If I choose to do that, it'll cost you a lot more than a one-time payoff. The million's fine for now. As for the future, I want backing, and I don't mean just that damned municipal contract. When the mayor's jurisdiction expands from Leaf Brook to the whole Empire State, I want to go along for the ride. I want a senator who'll do whatever it takes to back my projects, twist whatever arms are necessary to get me the votes I need. In return, I'll destroy all my sets of tapes—all but two. One I'll give to you, the other I'll lock up in a safe place. If, however, Stephen ever forgets where his loyalties lie, the other set of tapes will be released immediately to that shark Cheryl Lager, along with a transcript for her to print."

"What the hell are you babbling about?" Harrison blasted. "What tapes? What transcript? Have you lost your goddamn mind?"

Walker's jaw set. "Don't screw with me. It won't work. I'm talking about the tapes I have of my conversations with Stephen. The incriminating ones where I lay my cards on the table, and he agrees to bend the law to keep his gambling from becoming public knowledge. The tapes that will land your son in jail and ruin your family. You should've listened more closely to my phone message. It was cryptic but decipherable."

"What phone message?"

"The one I left you this morning."

"You didn't leave a message. You spoke directly to Stephen. And he never said anything about tapes being part of this sick plan of yours. He probably didn't care. Not with his son's life at stake."

Philip's brows drew together. "His *life?* I had one of my associates take his baseball cap and scare his mother by dropping it off on her doorstep."

"The same associate who ran down Julia Talbot yesterday? What was that, spite? Because you know Connor's involved with her? I knew that's what prompted your choosing Connor's Benz to rip off for whatever chop shop you're dealing with. But now, I'm wondering if it went beyond the car. After what you've done to Brian, you're obviously capable of anything. So I doubt that hit-and-run was an accident."

"Hold it." Philip interrupted Harrison's tirade, shaking his head in total astonishment. "I feel like I'm in the Twilight Zone. You think I'm behind that hit-and-run? Forget it, Harrison. If I were orchestrating strategic car-thefts—and I'm not saying I am—I wouldn't hire guys who plow people down. Not accidentally, and certainly not on purpose. I also wouldn't rip off cars from places that would negatively impact me. In case you didn't know it, I invested a shitload of money in that mall. The lousy publicity that goes along with a woman being run down on opening day is the last thing I want."

"What do you care? You're leaving the country anyway."

Philip stared. "Where do you get your information?

I'm not going anywhere, I never laid a hand on your grandson, I wasn't behind Julia Talbot's hit-and-run, and I have no idea who took Connor's car. Oh, and I didn't speak to Stephen this morning. I left a message on your cell phone."

It was Harrison's turn to stare. Slowly, he pulled out his cell phone, which had been switched off since he'd walked into the fiasco at Stephen's house. He punched it on.

One message. Left at eleven twenty-seven A.M.

Almost exactly the same time Stephen had received the ransom call.

Harrison listened to Walker's voice, telling him they should meet to discuss the mayor's political future and how Walker Development could contribute to it. Then something about some great audio tapes he wanted him to hear, after which he'd be willing to bet the bank that Harrison would want his own set.

Aggravated and confused, Harrison punched off the phone. "What about the call to Stephen?"

"*What* call to Stephen?"

"Walker, I'm about to break you in two." Harrison's fists were clenched at his sides, and he looked furious enough to do it. "The only reason I'm controlling myself is for Brian's sake. Now, where is he? Where the hell have you stashed him? Because if you don't tell me . . ."

"Wait a minute." Philip stopped him in his tracks. "Are you saying someone kidnapped your grandson?"

"Are you saying you didn't do it?"

"You're damned right I am."

Harrison strode over, grabbed Walker by the throat, and shoved him against the wall. He was taller and broader than Walker in build, an advantage that was strengthened by the fact that he was fueled by rage. "You didn't demand five million in ransom so you could leave the country? You didn't tell Stephen where and when to leave the cash tomorrow? You didn't do any of that?"

"No," Walker croaked.

"Then who did?"

"I don't know." A choked swallow. "But I haven't seen your grandson since they went to Stowe."

Harrison's grip tightened. "How did you know that's where Nancy took him?"

"G-Greg Matthews."

"That's right, my son's other loyal colleague. He works for you."

A nod.

"So you hired him to grab Brian."

"No." Philip was starting to feel dizzy. "Stratford, for God's sake . . ." He yanked at Harrison's hands. "Let me go. I'll make some calls, find out what happened. If I don't, then you can choke me."

"I'll do worse than that." Harrison released his grip and shoved Walker aside. "You were right about my being willing to do anything to protect my family. Anything. So don't test me. I'll tear you apart. Now, get on that phone and find my grandson."

4:57 P.M.
Stowe, Vermont

Nancy's side was aching. So was her shoulder. She shifted position and flinched. The floor was hard. She'd been lying on it for an eternity, since she'd managed to topple the chair over. The impact had hurt, but at least now she had some mobility. Even with her wrists and ankles bound, she could squirm her way toward the telephone.

She'd wriggled free of the gag. Thank God for that much. The drugs had nauseated her horribly, and she was terrified that if she vomited, she'd aspirate it and choke to death.

Sometimes she was lucid. Other times, she felt foggy and oblivious to time and motion. She'd be in one spot, fade out, then regain consciousness realizing she'd moved a short distance without remembering how she got there.

But always, it was fear for Brian that drove her.

She had to find him. She had to reach that telephone.

She'd just stopped to gasp in air and regain some strength when she heard the footsteps.

She froze.

Should she try to yell for help? Her voice was barely a croak at this point. Besides, what if it was him again? He'd be furious, and God knew what he'd do to her.

She had to take that chance, to try, for Brian's sake.

Steeling herself, she gathered every ounce of strength she had and emitted a hoarse groan.

The sound was swallowed up by the front door as it exploded open.

Running footsteps, followed by a broken cry of "Nancy!"

It was the most familiar, the most wonderful sound in the world.

Tears she thought were long gone sprang to her eyes and slid down her cheeks. "Stephen," she whispered.

He couldn't possibly have heard her. But it didn't matter. He was beside her nonetheless.

"Oh, God. Baby, are you all right?" He didn't wait for

an answer. He was untying her ropes, freeing her limbs from the horrible confines of the past two days.

He rubbed the circulation back into her hands and feet, anchoring her against his chest as he did. She was as limp as a rag doll, unable to do anything but sag against him and weep.

"Are you hurt?" Stephen demanded, tipping up her chin. "Should I get you to a hospital?"

A weak shake of her head. "Brian," she whispered.

"I know. Don't talk." Stephen stood, scooped her into his arms. "I'm getting you out of here. There's water in the car. We've got a great nurse who's just a phone call away. She'll tell us what to do. And I'll get us home."

"Stephen." Nancy clutched his shirt, giving him a pleading look. "Tell me."

He drew a harsh breath. "Walker's got Brian. He wants five million dollars by noon tomorrow. Connor's getting it. He and Julia contacted the FBI. Their agents are working with Marty. We'll find him, Nance."

She could taste the salt of her own tears. "He must be terrified. Seeing me unconscious, then being dragged away by a man in a ski mask."

"The bastard knocked you out?"

"Chloroform, I think. And some pills he dissolved and made me drink. I've been pretty out of it." She frowned, seeing the late-afternoon sky through the kitchen window. "What day is it?"

"Sunday. When did he take Brian?"

"Friday. Just before noon."

"That makes sense. Greg must have followed Cliff up here on Wednesday, then reported in. Walker had one of his thugs drive up here first thing Friday morning."

Nancy shook her head. "It wasn't a thug. It was Greg."

Anger tightened Stephen's features. "You're sure?"

"Yes. The mask didn't cover his eyes. I recognized them. It was Greg."

"Then God help him when we find him."

Something about Stephen's tone struck her, a conviction that came from deep within. And his demeanor—there was a quality of solid strength that Nancy wasn't used to. Intently, she scrutinized his face. "You're . . . different."

"I'm me again. Or maybe for the first time. I don't know." His knuckles drifted over her cheek. "One thing I do know is that I love you. And if what Cliff said is true, if I'm lucky enough to still have you, I'll never abuse your love again. You have my word."

"You really mean that, don't you?"

He swallowed, hard. "More than I've ever meant anything in my life. We're going to start over, Nance. You, me, and Brian. I'm going to get help. I'm going to take control of my life." He pressed his forehead to hers, and she could feel the emotion shaking him. "I'm getting the hell out of politics," he said fervently. "Let my father run for office if he wants to. I don't give a damn. I want to go back to practicing law. And I want to be a husband and a father. If you'll still have me." He paused, his eyes damp as he awaited her answer.

It came without hesitation, and her tears drenched his shirt. "If I'll still have you?" she choked out. "Yes, I'll still have you. That's all I ever wanted—to build a life with you and Brian."

"Then let's go do that." He headed for the door. "We'll start by finding our son."

30

5:15 P.M.
Leaf Brook Memorial

The process had been set in motion.

Patricia Avalon had answered her page immediately and returned Julia's—rather, Meredith Talbot's—phone call. Using her mother's name was a precaution Julia had taken to protect the fact that she was supposed to be in a coma. Not to mention that Special Agent Avalon was better acquainted with Meredith than she was with Julia and would, therefore, be more apt to respond quickly.

She listened to what Julia had to say, asked a few terse questions, then told her to stay put and wait for her call.

She took care of the rest.

The NCAVC in Quantico, Virginia, was contacted, as was the FBI's New York field office. Together, they coordinated an immediate response, and a team was mobilized. Special agents were assigned to work with the Leaf Brook police, including Patricia Avalon, who would be the Stratfords' primary contact. Julia's hospital room would be their meeting point.

The plan was for Patricia to masquerade as Julia's older sister. It would be natural for her to be allowed in to visit her comatose sibling, where she would also lend support to their mother. It would be easy enough to pull off. Walker wouldn't be concentrating on Julia now.

Thanks to Connor's news leak, he'd have dismissed her as a threat. So would his accomplices.

As for the local authorities, by the time the FBI field office contacted Martin Hart, Stephen already had spoken with him, and the police chief was ready to throw his weight and the weight of the entire department behind the investigation.

So the connections were made on all sides, Patricia Avalon was on her way to the hospital, and FBI agents were out looking for Brian.

It was five-twenty when the phone in Julia's hospital room rang.

Connor and Julia exchanged a glance and a prayer.

Then Connor grabbed the phone. "Yes?"

"It's me," Stephen said simply. "I've got Nancy with me. She's all right."

"Thank God." Connor released his breath, giving a thumbs-up to Julia, who mouthed her own thanks to the heavens.

"Listen, Connor. Nancy says she's okay. But I'd rather hear it from a medical professional. Does Meredith Talbot think I should take her to the hospital? She's been tied up for two days, and she was drugged."

Connor could hear Nancy in the background saying, "I'm fine, Stephen." But he turned toward the door anyway, beckoned Meredith Talbot in.

She popped into the room, focusing intently on his explanation. Then she took the phone.

After asking a few questions and listening to the responses, she assured Stephen that Nancy was probably just dehydrated and woozy from the drugs she'd been given. She advised him to give her lots of water and make her rest during the ride home.

"Bring her straight here," Meredith concluded. "It'll be late at night by the time you arrive, so the hospital corridor will be relatively quiet. Dr. Tillerman will check Nancy out. That'll put your mind at ease. In the meantime, you both can stay close to the action. This room's been designated as the central meeting place for the authorities. Patricia's on her way here now. In fact . . ." She looked up and gestured at a trim woman with short, dark hair who was exchanging a quick word with Dr. Tillerman. "She just arrived."

"Does she have any news?" Stephen demanded.

"The FBI agent is there?" Nancy interceded. "I want to talk to her."

Meredith heard and seconded the request. "She'll want to talk to you, too. I'll put her on." She held out the phone as Patricia strode briskly across the room. "It's both parents," she informed the special agent. "Stephen just rescued his wife from the ski lodge in Stowe. She's unharmed."

Nodding, Patricia Avalon put the receiver to her ear. "Mayor Stratford? I understand your wife is with you. I'd like to speak with you both."

"I'll snap the handset into the cradle," Stephen replied. He did that. "Can you hear us?"

"Clear as a bell. You're uninjured, Mrs. Stratford?"

"I'm fine. All I care about is Brian. Have you found anything yet?"

Patricia unbuttoned her coat, tossed it onto a chair. "No, but it's been less than an hour. We will."

Nancy's emotional reserves were shot, and with them her customary composure. She let out a choked sob. "He's in second grade. He's just a little boy—*our* little boy. Please, you've got to find him."

"Our agents are already on it, Mrs. Stratford." Compassion underscored Agent Avalon's crisp, professional tone. "And Police Chief Hart is cooperating fully. Trust us to do our job. We'll bring Brian home."

"What's your plan?" Stephen asked. "How can we help?"

"You can help by answering a few questions. Mrs. Stratford, can you describe anything about the person who abducted your son?"

"I can do better than that. I can give you his name. It was Leaf Brook's city manager, Greg Matthews."

Patricia's brows rose. "He did nothing to disguise himself?"

"He wore a ski mask. But it had slits for eyeholes. I recognized his eyes. He and Stephen have worked together for a term and a half, the entire time Stephen's been mayor. It was definitely Greg."

"I see. Well, two plainclothes detectives have already checked out Greg Matthews's home and his workplace. They've done the same for Philip Walker. As expected, neither man is anywhere to be found. Then again, we know where Walker will be tomorrow at noon."

A small gasp escaped Nancy. "Tell me you don't plan to wait until then to find Brian. Please say you don't intend to let my son's rescue hinge on your staking out the airport, hoping that when you grab Walker, he'll tell you . . ."

"Definitely not," Patricia interrupted. "Finding Brian is our number one priority. Waiting was never an option. The process is already ongoing."

"What does that mean, exactly?" Stephen pressed. "You never did answer me when I asked what your strategy was."

"There was a reason I didn't get into procedural details. Two reasons, actually. Both are for Brian's protection. First, this is a nonsecure telephone connection. It would be foolish to discuss confidential details on it. Second, to be frank, the less tactical information you're privy to, the better. It's quite possible that Walker will contact you again. You're under enough duress. You don't need to worry about letting something slip. Just be assured that we're taking every precaution. We know what we're doing; that's why you made the right decision to come to us, regardless of Walker's threats. You have my word that we won't make any major moves without consulting you or conceal any major discoveries."

Nancy swallowed. "The way you say that . . . do you think Walker's hurt Brian—or worse?"

"Walker doesn't fit that profile. He's not a killer; he's an extortionist. Plus, he'd have no motive. All he wants is to get his money and get out of the country. But if he calls you tomorrow—which I believe he will to firm up the details of the drop—try to pin him down. Ask for proof that Brian's okay. And work out a plan for how you'll get verification of Brian's whereabouts before Walker's plane takes off. It's a logical request. Walker realizes you're aware that once he leaves the country, he'll find a way to escape extradition, and you'll have no recourse. You'll want to be sure that Brian's unharmed and that you can find him. I think you'll hear a man whose only focus is on vanishing rich."

"Can we ask to speak to Brian?"

"Sure, but Walker probably will refuse. He won't want to stay on the phone too long, in case you're tracing the call. He won't want to take a chance that Brian will blurt out something that would give away his whereabouts. And it's also possible that Brian and Walker aren't in the same location. Walker's probably holed up in some motel, and having a child with him would only make it harder for him to blend into the woodwork. So don't be too concerned if he refuses to put Brian on the phone. Just keep in mind what I said about his goal: minimum hassle, maximum cash, and quick getaway. Harming Brian isn't part of that agenda."

"Okay." Nancy felt old, weary, and ready to jump out of her skin. "In the meantime, there's nothing we can do. Nothing but pray."

"Mrs. Stratford, I know how difficult this is," Patricia said quietly. "But it will all be over soon."

Nancy squeezed her eyes shut. "The most horrible questions keep running through my mind. What if Walker decides to shut Brian up so he can't identify him? What if he manages to jet off without ever turning our son over to us or telling us where he is? What if he takes Brian with him for insurance?"

Patricia remained silent until Nancy was finished. Then she said, "We'll discuss your fears in person. For what it's worth, I don't believe any of those prospects is in the cards. Now, drive safely. We'll see you both soon."

"And if there's any news in the interim?"

"I'll contact you immediately."

Patricia hung up, gazing at the phone for a moment before turning to the occupants of the hospital room.

"Julia," she began, "how are you feeling?"

"Physically? Better. Emotionally . . ." Julia's shoulders lifted in a trembling shrug. "This is excruciating."

Patricia nodded. She turned, extending her hand to shake Connor's. "Mr. Stratford, it's good to meet you. I'm sorry it has to be under these circumstances."

He returned the handshake. "So am I. But Meredith and Julia swear by your skills." A hard swallow. "Brian's a special kid. He means the world to all of us. Bring him home."

"We will." She pulled up a chair and sat down. "Before I get more details from you, is there anyone else involved that you know of? Anyone we should be talking to?"

Julia's head came up. "Cliff Henderson."

"Definitely." Connor explained to Patricia how Cliff fit into the picture. "I don't think his guilt runs any deeper than that. But given his contact with Matthews, you'll want to talk to him. He might know something he doesn't even realize he knows, something only a pro would pick up on. My only request is that you not talk to him here. I don't want anyone else knowing Julia's conscious—just as a precaution."

"I agree," Patricia replied. "Let's keep those who know Julia is awake and talking down to a minimum. On the other hand, I do want Cliff Henderson questioned. The logical place for that to happen would be police headquarters, where Martin Hart can handle things." A quizzical look. "Will Mr. Henderson go willingly?"

"For Nancy's sake? You bet." Connor pulled out his cell phone. "I'll give him a call. I want to let him know that Nancy's all right, anyway."

That call took two emotional minutes.

"He's on his way to talk to Marty," Connor announced, punching off the phone. He frowned, seeing the absorbed look on Patricia's face. "What's wrong?"

"Hmm? Oh, nothing. I was just thinking about the fact that Matthews did the actual kidnapping. It raises some questions."

"It would explain how Brian's rabbit's foot got into Greg's car," Connor noted. "And why Greg got to Walker so soon after Julia overheard him making Walker's travel arrangements. He wanted her shut up, big time."

Patricia's contemplative air intensified. "That's a lot of personal involvement for a hired hand. Not to mention a lot of risk. With what guarantees? Matthews sounds like an intelligent man. It must have occurred to him that he'd be directly linked with the kidnapping. Henderson and Nancy are friends. Obviously, Henderson knew Matthews was on Walker's payroll. Just as obviously, Nancy had direct contact with Brian's kidnapper. She saw his height, his build, his eyes. Put those pieces together, and there's every chance that Henderson would open up to Nancy, and she would figure out who abducted her son. Kidnapping is a federal offense. Walker planned an out for himself. He'd be in Switzerland, free as a bird. What about Matthews? What out did he have? Did he plan to relocate with a new identity? Using what contacts? He's a city manager, not a major underworld figure. But what else could he do? He had to realize that he'd be brought up on criminal charges."

Julia sat up in bed. "So what are you saying? That you think Greg's going to jet off with Walker? That doesn't make sense. The flight arrangements I heard him make were for one."

"Tell me exactly what you heard."

Launching into Saturday's events, Julia filled Patricia in on every detail. She was just finishing up when Connor's cell phone rang.

"Now what?" he murmured. He punched TALK. "Yes?"

"It's your father." Harrison Stratford sounded more

wired than Connor had ever heard him. "Have you heard from Stephen?"

"Yes, Dad," Connor said carefully. "He got to Nancy. She's okay. Dehydrated and sore but okay. He's taking her to the hospital to be checked out."

"Good." A hard swallow. "Connor, listen, I'm in Lake George."

A frown. "What are you doing in Lake George?"

"I'm with Philip Walker."

Connor nearly dropped the phone. "What?" He stared at Patricia, gesturing for her to lean closer. When she did, he angled the phone so she could listen. "Did you say you were with Philip Walker?"

"Yes. He's got a place up here in the Adirondacks. That's not important now. What's important is that he denies orchestrating Brian's kidnapping. He insists he knew nothing about it. I'm beginning to believe him. One thing's for sure—he had nothing to do with ripping off your car or with your girlfriend's accident. For those, you can thank Greg Matthews."

Slowly, Connor digested that. "Let me get this straight. Walker's claiming he's innocent, that he's not involved?"

"Oh, he's involved all right. Just not with the major felonies like kidnapping and attempted murder. He's just your basic thieving extortionist." Harrison launched into an explanation of the tapes Walker had of Stephen and the call he'd made to collect on them.

"So the ransom call, you're saying that wasn't Walker?"

"I don't think so, no. Look, I came up here to negotiate with the SOB—with my cash or my fists, it didn't matter. Once he realized how serious I was and how deep he was in, he agreed to cooperate. He's standing next to me right now, sweating over the prospect of spending the rest of his life in jail. He made a few phone calls, on speaker phone so I could listen. He reached one of his friendly carjackers. It seems Greg Matthews called him Saturday morning and ordered him to go to the mall and steal your car, supposedly on Walker's instructions. The thug did as he was told. Except that after he'd done the breaking, entering, and hotwiring, Matthews appeared, said he'd take it from there. I guess the Benz's alarm system was too complicated for Matthews to manage on his own, and he's not an electronic whiz. But running down a woman who might blow his cover, that's right up his alley."

"Shit," Connor muttered. "Hitting Julia was a cold-blooded murder attempt?"

"She must have found out something she shouldn't have."

Connor refrained from confirming his father's suspicions, but he met Patricia's grim stare.

"As for the kidnapping, Walker swears he doesn't know a thing," Harrison continued. "None of his goons knew anything about it, either. And here's another persuasive bit of news. I see no evidence that Walker's planning to leave the country. But his pilot sure as hell is. He thinks he's taking Walker to Switzerland—at guess whose orders?"

"Greg's."

"Yup. Matthews made all the arrangements and promised the pilot a hefty bonus for making it happen, again supposedly courtesy of Walker."

The pieces fit—all too well.

"Dad, you didn't straighten things out with the pilot,

did you?" Connor demanded. "We need him to follow whatever instructions he was given so Greg won't know we're onto him. For Brian's sake."

"I'm not stupid. I told Walker to keep his mouth shut. He told the pilot he was just confirming final arrangements. At this point, he's as eager as we are to grab Matthews before he gets on that plane."

"*We're* not the ones who'll be doing the grabbing."

"What does that mean?"

"Hang on a minute." Connor covered the mouthpiece, arching a questioning brow at Patricia. "How much can I say?"

"By all means, tell your father the FBI's involved," she advised. "It'll scare Walker enough to clinch his newly offered cooperation. But first, get me Walker's Lake George address. I'll have an unmarked car sent over to his place. Then tell him to stay put. Reiterate that he shouldn't tip *anyone* off to Matthews's deception. We're going to beat Greg Matthews at his own game."

Connor nodded.

"Dad," he said into the phone. "What's Walker's address there?" He listened, then scribbled it down, shoving the paper at Patricia. She, in turn, whipped out her cell phone and went across the room to make the necessary phone call. "Got it," Connor acknowledged. "Now, keep Walker there. Tell him if he tries to run, he'll be spending a lot more years in prison than if he cooperates. The FBI's already contacted the Lake George police. An unmarked car is on its way."

"You brought in the FBI?" Harrison blew up, as Connor had known he would. "Do you know what kind of publicity that's going to generate?"

"Yup. And I don't give a damn. Neither does Stephen.

All we care about is Brian, finding him fast and bringing him home safe." A meaningful pause. "Let it go, Dad. You're not going to win this one. I doubt you really want to. This isn't about a political or social scandal. It's about your grandson. Would you really risk his life just to save face? The answer's no. Because if anything happened to Brian, even you couldn't live with yourself."

A heavy silence, after which Harrison cleared his throat. "I'll stay here till the cops arrive. Then I'll head back down. Call me on my cell phone if there's any news."

"I will." Connor punched END and turned to Patricia, who'd just made two more quick phone calls herself. "The questions nagging at you about the loopholes in Greg's strategy clearly had merit."

"Those loopholes were just closed." She pursed her lips. "Evidently, Matthews is a lot shrewder than we thought. He not only masterminded Brian's abduction and personally ran Julia down, he set things up so Walker would be framed for the whole shebang. It was a little added protection on his part. This way, he'd flee as an accomplice, leaving Walker to take the rap for kidnapping and attempted murder. Well, it's not going to go down as he expects. I've notified the field office and Police Chief Hart. We'll make the necessary adjustments in our investigation. There'll be a few surprises in store for Greg Matthews."

7:15 P.M.

Greg stepped into the shabby motel room and locked the door, reaching into his pocket and whipping out the microcassette recorder.

Fear was a great motivator. Brian Stratford had done exactly as he'd been told.

The pieces were rapidly falling into place. His improvised scheme, thought up solo and at the eleventh hour, was about to yield jackpot results.

With the kid stashed in a trailer on a Walker Development construction site, as well as the fact that all the arrangements had been made in Walker's name, Philip Walker was well and duly screwed. He was going down for the kidnapping and all the crimes connected to it.

And the only person who'd heard enough of the truth to upset the apple cart was in a coma, unable to share her suspicions.

He frowned, remembering the white panic on Julia's face when he'd veered Stratford's convertible straight at her and knocked her down. That part still haunted him. He wasn't a killer. And he certainly hadn't wanted to kill Julia. But what choice did he have? He had to shut her up fast, before she told any of the Stratfords what she'd overheard.

Well, the fates had been kind—to his conscience and to Julia. She was in a coma, which left hope for recovery. At the same time, the hospital report said she wasn't going to wake up any time soon. That served his purpose to a tee. All he needed was seventeen hours. Then he'd be gone, and she could open her eyes and sing out her suspicions to the Stratfords and the whole damned Leaf Brook police force. He'd be in Switzerland. He'd renounce his American citizenship, and extradition would be out of the question.

It would be smooth sailing for him.

His optimism resurged with a vengeance.

The Walker Development jet was reserved and would

be fueled and ready for a noon departure. His living arrangements in Lucerne had been finalized. Just one night separated him and a lifetime of affluence and freedom.

He'd make his second call to Stephen Stratford tomorrow morning at nine sharp. He'd reiterate his demands: five million dollars in Brian's sports bag, to be left at the airport at eleven-thirty on the dot. With one slight change in venue, just in case the mayor had decided to play hero by arranging some sort of ambush at the previously designated alcove. No chance of that, not with the updated instructions he was going to issue. Nope. The five million would be right there in the parking lot, nestled securely in the mayor's Explorer, a mere sprint away from Walker's private jet. He'd have plenty of time to stop off in the main departure lounge and stuff the envelope he'd brought into the hands of some skycap looking to make twenty bucks, before he picked up his cash and jetted off to freedom.

But not to get ahead of himself. First came tomorrow's phone call. He had to be sure the Stratfords were ready. And he had to put the icing on the cake by playing the tape for them.

Dropping onto the creaky motel bed, he glanced at his voice scrambler, remembering the terror in Stephen Stratford's voice during the first phone call. The second call would be even more agonizing.

The rush of power felt great. So did thoughts of the life that awaited him.

A self-satisfied smile curved his lips. He'd always been good at making money. But this time he'd really stepped in it.

31

April 16
8:25 A.M.

It was morning.

Brian's tummy gave a sick flip-flop. Today was the day something was gonna happen. The man in the ski mask had said so when he shoved the tape recorder in his face last night. He'd said Brian's dad would be paying a lot of money to get him back today. He'd made Brian talk into the tape recorder and say how scared he was.

He hadn't had to fake it. He *was* scared. His kidnapper had been rougher than usual last night. Meaner, too. He'd muttered something about how the mayor had better cooperate or else. Then he'd reached around, grabbed Brian's arms to make sure the ropes were nice and tight, and stomped out of the trailer.

Brian didn't want to think about what "or else" meant.

It had stayed dark outside forever. He'd finally fallen asleep but only for a little while. Even then, he'd had awful dreams. He'd jerked awake, all sweaty and shaking. For a minute, he thought he was gonna be sick. Luckily, he hadn't been. But he wanted his mom, he hurt everywhere, and he had to fight really hard not to bawl his head off.

What if no one ever came to get him?

Somewhere outside, a twig snapped. Then another.

Brian's head shot up. Someone was there. No, it was a couple of someones. A man's voice, then a different man's voice. Was one of them his kidnapper? It didn't sound like him, but Brian couldn't tell. They were talking really low and only a few words at a time. It didn't sound as if they were talking to each other. They were both talking at the same time, and their voices were coming from two different places—one from behind the trailer, the other from around front.

The voices got closer. Brian could make out their words now. He heard his name. Then he heard the static. And suddenly, he realized they were coming for him.

He started screaming at the top of his lungs.

8:45 A.M.

You could hear a pin drop in Julia's hospital room.

And not because the room was unoccupied. To the contrary, it was full.

Julia was up and dressed, unable to lie in bed a moment longer. Meredith was perched outside the door, Connor was pacing the floor, and Stephen and Nancy were huddled near the window.

The two of them had spent the night in the hospital, in the room right next door to Julia's. Louis had checked Nancy over thoroughly, verifying that there were no lasting effects from her ordeal. Physically, she could have gone home, but neither she nor Stephen could bear to do that. Not when Patricia Avalon was using Julia's hospital room as the FBI's central information point. And not when news could come at any time, news they were praying for.

Stephen had gone home long enough to pick up some

clothes for Nancy and to program his private line so that all calls would be transferred automatically to his cell phone. Before that, Patricia had spent a full hour with him and Nancy, getting additional facts and trying to assuage their fears. The latter proved to be futile. There were too many details she couldn't reveal and too many guarantees she couldn't make. True, it seemed logical enough that Greg wouldn't do anything drastic—he had no idea that Julia was conscious or that Nancy had been rescued and knew the identity of her assailant. As for silencing Brian, it seemed equally logical that he wouldn't do that, even if the worst happened and Brian recognized him. Why should he? By eliminating the chance of extradition, he'd eliminate the chance of prosecution. So it would cease to matter. But Nancy argued back that Greg was unstable, that anyone who'd run Julia down in cold blood couldn't be counted on to behave rationally.

In the end, the conversation had gone around and around in exhausting circles, and the night had been endless agony.

No one had slept. Everyone had stared at the phone and the door, praying for news that never came.

It was coming up on nine o'clock.

The door opened, and Patricia walked in. Everyone's head snapped around.

"Not yet," she said simply. "But soon."

"How soon?" Stephen snapped, jumping to his feet. "My son's been stuffed Lord knows where since Friday. The son of a bitch who took him will be boarding a plane in three hours. And we're just sitting here, doing nothing. God only knows if he's okay, if he's eaten, if he's even . . ." He heard Nancy's choked sob, and he broke off, tugging her against him and pressing her head to his chest. "I'm sorry," he murmured, kissing her hair. "I'm sorry," he repeated, meeting Patricia's gaze. "I realize you're working as fast as you can. I guess I'm just losing it."

"With good reason. He's your son." Patricia walked over to them, a purposeful look in her eyes. "When I said soon, I meant soon."

Nancy twisted around. "You have a clue?"

"Let's just say we've had a lot of territory to cover. But it looks as if we're closing in on our answer. I expect to hear something any time now. So hang on a little longer."

"Can't you tell us . . . ?"

Nancy's question was interrupted by the ringing of Stephen's cell phone. He and Nancy both jumped.

"Answer it," Patricia directed Stephen. "Remember that it's Walker you're supposed to be talking to. And Nancy, not a word. We want Matthews to think you're still bound and gagged in Stowe. Let your husband do the talking."

She nodded, her face sheet-white.

Stephen pressed the TALK button. "Yes?"

"All set for our exchange?" the scrambled voice inquired.

"The money will be ready by eleven," Stephen replied. "I'll drive it straight to the airport."

"Excellent. Now, remember, put it in Brian's sports bag."

"Right. And leave it in the alcove closest to . . ."

"No." The voice cut him off. "Drive your car into the parking lot closest to Hangar E. Leave the car, unlocked, right near the hangar—*with* the sports bag in it. At eleven-thirty sharp, take a walk into the main terminal.

Grab a cup of coffee in the departure lounge, and listen for a page. You'll hear your name called at twelve-fifteen. At that point, we'll both have what we want."

"What does that mean?" Stephen gripped the phone so tightly that his knuckles turned white. "Where will Brian be?"

"That's what the page you'll be receiving is about. Answer it promptly. A skycap will bring you an envelope with written directions inside. They'll tell you where you can find your son."

"Twelve-fifteen? You'll already be airborne."

"That's the idea."

"I'm supposed to trust you?"

"You have no choice."

Stephen sucked in his breath. "How do I know Brian's safe? Let me talk to him."

"Ah, I'm glad you brought that up. Here's a message from your son." A few fumbling sounds at the other end of the phone.

Then Brian's voice.

"Dad? Please do what the man says. I'm scared. I wanna come home." A shuddering breath, as he tried not to cry. "I'm really scared, Dad. Please bring me home."

Another series of muffled sounds, and Brian's voice was gone.

Stephen squeezed his eyes shut, tears burning behind them.

"Satisfied?" the scrambled voice asked.

Emotion too vast to contain welled up inside Stephen. "You sick, fucking bastard," he blasted, his entire body vibrating with fear and rage. "If you've hurt my son, you're a dead man. I don't care where you go or how far you run. I'll hunt you down. And I'll kill you. Count on it."

The magnitude of his fury must have conveyed itself, because there was a brief pause at the other end.

"No need for violence, Mr. Mayor," the scrambled voice assured him. "You do your part. I'll do mine. Now, get busy. You've got two hours and fifteen minutes—exactly."

Dial tone.

As if in a trance, Stephen pressed the END button, staring at the phone and mumbling, "He turned off the scrambler long enough for me to hear clearly. It was Brian's voice."

"Stephen?" Nancy interrupted, grabbing his arm. "You heard Brian? How did he sound? Was he okay? What did he say?"

The panic in Nancy's tone snapped Stephen out of his paralyzed state. He focused on his wife, catching her hand and bringing it to his lips. "Brian's okay. All I heard was a tape of his voice. And, yeah, he sounds scared, but he didn't sound hurt or weak. I really believe he's all right. I just want to choke the shit out of Matthews for putting us through this."

"Stephen," Patricia urged quietly, "tell us what was said."

He drew a steadying breath and relayed the entire conversation. When he got to the actual words Brian had used in his plea, he tried his best to soften the emotional blow.

It didn't work. Nancy was Brian's mother. She understood, and the pain of knowing her son needed her and she couldn't be there for him was too much to bear.

Covering her face with her hands, she began to weep.

Across the room, Julia averted her head, choking back her own sobs. This was not the time to fall apart. She had to be strong for Brian's family.

"So he's switched the drop site," Patricia commented. She didn't look surprised. "Another insurance step on his part." She would have said more, but her secure cell phone rang just then. She excused herself, walking off to converse in private.

Connor blew out his breath and made a quick check of the time. "I'll head off soon, just in case the money's ready ahead of time. My contacts were really pushing to make that happen." He went over to Julia, gently bringing her face around. "Hey," he said softly, tipping up her chin. "Are you okay?"

Moisture glistened on her cheeks. "I'm so sorry. If I'd had any idea Greg was capable of this . . ."

"You didn't. None of us did." His fingertips wiped away the tracks of her tears. "You've got nothing to be sorry for. You were there for Brian when he was hurting. You risked your life to save his and almost died in the process. Not to mention that you've been unbelievably strong through this whole nightmare. Even when I wasn't. My family's lucky to have you. *I'm* lucky to have you." He lowered his head, brushed her lips with his. "Thank you for showing me what's important."

Julia didn't have the opportunity to reply.

From across the room, Patricia abruptly snapped off her cell phone and cut across to the door in a few long strides.

Nancy shot up. "What is it?"

"Stay put. I'll be right back." The special agent left, the door swinging shut behind her.

Silence ensued. The room's four remaining occupants looked at one another.

"What was that about?" Stephen demanded.

"I don't know." Connor's gaze narrowed. "But it was obviously important."

"She must have learned something." Nancy ran a quavering hand through her hair. "But what? Oh, God, Stephen, what if Brian's . . . what if something's happened."

"Don't think that way," her husband commanded, wrapping a supportive arm around her shoulders. "Just don't."

Julia was staring through the small square window in the hospital-room door, intently studying her mother, watching her demeanor and her actions. Meredith had risen to her feet, her hands clasped, and there was an ardent, expectant look on her face.

"Whatever's happened, it isn't bad," Julia determined quietly. "In fact, I'm praying it's good."

As she spoke, her mother's lips curved into a smile, and she nodded, saying something to Patricia as she returned, then squatting down until she was no longer visible through the window.

Patricia poked her head into the room.

"Do you have an update for us?" Nancy asked pleadingly.

Genuine pleasure sparkled in Patricia's eyes. "I have something better for you. I have a visitor." She yanked the door open the rest of the way, leaning back against it so that Meredith could push a wheelchair into the room—a wheelchair containing whomever Meredith had been squatting to talk to a moment ago.

Their visitor was a short, huddled figure totally concealed by a blanket.

But only long enough for Patricia to shut the door and give Meredith the okay nod.

With a watery smile, Meredith reached for the blanket, tugged it away. "Okay, champ," she urged. "Go for it."

Brian's cherished face appeared—tired and tear-streaked but eager as a puppy's. He squirmed out of the blanket, clambering to his feet and peering around all at once.

"Oh, God," Nancy whispered. "Brian." She stretched out her arms. "Brian!"

He ran to her, a harsh sob escaping him as his mother grabbed him and scooped him up into a tight hug. "Mom," he choked out, hugging her fiercely.

"Oh, baby, are you all right? Are you hurt? Are you . . ." Nancy was crying too hard to speak.

"I'm okay, Mom." With that rare, amazing grown-up sensitivity Brian had, he consoled his mother between sniffles. "Honest, I'm okay."

He felt another pair of arms wrap around him from behind, and he turned, his whole face lighting up when he saw his father. "Dad!" He flung himself against his father.

Stephen gripped him securely, pressing his lips into Brian's disheveled hair. He was openly weeping, his shoulders shaking as he held his son. "Hey, you," he managed. "I missed you like crazy."

"I missed you, too." Brian's voice was muffled against his father's shirt. "I was really scared."

"So was I," Stephen admitted. "But it's over now. You're here with us, and you're safe."

"Mom, too?" Brian shot an anxious glance at his mother. "He made her drink some stuff that put her to sleep."

"I'm fine, baby," Nancy assured him, rubbing his back.

"Dad drove up and found me. And now that you're home, I'm better than fine." She smiled through her tears. "I'm a lucky woman. I've got two heroes—you and Dad."

That tribute impressed Brian enough to divert his lingering apprehension. "A hero." He considered the idea, his sniffles subsiding. "That sounds pretty cool."

"It is," Stephen confirmed. "I'm so proud of you. You watched out for Mom, and you came through this like a trouper. I don't think I've ever seen anyone so brave."

"Me, either," Nancy agreed. She smoothed Brian's hair off his face, assessing him with a mother's practiced eye. "You must be starving."

"Yeah." An emphatic nod as the priorities and the rapid-recovery ability of a seven-and-a-half-year-old surged to the forefront. "Can I have a cheeseburger and fries?"

At the moment, Nancy would have bought out McDonald's, she was so relieved. But she forced her more practical, maternal instincts to prevail. "Sweetie, I don't think the first thing you eat after three days should be . . ."

"I ate yesterday and the day before," Brian protested. "Just not today."

Nancy and Stephen exchanged puzzled looks.

"Today's Monday, Bri," Stephen explained. "You were taken on Friday."

"I know. I counted the nights. They were dark and creepy, and I hated them. Anyway, the mornings were when I ate. Mr. Matthews brought me cereal and Gatorade."

"He did?" Stephen asked in surprise.

"Uh-huh. And after that, he untied me so I could go into the woods and . . . well, you know."

His father's lips twitched. "Yeah, we know."

"Brian?" Patricia Avalon interrupted the reunion. "Did you say Mr. Matthews?"

"Yeah. That's the guy's name. He works for Dad."

She blinked, glancing at Stephen. "We never referred to the kidnapper by name," she explained. A quizzical look at Brian. "Did Mr. Matthews not wear a disguise? Is that how you knew who he was?"

"Nope," Brian refuted. "He wore one of those robber's ski masks. He never took it off."

"Then how did you . . ."

"His voice," Brian explained patiently. "I'm real good at recognizing them. Just ask Dad. When I answer the phone, I always know who it is before they tell me. Anyway, I've heard Mr. Matthews's voice lots of times, whenever I visit Dad's office."

"I see." For the first time, Patricia looked taken aback. "Your parents are right. You're quite a guy."

"Thanks." Brian frowned. "Mr. Matthews got pretty mean and scary sometimes. I think it's because he wanted that money really bad. But he didn't hurt me, except for how tight the ropes were. I guess he figured Dad would punch him out if he did." Brian shot his father an interested look. "Did you give him the money? It must have been a lot."

Stephen grinned. "It was. And no, he doesn't have it yet. Uncle Connor was on his way to get it when you wheeled in. Speaking of which . . ." Stephen released Brian, stepping aside so his son could see the room's other occupants. "I think you have a few more fans to greet."

"Uncle Connor! Miss Talbot!" Brian zoomed over and gave his uncle a high five.

Connor squatted down, his eyes suspiciously damp. "Welcome home, ace," he murmured, wrapping Brian in a giant bear hug. "The house has been much too quiet without you."

"Are you still staying there?"

"You bet I am. In fact, I think we should have a big welcome-home party tonight. Pizza. My treat. I'll bring in as many pies as you want."

"Can Miss Talbot come, too?" Brian asked the same question he'd asked at a memorable Saturday baseball game, sixteen days and an eternity ago.

"Yeah, ace," Connor said fervently. "She sure can."

Brian took a step toward Julia, then stopped, his frown returning. "Miss Talbot, why are you still crying? And why do you have that big Band-Aid on your head? And all those bandages on your arm and your hand? Did you get hurt, too?"

She nodded, stepping off the bed—ignoring whatever weakness and dizziness ensued—and, with her good left arm, tugged Brian toward her, giving him a resounding kiss on the cheek. "I had an accident. But I'm better. And I'm crying because I'm very, very glad to see you."

"I'm glad to see you, too." He scrunched up his face in a hopeful look. "Can you come over for pizza? Or do you have spelling tests to mark again?"

"No." She swallowed hard. "No spelling tests this time. And as long as Dr. Tillerman says it's all right, I'd love to come over for pizza."

"Don't be too sure of that," Nancy warned, laughing shakily through her tears. "You have no idea how much gunk Brian and Connor like on their pizza. When they say 'everything on it,' they mean it. It takes a giant crane to lift each slice."

"Ugh." Julia shuddered. "That's going to take some getting used to."

"You're not gonna change your mind and not come?" Brian asked anxiously.

"No way." Julia squeezed his hand. "I wouldn't miss this celebration for anything."

"Plus, Miss Talbot's going to be eating a lot of pizza with us from now on," Connor added. A corner of his mouth lifted, and he winked at Julia. "But I'll compromise. How about a couple of plain pies, or maybe a few that you and Nancy pick out, topped with your ingredients of choice?"

Julia smiled. "Sounds good."

"You're going to be coming over a lot more?" Brian interrupted excitedly. He hadn't missed his uncle's comment. "Is that 'cause of me, or 'cause of Uncle Connor?"

"Both."

"Even after you're not my teacher anymore?"

"Even then."

"Cool." Brian grinned. "That's the kind of getting used to I like."

"In that case," Connor said, "I have one more thing for you to get used to. I think you'll like this one, too, even though it's going to take some practice."

"Practice? You mean, like baseball?"

"Yeah, like baseball. Maybe better."

"Better than baseball?" Brian looked dubious.

"To me it is. I think it will be to you, too." Connor inclined his head, meeting Brian's curious gaze. "You're going to have to get used to calling Miss Talbot by a different name. Think you can manage?"

"What name?" Brian demanded.

Connor pursed his lips, as if he were carefully evaluating the options. "I don't know—how does Aunt Julia sound to you?"

It took about twenty seconds to sink in.

Then Brian let out a whoop. "You're getting married?"

"Yup."

"Wow!" Exploding with excitement, Brian turned to his parents. "Did you know?"

"We had a pretty good idea," Stephen said, grinning.

"And we're thrilled about it," Nancy added.

"Me, too." Brian was beaming ear to ear. "Now we have another thing to celebrate. Maybe we should get ice cream to go with the pizza."

"Good idea." Stephen's gaze drifted over his son—from his exuberant expression to his torn, dirty clothes—and his eyes misted over. "I feel like I have a lot to celebrate," he murmured, giving Nancy a hard hug. "I'm a very lucky man."

He turned to Patricia. "Thank you," he said fervently. "There's not much more I can say."

"You're very welcome."

"Yeah, the FBI was super-cool," Brian announced. "They broke open the door of the trailer I was in. I'm glad I spit out that gag, so I could yell when I heard them. I knew it was cops 'cause I heard those radio things they talk through. And I heard my name. So I yelled. And Police Chief Hart was there, too. He gave me a chocolate chip cookie for later . . . uh-oh." Brian dug in his pocket and pulled out a handful of brown crumbs. "I guess I squished it."

"I guess so." Stephen ruffled his hair. "Trailer?" he asked Patricia, finally requesting the details he'd put off asking for until he was sure Brian was okay enough to handle it. "Greg hid Brian in a trailer?"

"A construction trailer located on a deserted Walker Development site," she clarified. "Matthews planned this very carefully. He arranged all the evidence so it pointed to Walker being behind Brian's kidnapping." Patricia counted off on her fingers. "Walker's plane and pilot prepped for a getaway. Walker's trailer where Brian was being held. Walker's thug who broke into Connor's car, presumably to steal it—which, in turn, made Julia's hit-and-run look like an unrelated accident. It was a very clever plan. Matthews devised it so he'd not only escape scott-free, but he'd do it with everyone believing he was just an accomplice, with Walker masterminding the major crimes."

"So that's where your agents have been looking, at Walker's development sites?"

"Not just the sites currently under development. Those previously developed by his company or that his company's invested in. Plus his personal land holdings. Walker owns a great deal of property in his own name. Then there were his employees' homes and apartments, the residences belonging to everyone from his hired hands to his reputable staff members. Any of them could have been aiding and abetting Matthews in his attempts to frame Walker. Trust me, it was a tedious process."

"I'm sure." Stephen felt another surge of gratitude. "What made you zero in on this site?"

"We blew through the list of possible locations we'd compiled as quickly and methodically as we could. When we got to the site in question, we discovered that all construction there had been temporarily suspended. Which meant the site was deserted. Shut down. Walker's equipment was still there, but his workers weren't. No one would have reason to visit the place. It was perfect for keeping a hostage. Martin Hart checked it out personally. He spotted tire treads, fresh ones. The rest was easy. Our agents found Brian and transferred him to an FBI car. We kept him all wrapped up in that blanket, so his rescue could remain our little secret." Patricia grinned at Brian. "Brian here helped us out by yelling, stomping, making as much noise as possible so our people could find him."

"Kind of like what I do at a Yankees game," Brian explained to his father.

"Ah, then, no wonder they heard you."

Brian fidgeted, having grown bored with the recap of events. "Dad, can we go home now? And can we stop off for that cheeseburger and fries?"

Stephen's jaw set. He would have liked nothing better than to say yes, but he couldn't. Not with Greg still out there. For security purposes, it was imperative that Brian, Nancy, and Julia remained hidden until Greg's capture was a fait accompli.

He met Patricia's sober gaze and saw the confirmation of his reasoning reflected there.

"You know what, champ?" he told Brian. "Not yet. First of all, Dr. Tillerman's around here somewhere. And I'd really like him to take a look at you, just like he did at Mom. You had a pretty rough time yourself."

"I guess so," Brian grudgingly agreed. "Mr. Matthews didn't make me drink that stuff he gave Mom. But he did put something stinky over my face that made me go to sleep. He must have done it a few times, 'cause I don't remember the car ride."

Stephen wanted to choke Greg Matthews all over again. But this time, he kept his cool for Brian's sake. "Exactly. Also, you'll need more antibiotic for that ear infection of yours. You were supposed to be taking ten days' worth. So I think we should hang around for a while."

"I need a checkup, too, Brian," Julia told him. "I'm not allowed to leave without one, either. So we'll keep each other company." A teasing smile. "Only no curve-ball practice. My arm's out of commission for a while."

Brian's brows drew together sympathetically, the thought of not being able to pitch tantamount to torture. "What kind of accident did you have?"

Julia opted for a vague response. Brian had been through enough trauma for now. He didn't need more gory details. "I went to the mall to see your dad make a speech. The parking lot was really crowded. I got hit by a car that was driving too fast."

"Wow." Brian's eyes widened. "That's almost as exciting as my getting kidnapped."

"Almost," Julia agreed.

While Brian was occupied, Patricia turned to Stephen and Nancy, lowering her voice so that only they could hear. "I wish I could say go home, but I can't. Not yet. We have some unfinished business to complete."

"Nailing Greg Matthews to the wall," Stephen concluded.

"Right. He doesn't know anything—not that Walker's cooperating and in custody, not that Julia's conscious, not that Nancy's home. And certainly not that Brian's been rescued. We have to keep it that way, for obvious reasons." Patricia folded her arms across her breasts, gazing from Stephen to Nancy. "I realize you want to be with your family, to go home and put this behind you. I'm asking for a few more hours to complete our charade and set our trap."

"You don't need to ask," Stephen assured her. "You couldn't stop me. I want this guy locked up with the key thrown away."

"What do you want us to do?" Nancy asked.

"You stay here with Brian and Julia," Patricia instructed Nancy. "Meredith will take up her post by the door. I need Connor to pick up the cash, as planned, and Stephen to drive it to the airport. Stephen, follow Matthews's instructions to the letter, just as if Brian's life were still on the line. Leave the sports bag in your car, and go to the lounge. Wait for the skycap to give you your directions. By then, Matthews will be dealt with, and this whole masquerade will be over."

"The FBI's going to grab him in the middle of the airport?"

Patricia smiled. "Better and more subtle. Remember your concerns that Matthews might try to take Brian along with him as an insurance policy? Well, that thought occurred to us, too. So we sent along our own insurance policy to nip things in the bud, just in case." A quick glance at Brian. "Thank heavens it never came to that. Still, the strategy we implemented will keep the arrest quiet, with as little sensationalism as possible." A hint of biting amusement. "I'm sure that'll please your father. He's been rather vocal about his desire to keep things low-profile."

"Yeah, right." Stephen didn't need to ask what Patricia meant. The minute Harrison Stratford had blown back into town at midnight, he'd descended on the Leaf Brook police like an avalanche, making sure they were executing discretion at every turn.

Frankly, Stephen had steered clear of his father. He'd been consumed with just one thing: finding Brian. After that, well, he was still reeling from his father's part in Walker's scheme, especially given what it had snowballed into.

But when all this was over, he and the imperious Harrison Stratford were going to have quite a conversation. Stephen had a few choice words to get off his chest. After that, he'd drop the professional bomb that would close this chapter of his life for good.

"So," Patricia concluded, "If there are no more questions, let's get started. You do your part, and we'll do ours."

"Done." Stephen gazed across the room at his brother. "Hey, Connor, we've got an appointment to keep," he announced pointedly.

Connor understood. "Gotcha." He leaned over and gave Julia a tender kiss. "I'm going to help Stephen get that son of a bitch who ran you down," he muttered, his voice low enough so Brian couldn't hear.

Julia nodded. "Be careful."

"I will be." Connor's gaze softened. "In the meantime, tell Louis I'm expecting to take you home, so he'd better give you a clean bill of health. If you need TLC, I'll supply it—but in your bed, not the hospital's."

"I'll tell him," she promised, a hint of a smile curving her lips. "Hurry back."

"I'll just pick up the ransom money and help Stephen stuff it into the sports bag. After that, he'll take care of the rest." Another kiss. "In the meantime, start planning our wedding."

Her eyes danced. "And our honeymoon?"

"Especially our honeymoon. Pick somewhere you want to stay for a month. And a luxury hotel with great room service and a view from the bed. Because you won't be leaving it."

Julia laughed softly. "Yes, sir."

Straightening, Connor walked over and rumpled Brian's hair. "You and your future Aunt Julia get good checkups," he instructed in a normal tone. "We'll be whisking you out of here right after lunch. I'll be back before your dad is, so I'll bring cheeseburgers and fries with me. But you'd better not stuff yourself. I'm planning a pizza-eating contest for tonight. I expect you to be my main competition."

"Ahem," Stephen interceded, clearing his throat. "I think you're forgetting me. I can eat more slices than both of you put together."

A broad grin split Brian's face. "No way. Right, Mom?"

Nancy rolled her eyes. "Why is everything a competition to men?"

"It's in our blood." Stephen met his wife's gaze. "But this competition's just for fun. No bets on who the winner will be. No bets at all." A silent communication ran between them.

"Stay safe," Nancy murmured, laying her palm against his jaw. "No heroics. Let the FBI handle Greg. Brian and I need you."

"Good," he said softly. "Because you've got me."

32

11:30 A.M.
Westchester County Airport

Greg stood in the shadows, watching Stephen Stratford's Explorer pull into the parking lot. Excellent. Right on time.

He himself had gotten there at eleven and had sought out an eager young skycap to do his bidding. He made sure the guy understood the importance of delivering the letter to Mayor Stratford. It was a way of ensuring that his conscience was clear. After all, he didn't want the kid to die. All he wanted was to get his five million bucks and get out of the country.

He watched Stephen get out of the car. He looked drawn and haggard, as if he'd been through hell. Well, his hell was about to end—at least for now. Given the guy's compulsion for gambling, it wouldn't be long before he got himself into another jam. Soon enough, he'd be misappropriating campaign funds again, then relying on his brother to bail him out.

Eventually, Stratford would blow his marriage and his political career to bits and self-destruct.

Philip Walker wouldn't be the one to light that fuse. Not anymore. The slick bastard would be rotting in jail. After months of ordering Greg around like a flunky, he deserved nothing less. It was a little bonus Greg had orchestrated for himself, by dropping clues like bread crumbs. Walker would go down for the big stuff. It didn't matter that Greg wouldn't be there to witness it. Just knowing he'd bested Walker—and knowing that Walker would realize it, too—was enough.

He stopped musing as Stephen left his car and glanced around briefly before heading to the door leading into the airport.

Good. Almost home free.

Still, Greg gave it a full five minutes, just to be safe.

The minutes ticked by. No sign of Stratford returning to his car. And no sign of any cops or other Stratfords acting as backup for the mayor.

Long enough.

Greg strolled out to the Explorer. He could see the sports bag through the passenger window. Casually, he opened the door and swung the bag out and onto his shoulder. He unzipped it enough to check inside. The cash was there. With a quick slam of the car door, he walked away, heading in the opposite direction from Stephen, toward Walker Development's private jet.

He climbed on board, prepared for the questions that Jerry Baines, Walker's private pilot, would have.

Jerry came out of the cockpit, his brows drawn in puzzlement. "Mr. Matthews? What are you doing here? Where's Mr. Walker?"

"A last-minute change in plans," Greg told him. "Mr. Walker had an emergency stockholders' meeting. He wanted me to get his Switzerland deal under way. So he brought me up to speed. He said for you to fly me over there, then head directly back. He'll call during your return flight and issue instructions about when he'll need you to fly him over to join me. Don't worry. He'll give you a day or two's rest in between." Greg dug in his pocket and whipped out some bills. "By the way, here's your thousand bucks, plus a little extra."

Jerry took it. "Okay, thanks." He pointed at the sports bag. "I thought you said a large attaché case."

Greg had anticipated this, too. "Walker's got that," he explained. "Along with the papers he needs to close this deal. He'll be bringing them with him. All I had time to throw together were some preliminary notes, a change or two of clothes, and my shaving kit. Just enough to get started. After that, Walker will take over. I'll fly home commercial." Greg glanced into the cockpit, nodding a greeting at Jerry's copilot.

The guy nodded back. He was a young, clean-cut type, who was yakking on his cell phone. Greg had never met him, nor did he care to. All he cared about was getting the hell out of there.

"I checked," he prompted Jerry, turning to walk into the main cabin and get settled in his seat. "We've got clear skies and no turbulence. Takeoff should be prompt." He started heading in.

"Sorry, Mr. Matthews." It was the young copilot who replied. He strode out of the cockpit, angling himself so he blocked Greg's path. "Takeoff has been delayed indefinitely."

Greg's insides clenched, an ugly premonition forming in the pit of his stomach. "What does that mean?"

"It means you're not going anywhere. Except to prison." The copilot raised a pistol, simultaneously flashing an official ID in Greg's face. "Special Agent Carver, Federal Bureau of Investigation," he introduced himself. "I've been waiting for you." He reached over, unzipping the sports bag enough to peek inside. "You're under arrest for the kidnapping of Brian Stratford, the attempted murder of Julia Talbot, and a long list of other crimes that Police Chief Hart will be glad to tell you about."

For one frozen moment, Greg stared, watching his future disintegrate before his eyes. "But it's not even twelve o'clock yet," he muttered aimlessly. "How . . ."

"Because the mayor's got his son. We found him three hours ago. Now, let's go."

From across the field, Stephen watched Greg being led away and taken into custody. He looked dazed, as if he still didn't believe he'd been one-upped at the last minute. The cruel, greedy bastard.

Stephen continued to watch until Greg's head had disappeared into the backseat of the FBI's unmarked car and the car had pulled away. There was a finality about it that evoked a powerful sense of justice, retribution, and, most of all, closure.

The nightmare was over. The rest was up to him.

Infinitely lighter of step and heart, Stephen hopped back into his Explorer and headed for the hospital—and his family.

Time for starting over to begin.

33

~

April 23

The announcement of the mayor's resignation and withdrawal from the senatorial race was carried by all local and regional newspapers.

His decision to retire from politics and go back to practicing law, as well as the family crisis that prompted it, appeared in major newspapers throughout the state, as well as a host of tabloids and quite a few society pages. After all, the mayor was, first and foremost, a Stratford.

Media everywhere jumped on the personal interest story of how Mayor Stratford's son was kidnapped by Greg Matthews, the Leaf Brook city manager. The stories went on to describe Matthews's drugging of Nancy Stratford, his abduction of young Brian, and his attempted murder of Julia Talbot, Connor Stratford's fiancée and Brian's second-grade teacher, when she tried to reach the Stratfords with her suspicions of his involvement. The exceptional role of Leaf Brook police, in conjunction with the FBI, was reported, together with their successful recovery of Brian and their well-timed capture of Matthews as he attempted to flee the country with the ransom money.

On a less significant note, the stories mentioned that land developer Philip Walker was mixed up with

Matthews in criminal offenses consisting of money laundering, car theft, and extortion.

Walker, it was reported, had cut a deal with the DA and was serving a reduced sentence.

Matthews, on the other hand, was up on federal charges and wouldn't be seeing the light of day for a long, long time.

In response to the public's clamoring for an emotional and personal take on what had happened, Connor Stratford acted as the family spokesman. He gave an exclusive full-page interview to the *Leaf Brook Herald,* which just happened to be the chief competitor of Cheryl Lager's newspaper, the *Leaf Brook News*. In that interview, he described the anguish his family had endured during Brian's disappearance, as well as their overwhelming gratitude when Brian was safely returned and his captor apprehended. Connor gave a hats-off to the Leaf Brook police and the FBI for their incomparable dedication and professionalism.

He also gave effusive, if not unbiased, praise to Julia Talbot, speaking with pride of the role she'd played in Brian's rescue, as well as of her loving dedication to her students. He went on to discuss her commitment to children in general and her association with the APSAC. Speaking highly of the organization that had put him in contact with Patricia Avalon and subsequently with the FBI, he made sure to give the APSAC a strong plug and to advocate the workshops Julia and her mother gave at area hospitals.

The subject of hospitals brought the reporter back to Julia's hit-and-run, and Connor frankly admitted how much he'd agonized during the hours she'd remained unconscious and his inexplicable relief when she opened her eyes. He made no secret of his feelings for Julia and, on a more personal note, happily announced their upcoming wedding, which was set for June—giving Julia more than enough time to heal physically, then to return to her classroom and finish out the school year. The details of the ceremony and the reception would be released at a later date. Not so for the honeymoon destination. That was being kept under wraps for good, ensuring that the bride and groom enjoyed the privacy they deserved.

One entire paragraph of the interview was devoted to providing tongue-in-cheek praise for Cheryl Lager, who'd turned out to be an excellent, if unknowing, ally.

Elaborating, Connor explained that Ms. Lager's overzealous invasion of the Stratfords' privacy, particularly heightened during the ongoing crisis, had triggered his idea to use her to feed information to the kidnapper rather than to follow his original intent, which was to sue her for slander and harassment.

To that end, he'd supplied Ms. Lager with the false lead that Julia remained comatose, knowing full well that the reporter would jump on the opportunity to print an exclusive story, embellishing on it in her customary manner. And it had worked beautifully.

The word *pawn* was, of course, never used.

As for his brother's decision to retire from politics, Connor addressed that by explaining that the threat to Stephen's family had shaken him badly and caused him to reevaluate his priorities. Being a Stratford was hard enough. It meant living in the public eye on a constant basis. Being a Stratford *and* in politics meant exposing his family to more danger than Stephen was willing to risk. So, while his commitment to Leaf Brook and to the

State of New York as a whole was as strong as ever, he'd decided to fulfill that commitment through less personally hazardous channels.

The result of the interview was to heighten the already widespread empathy and pride that had been intensifying since the story of Brian's kidnapping first got out—empathy for Mayor Stratford and all he'd endured and pride in his determination to protect his family at all costs. His political followers were disappointed but supportive. After all, he might be retiring from political life, but he was doing it with honor and achievement. Ultimately, he'd rid the city of an animal like Greg Matthews and a crook like Philip Walker. He'd taken care of his constituents, as always. And when he realized he could no longer do that without reservation or compromise, he was ethical enough to walk away rather than stick around and do a half-assed job.

In short, in the eyes of Leaf Brook residents, Mayor Stratford stepped up to become an even greater hero.

Of course, there were a few details Connor neglected to touch on in his interview.

One was the unofficial deal they'd cut with Martin Hart. Marty had agreed to sit on what he knew about Stephen's gambling, including his temporary misappropriation of campaign funds, in exchange for his resignation. The police chief's decision was rooted not only in loyalty and compassion but in common sense and reason. Stephen had done great things for Leaf Brook, including throwing his full support behind the needs of the police department. Plus, he was a good man, a decent man, and Marty respected him—weaknesses or not. In the police chief's opinion, Stephen had already paid dearly for his indiscretions. He'd been beaten and blackmailed and had come close to losing his wife and son. He'd been pushed to the limit, and he was owning up to it by seeing a therapist who'd help keep him on the road to recovery. Whether for his own future or that of the city and the state, he'd resigned as mayor and relinquished his political future.

Enough was enough. Marty was more than happy to let Stephen leave office with an emotional sendoff and an untarnished reputation.

Then there was Harrison Stratford, whose reaction had been anything but agreeable. He'd pitched a fit, blasting Stephen from today until next week when he heard what his older son intended to do with his future.

Stephen had blasted him right back, armed with a conviction that Connor had never seen and a self-confidence that was indicative of the progress he'd made. He laid it all on the line—from the childhood manipulation that had screwed him up, to dreams their father was living vicariously through him, to his flat-out, unequivocal declaration that he was now going to live *his* life, not his father's. As for whether or not Harrison would ever be a part of that life, the jury was still out.

Their father was flabbergasted. Actually, it was the first time Connor had ever seen the man speechless. The interesting part was that despite his bitter disappointment and anger, Connor could swear that Stephen had earned their father's respect for the first time.

It was fascinating how things worked out. Stephen got a shot of much-needed self-esteem, and their father got a shot of equally needed humility.

Things with Cliff had been almost as dicey. Obviously, his relationships with both Stephen and Nancy had taken huge hits. He was painfully aware of that. Still, fueled by a decade of friendship, he'd driven to their house the day after Brian's safe return to express his relief and, once again, his contrition.

Stephen could have thrown him out. But he didn't. He, better than anyone, understood human weakness and the impact it could have on one's life. He also understood the amount of guts it had taken Cliff to come to their home and face them, not to mention the courage it had taken to own up to his failings, face his mistakes head-on, and try to rectify them.

Stephen would be a damned hypocrite if he ignored the parallel between Cliff's situation and his. And since he was moving on, didn't he owe Cliff a chance to do the same? Ultimately, he'd talked it out with Nancy, and she'd agreed. They'd try to put their friendship with Cliff back on track.

The three of them began together by dissolving Stephen's senatorial campaign, carefully refunding every dollar that had been contributed. It was a symbolic step as much as an absolute one, severing a piece of the past that they were more than happy to bid good-bye.

After that, there were legal ideas for Stephen and Cliff to bat around as Stephen reopened his law practice. Maybe someday there would even be cases to collaborate on. On the social front, Nancy had an interesting report for Stephen when she came home from one of her matron-of-honor gown fittings for Julia and Connor's wedding. Julia had decided to pair off Robin Haley and Cliff at the reception. Subscribing to the old adage that opposites attract, she was convinced that the two of them would hit it off. And, having met Robin that day at the bridal salon, Nancy had to agree.

The outlook appeared promising. Especially after Nancy teasingly assured Stephen that aside from the fact that they were both natural blondes, she and Robin bore not the slightest resemblance to each other.

With a wedding to look forward to and so many new beginnings in the works, life was suddenly filled with hope.

And the necessary building—and rebuilding—was begun.

Epilogue

August 26

The silver LearJet sliced through the night sky. Its motion was smooth, the steady hum of its engines a soothing purr that shut out any other sounds. It had lulled her to sleep. Now, it coaxed her awake.

Julia Stratford stirred, her gaze automatically flickering to her wrist to see the time. According to her watch, which was the only thing she was wearing, she'd been asleep for about an hour.

She sighed, gazing out the window of Connor's private jet.

Outside was the moon, a spattering of stars, and, way down below, the Pacific Ocean. Inside was only the two of them.

At twenty-five thousand feet, the world seemed very far away.

Feeling languid and happy, Julia snuggled closer to her husband. They were entwined on the cabin's plush divan, her body draped over his, their clothing a tangle on the floor. This mode of travel had become a favorite of theirs as they'd winged their way from Europe to the Far East to Hawaii over the past few months.

"Hey, sleepyhead," Connor greeted her softly, his fingers drifting lightly up and down her spine. "Did you have a nice nap?"

"I never sleep on planes," she informed him, turning her face so she could brush her lips across his chest. "I'm not relaxed enough."

"That's a shame. Then again, we just found out that you have other reasons for needing your rest now. Right?" His hand slid around to cup her breast, his thumb skimming lightly over the nipple, teasing it into a tight, hard point.

"Right," she managed.

"Although, the way I remember it, you seemed pretty relaxed when you drifted off." His thumb rasped more fully across her nipple—once, twice—then again and again. "Or was that my imagination?"

"N-no. I was relaxed." She shivered. "But not anymore."

"No. Not anymore." He lifted her up to his mouth, tugging at her nipple until she cried out, then shifting to do the same to its mate. He loved how responsive she was, now more so than ever.

Like her recent fatigue, that was for a specific—and spectacular—reason.

The very thought of it was enough to make him reach for her again, settle her astride him.

They made love with the same hungry intensity as always, the pleasure so acute it was almost unbearable.

When it was over, Julia drew a shuddering breath, whispering Connor's name as she sank against him, going blissfully limp.

A twinge of worry inserted itself, one that hadn't been there before that morning's confirming test. "Julia?" Connor studied her, lying utterly slack against him. She looked a little too wiped out to suit him, and his brows knit with concern. "Was it too much?"

"Um-um," she refuted, easing his angst with a slight shake of her head. "Not even a little. It was perfect. *We're* perfect."

"Which we?" he persisted. "You and me we? Or you and . . ."

"*All* of us. You and me . . ." Her palm slid between them, rested against her abdomen. "And me and the baby. Stop worrying."

"Forget it. I've just started." He sifted strands of her hair between his fingers. "You're sure you made that appointment with your doctor?"

Julia began to laugh. "Connor, I'm pregnant, not senile. I called from our hotel room. I've got an appointment the day after tomorrow. But I described my symptoms to the nurse and then again to my mother, whom you also insisted I call. Both RNs assured me that everything I'm experiencing is perfectly normal. My parents are thrilled, by the way."

"I'm glad. Still, I'll feel better after you've been examined."

"Maybe for an hour or two you will." Julia propped her chin on Connor's chest. "Then you'll start worrying about the next phase. Honestly, I thought venture capitalists had nerves of steel."

"They do. With investments, not pregnant wives."

She reached up and traced the line of his jaw. "You are happy about the baby, aren't you?"

"Happy?" Connor caught her wrist, brought her palm to his lips. "I've been fantasizing about getting you pregnant since the first time we made love."

"Me, too," she admitted softly.

"You're going to make an incredible mother." Connor could just picture her nurturing and loving their child, providing all the fundamentals that he'd missed out on. Things he'd never regarded as viable, much less necessary. Her idealism, her sensitivity, and that core of inner strength—she'd make the kind of mother every child should have.

"I love watching you with Brian," Julia told him, tracing his mouth with her fingertips. "I always did. You come alive, let down your guard. I always wished you'd do that more often."

"And now?"

She smiled a radiant smile that warmed Connor inside and out. "Now that guard's down for good, at least with me." She sobered, a tender glow in her eyes. "You're going to make a spectacular father. I can't wait to see you with our child."

That swell of emotion that still caught him off guard each time he felt it tightened his chest. Theirs was going to be one lucky baby. Just as he was one lucky man.

"I love you, Mrs. Stratford," he murmured huskily.

A tiny shiver rippled through Julia. "Is it possible to be this happy?"

"Not just possible, permanent. You can count on it." He reached down and pulled a blanket over them. "Now, rest. You and the baby need it. And if you don't, just humor me."

"I can manage that." Julia sighed as Connor wrapped the blanket more securely around them. "Mmm . . . I hope we don't hit turbulence," she murmured. "This would be a very inconvenient time to have to put on our seat belts."

Connor chuckled, his arms tightening around his wife.

"Don't worry. My pilot said we had clear skies between Hawaii and the mainland. Which means another few hours before we have to think about turbulence." He nuzzled her hair. "At least, the atmospheric kind."

Julia considered that. "I just realized—after this trip, we've officially joined the Mile-High Club."

"Sweetheart, after this trip, we're Gold Club members."

Her breath of laughter warmed his skin. "I guess that's true. We've taken almost a dozen plane trips since we left in June. Most of them have ended up like this."

"Um-hum. Every one that exceeded two hours. As for the shorter flights, we made up for those when we reached our hotel rooms."

"Does that mean we get frequent flyer miles? Because I'd love to cash them in and do this again someday."

"Someday. But not for a while. I have other plans for you—for our family. A little surprise I've been working on."

An intrigued lift of her brows. "What kind of surprise?"

Connor's expression said he'd been savoring this moment. "Our house."

Julia's head came up. "Our *what?*"

"Our house." A corner of his mouth lifted at the excitement in her voice. "I conferred with your parents, got a better idea of what you'd like. I realized I was taking a risk, that you might be royally pissed that I did this as a surprise. But I wanted to give it to you as a belated wedding gift."

"Connor." She was having trouble processing the enormity of what he was telling her. "You bought us a *house?*"

"Well, it's not a house yet," he corrected, gauging her

reaction to see if she was thrilled or furious. "It's a site. It'll be a house in about six months."

"Where is this site?"

"About twenty minutes north of Stephen and Nancy's place, on ten of the most gorgeous wooded acres you've ever seen. It's less than a half hour from your school and just a little farther than that from your parents. It also has easy access to Manhattan. So we've got proximity to our families and our work. I bought the land right after you got out of the hospital. Then I commissioned a top-notch architect and gave him the specs your parents and I came up with. He drew up the plans, along with a few ideas for layout variations, so you can choose whichever floor plan you like best. And I'll leave all the decorating to you, starting with the nursery. The building permit has been issued. The construction crew is poised and waiting. All you have to do is give the drawings your stamp of approval, and the groundbreaking can begin."

Julia was still staring dazedly at him. "You said it would be ready in about six months?"

"Yup. Five if we push it. Which we'd better, now that I think about it. The baby's probably due at the beginning of April. I want you all settled in with plenty of time to spare." A decisive nod. "We'll be in by February first."

There wasn't a doubt in Julia's mind that they would be. Connor Stratford made things happen. More than that, he moved mountains.

"Till then, we've got your apartment and mine," he concluded. "We can follow our original plan—live in the city and the suburbs. But for the future, for us and our kids, I want roots." He broke off, searching her face for a final verdict. "Is that okay? Because if you're not happy, I'll sell the house right after it's built."

"Don't you dare." Julia rose up and gave him a long, effusive kiss. "I'm just stunned. I can't believe you managed all this. As for selling, forget it. This is one investment you're holding on to." Her lighthearted banter vanished, and she kissed him again, this time slowly, deeply. "Thank you," she whispered. "You thought of everything. You're amazing."

A heated look darkened his eyes, and his embrace tightened as he drew her mouth back to his. "Amazing, huh? Well, we've still got a long trip home. I'll show you just how amazing I am."

August 27

Brian was hopping around like a jumping bean on the observation deck of the airport as he waited for his uncle's private jet to land.

"Dad, where are they?" he demanded.

Stephen leaned back on the bench he and Nancy were sitting on and looped an arm around his wife's shoulders. "Let's see." He squinted, searching the brightly lit sky through the glass-paned walls. "I'd say, about there." He pointed off to the west.

"I don't see anything," Brian announced, following his father's line of vision. "How do you know that's where they are?"

"Because Uncle Connor called me a half hour ago and said they'd be landing within the hour. Which means they're almost close enough to see."

"If you say so." Brian didn't sound too convinced. He continued to dart from spot to spot, trying to get a better view of the runway that would serve as his uncle's landing strip.

Nancy grinned, resting her head on Stephen's shoulder.

"Tired?" he asked, pressing a kiss into her hair. "We were up pretty early this morning."

"Surprisingly, no. I guess I'm excited. I'm really looking forward to having the newlyweds home. I'm sure they have lots to tell us."

"And we have lots to tell them."

"True." Nancy smiled and tipped up her chin so she could see her husband. "Do they know your father's asked you to serve as counsel on that huge corporate acquisition?"

"Nope." A wry grin. "I wanted to see Connor's face when I told him that our father came to the surprising, if belated, conclusion that I'm actually a pretty good lawyer."

"A *very* good lawyer," Nancy amended. "You know Harrison well enough to know he doesn't compromise where business is concerned. No bones are thrown, not even to family. He works only with the best. Period. You just happen to be the best."

"Spoken like an objective bystander," Stephen teased lightly. He silenced his wife's objections by pressing a finger to her lips. "Seriously, Nance, I appreciate your vote of confidence. It means everything, coming from you. As for my father, who knows what makes him tick? Maybe he's finally caught on to the fact that I'm not going to change my mind and run for office, no matter what he says or does. Maybe this is his way of accepting my decision. After months of a cold war standstill, maybe he's elevating my status to lukewarm, especially with the news you and I just gave him. Maybe he's finally catching on to the fact that family means more than a name to protect and a financial empire to bequeath. After all, he nearly blew whatever flimsy relationships he had with Connor and me by conspiring with Walker. That might have shaken him up enough to make him think. I hope so, for his sake. But either way, it's his problem, not ours."

It was the truth. In fact, Stephen was as emotionally untouched by his father's job offer as he was intellectually fired up. Whatever anger and bitterness he'd felt toward the man who'd sculpted his life like a piece of clay had faded these past few months. Thanks to hours of soul-searching therapy, he'd gotten to know himself a lot better. He was able to separate his own weaknesses from his father's, to take responsibility for the former and detach himself from the latter.

Well, the need to dominate and micro-manage definitely fell under the second heading.

Ironic, the way life worked out. Stephen was finally getting his father's approval. And thanks to his counseling sessions and some overwhelming support from his family, he no longer needed it to feel good about himself.

The gambling, the self-doubts, the despondency—those were part of the old Stephen.

As for the new Stephen, damn, he was happy.

"Are you sorry you accepted Harrison's offer?" Nancy was asking. "Between your own networking contacts and all the corporate referrals Connor's sent your way, you're swamped. You certainly don't need the work."

Stephen shook his head. "Not at all. I'm actually looking forward to the challenge. This acquisition's not just a big one, it's a delicate one. It's going to take some major finessing to make it happen without stepping on too many toes." Another wry grin. "Guess I didn't retire from politics after all. Anyway, between some well-placed diplomacy and hours of good, old-fashioned hard work, I think Cliff and I have the collective smarts to pull it off."

Nancy shot him a quizzical look. "I notice that you and Cliff have been enjoying your collaborations lately. You're not just going through the motions anymore. It's getting better, isn't it?"

"Yeah, it is. Our friendship's getting back on track." Stephen kissed the bridge of her nose. "Of course, it helps that you and I are rock-solid again. And that Cliff and Robin are so tight. Because if he ever looked twice at you again, I'd have to punch his lights out."

"He won't. He's in a good place emotionally, at long last. He's found someone who reciprocates his feelings. So I'm no longer in the picture. Not that I ever was. My heart's always been right here." She pressed her palm against Stephen's shirt, directly over his heart.

A tender look. "Lucky me."

"Lucky *us.*"

Stephen released his breath on a contented sigh. "It doesn't get any better than this. I've got everything I want, plus a memorable Valentine's Day gift waiting in the wings." An awed gleam lit his eyes. "Talk about new beginnings. I'm more than lucky, I'm blessed. With all that going for me, I can afford to be charitable when it comes to Cliff."

"They're here!" Brian's shriek interrupted his parents' conversation and startled three gulls hovering outside the observation deck into taking flight. "They're landing!"

"Sure are," Stephen agreed, watching as his brother's jet touched the ground, then glided down the runway and came to a graceful halt. He stood, gripping Nancy's hand

and tugging her to her feet as he waved Brian on. "Come on, champ. We're the welcome party. It's time to do our stuff."

"Yeah!" Brian needed no second invitation. He shot by his parents, destination ground floor.

Julia and Connor had only gotten halfway across the field when Brian burst out of the building and flew at them, slamming into his uncle like a small freight train.

"Finally!" he panted, regaining his balance. "We've been waiting and waiting!"

"Hey, champ!" Connor grabbed his nephew under the arms and swung him around, then plopped him onto his feet with an exaggerated stagger and a groan. "You weigh a ton. I think you grew more muscles and at least an inch over the summer."

"I did." Brian gave a proud, emphatic nod. "Mom's complaining that I'll be growing out of my new uniform by Halloween, and I just got it last week. Wait till you see it. It's so cool." He didn't pause to breathe but whipped around to Julia. "Thanks for the rabbit's foot, Miss Talbo—" A crooked grin lit his face. "I mean, Aunt Julia. It worked great. I pitched two no-hitters and a shut-out in my summer baseball league."

"Congratulations." Julia bent to give Brian a hard hug. "We missed you. I can't wait to see your new uniform and that new fast ball you told me about on the phone. Is there a game this Saturday?"

"Yup. The last one of the summer. And I'm pitching."

"Then we're coming," Connor informed him. He raised his head, smiling as Stephen and Nancy approached them, walking hand-in-hand.

"Welcome home," Stephen greeted them, kissing

Julia's cheek. "You both look fantastic." A teasing look at his brother. "Not very tan, though."

"You know Europe," Connor replied, straight-faced. "It rains a lot."

"Right. In Hawaii, too, I'll bet. Especially inside those five-star hotels."

"Cut it out." Nancy laughed, hugging each of the newlyweds in turn. "Don't pay any attention to him."

"I never do," Connor assured her.

"You both look fabulous," Nancy declared, taking in the gleam in Connor's eyes and the glow on Julia's cheeks. "Marriage agrees with you."

"We're not the only ones it agrees with," Julia replied with a twinkle. "You look so happy, all of you." She gazed at Brian, filled with relief and delight. He was Brian again.

"You said you had a big surprise," he was now reminding his uncle.

"Did I?" Connor pursed his lips in feigned contemplation.

"Yeah. When you talked to Dad before, you said he should tell me you were bringing home a big surprise."

"Hmm. I must have been talking about all the souvenirs and presents we bought you."

"No." Brian shook his head. "You told Dad it wasn't that kind of present. You said it was something you'd tell us when you got off the plane. What is it?"

"Oh, *that* surprise." Connor snapped his fingers. He turned to Julia, gave her a lazy smile. "Do you want to tell him, or should I?"

She smiled back, then leaned over to meet Brian's curious gaze. "Actually, the surprise means a new job and lots of help from you."

"Huh?"

"Your Uncle Connor and I were hoping you'd make room at next summer's baseball games for one more spectator. A very small one, mind you, but one who'll yell really loudly, I'm sure. We're also hoping you'll give that spectator some curve-ball lessons in a few years—when he or she is old enough to pitch."

Brian's face fell. "How'd you know?"

"Know what?"

"About the baby."

Julia started, and her head came up. She and Connor exchanged stunned looks.

"A better question is, how did *you* know?" Connor demanded.

"Mom and Dad told me two weeks ago." Brian looked utterly deflated. "But they said *I* could be the one to tell you." He glanced quizzically at his father, his expression rife with disappointment. "Dad, why'd you tell?"

"I didn't," Stephen countered, realization dawning in his eyes. "Neither did Mom."

All four adult Stratfords stared at one another.

"Why do I get the feeling we're talking about two different babies?" Connor noted aloud.

"Because we are," Stephen confirmed.

"You're pregnant?" Julia turned to Nancy, excitement lacing her tone.

"Yes." Her sister-in-law grinned, laying a palm on her abdomen. "Almost four months. I'm due on Valentine's Day." A questioning lift of her brows. "And you?"

"We just found out," Julia acknowledged with a joyous nod. "I'll be confirming my due date with the doctor tomorrow. But I'd estimate it to be the first week in April."

One moment, they were all standing there, gaping at the unexpected and wonderful coincidence. Then they were hugging and congratulating, laughing about the timing, marveling at the fact that by next summer, there would be two new Stratfords to expand the family circle.

"Dad might just crack a smile when you give him your news," Stephen predicted, slapping his brother on the back. "He came damned close when Nancy and I made our announcement. And now a third grandchild, right on the heels of a second? I think his pride actually might exceed his desire to see this splashed across the newspapers."

"Maybe." Connor wiggled his palm back and forth in a gesture that said the jury was still out on that one. "But let's not get our hopes up." He clapped a congratulatory hand on Stephen's shoulder. "This is great. I'm so thrilled for you guys."

"Same here."

"Hey, Dad." Brian interrupted the excitement to tug at his father's sleeve. "Does this mean I'm getting a brother or sister *and* a cousin, too?"

"Yeah, Bri, it sure does."

"Then I'll be a big brother *and* a big cousin, almost all at once."

Nancy and Julia laughed. "That's exactly what you'll be," his mother verified.

Brian stood up a little straighter, his forehead creased as he considered his new and crucial role. "Aunt Julia, your dad's a teacher, too. Does he get summers off like you do?"

Puzzled by the surprising change in subject, Julia replied, "Unless he teaches summer school, yes, he's off for most of the summer. Why?"

Intently, Brian counted on his fingers. "Okay, then, six or seven summers from now, do you think he could not teach summer school? Because you and I could sure use the help."

"The help?"

"Yeah," Brian explained patiently. "We're gonna have two kids to teach a curve ball to. And both of them might not be as good as you and me. So we better get your dad's help. We better sign him up now. The way the Yanks sign up their coaches when they want to keep them around. That way, he'll be all ours when the time comes."

Laughter bubbled up in Julia's throat, and she gave Brian the thumbs-up. "That's a great idea. We'll call him today and offer him a long-term contract. I'll bet it won't take much arm twisting."

Brian beamed. "I'll bet not."

"You know," Connor pointed out with a grin, "if you, Aunt Julia, and her dad are going to be coaches, you'll need a bullpen to practice in. I've got a great spot in mind for setting one up. It's on a tract of land big enough for a private bullpen, a playing field, and a couple of bleachers. Of course, the land won't be ready until spring, but then again, Aunt Julia won't be able to pitch until then, anyway."

"Really?" Brian was practically vibrating with excitement. "Where?"

"That's part two of the surprise we brought home to tell you. I'm building a new house for Aunt Julia, our baby, and me. It'll be only a few minutes away from your house. We've got tons of property, more than enough to make a clearing for all your baseball needs. What do you think?"

"Wow!" Brian gave an enthusiastic leap. "That's the best!" He whirled around to face his father. "*Now* I know why you said what you did to Mom. You were right!"

Stephen looked blank. "I'm glad. But what did I say to Mom that I was right about?"

"You said Aunt Julia was the best thing that ever happened to Uncle Connor. And, boy, is she ever!"

The whole group laughed.

"You know something, Brian?" Connor wrapped a possessive arm around his new wife, gazing at her with an emotion he'd only just discovered and couldn't imagine living without. "I couldn't agree more."